William Alexander Hammond

On the Susquehanna

A Novel

William Alexander Hammond

On the Susquehanna
A Novel

ISBN/EAN: 9783337002480

Printed in Europe, USA, Canada, Australia, Japan

Cover: Foto ©Andreas Hilbeck / pixelio.de

More available books at **www.hansebooks.com**

ON THE SUSQUEHANNA

ON THE SUSQUEHANNA

A NOVEL

BY

WILLIAM A. HAMMOND

AUTHOR OF "LAL," "DOCTOR GRATTAN," "MR. OLDMIXON,"
"A STRONG-MINDED WOMAN," ETC.

"On Susquehanna's side."—CAMPBELL

NEW YORK
D. APPLETON AND COMPANY
1887

ON THE SUSQUEHANNA.

CHAPTER I.

"AND this is death!"

There were two persons in the room, a woman and a man. The woman stood by the side of a bed; the man lay upon it. She was apparently about twenty-five years of age; he looked as though he might be forty-five. Though evidently weary, both in mind and in body, she exhibited no signs of feeble physical or mental health; on the contrary, she was tall and robust, and though her cheeks were pale, and her movements somewhat languid, it was easy to see that these were temporary conditions, that would disappear as soon as she could get out to inhale the fresh air of the mountains that rose, like black walls, almost within a stone's throw of the house.

The expression on her face was not only one of fatigue, but it was one of poignant sorrow; and well it might be, for the man that lay on what was evidently his death-bed was her father; her friend and companion of many years, the only being in all the world that she loved, and almost the only one that she knew.

It was easy to see that he was ill unto death. His pale, haggard, and emaciated face, his sunken eyes, his pinched nose, his half-open lips, through which the breath came quickly and irregularly, his thin hands, which he moved nervously and aimlessly over the bedclothes, picking with them here and there at imaginary threads, all went to show that his vital powers were flagging, and that unless some extraordinary turn took place his stay on earth would be of short duration.

The four words he had spoken were uttered in so low a tone that no one not very close to him, or not on the watch for the slightest sound he might make, would have heard them.   But she had had her perceptive faculties on the stretch almost continuously for many days and nights ; the more she became exhausted, so far as bodily strength or the power of thought was concerned, the sharper her senses seemed to get, until now the slightest murmur that escaped his lips, the least shade of a change in his expression, struck her with tenfold the natural force.   She heard the words that he had breathed rather than spoken.   Had the end then come at last ?   She clasped her hands together and gazed into his face with a look of anxious, inquiring agony. Doubtless it was near, but it had not yet come.   She was becoming experienced in the knowledge of the signs of death. It was only one of those sudden paroxysms of faintness to which he was liable, though certainly the most severe one that she had yet observed.   How many such steps toward the grave would he take ere he reached his destination ? She asked herself this question, and then, without trying to answer it, seeing that the collapse was passing off, and that there was no immediate danger, she gave a sigh of relief, and turned away to busy herself with the preparation of a draught that his sudden exclamation had interrupted. Then, having completed her work, she again approached the bed, taking with her the goblet containing the potion she had mixed.

His eyes were closed, he was breathing more quietly, and his fingers had ceased to clutch automatically at the silken quilt that covered him.   She laid one hand on his head, and with the other held the glass toward him.

"Father!" she said, "take this. The doctor was very strict about your not missing a dose."

Her words roused the sick man from the state of dreamy abstraction into which he had fallen, for he turned his head and looked at her inquiringly, as though he was not quite certain in regard to her identity, and was striving so to collect his thoughts as to bring her once again into his memory. But his troubled expression was only momentary, for his face soon lighted up, and a smile of recognition passed over his countenance.

"Will you take it now, father?"

"Yes, give it to me; but what is the use? Its effects last only for a few minutes, and then all the old feelings return."

She did not answer, but, putting one hand under his head, raised it from the pillow, while with the other she held the glass to his lips.

He drained it to the last drop, and then motioning to her to sit by the side of the bed, he lay for a little while without speaking.

But a more decided change was gradually taking place in his appearance. His eyes became brighter, the deep lines in his face disappeared, and a faint flush was visible on his cheeks. Suddenly and with apparent ease, he raised himself in the bed till he sat bolt upright, supported only by the pillows that his daughter placed behind him.

"Now," he said, in a voice that could have been heard throughout the large apartment, "I am good for another hour. It's a powerful medicine, my dear, but I shall soon be beyond its aid, perhaps, by the time the next dose is due. I think I had better tell you all I have to say, for it may be the last chance I shall get."

"O father, keep your strength for more important things! Don't worry about me."

"There is nothing more important to me than your wel-

fare. You have had a hard life, an isolated life, all through
your love for me. In a little while you will be free. When
I think of all the care I have given you, I should not be
surprised to see you dance around the room with joy at the
thought that the old man that has been such a burden to
you all these years was at last about to go the way of all
flesh." He smiled feebly as he spoke, and she, knowing
that he did not mean what he said, made no other answer
than to take his wasted hand in hers and raise it to her lips.

"I felt it just now," he continued. "It was not a
pang, and the words that escaped me were expressive of
my surprise at the pleasantness of the sensation. It was
so different from what I had expected. A soft undulation,
as it were, passed through my brain and seemed to waft me
to the edge of a high precipice, down which I began to fall,
though so very slowly that I thought I should never reach
the bottom. Then it appeared to me that you stretched
out your hands and caught me as I was gradually falling,
but not till I had obtained a glimpse of the glorious prospect below. I was very near to death then. A little less
strength in the heart, and all would have been over in this
world. But if what I saw was the valley of the shadow of
death, I am not afraid of it."

"It was the crisis of your disease. You are stronger
than you have been for several days past."

"Yes, I am stronger. I called Dr. Arndell back this
morning and I made him tell me how long he thought I
should live, and he gave me forty-eight hours. I have
forty-five left."

"He does not know. He told me he had strong hopes
that you would get better."

"Ah, yes, he told you that because you are a woman,
and he did not wish to take away all hope from you; but
now, my dear Alana, we must look the matter in the face.
If I did not know that I am about to die, I would never tell

you one word of what I feel it to be my duty to tell you. But I know that you would be sure to hear it some day, and very soon, too, from other lips than mine, and then you would be grieved a thousand times more than when you learn it from me."

"No, keep your strength. I do not want to hear it. What matters it how it comes to me? The doctor said that you were not to be excited." She knelt down by the side of the bed as she spoke, while sob after sob broke her utterance.

"My poor Alana!" he said, tenderly, laying his hand on her head and stroking her hair. "I believe you love me with all your heart, and that you would rather have me with you, sick and burdensome as I am, querulous and self-ish as are most old men even when they are well, than to be the sole disposer of all my wealth."

"Oh, you know I would; and as to this knowledge that must come to me, what matters it how I hear it?"

"It matters a great deal, my dear, both to you and to me. There is much in the telling of a story, and while I shall not try to shield myself, there are circumstances that, painful as the duty will be, had far better be told you now than to have them reach you from unsympathizing and malicious persons."

"Is what you have to tell me about my mother?"

"Yes," he answered, "your mother, whom you have not seen since you were a babe, of whom you have no recol-lection, and of whom, till now, I have never spoken to you, avoiding as best I could all the questions and surmises that your heart prompted."

"She is not dead?"

"No, she is not dead. Would you like to see her? Stop!" he continued, seeing from her face that she was about to say "yes"—"stop till I tell you enough about her to enable you to answer intelligently. Yes, I will leave the matter to you. If, after what I am going to say, you can tell me that you wish to see her, she shall come at once, and if possible ere it is too late for me to repair any wrong I may have done her."

What could her father mean? Alana felt her heart sink within her as she heard words that seemed to imply disgrace or wrong of some kind. To her, her father had always been good and kind, but she was aware of the fact that he was not generally liked by those with whom he was thrown, and she had once been present when a man, who had come from Philadelphia to see him on business, accused him of cruelty and even of falsehood. To be sure, he had resented the insults by striking the man and putting him out of the house, but during the scuffle the intruder had shouted out something about "the mother of that young lady there," that, although not entirely understood, was enough to reveal to her the fact that there was a mystery of some kind or other of which her mother was the subject. That it was a sorrowful one she felt very sure. The silence that had been observed all through her life in regard to her mother, the avoidance of everything on her father's part that could possibly have any reference to her, and the fact that her acquaintances seemed to take it for granted that her mother was dead, when she had reason for believing that she was still alive, all went to convince her that there was something wrong. But her love for her father and her faith in his honor were so exalted as to prevent the idea that he had been guilty of evil-doing. Nevertheless she was fully aware of the fact that there were circumstances that he did not wish to discuss, and of which he desired her to remain in ignorance.

Often she had called to mind that many years previously, when she was quite a child, she had once asked her father where her mother was, and that he had answered that she was dead.

"Dead, and in heaven?" she had inquired.

"She is dead to you and dead to me. Never ask me about her again."

At that time, this answer had in a measure satisfied her, for she thought that her father's shortness of speech had proceeded from the sorrowful recollections that were evoked by reference to his wife ; but as she grew older, the peculiarity of the reply became more apparent to her. "Dead to her and dead to him." That could only mean one thing. It meant that though the woman, her mother, might be and probably was alive, she was to all intents and purposes dead so far as they two were concerned, and that, therefore, there was no likelihood that this essentially dead woman would ever come into the current of their lives.

Then she had over and over again, as she grew into womanhood, asked herself questions in regard to this mother who was to be regarded as dead, that she answered in a hundred different ways as often as they arose in her mind. She was afraid to go to her father and beg him to tell her who her mother was, and why she was to be regarded as dead, for the knowledge that had come with mature years told her that there must be something in that mother's life that it would be better her daughter should not know. So she had kept silent, though, nevertheless, wondering what could be the mystery surrounding the woman who had brought her into the world.

But now the words that her father had spoken seemed to her to imply that whatever disgrace or wrong there was rested on him, and not on her mother. She was unprepared for this, and the shock was therefore correspondingly great. Her mother was not dead ; the mystery was to be unfolded, and then she was to say whether or not the woman who for nearly twenty-five years had been separated from her child and its father should be allowed once more to come into their presence.

It did not take long for all this to pass through her mind, and her answer was ready before her father could begin what he had to say.

"Yes !" she exclaimed, "I wish to see her. Whoever she is, whatever she may be, I wish to see her. She is my mother—that is enough."

"Perhaps you are right. At any rate, you are filial, but I warn you that you are acting ignorantly. Take a little more time for reflection, and hear first a story that may cause you to change your mind."

"Nothing can make me change it. If my mother lives, though it be in a prison, or a poor-house, or on the streets, if she is the most wretched or the most wicked woman on the face of the earth, I want to see her, if only once to call her mother !"

She had risen to her feet, her hands were clasped together, tears were streaming from her eyes, but her look was resolute, almost defiant.

"You shall have your own way, for I feel that you are right; but oh, my dear child, my poor Alana, how grievous is the wrong I have done you, and what a terrible blow is about to fall on your head !"

"I shall forgive the wrong. The blow I can endure."

"Yes, you are charitable, and you are strong. You know how to pardon and how to suffer. God help you ! for there will be ample occasion for all your kindness and all your strength. Sit there and write the telegram to your mother that I am going to dictate."

She placed herself at a little desk that stood at the other side of the bed, near one of the windows, that opened on an extensive lawn. Beyond, were several large and ugly buildings, with tall chimneys, pouring forth smoke and flame ; and still farther on, the wall of mountains rising dark and gloomy high into the air, and casting their shadows even to where she sat.

She looked out of the window for a moment, thinking of what her father had said. The solemnity of his words awed her, and she felt sure that there would be many painful circumstances attendant on the act she had expressed herself as so anxious to perform. Should she do it? It was still within her power to decline. Yes, she would see her, she must see her; and perhaps, if there had been wrongs on either side, they could be righted now at the death-bed of one of the wrong-doers.

"I am ready, father," she said.

He turned his face toward her, and spoke in a low voice, for he was beginning to be exhausted with excitement and fatigue.

"You can not know, my dear, whether you are doing right or wrong. You are acting from impulse and emotion. Let me tell you the story first, and then, if you will, you shall send the message."

"That would be disloyal to my mother," she answered. "It is my duty, now that I know she lives and is within reach, to bring her to you, and to me, without any doubt of her fitness to be with her child. She is my mother. That is all I care to know, to make me wish to have her here at once."

"Well, well!" he resumed, a little wearily and bitterly, "youth is always full of confidence. It is well that it is so, for otherwise the world would be either a poor-house or a lunatic asylum. Now write:

"To Miss Sarah Mullin—"

"I thought the message was to be sent direct to my mother," interrupted Alana.

"You are right: Sarah Mullin is your mother's name."

"How can that be, if she is your wife?"

"She is not my wife." He covered his face with his hands as he made this avowal, as though to shut out from his eyes the look of astonishment and reproach that he knew would be turned upon him.

"My mother!" exclaimed Alana, "and not your wife?"

"Oh, the shame of it!—the shame of it!" he cried, excitedly. "That a father should be forced to make such a confession to his daughter! Yes! your mother, and yet not my wife."

"You will make her your wife, as soon as she can get here," said Alana, rising from the desk, and falling on her knees by the side of the bed. "You will do this for my sake, if not for hers. O father! dear father! it may be the last request that I shall ever make of you."

The sick man made no answer. His hands still covered his face, but his whole body was trembling with the emotion that raged within him.

"Father, did you hear me? Give me the address, and let me send for her at once. Then when she is here you will do what justice and honor require."

"Send for her," he said, feebly; "but as to marrying her, that is impossible."

She bent over the bed, and, taking his hands in hers, drew them away from his face. "Dear father," she said, "you have never broken your word to me."

"No, dear, I have kept faith with you, I think."

"Last year, when I was very ill," she continued, with a trembling voice, "you knelt by the side of my bed, just as I am kneeling now, and you took my hands in yours as I have yours at this moment, and you said that if I would get well you would do anything I asked you."

"Yes, yes, I remember."

"I thought then that when I was well enough I would ask you to tell me about my mother, but after I recovered I was afraid. I dreaded that she had done something that would make me lose the love I had for her, even though she had passed from my memory. But now I am no

longer afraid. The worst is known to me, and it is from
you, not her, that reparation must come, and I ask you to
remember your solemn promise and to grant my request."

"Suppose that you were to ask, instead, that I should
kill you, do you think I would be bound by my promise?"

"No, for I should be asking you to do me an injury
and to commit a crime."

"For me to marry your mother and to have her here
as I should have to do, would be almost as great a wrong
to you, ay, worse, than if I were to strike you dead! Do
you not know that as my widow she would be mistress
here, and that one third of my estate would go to her?"

"It matters nothing to me if she gets it all. She is
my mother."

"Yes, that is all you see in the matter. She is your
mother, and, knowing nothing else than that fact, you are
willing to risk your happiness in order to have an act of
fancied justice done to her. Give me another dose of the
mixture," he continued, in a voice scarcely above a whisper.

She mixed the medicine for him, and he drank it at a
draught.

"It is a wonderful remedy," he resumed. "It acts on
the very instant. In one moment I shall be able to go on.
Now," after a little pause during which he was not only resting but was trying to arrange his ideas in a coherent form,
"where was I? Oh, yes, 'act of fancied justice.' My
dear child, I verily believe I am on my death-bed, and that
I have but a few hours to live. On the very brink of the
grave I say to you these things. It was from no fault of
mine that I did not marry your mother. When I thought
her, as I once did, more sinned against than sinning, I was
prepared, nay, anxious, to make her my wife. But I was
then only a student, and with barely enough means at
my command to finish my education as a mining engineer,

and she had no intention of marrying a poor man, or, indeed, as I afterward ascertained, of marrying at all."

"Go on," said Alana; "I can bear it all. There can not be anything worse than what you have told me."

"Yes, there is worse to come. She was the daughter of the woman with whom I boarded. She was very beautiful, but coarse in manner and speech. I was only twenty years of age. She was thirty. Before you were born, I urged her over and over again to marry me, but she refused. I even went so far as to endeavor to accomplish by stratagem what I could not effect by persuasion, but she discovered my plan and I was foiled. Understand me, that I was actuated not by love for her, for that had been only a transient feeling, but by an honest desire to save her from disgrace, and to protect my unborn child."

Alana's face was pressed close against the bed. If she had raised it, her father would have seen that it was crimson with shame.

"I sent her into the country, and there you were born. From time to time I heard that all was going well. Then I ceased to receive further intelligence. I wrote, but my letters remained unanswered. Finally, I went to the village, only to learn from the woman with whom I had placed her, that she had disappeared in the night, leaving you at the door of the county poor-house to be cared for by public charity.

"You may think it strange," he went on, after trying in vain to soothe Alana, who was sobbing and moaning with her face buried in the bed, "that I can speak about all this without showing any emotion, while you, my poor child, are overwhelmed with grief; but long familiarity with the matter has blunted my sensibilities. I have become hardened to the contemplation of events that at first almost made me insane. I have looked forward, too, through many years to this hour. I knew it had to come, and that I should be obliged to reveal to you the fact of my and your mother's dishonor, or leave you to learn it from other and perhaps unfriendly lips.

"There is not much more to tell. I had, of course, no difficulty in reclaiming you. I committed you to the care of a good woman till I had secured for myself a home to which I could bring you. You were then only five years old, and ever since we have lived together, almost undisturbed by the woman who is only your mother in that she brought you into the world.

"I say 'almost,' for once she came here with her brother. I was then rich, and she had gone down lower and lower, till she had reached a depth that I had not thought it possible for even her to reach. I had heard nothing of her from the time that she deserted you till then. She remained at the village inn, while her brother came here and tried to scare me into acknowledging her as my wife, on the ground that I had married her when I was drunk. You were present at the time, and you doubtless remember how the attempt ended. I offered an allowance, liberal enough in all conscience, but I refused to regard her as my wife. Now, do you still wish to see this woman, and do you still think I ought to marry her? It is for you to decide. I am in your hands. Do with me as you will."

She raised her head. In presence of the momentous issue forced upon her she had been calm. She bent over and kissed her father's forehead and then his lips.

"You have suffered for your sin," she said, "but you have been noble and good through it all. God has forgiven you. As for me, I have nothing to forgive. But I think I see clearly that, bad as my mother was, perhaps is, she is still my mother and ought to be your wife. It is for us to do what is right, and who knows but that yet her soul may be saved alive!"

"Yes," he answered, absently, as though thinking of something else, "who knows ? Send the telegram. My expiation shall be complete ; and, as for you, God will protect you through your own goodness and strength."

She kissed him again, and then, going back to the desk, prepared to finish the message she had begun, and which had not got beyond her mother's name.

"Miss Sarah Mullin," he repeated—"I am not sure about the name ; she has changed it several times. The checks all came back indorsed with that name, but I have heard that she has been known by several others. You will have no trouble with her after I am gone, if you should yet decide not to send for her."

He uttered these last words in a pleading sort of tone, as though still hoping that the message calling her might not be sent. "All you will have to do will be to continue the allowance, and remain firm against all attempts to blackmail you. She is an adept at that business, and so is her brother ; but a little firmness and a few threats always brought them to reason. My dear Alana," he continued, still more feebly than he had yet spoken, "I am very tired. No one here knows anything about it. You are safe so long as you pay the allowance. It is too late ! The valley of the shadow of death again ! Alana, my darling !"

In a moment she was at his side. A smile was on his face. Hurriedly she mixed another dose of the invigorating draught and held it to his lips. "Father !" she cried —"father !"

He was still smiling. He opened his eyes for an instant, as she gazed anxiously into his face, and then he closed them forever.

Francis Honeywood was dead.

CHAPTER II.

THE "Susquehanna Iron-Works," to the ownership of which Alana Honeywood succeeded by the terms of her father's will, are situated on the left bank of the picturesque river from which they receive their name, and that courses from north to south through the State of Pennsylvania. The only town very near, is the little village inhabited by the workmen and their families, and the few others that minister to their wants. It had not been thought necessary to give this collection of about a hundred houses any special name, though attempts had been made by the outsiders to call it Honeywoodville—attempts that both Mr. Honeywood and his daughter had strenuously and successfully resisted. The place was the "Susquehanna Iron-Works," and that was also the designation given by the Post-Office Department. Proprietorship and official sanction had thus prevented the imposition of the barbarism "Honeywoodville" upon the pretty little village that lay deep in the shadows of Peter's and Berry's Mountains, where the Susquehanna, in ages long gone by, had broken through the range that then stood like a vast dam across its stream.

Fifteen miles to the south, and on the other side of several ranges of mountains, is the city of Harrisburg, to which place there is easy access by a good road that winds round the mountains along the river-bank, as well as by the Northern Central Railroad.

Mr. Honeywood had been dead two years, and during

that time no very notable events had occurred to disturb
the peace that Alana courted. She had made many attempts to discover her mother, but all had resulted unsuccessfully. She had been unable to find her father's private
check-book, or any of the paid checks, that must, of
course, in the ordinary routine of business, have been
returned to him. She had no clew to her mother's address, and no demand had ever been made on her for
money. A few weeks after Mr. Honeywood's death, she
had gone to Philadelphia, and, taking a city directory, had
found that there were eleven women of the name of Sarah
Mullin, whose residences were given.

Then she had gone to each one of them, occupying the
greater part of the day in the undertaking; but it was
quite certain that no one of those bearing the name was
her mother. A like procedure in Baltimore and in New
York had led to an almost identical result; I say "almost,"
because, in the latter city, a woman, calling herself Sarah
Mullin, had come to see her at her hotel, and had repre-
sented herself as being the person of whom Alana was in
search. She described Mr. Francis Honeywood very accurately, and claimed that Alana was her daughter; but a
little sharp cross-examination on the part of Mr. Wade,
Alana's legal adviser, who had accompanied her to the
city, was sufficient to show her to be a badly informed impostor.

During all the time that she was conducting the search,
and for several months subsequently, she had had an advertisement in the following terms kept standing in the
most prominent Philadelphia and New York newspapers :

"Sarah Mullin, who, in the year 1855 or thereabout,
in the city of Philadelphia, made the acquaintance of Mr.
Francis Honeywood, is requested to communicate without
delay with Mr. William Wade, attorney-at-law, Susquehanna Iron-Works, Dauphin County, Pennsylvania."

Many answers were received to this advertisement. Some of them were intended as jokes, some as insults, others appeared at first sight as though they might lead to some certain information; but full inquiry always showed them to be either written in ignorance or as clumsy attempts at fraud.

Then, feeling that she had done everything in her power to discover her mother, and thus to rescue her from the sinful and criminal life that there was reason to believe she was leading, Alana gave up all active prosecution of the search, though Mr. Wade had instructions to follow up any line of investigation that might be presented.

Certainly the ill success that had attended upon her efforts was very astonishing, and, as Mr. Wade admitted, absolutely incomprehensible. Here was a woman, who, according to her father's dying words, had been for many years in the receipt of a large annuity, paid quarterly, as he had declared, and by checks, suddenly disappearing on the death of the man who had given her the means of support, and leaving no signs behind her by which she could be traced. Of course, inquiry had been made of the banks with the view of ascertaining by whom the checks had been presented. Mr. Honeywood, it was known, had kept funds in two banks in Philadelphia and in one in Harrisburg; but from neither of them had any information bearing upon the subject been received. Indeed, the books of the institutions showed that no sums of money of a fixed amount had been regularly drawn by Mr. Honeywood's checks, nor had the officers ever been called upon, so far as they knew—and they were certain on the point—to pay money on his order to any woman during all the years that he had had business with them, except to Miss Honeywood. Clearly there must have been another bank, probably out of the State, in which he had kept enough money to meet his checks in Miss Mullin's favor, and for no other purpose. Or, for greater secrecy, he may have had funds in some private person's hands, and have given his checks on him. Nevertheless, a circular, sent to every public bank in the United States, failed to bring any response, and no private person made any sign that he had had pecuniary relations of the kind mentioned with Mr. Francis Honeywood.

Mr. Wade was astonished, even more than was Alana. He had been, for many years, her father's legal adviser. He owned a large tract of mountain-land in the immediate vicinity of the Susquehanna Iron-Works, on which he had erected a sort of round tower, in which he lived during the summer, when the courts were, most of them, closed, while in winter he resided in Harrisburg. Being a bachelor, and well advanced in years, he could do pretty much as he pleased, and he did it to his heart's content. This tower overlooked the river, being placed high up on the edge of the mountain, where once the river had flowed; it was, of all structures in the world, one of the most uncomfortable for an average human being to live in. It was three stories high, with only one room on a floor, and this round and of about thirty feet in diameter. On the inside was a winding staircase, made of iron, and just wide enough to admit of the passage of one person at a time. Mr. Wade was tall and thin, and was therefore able to ascend this special arrangement without much difficulty, but a person of very little more than his amplitude would certainly have been unable to pass between the newel-posts at the bottom. The lower floor was his dining-room, the next his library and sitting-room, and the third and topmost was where he slept. The kitchen and a room for the man-servant and woman-servant—husband and wife—that he kept, were entirely detached from the tower.

The result of the search for Miss Sarah Mullin had disturbed Mr. Wade very greatly. Alana had at once given him her full confidence, and had succeeded in obtaining his interest in the inquiry she was about to make. At first he had said that there would be no trouble in the matter; that the power of money was such that, when the time came round for the payment of Miss Sarah Mullin's quarterly allowance, the lady would not let the matter go by default, for more than a day or two, before a reminder, couched probably in no gentle strains, would be received at the Susquehanna Iron-Works. But as month after month went by, and no demand was received, he confessed that it was the strangest case that had ever come under his observation, and that nothing like it was to be found in any "Reports" of which he had knowledge.

"It's strange, too," he said one night, after about a year had elapsed, and he was sitting on the balcony that he had built around his tower on a level with the floor of the second story—"it's strange that I have never heard anything of this woman during all the years that I knew Honeywood. What an awful blow it must have been for that poor girl, but how nobly she bears it ! Not one woman in a thousand in her place would have wanted to be brought into contact with such a mother as Miss Sarah Mullin must be. I shudder when I think that some day she may turn up, and disgrace her daughter with her presence.

"I hope she is dead—I think she must be, for otherwise the failure to pay her allowance would have brought her here as fast as steam could bring her. I don't understand it at all. No trace ; not as much as would have been left behind if an earthquake had swallowed her, and every one connected with her. Well, for my part, I'm devilish glad that Honeywood died before he could tell anything more about her. And, by George, I'm not by any means sure that what he did tell was correct ! Seeing that his daughter was determined to have her mother come, he may have given a false name, for the express purpose of putting

her on the wrong track ; still, he would scarcely have been
such a scoundrel as to tell her that her mother was not his
wife unless it were true ! He wasn't that kind of a man ; I
never knew him to do anything dishonorable, and it's hard
that his one act of youthful folly—one, too, that he tried so
hard to repair—should now bear so hard on his daughter.
Poor girl, poor girl ! How keenly she feels the disgrace !
How well she sees that success in her search can only add
to her shame, and make public a circumstance that, so far
as I can see, she and I only know ; and yet she perseveres
as steadfastly as though the result would only redound to
her honor ! And so it will," he added, after he had watched
a long train of cars wind round the base of the mountain ;
"what can be more honorable to her than the self-sacrifice
she is trying to make ? By Jove, it is sublime, simply sublime !

"Let me see," he continued, having in the mean time
gone into the room, and returned with a lighted cigar
in his mouth, at which he was puffing energetically.
"Twenty-six years ago, and she was then, so he said, ten
years older than he. He was forty-five when he died, and
he has been dead a year. That would make her fifty-six
now. Quite old enough, she is, to throw off the follies of
youth, and settle down as a respectable woman.

"There's nothing like a cigar for quickening the intellect. Now, with all our inquiries neither of us thought of
trying to find the woman with whom Honeywood boarded
when he was a student, and whose seductive daughter, ten
years older than himself, lured him from the paths of virtue. That was very stupid, and I'll make amends for my
idiocy by going to Philadelphia to-morrow, and starting
inquiries in that direction. In the mean time, nothing shall
prevent my hoping that this, like all the other leads, may
result in nothing. I believe that, if the woman should be
found, Alana would give her a third of the property, just

as though she had been her father's wife. If she should
turn out, after all, to be a decent woman, that would be
very well; but if she's the sort of an old reprobate that I
take her to be, it would be casting pearls before swine.

"It's well Honeywood made a will, or there might some
day arise a question as to Alana's right to inherit. I don't
know that he left any relatives, but, after a man's dead, it's
astonishing how the cousins turn up in all quarters of the
earth. Where the carcass is, there shall the vultures be
gathered together. That's as true as gospel. By George,
I believe it *is* gospel!"

The next morning, early, without speaking of his intentions to any one but old Jacob Schwartz and his wife, who
looked after his domestic affairs, Mr. Wade departed for
Philadelphia. Arriving there, his first business was to go to
the university, in order to ascertain all the facts in regard
to the collegiate record of Mr. Honeywood that bore upon
the question in which he was interested. He had no difficulty in finding out that the young man had been a student
of the Scientific School, and the old janitor professed to
have a very distinct idea of his personal appearance and
manner of life.

"I recollect Mr. Honeywood," he said, "just as well as
I recollect my own son, and he's been dead just twenty-six
years. Mr. Honeywood sat up with him two nights during the last illness the poor boy had, and helped me to give
him a decent funeral. You see, then I was only a sort of
helper to the janitor. Now I'm the janitor himself." And,
with these words, the old man drew himself up proudly,
as though fully conscious of the honor attached to his
office.

"Then he was a very correct young man?" said Mr.
Wade, interrogatively.

"Yes, sir; just as straight as a die. Never going off
with the other boys, and always attending to his work. I

hear he's got to be very rich ; but he hasn't forgotten Peter Mitchell, I'll be bound."

" He's dead, and I have come to get some information from you as to where he lived, when he was a student here."

" I'm sorry he's dead—he was good to my boy. I hope he's better off in the next world than he was in this, though, from all I've heard, he had a pretty good thing of it here. I heard Professor Franborough say, in one of his lectures, that Mr. Honeywood's furnace was a model for them to study. But what do you want to know ? "

" As I said, I want to know where he boarded."

" Well, he had a room at Mrs. Mullin's"—Mr. Wade started at the name ; at last, he thought, he had struck the right track—"in Sansom Street, above Broad. He wasn't rich in those days, I can tell you, so he had to take care of every penny. I went there once to tell him of a bad night my boy had passed."

" Do you know anything of Mrs. Mullin's family ? Did she have a son or—or a daughter ? "

" She had a son, for he used to come to the college on messages for the young gentlemen that boarded with his mother, but I never heard of a daughter. And I'm pretty sure there was only one son."

" Then she had other boarders from among the students ? "

" Oh, yes, three or four ; but who they were, I can't tell you now. But Bill, the boy, was a bad fellow. He got into a fight with the police down in Southwark, or what used to be Southwark—I'm so accustomed to the old name that I can't get used to this new-fangled thing of consolidation. Well, as I was saying, he got into a fight with the police about some old junk he was trying to steal, and he got knocked on the head with a locust club, and in a day or two afterward he died. You see I know all about that, for he was taken to the hospital in Pine Street, and Professor Mangum lectured on him. The next day he was dead."

"So he is dead! And when was this?"

"Let me see," answered the old man, reflectively. "It was the night of the election of Lincoln the second time, or the night after. I know it by the fact that they were firing cannon while Professor Mangum was giving his lecture on Bill's case. Bill died on the second day after he was struck. The professor objected to the firing, he said, because it made such a noise that he could not hear himself speak, but the boys said it was because he was a Democrat."

"Then it must have happened in the early part of November, 1864?"

"Yes, I guess you are right."

"I am much obliged to you. You don't recollect Mrs. Mullin's number?"

"No, but it was just a couple of doors above the Academy of Natural Sciences. They've made a hotel of it since."

"Of the house?"

"No, of the academy. And didn't you know that? I thought everybody knew that."

"If I did, I had forgotten it. I'll find the place."

He found it without much trouble. People in Philadelphia don't change their residences often, and the occupants of the house had been in it nearly twenty years, being the immediate successors of Mrs. Mullin. The old lady, however, who appeared to be the mistress of the house, knew nothing of her predecessor, nor whether or not there was a daughter. So the end was that Mr. Wade returned to his round tower on the Susquehanna, no wiser than when he left, except that he had discovered that there had been a Mrs. Mullin, that there had also been a son, and that this young man, after leading a disreputable life, had been killed by a policeman in the early part of November, 1864. All

this was not much, but it might be the means of leading to
something more definite, and therefore was not to be de-
spised.   He had been a lawyer long enough to know that
facts of this kind, slight as they may at first appear to be,
are sometimes the determinating factors in important investigations.

For some time after this event, Alana had actively carried on the search, but eventually, after persevering for two
years without meeting with the slightest encouragement,
she had, as I have said, allowed the matter to subside, though
it was rarely for any considerable period entirely out of
her mind.

In the mean time, everything of a material character
had gone well with her.   The works of which she was now
the owner were in the most flourishing condition.   The
mines of iron and coal that supplied the forge, and that
were almost within a stone's throw, had never been more
productive.   She had begun the erection of another and
larger furnace, and had more orders for iron than she
could fill.   The fact that she owned the ore that she
worked, and the coal with which she worked it, and the
close proximity of the mines, gave her advantages over her
business competitors that told greatly in her favor.   Besides, the product of her works was of a very tough and
fibrous character, and was in demand for the purpose of
being manufactured into wheels for locomotives and rail-
way-cars, and the number of furnaces in the country that
could turn out the kind of iron requisite for these uses was
exceedingly limited.

Mentally she had suffered much, and this fact was made
apparent by the change that had ensued in her countenance, as well as in her manner and character.   Previous
to the death of her father, she had been remarkable for her
radiant though somewhat stately beauty ; but now, while
her features had undergone little if any alteration, the ex-

pression had altogether changed. The stateliness seemed to have increased, while the radiance had correspondingly diminished. The joy that comes from a mind at ease with itself and all the world, and which alone often stamps a commonplace face with an expression that constitutes beauty, had gone, and in its stead had appeared a gravity, a seriousness, that were scarcely ever absent. And when she smiled, which was rarely the case, this peculiar tone of sadness was there to modify the exhibition of pleasure, and often to remain mistress of the facial field.

She had never had many companions. There was little or no society in the immediate neighborhood that interested her; and Harrisburg, where there were a few people that she might have liked, was rather too far away for social intimacies. Occasionally she had passed a few days at a time with a friend, a widow, a Mrs. Priestly, who had two very charming daughters, much younger, however, than Alana, and who had also a well-appointed residence on the river-bank, or "The Bank," as it was generally called. Then the visits were returned by the three ladies, and thus a mild form of intimacy had been kept up. At the works or in their vicinity there were but four persons outside of her own house with whom she had intimate social relations, and these were all of the male sex. First, there was Mr. Wade, with whom the reader has already made acquaintance; next, there was Dr. Arndell, who has been mentioned as the physician who attended her father, and who had for five or six years had the medical charge of the workmen and their families, as well as of her own household; then there was the Rev. Mr. Trevor, who cared for them all spiritually, and who was the rector of the little church that, soon after erecting his furnace and its accessories, Mr. Honeywood had built; and last of all socially, but by no means last in importance, was Mr. John Benham, the superintendent of the establishment, forge,

iron-mines, coal-mines, lime-kilns, in fact of everything,
and of every person concerned in the getting of the iron out
of the earth, and its manufacture into the pigs that were
piled up in great cubical masses at almost every place about
the works where room for them was to be found.

Alana very soon discovered that it would not do for her
to yield to the depressing emotions that crowded upon her.
Her position she felt most keenly.   She knew that she had
in reality no legal right to her father's name, and, being
naturally of a high-spirited nature, the thought galled her
to a degree that was almost unbearable.   She had, previously to her father's death, been rather proud of her ancestry.
The Honeywoods were one of the most eminent families of
England, going back in a direct line to the time of the
Conqueror, a Sir Guillaume de Bois-Mielleuse having been
one of the most redoubtable knights of Duke William's
army with which he had overcome Harold at Hastings.
Now, the consciousness of possessing a noble ancestry was
taken away from her, and in a manner, too, to shake her
pride to its very foundations.   There was a blot upon her
pedigree that, so far as she could perceive, there was no possibility of her effacing, and of the existence of which she would,
to the last day of her life, be painfully conscious.   The
more she thought of the matter, the worse it appeared to be.
Everything that her father, in the course of his recital of
the story of his life, had said relative to her mother, was of
such a character as to cause her heart to sink within her
at the idea of that mother's life of shame—perhaps, now,
still more shameful than it had ever been before.   She
knew little of the evil ways of the world, for her life had
been, as we already know, a comparatively secluded one,
but she had dim and uncertain ideas that there were
depths of depravity into which women sometimes fall, and
that it was almost an act of impurity for her to think of.
Had her mother sunk below the surface of the current so

as to be out of the course through which the life of the world passes? Yes, it must be so, and that was doubtless the reason why no trace of her could be discovered. Perhaps it would be well if she were dead, for then, at least, she would have closed her account on earth, and no further sins could be charged against her.

But, as often as this thought occurred to Alana, it never stayed long in her mind. From the very first she had resolved that it was her duty to leave nothing undone that could by any possibility lead to the discovery of her mother, and her reclamation to an honest and decent life. The failure to find her had been a great disappointment, and, what was more, a great sorrow. It was for a long time almost impossible for her to avoid making ideal situations in her mind, in which her mother appeared as the chief personage, sometimes as a pauper, again as a criminal, always in some degraded position from which a daughter's love and power might, were there an opportunity for them to be exercised, be potent factors in her salvation.

Alana was endowed with one of those minds that are capable of self-protection. It is true that she had, almost throughout the whole period of her existence, been accustomed to rely on her father as her guide in all matters in which she required advice. But the potentiality for independent action existed, although there had not heretofore been occasion for calling it into exercise. She found that the concentration of her thoughts upon one subject was making her morbid. She was beginning to enter into that condition in which the person sees everything with a jaundiced eye, and in which even the most cheerful subjects are distorted into a melancholy tint. She was sensible enough to perceive that this was all wrong, and to determine to break loose from mental associations that she was convinced would, if kept up, not only render her supremely unhappy, but, what was of more importance in her estimation, prevent her doing the good that she wished to do with the large pecuniary means at her disposal.

While her father lived, she had not taken much interest in the " Works," as they were generally called by those who had anything to do with them.   She had heard the state of the markets, the tariff, the price of labor, and other matters bearing on the business, discussed by her father and Mr. Wade, or Mr. Benham, and sometimes even with Dr. Arndell and Mr. Trevor.   She had frequently ventured to excite the interest of her visitors or to gratify their curiosity by showing them, under the guidance of Mr. John Benham, through the forge, and even to descend into the iron and coal mines.   On such occasions she had wondered as much as did her friends at the mechanical appliances that she saw and the skill with which they were used.   She had also admired the big, burly fellows that, bare to the waist and dripping with perspiration, handled the large pots of melted iron as though they were tin pails, and poured the red-hot metal that dazzled her eyes into molds with as much ease as a boy would handle a ladle of melted lead when making bullets.   But, for all this, she had concerned herself very little with the every-day routine business of the works, and but, as I have said, for the purpose of gratifying her friends, would never have put her foot inside of forge or mines from one year's end to the other.

But now, when in her tribulation she resolved to make a mighty effort to get rid of the depressing emotions that were bearing so heavily upon her, the idea occurred to her that nothing could be more effectual in assisting her to accomplish her object than the active occupation for both mind and body that would be secured were she herself to take her father's place as controller of the works.   She was owner, the mistress of a large establishment doing an important work in adding to the productiveness of the country ; the destinies of several hundred men, women, and

children were in her hands : was it not her duty, more than
for her own sake, to exercise some degree of personal supervision over these great interests ? Had she not a stew-
ardship of which she would some day be called upon to
render an account ? Yes, here was her field for the work
that would not only clear her mind of the "perilous stuff"
that filled it, but that would also make her once more
an active power in doing good to those dependent upon
her.

For a full year she had, so far as any personal interference of hers was concerned, allowed matters connected
with the works to go their own way. But they had not,
for all that, been neglected. Her father had trusted John
Benham as fully as it was possible for one man to trust another. There had been no restrictions on his management
of all the many details connected with the large business,
reserving to himself only the dictation of the general policy
of the establishment and the final word in all large transac-
tions. Even in these, however, John Benham's advice was
usually followed, and, as a rule, all negotiations, whether
for the purchase of new ore-beds or for the sale of manufactured iron, were first or last passed upon by him. Only
the day before he died, Mr. Honeywood had, while telling
Alana of the responsibilities that after his death would
rest upon her, expressed the satisfaction he felt that a man
like John Benham was in charge of the works, and that
therefore her load would be lessened in weight.

Alana had at first taken her father's commendation for
more than it was meant to imply, and had never asked a
question or made a suggestion in regard to the business.
Certainly, so far as the material prosperity of the works
was concerned, she could not have done better, for never
before, in all their existence of nearly twenty years, had
things been in better condition than during the year that
John Benham had had full swing, with no one to interfere

with him.   Already he had suggested the enlargement of
the works in order to be enabled to take the great number
of orders offering that they were, for want of facilities,
obliged to decline.   Even Mr. Wade, who was naturally of
a suspicious and untrusting disposition, had admitted that
John Benham was a man that could be depended upon in
any emergency, and that could be relied upon to render an
honest account of his trust.   Mr. Wade based his assertions
not on emotion or on guess-work, but on the thorough inspection that he had made of the books and accounts, and
on the fact that the sums that John Benham turned over
at the end of each quarter were larger than any that had
been before rendered, and had exactly agreed with the figures that he (Mr. Wade) had obtained from his examina-
tions.

Matters had, as I have said, gone on without the occur-
rence of any events worthy of being noted, till two years
had elapsed since Mr. Honeywood's death.   For about a
year Alana had been exercising a general supervision over
her affairs.   In order to do this to the best advantage, it
had been necessary for her to become acquainted with the
numberless details of the large establishment, and with the
methods of transacting business.   For the accomplishment
of this object John Benham's assistance had been absolutely
necessary, and it had been given with a sincere desire on
his part that Miss Honeywood should acquire all the information essential to the accomplishment of her purpose.
As soon as she had determined upon her course, she sent
for him and told him of the resolution she had formed, and
the reasons by which she had been actuated.   She did not
ask him what he thought of her intention, and he did not
venture to tell her that it met with his approval.   He only
promised that so far as he was concerned she should receive
his aid right loyally.   Then, after arranging for the beginning on the morrow of a thorough inspection of the whole

establishment as a preliminary to her work, he bade her good-morning, and went about the business he had in hand.

"To-morrow, then," exclaimed Alana, as soon as the door had closed upon the superintendent, "I begin a new life." A year of this life had elapsed when we again take up the thread of her history.

CHAPTER III

"So you think we should decline the order of the Pennsylvania Railroad Company?"

"Yes, Miss Honeywood, I do. The price offered is considerably below the market value, and if we accept it we shall, with our present means, be unable to execute the order of the Union Pacific, which is worth more to us."

"When do you expect to have the new forge ready?"

"Certainly not for a month, and perhaps two. The contractor had a strike among his men yesterday. All the brick-layers quit work without a minute's notice, simply because he had discharged a foreman that they liked. But for that we should be in it in less than two weeks."

"He can get other workmen, I suppose?"

"Yes, he has gone to Harrisburg, and has telegraphed to Philadelphia for others, but still the loss of time will be considerable. He will lose money too."

"How is that?"

"Don't you recollect, Miss Honeywood, that he is under a forfeit of two hundred dollars for every day after the 15th of September that the stack remains unfinished? It is now the 5th. He will probably be behindhand fifteen days, perhaps more."

"He shall not lose money on that account, if the delay is owing to the strike, and the strike was, as you tell me, due to his dismissal of a foreman. Assure him of that, Mr. Benham. What kind of a man is this foreman?"

"A worthless fellow, lazy and drunken. If he had

been capable and faithful, we should be using the new forge to-day."

"It seems strange to me that Mr. Byles should have employed such a man."

"He made a mistake, as others wiser than he have done before him, and as others will do after him."

"Yes, I suppose so," assented Alana, turning over some papers that lay on the table at which she was sitting, and looking carelessly at the indorsements. "I had a letter this morning from the foreman. He complains of having been badly treated, and asks me to interfere in his behalf."

"I know something about him of my own knowledge," continued Benham. "Last night the work that had been done on the stack was torn down, and the structure is now a mass of ruins. Of course, it was done by the striking brick-layers. I went by there this morning early, and I found this rule"—taking, as he spoke, a folding rule from his pocket. "The foreman's name is cut on it," he continued, looking at it closely—"Alexander Todd." He handed the rule to Alana as he spoke, and then rose as if to go.

"Yes," she said, "here is the name, sure enough. This is pretty strong proof, Mr. Benham, that the late foreman was one of the party that pulled down the stack."

"Yes, although not absolutely conclusive. Somebody may have put it there in order to create that impression. Still, his character is so bad, that I strongly suspect him of being the leader in last night's depredations; and Mr. Byles, the contractor, is so sure of the fact that he has gone to get a warrant for Todd's arrest."

"But where was the watchman? Surely, there should have been some one there to look after the property at night."

"There was a watchman, but they tied and blindfolded

him so that he was prevented giving the alarm. Of course there was a gang of men at work in the forge, but they were busy, and did not hear what was going on."

"Will you kindly find out for me where Todd lives? I will go and see him."

"You go and see him, Miss Honeywood!"

"Yes, I wish to hear what he has to say in his defense. He has written me a very well-worded and plausible letter, and I shall answer it in person."

"If you will allow me to say so, I think you will run some risk of being unpleasantly treated. He was very drunk yesterday."

"Oh, I am not afraid." .

"Will you permit me to go with you?"

"You are very kind, Mr. Benham, but I think I should prefer to see him alone. Has he a family?"

"Yes, a wife. They live in the ravine just beyond the church, in the house that was built for one of the master workmen. I let him have it at a small rent, which, by the by, he has never paid."

"That looks bad, to begin with. Good-morning, Mr. Benham. Oh, I almost forgot—did you not tell me that Mr. Wade had found a large deposit of iron on his land?"

"Yes, and that it would be well for us to secure it, for it will be very easily worked, and we shall need more ore after the new forge is in operation."

"I will think of it. Good-morning."

Mr. Benham took his departure, and Alana was left alone. She sat for a few moments with her head resting on her hands, her elbows on the table. The room was the same that her father had used as an office, and was in a wing of the house, having a separate entrance of its own. She had made very little alteration in it, preferring to keep it as nearly as possible as it was when he occupied it. In fact, she had added nothing to its furniture but a portrait of him that she had had painted from an excellent photograph, and had hung on the wall immediately over the table at which she sat.

To-morrow would be the anniversary of his death. Two years had elapsed, and she had accomplished nothing in the matter of her search for her mother. With a sigh she turned to the work before her, which consisted of reading some dozen or more letters, and indorsing on each the disposition to be made of it. Then she touched a table-bell near her hand.

"Give these to Mr. Bowman, please," she said to the boy that made his appearance from the adjoining room.

Mr. Bowman, it should be stated, was her secretary, and occupied an apartment separated by the room from which the boy came, from that in which she was. There were several clerks besides, but they were connected with Mr. Benham's office, which was in a separate building between her house and the forge.

Having finished her morning's work, she went through a passage that led from the wing to the main building, and, going to her own room, put on her hat and a light shawl, and, without a word to any one, started out on her visit to Todd's house.

She crossed the lawn, and went out through the gate upon a well-shaded lane that led to the entrance of the ravine in which Todd's house was situated. She passed the little stone church that her father had built, and, seeing that the door was open, looked at her watch, thinking that she might possibly be in time for at least the conclusion of the morning service. For Mr. Trevor was a strict churchman, and thought it his duty to have prayers every day whether anybody came or not. Generally he had three attendants at his daily ministrations. These were Mrs. Winebrenner, her housekeeper, who, having begun life as a Lutheran, had been converted from the error of her ways through the teachings of Mr. Trevor, and had, of course, gone to the farthest extreme in her efforts to reach ecclesiastical rectitude; Mrs. Barton, an Englishwoman, who kept a little shop at which the wives and daughters of the workmen might refresh themselves with the so-called latest New York and Paris fashions; and little Miss Pink, who managed a similar shop, but on a somewhat larger scale as regards scope, though considerably less in actual size. If there was a fourth, it was when Alana made herself one of the congregation. The look at her watch showed her, however, that she was too late, and she was about resuming her walk, when Mr. Trevor came out of the church, and, seeing her, raised his hat and bade her good-morning.

"You are late, Miss Honeywood," he said, as he joined her. "Service has been over half an hour. I stayed to talk to Mrs. Todd, the wife of one of the workmen on the new forge. She appears to be in great trouble. She tells me her husband has been discharged from his place as foreman, and that they are in want of the necessaries of life."

"I am going there now. I would ask you to go with me but for the fact that I wish to have a little private conversation with her husband. If they are suffering as you say, it is probably on account of his bad habits. I hear that he is a great drunkard."

"Let me walk with you at any rate as far as the house," said the clergyman, placing himself at her side without waiting for an answer to his request. "I am afraid you are correct in what you say. I saw him this morning going down the lane toward the river, doubtless to old Cooney's grog-shop. He was staggering then, and he was staggering still more when he passed on his way back an hour afterward. I hardly think it is safe for you to go alone to his house."

"Oh, I am not at all afraid; I have encountered several drunken men in my time. If I find that he can not talk intelligently or understand me, I shall soon leave him."

"But you might find him troublesome. I really think you had better let me be present."

"No, I must beg you to allow me to see him alone," she answered, smiling. "Mr. Benham was, equally with you, solicitous for my safety when I told him where I was going, but I answered him, as I do you, that I prefer to be alone."

"Well!" exclaimed Mr. Trevor, with a hearty laugh, "I certainly have no right, then, to feel slighted, for Mr. Benham is worth five times more as a defender than I am. He would make short work of Mr. Todd, or indeed of any one else about here, if he chose to let his strength out. But here we are at the mouth of the ravine, and if you are obstinate, or shall I say firm, in your desire to be alone, I shall take leave of you here. I don't suppose that you run much risk." He bowed, turned back, and Alana went on her way.

She did not have far to go, the house not being much over a hundred yards from the place where Mr. Trevor had left her, but the road had now degenerated into a path which, being a little rough, required her to take care where she stepped. There was a wagon-road up the ravine, but it was on a level of fifty feet below where she was walking, the path being on a plateau that skirted the edge of the hill. The house was built on an expansion of this plane, there being at most an acre of ground around it. There was another path still higher up that ran around the mountain spirally, and by which the ascent to its top could be made, but at the point where she was it was probably at least a hundred feet above her. Somebody was traversing it, for every now and then a stone was detached and came rolling down the mountain-side across the path she was on, and down into the road at the bottom of the ravine. The two paths were nearly parallel for the first part of their course ; but they soon diverged, the one keeping up the mountain, and the other descending gradually till it joined the road. Whoever he was, the person on the upper path was going much faster than she was, for the stones that at first fell close to her were now rolling down the side a dozen or more yards in front of her. She wondered who it could be that was going so rapidly up the mountain, and then, without stopping to examine further into the matter, she went on till she found herself standing in front of Todd's house.

She stopped for a moment or two to think before knocking at the door, for she had formed no clear idea of what she proposed to accomplish by the visit she was about to make.

And, indeed, when she came to think of it, there was no reason why she should make the visit at all. Had she wanted merely to give Mr. Todd an answer to his letter, she could have done it in writing, or have sent for him to call upon her at her office.

And now she almost made up her mind to go back and adopt one or other of the alternatives mentioned. Then the thought of what Mr. Trevor had told her of Mrs. Todd caused her to decide to go in. It was possible that she might be able to do something to make the life of this woman more tolerable than it appeared to be while she was left to the tender mercies of her husband. So, acting at once on her determination, she knocked on the door with the handle of her parasol.

There was a rather confused sound of voices from within ; which, however, stopped on her knocking, and the door was immediately opened by a sad, pale-faced woman, who, recognizing her visitor, with many apologies for her personal appearance, and for the dilapidated condition of things in the room, invited her to enter.

She had hardly put her foot beyond the threshold, when a man came forward with a staggering, slouching gait.

"I'm glad to see you, Miss Honeywood," he said, with the thickness of utterance exhibited by drunken people. "I was sure you'd come yourself, to see how poorly we're gettin' along, just because o' that purse-proud Byles, the contractor for the brick and stone work of your new forge."

While Todd was speaking, Alana had a good opportunity to examine the man. Certainly he was not a prepossessing-looking person. He was in his shirt-sleeves; his trousers were tucked into his boots, he was dirty, and he was evidently drunk. He had his hat on when Alana entered, and he did not remove it. He staggered over to a distant part of the room, however, and brought a chair for her. As he turned, the sunlight streaming in through a window in the side of the house fell full upon his face, and gave her a better view of it than she had had, and then she perceived that she had seen it somewhere years ago. Where or when she could not tell, but certainly she had seen it before this day.

"I've come, Mr. Todd, to hear from you the cause of your dispute with Mr. Byles."

"Well," said Todd, not sitting down, but walking the floor, and gesticulating vehemently, "there ain't no cause but his spite. He never did like me, and at last his spite got the better of him and he sent me off."

"Mr. Byles says he had ample cause; that you drank too much, and neglected your work."

"Then he lied—that's all there is in it. I don't drink as much as he does, and I have done my best with the work."

"Don't talk so loud, Alec," said Mrs. Todd; "Miss Honeywood ain't deaf."

"Who's a-talkin' loud, and who said she was deaf?"

exclaimed Todd, angrily. "You just mind your own business, will you?"

The woman made no reply, but pretended to be busy
arranging some plates on a shelf that hung against the wall.

"I am very sorry, Mr. Todd," said Alana, "to be obliged
to say that I think there is ample foundation for his actions. You are also accused of having led the men that
demolished the work that had been done on the stack."

"Then that's another lie! Who says that about me?"

"This," said Alana, calmly, at the same time taking the
rule from her pocket and laying it on the table. "It was
found this morning amid the ruins. It has your name
on it."

For a moment the man was dumfounded. He picked
up the rule, looked at it closely, and then, putting it into
his pocket, said :

"Did you find this?"

"No; Mr. Benham found it."

"He's another one of them that's down on me. But
that ain't no matter, if you'll get Byles to take me back."

"I am afraid I can not ask Mr. Byles to hire you again."

"Then give me a place under you. You must have
lots of places that I'd fit into."

"No, I can not employ you here. At the same time,
I do not wish your family to be in want. Mr. Byles will
probably have you arrested for destroying his work last
night, and I must say that you deserve punishment for
your conduct, which seems to have been prompted by mere
wantonness, or worse, a spirit of revenge."

"Then you're agin me too. It's the old story of wealth
agin honesty, capital agin labor. I'd like to know what
right you have to all the mines, and forges, and houses,
when I'm cut out of the chance of earnin' my bread?"

"It is not necessary for us to discuss that matter, for
it has nothing to do with what I came to talk about. I

want to be of assistance to your wife. She may continue to occupy this house, and I shall see that she does not want for food and clothing."

"That's very kind, I'm sure," said the man, ironically. "You'd do her more good by helpin' me than in any other way."

"Is Alec to be took up?" inquired Mrs. Todd, anxiously.

"Mr. Benham informed me this morning that Mr. Byles had gone to get a warrant for his arrest."

"Well, I'd like to see any constable in these parts take me!" exclaimed Todd, opening a drawer and taking a pistol out of it. "I'd put a bullet into him just as soon as I'd put it into a mad dog!"

"I think a better way for you to avoid the constable would be for you to escape. There is plenty of time for you to get out of the country before Mr. Byles returns."

"Yes, you'd like me to go, wouldn't you?" replied the man, sneeringly; "well, I don't mean to, and, what's more," he continued, approaching Alana, and looking impudently and defiantly into her face, "I mean you to give me work."

"O Alec!" cried Mrs. Todd, coming forward and putting herself between her husband and Alana, "don't talk that way to Miss Honeywood. Haven't you had this house rent-free, and didn't she come here to-day to do us a kindness?"

"Well, now that she's here," exclaimed the man, "she's got to promise me work. As to you," he continued, seizing his wife by the arm and slinging her with all his force, "take that!" He let go as he spoke. The woman went reeling into a corner of the room, striking violently against a cupboard, and falling senseless on the floor.

"You brutal fellow!" exclaimed Alana, rising and hurrying to the woman, who was moaning, but was unable

to get up. "You have hurt your wife—yes," as she knelt
down on the floor and took the woman's head in her hands,
"you have injured her severely. Do you see that blood?
Look at what you have done!"

The blood was streaming down his wife's face from a
long and apparently deep cut in her forehead. The sight,
however, so far from calming the man, seemed to enrage him
still further.

"Yes, I see it," he said, rolling up his shirt-sleeves as
he spoke, and looking menacingly at Alana, who still knelt
on the floor beside the senseless woman. "That's what
people get here when they meddle with other people's business. It's a lesson for you, I guess; but I am goin' to give
you a stronger one. You get out of here, but before you
go I'll take what things a rich woman like you are likely
to have, and then we'll have a little talk about the place
you're goin' to give me in the mines. I'd like to be the
superintendent of the Colerain mine, and I guess you'll give
it to me, too."

Alana felt now that she had been imprudent in coming
into the presence of such a brute without the protection
that Mr. Benham and Mr. Trevor had offered her. She
was frightened, but was far from being so terrified as to
lose her presence of mind. She rose to her feet as the man
approached her, determined to rush by him, and escape
through the door, being quite sure that in his drunken
state he would be incapable of following her. Her whole
course of action was resolved upon in an instant.

"Here," she said, approaching the fellow, and holding
out her watch to him, "take this. Is there anything else
you want?"

"I'll take the money you have in your pocket, and then
I'll take a finger off that pretty hand of yours, for calling
me a brute, unless you'll promise on your bended knees to
make me superintendent of the Colerain mine."

Things were indeed in a desperate state, for she was at the mercy, unless she could manage to dash by him, of a ruffian who would evidently stop at nothing. Still, she kept her senses about her, and, taking out her pocket-book, handed it to him. "I think there are fifty dollars in it," she said. "Count it."

"Well, I'll see, and if there ain't, I'll take a finger off the other hand!"

He stood with his back to the door, between it and Alana. It was her intention, as soon as he opened the pocket-book, to make the attempt to reach the door. She had, while talking to him, been examining it so as to get the exact position of the latch, and thus to lose no time in opening it. The pistol, she saw, was on the table at the other end of the room.

But the man had no sooner finished his speech, had not had time, in fact, to open the pocket-book, when the door was suddenly burst open, and a large and powerfully built man advanced into the apartment. To seize Todd by the collar of the coat with one hand, and to deal him a terrible blow on the side of his head with the closed fist of the other, were acts that did not take ten seconds to accomplish. At the same time he jerked the fellow backward, and he lay a confused mass on the floor, stunned by the combined effects of liquor, the blow, and the fall.

"Mr. Benham!" exclaimed Alana.

"Yes, Miss Honeywood, I knew what a bad fellow Todd was, and I thought it would do no harm to watch him a little. I missed my way, however, and barely got here in time to be of service to you."

"It was you, then, who hurried so rapidly up the mountain road?"

"Yes, I was afraid that, if you saw me, you would not allow me to accompany you, and I knew how necessary protection was to you. I went too far, before coming down

the mountain, and thus got beyond the house. I hope the
fellow has done you no harm."

"No, he did not touch me ; I was just getting ready to
make a dash for the door when you opportunely came in.
I am very much obliged to you. I was exceedingly foolish
not to take your advice this morning."

He bent his head in acknowledgment of her thanks.

"Will you look at his wife ?" continued Alana. "She
is severely injured, I am afraid."

"Good heavens ! I did not see her. Yes, she has an
ugly wound in her head, and, from the quantity of blood
that is escaping, I fear an artery has been cut. Do you
think you can go home now, Miss Honeywood, and send
the doctor here ? I will remain and look after the poor
woman till he comes."

While he was speaking he was diligently engaged in
binding his handkerchief around Mrs. Todd's head, and
thus making an effort to stop the bleeding. It was evident,
however, that the attempt was not very successful, for the
handkerchief was rapidly becoming saturated with blood.

Alana did not stop for further speech, but rushed off
down the road along the mountain, and then through the
lane, past the church, and then through another lane at
right angles to the first, till she came to Dr. Arndell's
house, at the distance of a couple of hundred yards from
the turning.

Fortunately, the physician was at home. It did not take
her long to explain her errand, and in a few minutes he
was on his way, with the understanding that he had a case
of partial division of one of the temporal arteries to deal
with, complicated perhaps with injury to the brain. Alana
had said nothing about her own danger and rescue by Benham. There would be time enough for that hereafter.
She went on to her own house, and calling Mrs. Winebrenner, desired her to send at once for a woman who did what

nursing the people of the village required, in addition to keeping a cake and candy shop, for the delectation of the youth of the place that possessed the necessary wherewithal to enable them to avail themselves of her luxuries. On Mrs. Knepley's arrival, Alana sent her at once to Mrs. Todd's assistance, with instructions to remain with her as long as the doctor thought necessary.

An hour afterward, while sitting on the broad veranda that went around the house, she saw the constable and another man escorting Mr. Todd to the railway-station, doubtless on their way with him to the county jail at Harrisburg. Seeing her, the officer of the law left the prisoner in charge of his assistant and brought her her watch and pocket-book that she had been forced to deliver to the amiable person now in custody.

"I found them in his pockets," he said. "It's a clear case of robbery, and I guess it will cost him ten years in the penitentiary."

3

CHAPTER IV.

JOHN BENHAM's house was a substantial stone cottage that had been built for him soon after Alana had come into possession of the property. Previous to that event he had been alone, and had lived with Mrs. Barton, the purveyor of fashion, who, having two second-story rooms that she did not occupy, had been kind enough to rent them with board to the handsome young superintendent.

Mr. Honeywood was the first to give him employment, and he did so on the recommendation of his old friend Prof. Chalmers, of the Scientific School of the University of Pennsylvania, and his statement that the institution had never turned out a closer approach to the ideal metallurgist than was John Benham, nor a truer-hearted gentleman. Benham's father lived in Harrisburg, and, though not rich, was in comfortable circumstances; but at about the time Mr. Honeywood died he died also, and then it was found that he had invested all his means in petroleum companies, most of which were more or less fraudulent, and, of course, worthless. Then the necessity had arisen that John should take care of his mother, and then it was that Alana had built for them the pretty little cottage not far from her own house, and, indeed, standing in the same grounds, though nearer the forge.

John Benham's claims to being a gentleman were as good as those of Mr. Honeywood, but he was as proud as Lucifer, and had always, as it were, kept his employer at a distance. He had come to the Susquehanna Iron-Works to fill a subordinate position; he knew that Mr. Honeywood was disposed to be haughty and austere with those whom he deemed to be his social inferiors whenever they attempted to treat him as an equal; he had seen several instances of his manner of acting to such people, and he had heard of others long before he made Mr. Honeywood's acquaintance, and he had at once determined that he would never allow himself to forget the fact that he was in a position that made him socially the inferior, for the time being at least, of the rich employer. He was, in fact, only an upper servant.

It is due to Mr. Honeywood to say that he had never, by word or deed, given any occasion for John Benham to suppose that he would be treated in a supercilious or unkind manner. When the young man arrived, Mr. Honeywood invited him to stay with him till he could procure suitable lodgings in the village; but Benham had already made his arrangements with Mrs. Barton, and went at once to the rooms that she had prepared for him. "I can do my work better," said Benham to himself, as he walked along the road to Mrs. Barton's, "if there are no familiarities. I shall not be in danger then of forgetting my place as his servant, nor he of forgetting his as my master. When I was in the 250th Pennsylvania Volunteers as a sergeant during the war, it would not have done for me to have messed with my captain, though it was known I was a gentleman and he was a dealer in old clothes. No, I shall be perfectly independent. I shall treat him with the respect due to his position, and he shall act in like manner to me; but no familiarities on either side."

A few days after his arrival Mr. Honeywood had invited him to tea, and this invitation he thought it would be churlish in him to decline. He laughed, however, as he went to his work on leaving his employer. "It's not exactly the same kind of a relation," he said, "as that that existed between Captain Braumiller and Sergeant Benham." At tea he had been presented to Alana. He knew that Mr. Honeywood had a daughter, but he was unprepared to see so beautiful and in every way so attractive a woman as was she who sat at the head of her father's table. Here, however, was additional reason for the reserve as regarded social matters that he had resolved upon adopting. Nevertheless, he recognized the fact that while a guest of Mr. and Miss Honeywood, it was his duty to do all in his power to make himself agreeable, and he had accordingly exerted himself in the direction of trying to cause the evening to pass pleasantly. After he had gone, both Mr. Honeywood and Alana expressed the opinion that rarely had they encountered a more polished and accomplished gentleman. He had shown, by his conversation, that he had been a close observer of men and things, and, as Mr. Honeywood remarked, that he had the stuff in him of which successful men are made. "I shouldn't wonder," he said, with a laugh, "to find John Benham my partner before ten years are over. He'll make a reputation for himself, and will be offered a better position with a higher salary than he gets here, and I shall have found him so indispensable that I shall be glad to give him an interest in the works for the sake of keeping him."

"He's handsome, too, father," said Alana, "and I should think good-tempered."

"Yes, good-tempered so long as he is not improperly interfered with. It would go badly with a man that should attempt to impose on him. He is fully capable of taking care of himself."

As to Benham, he had walked to his home at Mrs. Barton's, his mind in a whirl such as he had never before known it to be in. He more than ever recognized the fact that expediency, to say nothing of any other motive, required that his relations with the Honeywoods should be marked by the formality usually existing between the employer and the employed. So long as he did not allow himself to regard Alana as within his reach, he could permit himself to see her at least from afar off, as a child might look at the moon and admire it, while knowing that he could never get it within his grasp. But if he were to see her often, and on terms of equality, he felt sure that he should lose his heart, and, in that event, there would be danger of his head going also. He knew enough of human nature to be aware of the fact that a man in love is very likely to be unfit for the every-day practical duties of life such as it was incumbent on him to perform, and to which his whole powers should be given.

Moreover, it would be conceived to be the height of impropriety for him, occupying as he did a situation of subordination, to fall in love with his master's daughter. It would be disloyalty in a high degree. It would be taking advantage of his position to do that which Mr. Honeywood certainly would not like. Even if his love should be returned, it would not make him any the more justified ; on the contrary, his conduct would then place him in a still more contemptible position in the minds of all high-minded persons. He knew how the world generally regards the successful lover, even if he has descended to the perpetration of acts that if done in any other cause would be regarded as ungentlemanly. He knew that the adage, "All is fair in love," is made to cover lies, treasons, and all other kinds of villainy and shabbiness short of felony, and that even *that* is sometimes extenuated or pardoned if the offender can only show that love was the real incentive to his crime. He knew all this, but it did not cause him to look at the matter before him with any the more lenient eye. He believed that it would be dishonorable for him to attempt to gain Alana Honeywood's heart, and that was enough.

Perhaps he judged himself too severely and with too narrow a mind. He was not an austere man, neither was he wanting in mental amplitude. But he had been brought up in an old-fashioned school, the representatives of which are fast disappearing from the face of the earth in all civilized countries. Most young men of his time would have thought it a very fine thing for them, if placed in his position, to at once lay their plans, not only for capturing the daughter, but for obtaining a partnership in the business at the earliest possible moment, the chief object in view being the aggrandizement of number one. Such smartness was not, however, an ingredient of John Benham's character. Of course, he expected advancement; he looked forward to the time when, if he had proved himself a valuable and faithful servant, he should have a partnership offered him, but he intended to get it by doing his duty as the superintendent of the Susquehanna Iron-Works, and not by forcing himself into the owner's family by marrying his daughter. Perhaps, when he stood upon the same business plane with Mr. Honeywood—but that was too remote a contingency to be considered now. So he kept himself aloof, rarely meeting Alana, and when they came into association never "laying himself out," as the somewhat slangy but abundantly expressive phrase goes, to make himself especially agreeable.

Of course, both Alana and her father noticed his manner, and the fact that they did not think it particularly out of the way, was perhaps an indication that Benham was not far wrong in the principles that governed him in the matter. Nevertheless they gave him the character of not being what is called a "society man." "I have several times had occasion to go to his rooms in the evening," said Mr. Honeywood to his daughter, one day when they were discussing the superintendent, "and I have always found him studying some work relating to metallurgy. He has accumulated quite a good-sized library, and is besides conducting a series of experiments relative to smelting ore, by which he expects that a great saving in fuel and labor will be effected. Depend upon it, my dear, he cares more for his profession than he does for our society."

"That is very evident," said Alana, laughing : "but don't you think he would be more consistent if he avoided *all* society ? Mr. Trevor and Dr. Arndell and Mr. Wade tell me that he visits them quite frequently, and invites them to his rooms."

"It must be you, then, my dear," rejoined her father. "You are the formidable obstacle that stands in the way of his coming here. However, I shall not be able to keep him out of his partnership ten years if he goes on as he has begun."

Then, when Mr. Honeywood died, and Alana was left the sole mistress of the works, it was still more necessary, so John Benham thought, for him to be circumspect and reserved in his conduct. It was a hard struggle that he had with himself now. He had not lived at the Susquehanna Iron-Works for three years without, notwithstanding his isolation, having seen a good deal of Alana Honeywood. He had observed her when she had no idea that she was being looked at ; he had heard her talk when she did not know that he was within ear-shot ; he had thought of her when she did not dream that she ever crossed his mind except when some matter of business was concerned. He loved her with all his heart. Not madly, for, notwithstanding his fears when he had first come into association with her, he had not lost his head ; and no one in all the world, not even the object of his devotion, imagined that John Benham's heart was big enough to hold his profession and a woman at the same time.

Outwardly there was no change in his manner, except such as was necessary in order for him to adapt himself to the relation of having Alana instead of her father for his superior.   For a year she had, as we have seen, left everything to him ; then she had taken the reins, and he had fallen naturally and easily into his old position—still, however, as in her father's time, exercising the real power that governed the establishment.

Then the death of his father had rendered it necessary that his mother should in the future find her home with him, and in order that he might make the requisite arrangements he had requested and received permission to be absent for ten days.   He thanked Alana for granting him the favor, and was turning away to avail himself at once of his privilege, when she stopped him.

"Is your mother in Harrisburg ?" she inquired.

"Yes."

"Will you be kind enough to defer your departure till to-morrow ?   For I would like to go to Harrisburg to-day to see your mother, to express my sympathy with her in the death of your father, and to ask her to stay with me till the house that I have directed to be built for you is finished."

"Miss Honeywood !"

"Yes, it was my father's intention to build a superintendent's house.   He often spoke of the matter to me, and even selected the ground for it.   I think, too," she added, reflectively, "that he had plans for it drawn, and that they must be somewhere in this room."

"I scarcely know how to thank you, Miss Honeywood."

"No," she answered, smiling, "but you know something better ; you know how to manage iron-works, and to increase their revenue over any previous year.   It is only right, therefore, that you should be well housed, especially as you will now have your mother with you."

"It is very pleasant to me to know that you appreciate my efforts in your service."

Alana thought for a moment. She liked him, and she wished to be his friend, but here he was accepting her gifts as a general might accept a decoration or a sword given him by his government for distinguished military services. He had done his duty, and her appreciation of the fact and her mode of showing it were gratifying to him. He was as distant as ever—as unapproachable as on the day he had entered her father's service. She liked strong characters, and certainly she had one to deal with in John Benham. He had made no specific allusion to her expressed intention of visiting his mother, and of inviting her to be her guest till his house was finished, but from what she knew of him he would have been prompt enough to decline if he had had any objections to make to the arrangement. But he had no notion of treating her kindness with boorishness.

"My mother will be glad to see you, I am sure," he said. "Such sympathy as yours will be soothing to her. I can go as well to-morrow as to-day, and, as you say, both of us ought not to be absent at once. It seems to me, however, that she would be incurring a very great obligation were she to accept your hospitalities during the whole time that the new house is being built."

"No, Mr. Benham, the obligation will be the other way, for I am at times very lonesome. This house is so large that I often feel lost in it, with no one to keep me from thinking of the past."

"She will be gratified by your invitation, but you will not find her a cheerful companion. Her loss is more recent than yours, and the memory of it is fresher. But I am sure she will be grateful for your kindness, and anxious to do anything that she may think will please you."

Alana went to Harrisburg, saw Mrs. Benham, and induced her to accept the invitation to her house. For six months she was a member of Alana's household, and during this period the unofficial meetings between the iron-mistress and her superintendent were numbered with the days. Still, he was always the same, always respectful, always polite, always considerate, but never venturing on the slightest familiarity, or advancing an iota beyond the line he had established. Alana wondered at him more and more. Was this man made of stone, that she could make no impression upon him ? Then she resolved to accept the situation, to make no further advance, to treat him with the same formality that he observed toward her, but never-theless to regard him as a man to be trusted in all the de-tails of the business, and as one to be relied upon in any emergency that might arise. Occasionally she visited his mother, at times when she knew he would not be present, and Mrs. Benham, sometimes accompanied by her son, but generally alone, returned the visits. There were mutual respect, kindness, and a deep-seated regard, but attended by all the formality that the greatest stickler for etiquette could have desired.

I think the majority of my readers will decide that John Benham was somewhat straining principles very good in the abstract, but capable of being perverted to the origi-nation of conduct bordering on the absurd. He was a man with the utmost faith in himself, and yet he appeared to be afraid that, should he venture upon the slightest de-gree of friendly intimacy with Alana, he should be in dan-ger of going further than a due regard for their relative positions would warrant. It should be borne in mind that these relations had changed with the death of her father and the advance of time. She was not a girl in her teens under guardianship ; but a woman twenty-six years of age, her own mistress, possessed of excellent mental capacity, and fully able to judge for herself in all matters that affected her. There was no reason, therefore, why John Benham should not have laid siege to her heart, and have captured it, had she been willing to surrender. Whether she would, or not, he could doubtless have ascertained had he allowed himself a little more freedom in his intercourse with her. Still, it must be admitted that the situation was not without its peculiarities. It was a matter about which there would have to be absolute certainty before he could dare to lay bare his heart to her. Rejection would mean, of course, the severance of his business relations with Alana, and his immediate departure from the Susquehanna Iron-Works. The retention by a rejected lover of an office that he held from the woman who had refused him, would be out of the question.

And, as a matter of fact, Alana did not love him. She admired him for his supposed possession of certain qualities that stamp their holder as a good man in the largest sense of the word, and she respected him for his independence of character and devotion to his duty. If she thought at all of the matter, she admitted that it would be perfectly safe for her to trust herself with him for all her life. He would look after her interests, protect her, cherish her, love her after a fashion; but she was a warm-hearted woman, and that would not have been sufficient for her.

But there was another reason that was still more powerful in causing Alana to dismiss from her mind as a thing past recall the idea that she could ever marry Benham, or, indeed, any one else, and that was the fact of her disgraceful parentage. True, no one, so far as she was aware, knew of the circumstance but herself and Mr. Wade, but that made it none the less humiliating. Indeed, in some respects it was worse than if all the world understood who and what she was; for she felt that she was as it were a living lie, a woman passing herself off for what she was not. She had heard of rogues being sent to prison for getting money under false pretenses. Were they really worse than she? Was she not getting a position of respectability in the world by false pretenses? Would Mrs. Priestly allow her daughters to visit her if she knew that her mother had never been married, and that she not only belonged to the very lowest stratum of American society but was in all probability a member of the criminal class? Well, there might be, she confessed, some doubt as to Mrs. Priestly's course of action. Wealth covers a multitude of blotches, not only on escutcheons but on bodily form and mental characteristics. She could thank God that there was no reproach against her on either of these latter scores, and doubtless Mrs. Priestly would forgive her the rest, so long as she owned the Susquehanna Iron-Works.

As to John Benham, to think of him as a possible husband would be worse than a folly; it would be a crime. How could she, as an honest woman, allow an honest man to marry her with the taint that was inherent in her coursing with the blood through her veins, and making her unfit to be the wife of his bosom and the mother of his children? No, it was impossible, not only that she should marry him, but, in fact, any other respectable man.

But John Benham had good, sound common sense, and was apparently free, to a great extent, from the narrow-minded prejudices that so-called practical men generally exhibit. He would think no less of her if her mother were tenfold lower—if it were possible—in the dregs of humanity. He was generous, too, and if she loved him, and he loved her, and she were—as in duty bound she should be—to tell him all that she knew of herself, he would only cling to her the closer. That she knew. She had studied him enough to comprehend his character—better, perhaps, than he himself comprehended it. And then, too, while love does not, like wealth, cover mental and social deformities, it prevents them being seen, by rendering the observer blind, so that the result is just as satisfactory—while the love lasts.

Yes, so far as he was concerned, if she loved him, and he loved her, she should have no fear. She felt, however, that she should be disgracing him, no matter what he might think. The world would judge her even more severely than she judged herself, and it would say that she had committed an outrage on an honest man—and, and— Well, the world would be right.

It may be contended that a woman that could reason, in this way, in regard to a man, associating herself in her mind, with him, in situations implying the existence of love between them, must have had more than a liking, or friendship, for that man, even though she might not be fully aware of the state of her heart. I am not sure that it was not so with Alana Honeywood. It may be that she had, for a long time, loved John Benham without knowing the fact. There is such a form of the emotion as latent love, just as there is a form of heat known as latent heat. Like latent heat, latent love is only exhibited under certain circumstances. For the development of the one, there are well-known causes, but for making unconscious love conscious we have no idea what the excitations may be, till the instant that they arise. Doubtless, there were factors that could at once have made Alana's love sensible to herself, as well as to its object; but no one knew what they were, and there were apparently no causes likely to develop them.

Thus matters stood when the incident at the house in the ravine occurred. Perhaps, that was to be the spark to fire the mine.

CHAPTER V.

THE attack made by Todd on Miss Honeywood, and her narrow escape, through the interposition of John Benham, were the topics of conversation all that day at the Susquehanna Iron-Works. It was well for Mr. Alexander Todd that he was safe on his way to jail, in Harrisburg, ere the fact of his misconduct became generally known among Alana's workmen. As it was, about fifty of them started off for his house, as soon as they heard the news, prepared to take summary vengeance on him, as they declared, by tying him to a tree, and giving him a hundred strokes with a cowhide on his bare back ; but they found only his wife and her nurse, the former lying in bed, and still in an unconscious state, notwithstanding the vigorous treatment initiated by Dr. Arndell.

Then they returned to the works, and gathering together all the men that could be spared from their labors, they formed a procession, and marched to Alana's house, making the air ring with their cheers, and preceded by the Susquehanna Iron-Works band, that discoursed very emphatic music, even if it was not the most harmonious. Alana saw them coming, and knew what their object was, so she sent a servant to Mr. Trevor, with a note, requesting him to come at once, and make the speech, in her behalf, that she knew the men would require from some one.

But, before the messenger reached the reverend gentleman's house, the procession was at Alana's door, accompanied by all the population, men, women, and children, of the village, available for the occasion. They formed in a line in front of the house, and, while the band continued to play an inspiriting popular air, Messrs. Michael Maloney, Joseph Witler, and Peter Fink, a committee appointed for the occasion, left the ranks, and, advancing up the terrace, rapped at the door, and, on its being opened, requested that they might have the pleasure of seeing "the mistress," that being the designation given to Alana by the workmen, and, in fact, by most of the inhabitants of the village and the neighboring region. Alana saw that there was no escape, and at once sent down a request to the committee to wait in the library, where in a moment she would join them. She was not long in following.

"We have come, mistress," said Michael Maloney, who had been made spokesman for the occasion, "to tell ye how pleased we are to learn that ye suffered no inconvanience from that villain Todd. We felt that we wouldn't be returnin' all the kindnesses ye've done to us, and our wives and little ones, if we left this chance to go by without offerin' our congratulations to a lady whose workmen we are, and proud we are of the fact. May God Almighty bless you, and—and—" With this the honest fellow broke down, and, covering his face with his hands, sobbed like a child.

"You see, mistress," said Witler, while Alana, down whose face the tears were coursing at this manifestation of love from her workmen, tried to give him her attention, "we were shust goin' to make it hot for Mr. Todd. I don't forget how, when mine leetle Gretchen was down mit de fever, you come and stayed mit her a whole night; me and mine wife don't forget dem dings," and then Witler, like his predecessor, "went to pieces," leaving Fink to finish the address.

"If the mistress," he said, "would come out on the veranda, and let the people see that she was all right, it would be a great pleasure to them. There isn't a man on the place that wouldn't go to—do his best to serve the mistress, and, if she'd just show herself, it would please them mightily."

"Your kindness overwhelms me," said Alana, much moved. "It is worth while going through some danger to find that I am so greatly beloved by you whom I have known and respected for many years, and who have served my father and me so faithfully. Yes, I will go out and see the rest of my friends."

She led the way, and the committee-men followed.

As soon as she appeared at the door, a shout was raised that made the mountains echo and re-echo the sound, while the band played with renewed vigor. Silence was at length obtained, and then Alana, in a few words that they all saw came from her heart, thanked them for the interest they took in her welfare. "And," she continued, "there are two things I am about to do for you that may serve to show that I am not unmindful of your faithfulness and uniform kindness to me. First, I have long thought that it was something of a hardship that those of you who belong to the Roman Catholic Church—a majority, I think—should be obliged to go to Dauphin to attend services. I had an interview with your bishop at Harrisburg a few days ago, and he has promised that, if I will build the church, he will see that it is supplied with a pastor. To-morrow the ground will be broken, and before long I hope you will have your own building within easy access to you winter and summer. I shall ask Mr. Benham to confer with you immediately relative to the best situation for the edifice.

"Then I have thought that you ought to have some place at which you could spend your leisure hours—you, and your wives and children—and, at the same time, read the newspapers and entertaining and instructive books. I

am going, therefore, to erect a building in which there
will be a library and a hall, at which concerts and lectures
can be given and meetings held. This will be open every
day till ten o'clock at night, and I hope to have it in
operation in three months from this time.

"It is only right, my friends, that I should tell you
that it would probably have gone hard with me if Mr.
Benham, our superintendent, had not arrived just in time
to interpose his strength against that of my assailant.
Again I thank you."

This short address was frequently interrupted by vocif-
erous applause, and, at its end, with "Three cheers for the
mistress!" The assemblage then, by common consent, repaired to Benham's cottage, where they gave the superintendent what the Harrisburg papers of the following day
described as a "second ovation," the first having been the
demonstration at Alana's house.

While they were still filing away from the door, Mr.
Trevor made his appearance, very much out of breath, for
he had run nearly all the distance from his house to
Alana's. She had just re-entered the door, when the
reverend gentleman dashed up the steps.

"My dear Miss Honeywood!" he exclaimed. "what's
all this I hear? Surely, it is not true that that scoundrel
insulted you! And how kind of the men and the women,
and the children too, to turn out in force to congratulate
you! I'm sorry I could not get here in time to spare you the
trouble of making them a speech, though doubtless you were
much more satisfactory to them than I would have been."

"I don't know," said Alana, smiling; "I said what
came into my mind. I believe I did get through better
than I expected."

"Ah! you ought to have allowed me to go with you to
Todd's house, and to have remained to protect you."

"Mr. Benham was there."

"Mr. Benham! I did not know that he was to be with you. If I had, I should have felt easier in regard to your safety."

"I did not know it either."

"Then it was by accident," said Mr. Trevor, with an air of relief. "It was fortunate, then, that he arrived just in time."

"No, it was not by accident. I told him I was going; he said it was not safe for me to go without an escort, but I thought differently, as I did when you kindly offered your services. Still, so strongly was he impressed with a sense of the danger I ran, that he followed me, and, taking the mountain-path so that I should not know of his movements, arrived at the house just in time to save me from injury; but unfortunately, as he missed his way, not soon enough to prevent the brute inflicting a serious wound on his poor wife, by which she was rendered senseless."

"Yes, he knew the fellow better than I did. I hope you were not greatly frightened?"

"I was frightened, but I tried to prevent losing my presence of mind. I think I might have got away even if Mr. Benham had not come in time; but if I had failed, the man would certainly have cut off one of my fingers as he threatened."

"Good heavens! You don't mean to tell me that he went so far as that?"

"Yes; but I must beg that you will now dismiss me from further consideration. I am greatly worried on account of his poor wife; she is grievously injured, I fear. Dr. Arndell arrived as soon as possible, but I am sure he is alarmed for her life." .

"Did *you* go after the doctor?"

"Yes; there was no one else to go, for Mr. Benham was obliged to stay with Mrs. Todd, to prevent her bleeding to death from the wound in her head."

"My dear Miss Honeywood, I shall never forgive my-self for leaving you alone in the ravine. I ought to have insisted on going with you."

"But you will recollect," answered Alana, laughing, "that I sent you away."

"Yes, but I ought to have gone, for all that. Now I shall make amends by going at once to see how Mrs. Todd is doing, and I'll come in this evening and report. I can never"—he continued, holding out his hand to Alana—"be sufficiently thankful to God for having saved you from harm." He turned away much-moved, and Alana went on her way into the house.

"It's all very well for him to thank God," exclaimed Mrs. Winebrenner, who had been present during the conversation, but had had no opportunity of getting in a word, "but he might have been a little more thankful to Mr. Benham. *He* go with you! I'd like to know what good *he'd* be in a mess with a fellow like Todd! Now no one, I guess, reverences the clergy more than I do. My father was the pastor for forty-two years of the Lutheran church in Hummelstown, and I was, from a baby, in the society of the members of the synod; but there wasn't one of them that would have been worth a cent in a row, and they were all bigger men, too, than Mr. Trevor. He'd better stick to his church, I think, and let such men as Mr. Benham do all the fighting that may be necessary."

"I think I've read of 'fighting parsons,'" said Alana, with a smile. "Perhaps Mr. Trevor comes under that head. He will probably stay to tea; so have the table prepared, please."

"Stay to tea! I think you give him too much encouragement."

"Encouragement! What do you mean?"

"You know, Miss Alana, I've lived in this house nearly fifteen years, and I feel more like a mother to you than a housekeeper, though I don't think I've forgotten my place often. You'll not be angry with me if I speak my mind freely, especially when I do it for your good."

"You've always been very kind to me, and I have a great affection for you. As you say, you have stood in the place of a mother to me, when there was no one else to do so. I don't think I could be angry with you for anything you might say to me in kindness."

"Then I'll speak out, if I never say another word. It's very clear that Mr. Trevor is in love with you."

"Stop, please!" exclaimed Alana; "I don't think it's at all clear. He has never said a word to me that would lead to that inference. It is scarcely worth while, therefore, for you to say anything more on an assumption that has no foundation."

"Ah! my dear—you mustn't mind my calling you 'my dear'—I've known you since you were a mere child—"

"You may call me your 'dear,' of course," interrupted Alana. "I hope you will always love me."

"I'm sure I shall. Well, as I was going to say, I'm a better judge than you are, for I've seen his looks and observed his manner, and there can be no doubt that he is deeply in love. He will speak before long, depend upon it."

"I think you are mistaken, for there has been absolutely nothing that I have observed. Of course, Mr. Trevor comes here often, for there are many things that we have to talk about. Oh, yes, I am sure you are wrong!"

"No," persisted Mrs. Winebrenner, "I am not mistaken; I know men too well not to understand the meaning of looks and conduct, even though not a word be spoken. He will speak soon—perhaps this very night. He would have done so to-day if I had not been present. Now, my dear, there are two very powerful reasons why you should not marry him."

Alana started. Had Mrs. Winebrenner become acquainted with her secret? That was almost impossible, for no one at the works, except Mr. Wade, so far as she knew, was acquainted with the story of her parentage. Besides, if Mrs. Winebrenner had heard any rumors affecting her, she would not have given expression to them in so resolute a way. She smiled, therefore, at the old housekeeper's earnestness.

"Tell me the reasons," she said; "one is generally sufficient for the rejection of a marriage proposal. I shall be doubly armed."

"Yes, my reasons are two; one concerns you, the other him. In the first place, clergymen don't make good husbands for rich women. I have watched them pretty closely, and they all relax in their labors as soon as they marry women who have enough to support them. Then they know so little of business matters, that they are not fit to take the charge as husbands should of their wives' interests. If Mr. Trevor had the management of the works, they would go to ruin in a year. If you were in love with him, and determined to marry him, it would be better for you to give up your wealth, and go to the parsonage as a clergyman's wife solely, and not bring him here to spoil everything. That's one reason."

"Now," said Alana, laughing heartily, "what is the other reason why I should not marry Mr. Trevor? You said that it concerned him. Perhaps I should not make him a good wife."

"Ah, my dear, you'll make a good enough wife to the man you love. But this reason does concern him and him alone. You know I was brought up a Lutheran, but that through the ministrations of Mr. Trevor I became a member of the church four years ago. I've read a good deal on church matters, especially on those relating to the primitive church, and I am convinced that the men to whom the apostles gave their succession should never marry."

"You are hard on them," rejoined Alana, still laughing, but not in a way to offend the old lady. "First you deny them rich wives, and next you would prevent them marrying at all."

"Yes, that is it. If Mr. Trevor were married, his usefulness in this parish would be destroyed; if he were married to you, he would not only be injured as a priest of the church, but the Susquehanna Iron-Works would in a year's time be deserted."

"Well, my dear friend," said Alana, seriously, "keep your soul in patience. I shall never marry Mr. Trevor or any other man. I am cut out for an old maid."

"You are not quite twenty-seven. You ought to marry soon; you would make a good wife to a good man."

"There is Mr. Wade. He's a good man," replied Alana, feeling inclined to humor the old lady and to elicit her views.

"He's too old and too coarse."

"Too coarse!"

"Yes. I met him the other day on the road, and he stopped me. 'Hot day, Mrs. Winebrenner,' said he. 'Yes,' I answered, 'it's a warm day.' 'I never perspired so much in all my life,' said he. 'I'm parboiled; cooked in my own juice like a scalloped oyster.' I think that was very coarse."

"It wasn't very refined, I admit, but then I'd polish him."

"You'd never polish William Wade. His ways are burned into him and are part of him, as much as his ridiculous notion of living in a round tower. He'd never leave his tower, and you would not consent to go there."

"I am afraid the tower would be an insuperable obstacle. But, then, there is Dr. Arndell."

"Dr. Arndell! An infidel, a deist, an atheist, a scoffer, a man who never puts his foot inside of a church! You could not unite yourself with a man like that!"

"If I intended to marry at all, I don't see why I should not marry Dr. Arndell. He's a gentleman, is well educated, refined, kind to the poor. He likes me, too, and—and—" she added, mischievously, "I like him."

"Yes, he likes you. He loves you as much as Mr. Trevor does. I've watched him, too; but, my dear, you'd never throw yourself away on a man of no principles like Dr. Arndell. Oh, if I thought you'd do such a thing, I should be very unhappy."

"But I will not admit that Dr. Arndell is a man without principles. He is a generous, kind-hearted, liberal-minded gentleman, and I say again that if I had any intention of marrying, I might—now mind, I only say 'might'—if he were to ask me, take him with a 'Thank you, sir.' But he is not 'keeping company'—as they say about here—with me."

Mrs. Winebrenner looked at the girl for a moment, and then, bending forward, laid both hands on her head. "What makes you so light-hearted to-day? I don't think I have ever seen you in a merrier mood. You look as if a ray of sunshine had rested on your face and was never going away."

"Do I look happy? Well, I *am* happy. Is it not a great thing to be rescued as I was so bravely and disinterestedly? Is it not another great thing to be the recipient of such affection as every one has been showing me? When I think of it all, I feel glad, and I suppose it shows in my face."

"Mr. Benham is a brave man and a stanch friend. He knows something of women, too. He did not stop to controvert your assertion that there was no danger in your going to Todd's house. He knew there *was* danger, and he had the courage of his opinion, which is more than Mr. Trevor had, and more than Dr. Arndell would have had if the chance had been offered to him as it was to the others."

"Come, now, you don't know what Dr. Arndell would have done, and you are therefore scarcely just to him. He also has courage and determination, and he, probably—as that seems to be a point of importance—knows more about women than both of them put together."

"Your mind seems to be set in favor of Dr. Arndell. Now, I don't believe you half thanked Mr. Benham for what he did for you."

"I thanked him very little. He is not a man that one can thank much. He looks as though he would not like it."

"It might be well to ask him here to tea this evening."

"No, but I think I shall ask Dr. Arndell. I am anxious to hear from his own lips how Mrs. Todd is doing. Won't you please send Moses to him with a note I am going to write?"

She sat down at a table and in a minute or two wrote a note which she handed to Mrs. Winebrenner, and the latter, with a half-stifled sigh, left the room.

Alana, as soon as she was alone, covered her face with her hands, and resting her head on the table before her, sobbed with the violence of the emotion, whatever it was, that overwhelmed her.

"Oh," she moaned, "I think I am the most miserable woman that ever lived! I can not endure this lie much longer. I have acted it till my heart is almost broken. The strain is more than I can bear; and yet I thought down to this day that I should be able to live through it—now I know it is impossible."

She spoke the last words in a low whisper, and, rising

from the chair, began to walk up and down the floor. Her face was as pale as a sheet, and she looked as though she could hardly stand, much less walk. She took but a few steps, and then, supporting herself against the window-frame, looked out over the lawn and beyond to the works, where the tall chimneys were giving out great volumes of smoke and fire, while the hum of the blast reached her ears.

"It is mine," she said, wearily, "but, oh, how readily I would give it all for the knowledge that my mother was an honorable and good woman! I have not even the right to the name that came with it," she continued, bitterly— "a name that I have borne falsely all my life, and that like an impostor with an *alias* I continue to keep. So did my mother before me. She had several names. I come honestly by the tendency to falsehood, at any rate. It is the one thing that I can not lose. To act a lie is worse than to speak one.

"How bravely he acted!" she said, more calmly, after she had lain down on a sofa that stood against the wall on one side of the window, and tried, though unsuccessfully, to compose herself to sleep. "Bravely but coldly.. From a sense of duty only. The duty of any man to any woman ; of any superintendent of iron-works to any woman that owns them and employs him. My God! if he would only do something for me that was not prompted by duty!" She sat up on the sofa and pushed back the hair from her face. "Yes, I would go on then, I think, and act my lie to the end ; for, God help me, I love him—I love him!"

She threw herself on the sofa as she spoke, and, burying her face in its velvet cushion, abandoned herself without restraint to the storm of emotion that she was helpless to resist, and that carried her whither it would. Yes, she loved him—she knew it now ; and with the consciousness came the recollection of the social degradation that she felt

4

was attached to her, and that in her estimation would stand as an adamantine barrier against her ever being the wife of an honorable man.

That was the way in which her thoughts ran. First, determining that if John Benham loved her she would keep her secret to herself, and be his wife if all the world stood in the way, so only that he asked her; then, becoming horrified at the idea of deceiving the man that trusted her, she would break out into self-reproaches, and declare that nothing should induce her to link her dishonored name with his.

She was still in the midst of her passion of tears when the door opened and Mrs. Winebrenner entered the room.

"Moses has just returned," she began, before she had the opportunity in the rather dark room of seeing where Alana was. Then looking around, she saw her lying with her face pressed against the sofa, and exhibiting a degree of agitation that more strikingly than words showed how deeply the girl was moved.

Mrs. Winebrenner saw that Alana had not yet noticed her presence. At first she thought she would endeavor to ascertain the cause of the grief that was evidently rending the heart of her young mistress. The old lady prided herself on the sympathetic qualities that she believed she possessed, and was always on the alert to soothe a troubled spirit with kind words and actions. The idea struck her that Alana's outburst of sorrow was probably due to recollections evoked by the fact that to-morrow was the anniversary of her father's death; but a little reflection sufficed to convince her that even the remembrance of that sad event would not produce such a whirlwind of passion as that which convulsed the agonized woman on the sofa. No, there was something more acute than the death that had taken place two years ago.

She stood for a moment undecided; then she turned

and very gently retreated from the room, with Dr. Arndell's note undelivered, and with Alana still sobbing on the sofa as though her heart were broken.

Probably she cried herself to sleep, and thus counteracted the effects that such a degree of emotional disturbance as she had experienced would otherwise have inevitably produced. At any rate, at seven o'clock she was waiting in the drawing-room to receive her two guests, and not exhibiting, except, perhaps, to a critical eye such as was Dr. Arndell's, any traces of the conflict that had raged within her.

CHAPTER VI

"I DO not want to appear illiberal," said Mr. Trevor, as he stirred the cream and sugar in his second cup of tea; "but it seems to me that you have not acted with your usual prudence in establishing a Roman Catholic church in the village. Do you think there is a Roman Catholic in all the world, situated as you are, that would build a Protestant Church?"

"I do not know whether there is or not," replied Alana, with a little tinge of vigor in her tone. "I did not stop to consider what others would do. I thought it right that the people who work for me faithfully, and many of whom are Catholics, should not be obliged to walk nearly four miles through the heat and dust of summer, and the cold and snow of winter, in order to worship God according to their consciences; and so I am going to build the church."

"Trevor is afraid that the priest will draw off some of his congregation," broke in Dr. Arndell, with a laugh. "He knows the bishop will send one of his strongest men to take charge of the church, and he is trembling for the consequences."

"If by building a Roman Catholic church, or any other church, Miss Honeywood should succeed in getting you inside of a building devoted to the worship of God, it would almost of itself justify the undertaking." The clergyman spoke in an irritated tone, and stirred his tea with renewed energy.

"If you could pound me in a mortar, now, as energetically as you are pounding the sugar in your tea," exclaimed the doctor, still laughing, "what an intense satisfaction it would be to you! As to Miss Honeywood, and my salvation, I doubt if her interest in me extends as far as that point."

"No, but don't you wish it did?" was on Mr. Trevor's lips, but he stopped the impulse before the words were pronounced, and made some commonplace observation about "doctors and atheists," that made the physician smile, but that elicited no remark in reply.

"At any rate, Arndell," resumed the clergyman, seeing that the doctor evinced no desire to get into a theological argument with him, "however poor a Christian you may be, you're a good physician. I suppose you told Miss Honeywood about poor Mrs. Todd before my arrival. Won't you be kind enough to give me your conclusion as to the probable result of her injuries?"

"Yes, I had just finished telling Miss Honeywood when you came in. Mrs. Todd is in a critical condition; I think she has a fracture of the base of the skull, and, if so, she will probably die. I am not sure yet; to-morrow will settle the matter past doubt. She must have struck the vertex of the skull when she fell against the bureau."

"What a wonderful profession yours is, Arndell! How are you able to say, when there are no external marks, and no means of seeing, or even of feeling the base of the skull, that it is fractured?"

"Oh," exclaimed the doctor, laughing, "I can't give you a lecture on the symptomatology of fractures of the base of the skull. It will be sufficient if I say that the bleeding from the ears indicates such an injury."

"If she should die, it will go hard with Todd, I should think," remarked Alana.

"Yes, but they can't hang him for it, I fear, for it would scarcely be murder in the first degree. He did not intend to kill her. You will be the chief witness for the Commonwealth."

"I suppose so. It will be very unpleasant to me, for, though the man deserves to be punished, I don't wish to be the means of bringing him to punishment."

"He'll have to be tried, too, for robbery, and for assault and battery on you. That will give him ten or more years in the penitentiary."

"Oh, I hope those charges will not be pressed!" cried Alana; "let them go. He did me no harm."

"You are too lenient," said Mr. Trevor. "It is just as necessary for the safety of society that Todd should be punished for his attack on you, as for what he did to his wife. In fact, more so, for he intended to do you a brutal personal injury, whereas it is pretty certain that he only meant to thrust his wife out of the way."

"I never knew a clergyman that was not in favor of the full measure of the law being meted out to all offenders," said the doctor, returning to the attack on his clerical friend, but from another standpoint. "Doesn't it strike you that it might be some gratification to Miss Honeywood to forgive this man, and that her wishes are entitled to some consideration?"

"My friend, I am sorry to say," spoke the clergyman, eagerly, for he at once perceived that he had caught the doctor in a weak spot, "that you have no clear idea of what you are talking about. Miss Honeywood's disposition to forgiveness is a faculty that I should be the last to attempt to curb. It is her duty to exercise it, and she does so with all the graciousness inherent in her; but she will, I know," as he looked at Alana, and bowed, "excuse me if I remind her of what doubtless she knows as well as I do, that she has nothing to do with the law but to obey it, and, as a good citizen, aid in its enforcement. If called upon, she will testify, of course."

"By the by," said the doctor, wisely changing the conversation, "I understand, since Todd's arrest, that all the striking brick-layers have announced their intention of going to work to-morrow morning."

"Ah! then we shall have the new furnace ready for use sooner than I expected this morning, from what Mr. Benham told me," said Alana. "And that reminds me," she continued, "that I shall be very glad if you two gentlemen, in conjunction with Mr. Benham, and Mr. Wade, and myself—if you don't object to having a woman in your company—would act as managers of the lyceum that is soon to be put in operation."

"Nothing would give me greater pleasure," said each of them in a breath.

"I shall be glad, too, if you would each, at your earliest convenience, give me a list of the books that ought to be purchased at the start. Doubtless you will, in many instances, name the same works, and it will be my task to go over all the separate lists and strike out the duplicates."

"You won't have much to do so far as Mr. Trevor and I are concerned," observed the doctor, in a matter-of-fact tone of voice, "for it is not at all probable that there will be any concurrence in our selections. He wouldn't be likely to name a single book that I've named, and I'm quite sure I shall not have a book on my list that will be found on his."

"So much the less trouble for me, then," said Alana, smiling, "and so much the greater variety of works for the library."

"I shall doubt the expediency of placing in the hands of simple, ignorant people, like ours here, such books as Dr. Arndell would be likely to select." Mr. Trevor made this observation with his eyes cast down, and as though he were only for his own satisfaction expressing a thought that was too strongly felt to lie dormant in his mind.

"Do you think I'm a fool?" exclaimed the doctor, angrily. "Do you suppose that I would attempt to cram these sucking babes in knowledge with food fit only for trained minds? Yet that is what you'll do, if Miss Honeywood permits you. You'll have Paley's 'Natural Theology,' and Butler's 'Analogy of Religion,' and Leslie's 'Short and Easy Method with a Deist,' and such like trash."

"There shall be no theological books of any kind," said Alana, with decision; "and, above all, no anti-theological books. History, biography, travels, popular science, books of reference, and a few good novels, will do very well to start with.—Ah, Mr. Wade," she continued, as that gentleman entered the room, as he was in the habit of doing, without ceremony, "I am glad you are here; I did not invite you to tea, for, the last three times I have asked you, you gave some indifferent excuse for not coming, so I resolved that the next time you should come of your own accord. I see my plan works well."

"It would be no slight matter that would prevent me accepting your invitation. Lawyers, like doctors, can't call their time their own. How often have you asked Dr. Arndell without getting him?"

"Never once," said the doctor, answering for her— "never once. I'd let every patient I have die of neglect before I'd refuse an invitation from Miss Honeywood."

"The hypocritical fellow!" said Mr. Trevor, to himself. "He thinks that speech will please her. She's not the kind of a woman to like that sort of thing. I never saw a man with less knowledge of human nature than Arndell."

"Then I should be very sorry," said Alana; "and I don't think you would do so, either. You have never neglected your patients."

"You are perfectly right," rejoined Mr. Trevor. "If

Dr. Arndell has any good point in his character—and I am free to admit that he has several—that of being a competent and faithful physician is the one."

"And that atones for a multitude of deficiencies—if he has any."

The doctor looked his thanks and bowed, but made no answer. He had never before had so decided a compliment from Alana, and it pleased him beyond measure.

In accordance with Alana's request, Mr. Wade, after congratulating her on her escape, seated himself at the table, and the conversation again turned on the events of the day. Then the party adjourned to the drawing-room, and the two younger gentlemen, thinking it likely that Mr. Wade had come on business, soon afterward took their departure.

No sooner had the door closed on them, than Mr. Wade began to state the object of his visit.

"I was in Harrisburg to-day," he said, "and it was there that I first heard of the danger you had been in. I heard of it from the perpetrator of the outrage, Todd himself."

"Todd! Have you seen him?"

"Yes, by some means or other the scoundrel heard that I was in the city, and sent for me to come to see him in the jail, alleging that he desired to retain me as his counsel."

"Is it possible he could be so presumptuous? He knows, of course, that you are my counsel."

"He declares that he did not intend to do you the slightest harm. He says he only wanted to let you see that you were powerless, in order that he might make sure that you would listen to him."

"I have not told any one yet, but I must tell you, that I am sure that I have seen the man before. I did not at first recognize him, but once his face was turned to the window and the full light of the sun fell upon it, and then I knew that I had seen it before, and I am sure, too, that the circumstances of the occasion were unpleasant. I can not recall time or place, but of the fact I have no doubt. Perhaps the matter will be made clear to me before long."

"Yes, it will come to you as other events do to all of us, in some mysterious way, when you least expect it. But in regard to my being counsel for Todd—I told him, of course, that if I had anything at all to do with the case as a lawyer, it would be by trying my utmost to have him receive all the punishment that the law allows."

"He wanted me to promise to give him employment, but after his conduct, and the record of him that Mr. Benham gave me, I refused. It was then that he threatened me. I don't know what makes me think so, but I believe he had some ulterior object in view that he had not disclosed when he was interrupted in his proceedings."

"Do you think so? That's very strange!"

"Why is it strange?"

"Because the same idea occurred to me while we were talking together in the jail. It seemed to me as though he had an idea that he had it in his power to compel me to act as his counsel."

"Can it be possible that he knows anything of—"

"No, no, that is out of the question. If he had had any knowledge on that subject, he would have revealed the fact long ago, or have used it to his advantage before this. No, my dear, I think you may make up your mind that your mother and all connected with her are dead."

Alana was silent; she had so often discussed with Mr. Wade all the points connected with her mother's disappearance, that there was nothing now to say about the matter. Her hopes and her fears had long since faded out of her mind. It was her own position that troubled her now, and that time could not reconcile her to enduring without regret.

"I have never told you," resumed Mr. Wade, "that some time ago I started off on an independent search of my own to find your mother, or at least some trace of her. I went to Philadelphia, and began at the university, where your father was a student. I found the place where he boarded, and ascertained that the house was at that time kept by a Mrs. Mullin. I also learned that she had a son who was killed by a policeman in the early part of November, 1864, but I could not ascertain that there was a daughter. By the by, can you recollect when it was that the man of whom you spoke to me once came to see your father? I mean the man that pointed to you, and said something about 'that girl's mother,' and whom your father put out of the house."

"Yes, I recollect the circumstance well, for it made a lasting impression on me. It must have been fifteen years ago at least. That would make it in 1868. It was in the summer, I know, for the windows were open, and the man went out of one of them, almost thrown out by my father. That same night an attempt was made to rob the office. The safe was blown open, and—"

"That was in 1868. You are right. I recollect the circumstance of the attempted robbery. But how do you associate the two events?"

"By the fact that father declared that the man whom he had put out of the house was the burglar."

"Good! that comes very straight. Now, my dear, if your mother's brother was killed in 1864, and of that there appears to be no doubt, it is very clear that he was not the man that came here, as your father asserted, with your mother in 1868, and that you saw in this very room."

"Yes, in this very room. My God!" she continued, starting to her feet with fear and astonishment depicted on her countenance, "Todd is the man! I know it. He stood just in front of you, there, and father sat here, and at something the man said, father sprang at him and struck him a violent blow in the face, and then forced him out of the house through that window. At last, then, a clew has been reached."

"A clew to the identity of Todd as the man that came here with a woman, whom your father did not see, and who the man appears to have said was your mother; but I do not see that we have any indication as to the fate or whereabout of your mother. Clearly Todd is not her brother, for the latter had then been dead nearly four years; and yet your father, as I think you told me, declared on his death-bed that the man was your mother's brother."

"Yes, he certainly said that."

"Then it appears to me that we have a greater mystery than ever. My information is very exact on the point that there was but one son. Now, that son died in 1864, and your father told you that it was he that came here in 1868."

"He told me that the man was my mother's brother. There might have been two sons; you did not find out that there was a daughter, but of course there must have been one. Your information, therefore, about the sons may not be correct."

"Yes," replied Mr. Wade, musingly, "there must have been a daughter, and there may after all have been another son. But if Todd is one of them, why has he not come forward and declared himself? He would, of course, know that he is your uncle"—Alana shuddered as Mr. Wade made the remark—"and that you would feel in duty bound to provide for him."

"It's all very mysterious."

"Yes, that's what I say; very mysterious and contradictory. If Todd is your mother's brother, he must, of course, be aware of the fact that she received, till your father's death, three thousand dollars a year, and he would certainly, from what I know of him, have found means—even if your mother died when your father died—to have had the allowance continued to himself. He would have known that he was the possessor of a valuable secret, and he would have endeavored to make it of use to him."

"He could not have done that. I should have told the story to the whole world if he had threatened me."

"Yes, you are not one to submit to black-mail, even from an uncle. But," he continued, rising as though preparatory to taking his leave, "if Todd is not your uncle, who is he? What was he doing in this room fifteen years ago? What did he mean by the words he addressed to your father? Who was the woman that remained at the tavern? For if Todd is not your mother's brother, the woman could not have been your mother, provided of course that your mother was Miss Mullin; and yet your father said that she was your mother. I am all mixed up. I don't understand what I have just said. I shall have to go home and think it all over after a night's rest. In the mean time, my dear, don't disturb yourself about Todd. If he knew anything that he thought might be regarded as distasteful or injurious to you, depend upon it he would have brought his information to market long ago. That ruffian your uncle! It's out of the question. You, one of the noblest and best of women, as well as one of the most beautiful, to be the niece of a beast like that, a mere dog coming from the scum of the earth!"

"Oh!" cried Alana, covering her face with her hands, "remember that such was my mother. I can never forget. Do I look like him?" she suddenly exclaimed, dropping her hands and approaching Mr. Wade, till she stood close in front of him. "Is there a feature of mine that is

his ; is my voice similar ; do I walk like him ; is there
anything in my body or mind that recalls him ? If he is
my uncle, there must be something in me that would remind you of him—some family trait or feature that we
both have. Todd my uncle ! Was my mother—*is* my
mother—as low, for a woman, as he is for a man ? Do you
think, as you look at me, that such a thing can be possible ?
See ! I am, they say, good-looking, I am well behaved, I
dress well, I go to church, I pray to God night and morning "—she clasped her hands together as she spoke, and
raised her eyes—"I try to do my duty to my Maker and to
my neighbor. I have never intentionally wronged a human
being. I take pleasure in books, in learning, in the refine-
ments of life. Now, could wealth and education and association so take the beast out of me as to make me different from that man, when, if I had been left to my own na-
tive mental and bodily filth, I should have been like him ?
Is it possible that the innate brutality that would have
characterized me, if that man's sister is my mother, could
have been removed by any influences that mankind can
control ? You look astounded to hear me talk thus, but I
am only giving utterance to thoughts that for two long
and dreary years have burned themselves into my very
soul !"

"My dear child, I *am* astonished ; you take the matter
too hard. I thought you had made up your mind to accept
the situation and to make the best of it. Yes, I do believe
that such associations as you have had could have raised
you up to be the peer of any woman that walks the earth.
What do I care who your mother was or who your uncle
is ? I know what you are. I have known you since you
were a little child : you were always gentle, always good,
always ready to do a kindness to any one in need. What
if your mother were worse than Todd ? Have you forgotten that your father's blood flows in your veins ? I don't

believe in this nonsense about heredity. A man or a woman
is the creature of circumstances; but, if there is anything
in it, your father and the race from which he comes must
count for something."

"I don't know—perhaps you are right; but it seems to
me now that, if such a man as Todd is my uncle, I must be
like him. You see, I may be concealing all my bad traits,
just as I have made you believe that I had ceased to care
who my mother was. They will come out after a while.
Blood will tell."

"You are getting morbid on the subject. You are not
speaking your real sentiments. You know that what you
say is not true. You ought not to speak to me in that
way." He spoke severely, and turned as though to leave
the room.

"Forgive me!" cried Alana, laying her hand on his
arm; "I did not intend to trifle with you, but, if I am morbid, have I not had enough to make me so? When I think
of what I really am—the nameless child of a wicked and
degraded mother—and of what I am forced to seem to be,
the daughter of Francis Honeywood, born in honor—I lose
command of myself and scarcely know what I say. It
seems to me then as though I owe expiation for my continued deception, and that I ought to reveal myself in my
true colors."

"My dear Alana," said Mr. Wade, "I understand
your position perfectly, and it is nothing like as bad as you
imagine it to be. Suppose your mother was the very dregs
of society, and that you—as seems to be established—were
born out of wedlock, have you nothing for which you
ought to be thankful? Your father was a good man.
Even if he did sin in his youth, he rescued you from the
ditch, acknowledged you as his daughter, brought you up
in wealth, education, and refinement, and then made you
his sole heiress. What difference does it make to you now

who your mother was ?   What if you are a bastard ?   The
word is a good one, and we need not displace it for eu-
phemisms.   Do you not know that some of the noblest,
bravest, most honorable and chaste men and women that
the world has ever seen, were bastards ?   It is no fault of
yours that you are illegitimate."

Alana was astonished ; she had never seen Mr. Wade so
thoroughly in earnest. He spoke as though he meant
every word to make an impression that would be lasting.
She could not answer, she could only stand and look at
him in wonder, at the frankness with which he spoke—a
frankness that he had never, though free from hypocrisy,
ventured to display to such an extent to her on any previous occasion.

"Now," he continued, stopping in his walk and laying
his hands on her shoulders, "if this matter is going to
change your disposition and to make you misanthropic, or
cause you to be eternally carrying on contests with yourself, I'll tell you what to do.   You spoke just now of sailing under false colors.   There is no occasion for you to do
that if you really believe that you are acting a lie.   I don't
see the matter in that light.   The world, probably, is not
bothering itself about you ; and, at any rate, it's none of
its business who your mother was, or whether you are, or
are not, illegitimate.   But if you wish to enlighten it, and
if you feel that the burden of your secret is more than you
can bear, out with it, and cease sailing under false colors !
Cleanse your heart of the 'perilous stuff,' and stand forth
in your true light."

"What !" she exclaimed, in horror, "reveal my shameful origin ?   You must be mad to give me such advice !"
She thought of John Benham and of his honorable lineage,
and of what he would probably think.   Certainly he
would not ask her, whose mother had been, if she was not
now, a strumpet, to be his wife and the mother of his chil-

dren. No, the idea was not to be thought of. She would keep her secret to herself.

"You say that you are acting a lie," resumed Mr. Wade, with merciless emphasis. "If that is true, it is your duty to tell the truth. If you imagine that there is one person who would think less of you, knowing who you really are, go and tell that person that you are a bastard, and that your mother probably died in the gutter or in a prison. I'm not going to spare you," he continued, as she moaned piteously, and covered her face with her hands, as though to hide her shame. "Desperate diseases like yours require desperate remedies. Go and blazon the truth to the world and be done with it! Then you will know how many true friends you have, and there will be no more morbidness and hysterical statements about your wickedness and your false colors and your acted lies. Or, if you shrink from personally proclaiming the truth, I will do it for you."

"A week ago I could have done this," said Alana, in a voice scarcely above a whisper, and as though speaking to herself. "I would have done it rather even than submit to imposition, but now it is impossible."

"Why impossible?"

"I can not tell you."

"Do you mean that you can not tell me because you do not know, or because you will not?"

"Oh, I know well enough! I do not wish to tell you."

"Then I have nothing further to say. Good-night!"

He held out his hand as he spoke.

"You are going away angry with me," she said, with an attempt at a smile, as she took his hand.

"No, not angry with you, but somewhat disappointed."

"You thought I was stronger than I am."

"I thought you stronger than you seem to be. Perhaps even yet you will show your strength."

"You have not spared me to-night. You have never before spoken so cruelly to me."

"Cruelty such as mine is kindness in reality. I wished to save you from yourself. Do you not know that most of the troubles of this life flee from him who faces them ? You are beginning to brood over this one of yours, and if you keep on as you have begun it will seize you in its pitiless grasp and perhaps destroy your reason. I have tried to-night to cut it out, as the surgeon cuts out a diseased part of the body. Good-night ! God bless you ! I love you as though you were my own child, and that is why I want to rescue you while there is yet time."

CHAPTER VII

THE procession, with the band, and followed by the greater portion of the women and children of the village, moved across the lawn to John Benham's house, and made a demonstration similar to that that had been shown to Miss Honeywood. He came out on the veranda and spoke his thanks in a modest sort of way, that gave the people more satisfaction than they would have derived from an elaborate speech. It was then that Tom Stickler, one of the leaders of the striking brick-layers, announced that to-morrow morning he and all the rest of them would go to work, and that they would take no wages till they had restored to its original condition the stack that had been pulled down during the previous night. This declaration was received with great delight by the crowd, for there were many men skilled in the working of furnaces that were in the village waiting to be employed, and whose chances had been suddenly taken away by the conduct of Todd and his friends.

Then, when the men had gone, Benham re-entered the house, and, going up-stairs, proceeded to a large room in the attic which he had fitted up as a laboratory, and where he pursued his studies and conducted his experiments.

He had as yet scarcely had time to think over the events of the afternoon. He had been kept more than an hour at Todd's house assisting the doctor, and watching his late adversary in order to prevent him making his escape. Then, after he had turned him over to the officers of the law, some matter at the furnace had required his attention, and he had barely got home, and told his mother what had happened, when the demonstration of the workmen had required his attendance.

Now, however, he was his own master for a couple of hours, and, as usual with him when his time was at his disposal, he spent it in his laboratory. He sat down at a table on which there were blowpipes, and crucibles of sand and black-lead, and various other chemical appliances, and began heating with a blowpipe a little mass of something that was held in an excavation in a piece of charcoal.

He worked at this uninterruptedly for several minutes, but apparently without getting the result that he wished; for he got up several times and paced the floor as though to abstract himself more thoroughly from the manipulation, and to concentrate his thought upon points that he had previously deemed of no importance. Then he returned to the table, and added something out of a wide-mouthed bottle to the little bead on the charcoal, and, again turning the flame of the blowpipe upon it, watched for the changes that might ensue.

But again he was disappointed, for, with an air of vexation, he extinguished the spirit-lamp that he had been using with the blowpipe, and, throwing the charcoal with its little mass upon which he had been working on the table, he pushed back his chair and rose to his feet.

"It is no use," he said. "Do what I will, I can not fuse it satisfactorily; and yet I am sure that the process is right, and that it must be something in the proportions that is wrong."

He took up from the table a sheet of paper covered with chemical and algebraic equations, and other notes and figures, and studied them for a few minutes.

"I'll go out and take a walk," he said, at last. "This is all wrong," crumpling the paper in his hand and throwing it on the floor. He stood for a moment as though un-decided what to do; then he arranged some of the appara-tus on the table, and, still looking annoyed, left the room.

As he went down the stairs, the door of a room on the first floor was opened, and an elderly lady, still handsome, and wearing the dress of a widow, came out into the hall.

"Are you going out, John?" she said. "I heard your speech to the men. I did not know you could be so elo-quent. They seem to be very glad that Miss Honeywood was rescued. I thought, if you were going out, I would get you to stop and present my congratulations to her. I would go myself, but my sciatica is so bad that I am afraid to make the attempt."

"Yes, mother," he answered, "I am going to take a walk. The excitement of the day has been too much even for me, and you know I am not easily affected by such things. As to stopping to give your message to Miss Honeywood, I'd rather not, if it doesn't make much differ-ence. Suppose you write her a note, and send it over by Eliza?"

"Yes," rejoined his mother, smiling, "I suppose Eliza can take the note; but I thought you might want to say something yourself to Miss Honeywood."

"All that is necessary has already passed between her and me. She thanked me, and I acknowledged her thanks, and expressed myself gratified at the fact that she had suf-fered nothing beyond a little fright."

"Well, well, I suppose you know best; but it does seem to me that you two might be a little more sociable with each other. How long has it been since you paid Miss Honeywood a visit?"

"You know I go there every morning."

"Yes, to the office."

"It isn't necessary, so far as I can see, that I should go at any other time."

"Certainly not necessary, but it would be kind, and at the same time respectful, if you occasionally paid her the compliment of a visit that was not official. You owe her something, I think, not only on your own account, but on mine."

John Benham gave no reply, while he made a show of brushing his hat and looking for a cane that he generally took with him when he went for a walk. At last, having used up all the time that these acts could, by the most liberal expenditure, require, he said:

"Doubtless I have been very negligent; I will try and do better in the future." He laid the hat-brush that he had been using so assiduously on the table, and, as he did so, a letter attracted his attention. He took it up, saw that it was addressed to him, and, opening it, read as follows:

"JUNIATA IRON-WORKS, RITNER, PA.

"DEAR SIR: We have been for some time contemplating making you the following proposition, but circumstances have, up to the present, prevented our so doing.

"We desire to secure your valuable services in the general management of our works, and, with that view, hereby offer you a one-fourth interest in the same. There are no debts beyond such as have been incurred in the running of the business, and which will all be paid off whenever the bills for the same are presented. Last year the net profit was $84,659.80, and the business this year, as well as the prices obtained for our iron, assure us that the net income will be considerably over $100,000.

"Should you be disposed to entertain our proposal our Mr. Cummings, with whom you are already acquainted, will call to see you at such time as you may designate, and arrange with you for an inspection of our works.

"We are, very respectfully, your obedient servants,

"CUMMINGS, JANSEN & JONES."

To say that John Benham was astonished at the contents of this letter, would very inadequately express the state of his feelings. For a moment he was overwhelmed, but it was only for a moment. He was one of those persons that rarely, if ever, lose their presence of mind, but who are always ready for any emergency that may be forced upon them. But it might well happen, even to a man of his strong mental organization, that he should be at the instant somewhat confused at the magnitude of the prospect so suddenly opened before him.

His salary at the Susquehanna Iron-Works, which originally had been three thousand dollars a year, had, just before Mr. Honeywood's death, been raised to five thousand. Then, as the reader knows, Alana had added a house, so that no fault could reasonably be found with his pecuniary situation. This offer of Messrs. Cummings, Jansen & Jones, if accepted, made him his own master, with an income of twenty-five thousand dollars a year, from a partnership given to him outright, in order that the firm might secure him. Certainly, it was very pleasant. He liked to be appreciated ; he was ambitious. Doubtless, the gentlemen who owned the Juniata Iron-Works knew what they were about, and were confident that, with him as a member of the firm, the profits of the establishment would be still further increased. The net income from the Susquehanna Iron-Works was about sixty thousand a year, and this all went to Alana. He believed that, if the experiments that he was now conducting were successful, the net profits could easily be doubled. However, he could not think of it now. There were too many questions to be considered before he could come to a determination. He would revolve some of them in his mind during his walk. Without saying anything to his mother, relative to the contents of the letter, he left the house.

Passing out of the grounds to the long street upon

which most of the houses occupied by the workmen and their families were situated, he turned to the west, and, in a few minutes, found himself on the bank of the Susquehanna. He stopped for a moment, to determine whether he should go north or south, but, concluding that he would have a better chance of being alone if he climbed the mountain, he turned to the left, and walked rapidly toward the ridge, now lit up by the rays of the setting sun.

He had about a mile to go before arriving at the base of the mountain, but it did not take him long to traverse this distance, and then he began the ascent, which at this point was easy. He intended to go about half-way to the top, and then, taking a path that he knew of, that inclined to the right, go partially around the ridge to a big rock that he often visited, and from which a view of the river, up and down the stream, was obtained. Here he meant to stop, and at his ease, and isolated from all disturbing influences, direct his mind to the task of settling the very important matter which the letter he had just received had brought up for consideration. At last the rock, an immense mass of limestone, was immediately in front of him, at the distance of about fifty feet. To reach the place on which he had generally sat, when he came here, it was necessary for him to pass around on either side, for it was on the south face of the rock, and was an excavation made probably at some very remote period by water, being in shape like a big arm-chair, and, as such things go, not uncomfortable.

He did not stop to think which path he should take, but automatically followed the one that led to the right. How slight a circumstance sometimes determines important events! If he had gone by the left path, or the one farthest from the river, he would not have been in the position to perform the timely act that, as it was, he *did* perform. For he would at once have been discovered by the parties courting secrecy, and they would have taken a speedy departure from the vicinity of the intruder. The difference between the two paths mainly consisted in the fact that the one to the right led to the top of the rock, and thence down to the natural seat, or, as it was called, "Washington's Throne," from a legend not, perhaps, well authenticated, that Washington had sat in it. The path descended till the front of the rock was reached, and then, by a few steps cut in the stone, the seat was reached.

Benham, as I have said, took the right or ascending path, and thus reached the top of the rock. He walked along the flat surface, and, just as he was about to descend, he thought he heard voices below him. Quietly approaching the edge, he looked over, and there, engaged in earnest conversation, were a man and a woman.

He was about to draw back, and return to the village, or seek some other spot for his meditation, when he heard the man utter Todd's name. This surprised him. He would have scorned to listen to any private conversation from mere motives of curiosity, or for the purpose of personal advantage, but he had ample reason for believing Todd to be a desperate and a dangerous character, and he had no doubt that it was his duty to find out all he could in regard to the fellow's movements and schemes. He therefore again approached the edge of the rock, and, bending over, took a good look at the pre-emptors of his objective point.

Being immediately above them, he could not see their faces. The man, however, was sitting in "Washington's Throne"; the woman was on the ground, below her companion. Both were, as well as he could determine, strangers to that part of the country.

For two or three minutes after uttering Todd's name they were silent. The last speech—it was the man who had made it—had apparently been of a kind to require reflection, and that, too, of no pleasant character, for the

5

woman was crying. Benham not only saw her wiping her eyes with a handkerchief, but he could hear her sobs. At last she spoke :

"I think we had better give the matter up ; I haven't the heart to go on with it."

As she said these words she turned and faced the man ; and, in order to see him, she had to look up, so that Benham, who had stretched himself out at full length, with only so much of his head protruding over the edge of the rock as enabled him to see the parties below, got a tolerably good view of her face. It was that of a woman apparently fifty or even fifty-five years of age, of handsome features, and still not uncomely-looking. Her hair was quite gray, but she seemed to be well preserved, and was evidently vigorous, and capable of enduring a good deal of physical hardship without suffering. She wore a close-fitting, dark-gray traveling-dress, of some woolen material, and a plain black hat, with a blue veil. She had the general appearance of a lady, and her speech showed that she knew how to speak the English language without falling into the errors common to the uneducated people of that part of the country. She clasped her hands together as she spoke, and the tone of her voice showed that she was suffering from strong feeling, either of fear or of sorrow.

"It's too late, now, for you to back out," answered the man, as he nonchalantly kicked his heels against the rock on which he was sitting. "Todd will be out in a few days, and then things will all go right again. Because he got drunk, and spoiled things, is no reason why you should be despondent or frightened. His wife will get well ; she won't appear against him, and by to-morrow morning the girl will be out of the way, and *can't* appear."

"I think we had better give it up till Alec is free again. I am afraid."

"I tell you it's too late to give it up ! Everything is

ready for to-night, and it must go on. If I had Alec here, though, I'd wring his neck, for acting as he did."

"What do you wish me to do?" asked the woman, apparently unable to contend with him very long.

"I want you to go to the house on Berry's Mountain, and stay there till I come with the girl, or at least till to-morrow morning. If I am not there, with or without her, by sunrise, you may know that something has occurred to stop the thing. You'll find the wagon at the foot of the mountain, just where we left it. All you've got to do is to follow that path till you come to it at the spring. Get in, and follow the road to the north, along the river, till you come to the aqueduct at Duncan's Island, then take the road to your right, or through Millersberg, till you reach a white house and a red barn. There, there is a fork; keep on to the right, and you'll reach the house on Berry's Mountain. I've got it all down here, in black and white," he continued, putting his hand into the breast-pocket of his coat and taking out a number of papers that he proceeded to look through. "Here it is." He reached out his hand with the paper, and she tried to take it from him, but the distance was too great; so he dropped it, and she picked it up and read it over.

"You know well enough how to drive, and you'll find your way there without trouble."

"Yes, I suppose I can. This is all very clear. I wish there was some way of my knowing before midnight that you have succeeded."

"Well, you can't know before midnight, for the thing won't be done before two o'clock; but if about that time you look out in this direction, you'll see the light from the fire I'm going to kindle."

"I don't see the use of burning any of the houses. For God's sake, let us commit no more crimes than are necessary! I feel as though I could never forgive Alec, and, if he had injured her, I think I should have killed him."

"Well, that would have been an unnecessary crime," answered the man, laughing; "so you needn't be so squeamish about what I'm going to do. Besides, it is necessary. Without it the whole thing would run a good chance of falling through. The fire will engage attention, and leave me and my proceedings unnoticed."

Benham had listened to this conversation with all the interest that he was capable of experiencing. Who were these people? What criminal acts did they contemplate? Evidently something against a woman, and clearly that woman was Alana. So far as he could judge, they proposed that night to abduct her. "With or without the girl, I'll be there before morning." That meant abduction, and then the wretch meant to set fire to the house at the same time. He could scarcely refrain from dropping a big stone on the scoundrel's head and knocking his brains out. He calculated the space between himself and the fellow, as he sat in "Washington's Throne," dangling his legs and talking coolly of abduction and arson, involving, perhaps, murder as well, and he came to the conclusion that the distance was not too great for him to seize the wretch by the collar of the coat and lift him bodily up to where he himself was. Then it would be no fault of his if he did not manage to prevent the contemplated crimes. It was not yet time, however, for him to interfere. Other revelations were coming.

"For God's sake, do her no injury!"

"Oh, never fear; I'll be as gentle with her as if she were my own daughter. It's not her house I'm going to set fire to. That would be destroying valuable property"—he laughed as he said these words—"that we may have need for. It's Benham's house that's doomed! He's the fellow that interfered with Todd this afternoon and secured his imprisonment, and I'm going to pay him for his trouble."

"I am glad he did; Alec would have injured her if he had been let alone, and then I should have injured him as sure as there's a God in heaven!" She spoke with great feeling, and raised her eyes as though to give additional emphasis to her exclamation.

"Well, she's safe, and won't be injured. But we're in danger of forgetting the object of our visit to this rock. You can't quite see the works from this side. Come round to the other side and I'll show you every house in the village, including the one she lives in, and that of the superintendent."

He made a movement as he spoke, as though to get down from his perch. and at the same instant Benham leaned over the rock, and, stretching out his right arm to its fullest extent, grasped the coat-collar of the man, and, exerting all his strength, raised him kicking and squirming to the top of the rock.

It is doubtful whether he or his woman-companion was most astonished. She, hearing the muttered exclamation of the man, looked up, and seeing him dangling in the air, and a strong arm lifting him higher and higher, gave a shriek of affright, and, rushing over the path that led to the plain below, was soon out of sight. As to the man, Benham did not give him much opportunity for seeking assistance. Besides, he was a small personage, and was as but a feather in the strong grasp of the determined man that held him in a grip of iron.

"Now, you scoundrel," exclaimed Benham, as he swung him to the flat surface of the rock and put his knees on the fellow's chest, "if I don't punish you here once for all, it's because I think you will do better in the penitentiary than as food for the crows. I heard you unfold your vile schemes, and I've a notion to choke you.   By Heaven, I can't keep my hands off of your throat!"

He seized the man by the collar as he spoke, and gave him a shaking that seemed as though it would knock the breath out of his body.

"Now, you rascal," he continued, still keeping his hold on the man but relaxing his grip on his throat, "who are you?"

"How can I speak," muttered the fellow, as though half choked, as he doubtless was, "when you treat me like that? Let me go, and I'll tell you who I am."

"I'll give you a chance to speak, but I have no intention of letting you go till I see you inside of the Dauphin County Jail." He looked around him as he spoke, as though hoping to cast his eye on a rope, or something that would serve to restrain the man's movements. It was a purely automatic act, arising from the habit he had, when in his laboratory, of looking for things, and generally finding what he needed close at hand. Of course, he did not this time see what he wanted. Suddenly an idea appeared to strike him, for he lifted the man till he stood upon his feet.

"Now," he said, holding him by the arm with a grip of iron, "come with me."

Of course the man came. There was no help for him. Benham would have been more than a match for two like him. Down the rock they went till they reached the ground; then Benham stopped, and, looking around him again, found this time what he sought in the form of a small hickory-tree. Holding on to his prisoner with one hand, he took from his pocket a large clasp-knife, and cut from the tree a long switch, almost as flexible as a hempen cord, and with this—all the time admonishing the submissive captive to keep still, or it would be the worse for him—he proceeded to fasten the man's hands behind his back, in such a way, and so firmly, that it was impossible for him to loosen himself, no matter how hard he might struggle.

"I think, my friend, that you are safe enough now," he said, "and, if you please, I'll hear who you are."

"You won't hear anything from me," answered the fellow, sullenly. "If I've got to go to jail, you'll have to make out your case without my assistance."

"All right; to jail you are going. as certain as that you are now on Peter's Mountain! As to making out a case against you, I heard enough of your conversation to know that you contemplated entering Miss Honeywood's house to-night and carrying her off; and that you also intended, in order to further your schemes, and to be revenged for my interference with your confederate, Mr. Alexander Todd, this afternoon, to burn my house down!"

"You'll find it difficult to make any crime out of words, I rather think, no matter what I said."

"There you are wrong. I shall be able to prove the existence of a conspiracy to commit arson, burglary. and abduction; and I am decidedly of the opinion that, under the laws of the Commonwealth of Pennsylvania. either of them is a crime. However, you'll have a chance to plead your case before a jury."

Nothing more was said till they reached the foot of the mountain, and were about turning into the road that ran along the bank of the river. Then the prisoner, who was walking in front of Benham, suddenly stopped and faced his captor.

"I don't care to pass the night in jail," he said. "I'll tell you who I am, and all about the matter, if you'll let me go."

"No, my friend; I have not the most distant idea of letting you go. I shall find out soon enough who you are, and all about your plans; for, as soon as I see you safe in the hands of Constable Keifer, I am going with half a dozen trusty men in pursuit of the woman, your confederate ; and as, from what she said, she seems to be rather lukewarm in her adhesion to your plans, doubtless she will tell me all that I care to know."

"You'll never find her," said the man, with decision. "If you think she's gone to the house on Berry's Mountain, you're very much mistaken. By this time she's far enough off to defy pursuit. She isn't a fool. You'd better make a friend of me."

"No, you are going to jail, and by the train that passes here in half an hour ; so move on."

"But I'm not going on the train in half an hour," saying which, the man deliberately lay down on the ground. "Now," he continued, "if you want me to be in time for that train, you'll have to get me there yourself, for not another step will I walk !"

"Very well, then !" exclaimed Benham, not losing his temper, but it must be supposed coming very near it. He cut another larger and stronger branch than the other, from a hickory-tree close by, and, tying the man's feet together in such a way as to leave a loop of the withe to catch hold of, he proceeded to drag him along the ground. "I think," he continued, after he had gone a few steps, at every one of which the man's head struck uncomfortably against the rough ground, "that I can stand it as long as you can ! You won't have much skin on your back by the time we get to Squire McElroy's ; for I mean to get you there, if I have to drag you every foot of the way !"

They went on along the road, meeting no one. It was nearly dark now, and in order to catch the train it was necessary to hurry. Besides, the business with the squire—as a justice of the peace is called in Pennsylvania—would probably take ten minutes. Fortunately, his residence was very near the railway-station. Benham looked at his watch; it was half-past six, and the train was due at five minutes after seven.

He looked back at the man he was dragging. The fellow was holding up his head, so as to keep it from rubbing against the ground, but it was very evident he was having a most uncomfortable time of it; for not only was his back getting hard usage, but, what was still more unpleasant, his hands, being tied behind him, were being scraped in a way that must, from the very beginning, have denuded them of their skin.

Benham looked back, but it was not with any pity in his heart for the man that he was so ruthlessly bent on delivering into the hands of the officers of the law. He was an obstinate man in some things, and rather disposed to be hard, even to the verge of cruelty, with evil-doers. But the weight was beginning to tell on him, and he had not yet gone a hundred yards since his prisoner had refused to walk. At the rate at which he was going, he certainly would not arrive in time to get his warrant from Squire McElroy, and deliver his prize to the constable in time to take the seven-five train, and he did not see what he could do to expedite matters. The survey that he hurriedly made of the man did not lead to any suggestions for increasing the speed at which he was going. There was nothing to do but to go on and get to the village as soon as he could.

But the man had watched the face that was turned toward him, and had seen that there was no glance of compassion or signs of yielding in it. The situation was for him more than uncomfortable; it was painful, and there was every prospect that ere long it would be agonizing. His clothes were worn through; the skin of his back was beginning to be abraded; that of his hands, where they had touched the ground, was gone after the first few steps, and if the thing continued all the way to the village there would be scarcely a vestige of flesh and bone, much less of skin, on either his back or hands. Evidently, his master for the time being did not care whether he got him in alive or dead. That he was going to drag him to the squire's house in any event was clear. He made up his mind. "Stop!" he cried; "I will walk."

"You will have to run now; walking will not do," answered Benham without relaxing one iota of his effort.

"Very well, then; I will run as fast as I can."

In an instant Benham stopped, and, cutting the hickory withe that bound the man's feet, allowed him to rise.

"Now," he said, indicating to him to take the lead, "go on as fast as you can, and I'll follow you. If you stop, I'll drag you again!"

At first the man showed by his movements that his muscles and joints were stiff, but in a short time he appeared to get over the ground with more ease. Just as they reached the confines of the village, they met a wagon coming toward them, driven by a man whom Benham recognized as one of his own people. He stopped the vehicle, and, after a word with the driver, ordered his prisoner to get into it. The man was nothing loath. He had had enough of the two kinds of locomotion with which he had experimented. Benham followed him. It was just ten minutes to seven when they reached the squire's house.

In the examination, Benham told his story without comment. The man declined to tell his name or to make any statement. At seven-five he was on his way to Harrisburg, under the charge of Constable Keifer, and with a pair of handcuffs on his wrists. There was even time for him to wash his hands, which were in a pitiable plight, and for Benham to apply a healing salve and bandages to them.

The man looked at him curiously while his captor was performing those charitable acts.

"I'm much obliged to you," he said, "but it won't be

sufficient to wipe out of my mind the remembrance of this day. I'll be even with you yet!"

"Well, my friend, I've had so much the start of you, that you'll have a good deal to do to catch up."

Men were sent in all directions, with the hope of intercepting the woman, but they returned at different hours through the night without even having caught sight of her. The house on Berry's Mountain was entirely deserted, and exhibited no signs of having been recently occupied. It was owned by a farmer, who occasionally lived in it for a few weeks at a time, when he was burning lime and charcoal on the mountain. A telegram to the chief of police of Harrisburg was answered to the effect that no woman such as was described had to his knowledge arrived in that city.

CHAPTER VIII

IN making his charge against his prisoner, Benham had said nothing in regard to the conspiracy to abduct Miss Honeywood, which he believed the man and woman contemplated, but had confined his allegations to what he had heard relative to destroying his house by fire. He judged it better to make this restriction, for the reasons that he did not wish to alarm Miss Honeywood, and that he thought he would be more likely to discover further details of the plot by preserving secrecy, and pursuing investigations, privately, and in his own way. He resolved, however, to institute a special system of guarding Miss Honeywood's and his own house by night, and, before he went home, he arranged with several of his men a service of the kind. At first he thought he would stop in and tell Miss Honeywood what had happened, and he went to her residence for that purpose. He ascended to the veranda, and was about pulling the bell, when he heard voices in the drawing-room, and listening for a moment distinguished those of Mr. Trevor, Mr. Wade, and Dr. Arndell. Not caring to relate his adventures before these gentlemen, he crossed the lawn to his own house, where he found his mother waiting tea for him. He told her what had occurred, omitting, however, all reference to the abduction plot. Of course, he knew that she would be alarmed, but as she was sure to hear the story in the morning as she strolled through the village, stopping at Mrs. Barton's and Miss Pink's, to make little purchases, but mainly for the purpose of hearing the news, and as her informants would doubtless descant with great volubility on her narrow escape from being burned to death in her bed, he judged it preferable that she should get the account from him.

"You need not be afraid, now, mother," he added; "the chief conspirators are safe in jail in Harrisburg, and there will be an all-night patrol, well armed, kept at this house and at Miss Honeywood's."

"But, my dear John, why should they want to burn your house? You never did them any harm! It's infamous! perfectly infamous!"

"Of course it is," said Benham, laughing. "As to why they desire to burn this house, it is perfectly clear to me that they wish to be revenged for the drubbing I gave Todd. In fact, the fellow I caught said so."

"How fortunate that you went to 'Washington's Throne,' instead of going up the river, as you sometimes do!"

"Yes," he answered, musingly, "it was very fortunate."

"It isn't often that you go off at that time of the afternoon. I saw you had something on your mind, that worried you, and I suppose you wanted to 'clear your brain,' as you say."

"Yes, I could not get my experiment with the new flux to work right, and I thought I would go out into the pure air and think over all the points. I can think much better when there is no ceiling over my head. I have heard of people that can't stay in a room without feeling terrified. I shouldn't be surprised if I had a mild form of the disease —claustrophobia, Dr. Arndell calls it."

"Did your letter worry you? The one, I mean, that you got and read just before you went out."

"No, I can't say that it worried me, but it gave me something important to think about. I am offered a partnership in the Juniata Iron-Works at Ritner."

"A partnership! O John, what a fortunate man you
are! But you deserve it all; no one ever worked harder,
or more faithfully and intelligently. Of course, you won't
have to give the matter much consideration."

"I don't know. At first I almost made up my mind to
accept, but the little reflection I have been able to give the
matter rather leads me to the opposite conclusion."

"My dear John, you could scarcely refuse such an offer.
What is the interest they offer you?"

"One fourth."

"And about what will that amount to?"

"Twenty-five thousand dollars a year, more or less;
probably more."

"And you would be your own master, with twenty-five
thousand a year, while here you occupy a subordinate position, with five thousand? I don't see how you can hesitate a moment."

"If I looked at the matter, mother, from a purely business point of view, I should not require a moment in which
to make my decision, but there are other considerations."

Mrs. Benham was not endowed with the ordinary
amount of curiosity of her sex, or, if she was, she did not
exhibit it in her relations with her son, for she had never
shown a tendency to pry into his affairs. She had not the
most remote idea that he was in love with Alana, or of the
struggle that had been going on in his heart, from almost
the first hour of his arrival at the Susquehanna Iron-Works.
She had believed that his disposition had undergone a great
change from what it was before he had accepted the super-
intendency of Mr. Honeywood's furnace. He was more
thoughtful, more sedate, and this extended very near to the
point of moroseness. He was often by himself, he was indisposed to converse, he had not the gayety that had previously characterized him. She attributed these changes
to the heavy responsibilities that rested upon him, to the

necessity that existed for his giving his attention to the work he had to do, and especially to his experiments, and to the fact that he was no longer a boy, but, being a studious man, had the temperament and disposition peculiar to persons of his type.

But she had always given him credit for possessing ambition to succeed in his business and profession, and the fact that he now showed a decided indifference to the proposition that had been made to him, disturbed her not a little. At first, she was disposed to think that he was actuated by an attachment for the place at which he had, as it were, begun life, and with which, therefore, he would naturally have many pleasant associations; but a moment's reflection was sufficient to convince her that that factor, even if it existed to a more than ordinary extent, was altogether inadequate to produce the result that apparently had been produced by something. The "other considerations," to which he had alluded, were certainly stronger than any that were at that moment in her mind. What they were, she could not divine. So far as she understood the matter, she believed it to be to his interest to accept the proposition that had been made to him, unless, indeed—and the idea struck her as one that was worth attention—he should be offered a partnership by Miss Honeywood. It might well be that, rather than lose so valuable a coadjutor, she would see it to be her interest to retain him, upon like terms to those offered him by the proprietors of the Juniata Iron-Works. All this passed through her mind in a few moments, and then she spoke.

"I think," she said, "that if you were to tell Miss Honeywood of the offer that has been made you, she would make you a similar one, rather than lose you."

"Yes," he answered; "I am quite sure she would. It would not, however, be a delicate suggestion for me to make to her, or, in fact, to do anything that might lead to the

supposition that I was trying to make the most of myself.
I would not like to be put in that position, especially to
her."

"I do not see it in that light. A man is worth just
what people are willing to give for him. Messrs. Cummings, Jansen & Jones think you are worth to them a
partnership. That is, a gift of one fourth of their property. It seems to me you ought to be worth more than
that to Miss Honeywood, for you know all the details here,
better than you could know them in a year at the Juniata
Works."

"Yes," he answered, with a smile, "provided Messrs.
Cummings, Jansen & Jones have made a correct judgment
of my value."

"But you have succeeded here; see how you have
brought up the business, till it pays better than it ever did,
and better and better every year."

"Very true; but I could not make up my mind to go
to Miss Honeywood, and say: 'Here, I am offered a fourth
interest in the Juniata Iron-Works; give me a like interest,
and I will stay with you; refuse, and I leave you.' Do you
think that would be a nice thing for me to do?"

"Not in those terms, perhaps, but in all essential points,
yes. Why should you not? Are you to stay here as a
superintendent all your life, when you have advancement
offered you? My dear John, I think you are very blind to
your interest."

"Perhaps I am; but I see clearly in regard to other
things, that are more to me than my pecuniary interest,
and I think I see that I can not leave this place. I suppose
that I shall be the superintendent as long as I live. Yes,"
he added, after a moment's pause, and rising from his chair,
and beginning to pace the room, "I shall probably stay
here all my life in a subordinate position. It is preferable
to wealth and independence elsewhere."

This was too much for Mrs. Benham; she rose also, and, putting her hand on her son's arm, said to him:

"My dear John, either your reasons are stronger than it is possible for me to imagine, or you are very impolitic. Is there any objection to your making a confidante of your mother?"

"No, my dear mother," he said, putting his arm around her waist; "I think I can be entirely frank with you. I love Alana Honeywood."

"That surprises me very much! I had no idea that you had any particular liking for her. You have always appeared to avoid her."

"Yes, because I was trying to overcome my passion, but to-day it got the better of me. It is useless for me to struggle against it any longer; I am deeply, hopelessly in love."

"Not hopelessly, John! Why do you say that?"

"Because I have no reason to think that she can ever love me. In all the years that we have lived in the same place, seeing each other every day, she has not by word, or sign, or tone of voice, or act, shown that she cares any more for me than she would for any other man that did her work as well as I have done it—unless, perhaps, to-day."

"I should think much less of her than I do, if she had. Perhaps, she has been struggling with herself, as you have been with yourself, and has been fully as successful. Now, I think she does like you more than she would another man that did her work as well as you do it. I think she likes you—loves you, because you are John Benham. I know women's ways better, my dear, than you know them, and I am quite sure of the truth of what I say. And why should she not?" she added, putting her arms around his neck, and drawing his head down till she could kiss him. "You are handsome and good; your family is as old and as respectable as hers. A Walter de Benham, or Debenham,

was a valiant commander under Edward III of England, at
the battle of Halidon Hill, and captured with his own hand
three standards from the Scotch. You are descended from
him in a direct line, and I doubt if the Honeywoods, good
as their family is, can go as far back as that. Besides, you
can, when you choose, make yourself very winsome with
women, though I must say you have not done much in that
direction since you have been here."

"I wish I could be sure that you are right. This offer
of a partnership seems to me to put me more on a level
with her than I was before. I would not tell her of it for
the world, but it certainly gives me more assurance than I
would otherwise have."

"Go to her, and tell her that you love her, and ask her
to be your wife. Go as you are, the superintendent; her
hired man, if you choose to give yourself that designation."

"But, if she refused me, I should have to go away, and
I do not want to go away."

"If she refused you, you can accept the partnership in
the Juniata Works. Yes, you would have to go away."

"But I don't wish to go; I must stay here."

"My dear John, that is nonsense. If she refuses you,
you will act like a man, I suppose, and not remain here,
as a rejected lover, to have your soul harrowed every moment of the day, and to make her situation more or less
embarrassing."

"Mother, I can not go; I have reason to think that she
is in danger. I shall have to tell you all I know of the
matter. You are entitled to that consideration, if only for
the assurances you give me that she cares for me."

In as few words as possible, Benham told his mother
what he had learned of the plans of the conspirators in regard to the proposed abduction that night.

"There seems to be a mystery of some kind," he said,
after the old lady had sufficiently expressed her astonish-

ment; "but I have bothered my mind over the matter to no purpose. What puzzles me most is the fact that, notwithstanding the woman's purpose of entering into the conspiracy to abduct Miss Honeywood, she evidently entertains a deep affection for her. Her denunciations of Todd were terribly earnest."

"Did you get a look at this woman's face?"

"Yes, and I am sure that I should know her again under any circumstances of dress or situation. She turned up her face once, while speaking to the man, but she was then weeping, and I saw it only for an instant; but I got a second, and a better look, as I was pulling her companion up to the top of the rock. Yes, I am certain I should know her again. She has a handsome face. I have sent after her, in all directions, but have no very vivid hope of intercepting her."

"Perhaps Miss Honeywood could throw some light on the matter. The woman may have been a former nurse, who has formed bad associations. Evidently, the object was to hold Miss Honeywood for a ransom."

"I think not. Such a thing could not succeed in this country. We are not in Sicily, or Greece."

"Oh, I think in some parts of this country such a thing could be done with entire success—in fact, in almost any part. It has been done repeatedly."

"I should not like to mention the subject to Miss Honeywood," said Benham, replying to the suggestion of his mother. "It would alarm her to know that she was the object of such a scheme. But," he added, as the idea occurred to him, "I shall tell the whole story to Mr. Wade. He will doubtless be able to give good advice in the matter."

A ring at the front-door bell interrupted him, and in a few moments a card was brought to Mrs. Benham. She glanced at it.

"Miss Pink," she said. "Is she in the parlor, Eliza?"

"Yes, ma'am. She said, if you were at tea, she was in no hurry, and could wait till you were through."

"Ask her to come in and take a cup of tea.—She's a good soul," continued Mrs. Benham, as the girl left the room, "and for picking up news there is not her equal in the State of Pennsylvania."

"She's horrid," said Benham; "she tacked herself on to me a few days ago, and I had almost to be rude to her before I could get away."

"Hush! here she comes," and, almost before the words were out of Mrs. Benham's mouth, Miss Pink entered the room.

"My dear Mrs. Benham!—Good-evening, Mr. Benham!" she exclaimed, before either of the occupants of the room had the opportunity to say a word. "I have just got back from Harrisburg."

"Sit down, Miss Pink," interrupted Mrs. Benham, while her son bowed without giving any verbal salutation, "and take a cup of tea. It will refresh you after your journey."

"Yes, thanks!" sitting down as she spoke, and taking the cup that John Benham passed to her. "As I was saying, I went to Harrisburg this afternoon to see my sister, who married Gotlieb Schillinger, the butcher. She's his second wife, you know, and I'm afraid Minnie isn't happy—not that she told me in so many words, but it's easy to tell when the worm of sorrow is eating at one's heart. Don't you think so, Mr. Benham?"

"Really, Miss Pink," answered Benham, with a good-natured smile, "I can't say that I am sufficient of a zoölogist to express an opinion of the habits of the 'worm of sorrow,' or enough of a physician to know the symptoms produced when it 'eats at the heart.'"

"Oh, you know what I mean! You practical men have no imagination; the beauties of diction are nothing to you,

you are so *very practical.* Well, as I was saying, it requires no adept at the knowledge of the signs of grief to
know when a woman is suffering. To add to Minnie's
troubles, her baby is a bottle baby, and it doesn't flourish.
It's apt to be the case with bottle babies—isn't it, Mr. Benham?"

"I don't even know what a 'bottle baby' is. I know
what a bottle fly is—a blue-bottle fly. Is this a blue- or a
black-bottle baby?"

"Oh, you know what I mean!" giggled Miss Pink,
shaking the corkscrew curls that hung low down on each
side of her face. "And, besides, if you don't, ask your
mother to tell you! Well, to go on : Minnie is of course
worried over the baby. She got a wet-nurse—there, it's out
at last, Mr. Benham !—But really she feels as if she couldn't
afford it. Twenty dollars a month, and two bottles of
porter a day ! It's enormous. I'd go out myself as a wet-
nurse on such terms, if— Well, as I was saying, that isn't
all. I was sure there was more and worse ; and at last
Minnie, bursting into tears, told me the whole story. Now,
Mr. Benham, what do you think it was ?"

"I can't imagine," answered Benham, assuming a very
grave appearance—"unless that, in view of the porter you
mentioned just now, the baby, from being a bottle baby, became a two-bottle baby !"

"No, it wasn't anything of the kind, and you know it !
As I was telling you, Minnie is Schillinger's second wife.
He has all his first wife's clothes carefully put away and
scented with lavender and sage, and he wants Minnie to
use them, as she's just about the same size as the other one ;
but Minnie says no ; for, you see, the first Mrs. Schillinger
died of the consumption, and she's naturally afraid she'll
catch the disease if she wears the clothes, especially the
ones that have been slept in ; and that worries her. Do
you think there's any danger, Mr. Benham ?"

"Ah!" he answered, unable to restrain a broad smile that almost became a laugh, "you'll have to go to Dr. Arndell for an answer to that question. My knowledge on such subjects, as you will soon find out, is limited."

All this time Mrs. Benham had never said a word, but was sitting at the head of the table, looking very grave and somewhat disgusted with Miss Pink, and what she considered her indelicate questions to John. It must not be considered that she regarded Miss Pink as her social equal. Mrs. Benham was very stiff in the matter of family. Her husband's, as we have seen, was an old one, and she was one of the Randolphs of Virginia, and prided herself accordingly. She had taken some notice of Miss Pink in a patronizing sort of way; but the younger lady, while accepting the notice, had declined to be patronized, and had at once, so far as she could, put herself upon a footing of perfect equality with Mrs. Benham. Of course, she could have been got rid of without any great difficulty had Mrs. Benham thought the matter of sufficient importance and been inclined to make an enemy. Being, however, of a peaceable disposition, and indisposed to hurt anybody's feelings, she had allowed Miss Pink not only to retain the ground she had won, but to encroach, little by little, till she had at last reached the point of considering herself an intimate friend of the Benham family. In the long run, aggression such as was that of Miss Pink will win in ninety cases out of a hundred.

Miss Pink had rarely had such an excellent chance of getting at John Benham as that of which she was now taking advantage. She had long secretly admired him, had often stood unseen at her window when he passed, and had, unseen, kissed her hand to him. She thought it not at all outside of the range of probability that with opportunity she could succeed in bringing him to her feet. True, she was at least ten years older than he, being at the time she is introduced to the reader on the shady side of thirty-eight ; but she did not consider that an objection. On the contrary, she had advanced the doctrine, and had adduced from her reading many examples of its truth, or at least of its expediency, that the wife should be much older than the husband. "The happiest marriages," she was wont to say, "are those in which the age is with the woman. To be sure, if I were to marry now, I should have to mate with a mere boy, for I am just turned twenty-six, a year younger than Miss Honeywood ; and the very least difference that is admissible is ten years. But I shall not marry yet—no, not yet," she would add, with a mournful shake of the head, "although by adhering to my resolution I make two loving hearts miserable !"

Miss Pink's besetting sin was vanity. She had not a good feature in her face. Her long and sharp nose, her wide mouth with its irregular and spotted teeth, her large, washed-out blue eyes, her sallow complexion, made an *ensemble* that was altogether devoid of beauty, and yet she spent a great part of every day in looking at herself in the glass, and in twisting her countenance into all sorts of possible shapes such as she thought would be exhibited under the influences of the various emotions of which the maiden heart is capable. There are very few women that are good judges of their own faces. They are more likely either to think themselves particularly plain or particularly beautiful, instead of forming a dispassionate opinion. The difference among them in this respect is not shown in the judgment they give on the question of their personal beauty only, but is likewise exhibited in all the affairs of life with which they have anything to do. Miss Pink was an optimist of the most decided kind. When she did not express optimistic views, it was merely in order that she might, by exciting opposition, have those that she really entertained confirmed and strengthened. She was not even gifted with good sense, but she had few very vicious traits. Notwithstanding this fact, however, she was one of those women that always, without intending it, keep those about them in hot water.

After finishing her story about her sister, she turned her attention to drinking her tea, while Mrs. Benham and her son preserved a discreet silence, fearing to ask a question or to make a remark, lest it should serve as a starting-point for a fresh display of volubility. But Miss Pink required no one to act as starter to her, for she possessed in an eminent degree that happy faculty of being able to amuse one's self, that renders its possessor happy whether in a palace or a prison. In a minute or two she had gulped down her tea, and munched a piece of toast, and then she was ready for renewed demonstrations.

"I was so interested in poor Sister Minnie," she went on, "that I forgot all about what I really came for. Sister hasn't my exuberance, my happy disposition, that enables me to see a silver lining to every cloud. But although she doesn't see it, I do, and that's something—isn't it, Mr. Benham?" She shook her corkscrew curls at this question, and fashioned her face into an expression which, however wide of the mark it might be, she intended should denote a radiant frame of mind.

"I suppose it is something," answered Benham, rising as he spoke and approaching the door, evidently with the intention of making his escape. "I have some work to do in my laboratory to night," he added, "and—"

"Now do sit down, if only for a moment," she interrupted, "for I must tell you the news, and it concerns you too. Never mind about the 'silver lining.' This is of much greater importance. Now listen!"

Benham resumed his seat, and Miss Pink went on:

"I stopped in Mulberry Street to see my old pastor, Mr. McClure. I come of a good old Scotch Covenanter stock,

Mr. Benham. There's no Pennsylvania Dutch blood in me, thank God! And the one thing that I don't like about this village is, that there's no place of worship to which I can go with a clear conscience. Of course, I *do* go to hear Mr. Trevor; but, for a woman who comes in a straight line from John Knox, that is pretty hard. Don't you think so, Mr. Benham?"

Benham was beginning to lose his patience. "No, Miss Pink," he said, "I do not. I think any one might well be satisfied with Mr. Trevor."

"Even a descendant of John Knox," joined in Mrs. Benham, a little stiffly.

"Well, well! dear me! How people do differ! But we won't quarrel about that—will we, Mr. Benham? However, as I was saying, I stopped in to see Mr. McClure, to get a little spiritual consolation about the matter of poor Sister Minnie, and, as good luck would have it, he had just got back from the jail. He's the chaplain of the jail, and has prayers every afternoon on week-days, and twice on Sunday. He was greatly fatigued, and I really pitied him, for, as he told me, he had been wrestling with Satan, who had taken up his abode in the soul of a poor man that had just been brought in, and the fight was a severe one, lasting over two hours, and Mr. McClure not quite satisfied with the result either. To wrestle with Satan for two hours, and not gain the victory, is somewhat discouraging. Don't you think so, Mr. Benham?"

"I certainly do, Miss Pink. I speak emphatically," he added, "for I know the fact from my own experience."

"Ah! but you are generally victorious, I'm sure," said the lady, in her most encouraging tones. "You are *so* strong, *so* self-confident, that you are not only capable of whipping Satan in a fair fight, but you would be able to protect any weak soul with nothing but its own inherent weakness to rely on," and Miss Pink rolled her eyes, and

6

clasped her hands together, and for a moment was silent, lost in the contemplation of John Benham as her protector.

"He was sober, when he got to the jail," she went on, suddenly—"Todd, I mean, not Mr. McClure, but of course he was sober too."

"Todd!" exclaimed Benham; "did Mr. McClure talk with him?"

"Talk with him! yes, of course he did. That's what I came to tell you about, but Sister Minnie put it all out of my head. He swore to be revenged on you, for he said it was through you that he was in jail."

"That's true!" said Benham, smiling grimly, "however false everything else he said may be."

"Yes, and I came to warn you against him. He's a very wicked man, and Mr. McClure said he had never met with such opposition—no, not even when, during the Buckshot War, he had a Philadelphia rowdy to deal with."

"I'm much obliged to you," said Benham. "It was kind of you to come; but threatened men, you know, live long. I shall try to protect others, as well as myself, against Mr. Todd."

"Yes, and that reminds me: he said that you had no right to interfere between him and Miss Honeywood. He said he had rights that he'd make you respect, and that he hadn't intended to do her any harm."

"He could scarcely have recovered from his drunkenness, I am afraid," said Benham, rising again, as though to leave the room.

"But that was not all!" resumed Miss Pink; "he said," rising also, and approaching Benham, and dropping her voice to a whisper—"he was her uncle!" Then she started back, and tried to put on an expression of horror and amazement at the magnitude of the statement.

"Miss Honeywood's uncle!" exclaimed Mrs. Benham, while John Benham's face assumed a thoughtful look. He was thinking of the woman he had seen that afternoon, of her evident affection for Alana, and intimacy with Todd.

"Yes," repeated Miss Pink, feeling the importance of the communication she had made, "Miss Honeywood's uncle; his exact words were, 'She's my niece, I guess, and I've more rights with her than Mr. John Benham has.'"

"The man was certainly drunk," said Benham, recovering his presence of mind. "You may take my word for it, Miss Pink, that Todd is not Miss Honeywood's uncle. You have only to look at the two to be sure of that."

"Yes, so I said to myself. Blood will tell, Mr. Benham. Families, however, go down. Now, here am I, only a humble member of society, and yet the blood of Robert Bruce runs in my veins. What we have to do, is to do our duty in the sphere of life to which we are called. Don't you think so, Mr. Benham?"

"Did he have anything further to reveal?" inquired Benham, without seeming to notice Miss Pink's question. "Did he say anything about his companions?"

"No, I think not. Yes, he did," she added, hastily correcting herself; "he said that he had friends who would look after his welfare; that a writ of *habeas corpus* would be applied for to-morrow, and that he would be out on bail before another night had passed. He may have said a good deal more, but that is all Mr. McClure told me."

"Nothing about a woman?"

"Oh, no, that I'm *sure* of. Is there a woman mixed up with them, Mr. Benham?"

"I have reason to think that there is."

"Then you know something about their plans, and you'll be prepared for them?"

"Yes, I think I know something about them. But now," he continued, for he had no idea of letting Miss Pink into his confidence, knowing full well that anything he told her would be all over the village the next day, "I must bid you good-night; I have a good deal to do before I go to bed.   Many thanks for your kindness in coming here, to tell us about Todd and his threats."

"Have I really done you a service, Mr. Benham? Oh, I'm so glad!" and Miss Pink clasped her hands together, and looked ecstatically at the ceiling, as though there were some one there whom she was addressing; "it's so little that we women can do for men, that when anything comes in my way by which I can oblige them, I'm always glad to do it.   And then, when it's a man like you, Mr. Benham, it is a tenfold greater privilege."

"Thanks, you are very kind.—Good-night, mother," kissing her as he spoke; "I shall be up late, but shall probably not see you before we meet at breakfast."

"Good-night, John.   Don't sit up too late."

"You need not be afraid," he said to her, in a low voice, not intended for Miss Pink's ears; "all will be well watched."   Then he left the room, and soon afterward Miss Pink, feeling that she had made an impression at last that might be enduring, also took her departure.

CHAPTER IX.

JOHN BENHAM did not go to bed till daylight began to break. He passed the greater part of the night in his laboratory, working at the experiment that in the afternoon had baffled him. At intervals he looked out of one of the windows, and again and again went down-stairs, and out of the front door, on tours of inspection around Miss Honeywood's and his own house. All was quiet, and the watch that he had set on both buildings was vigilant. Toward morning, in fact, just as the first faint streaks of dawn were showing themselves over the top of Peter's Mountain, the little bead of metal in the cavity in the piece of charcoal underwent the reaction he wanted. His experiment had succeeded. He had discovered a method by which iron made with anthracite coal could be rendered as tough, as ductile, and in every way as good, for all purposes for which iron is required, as that made with charcoal. He owned a secret that had in it the power to make him one of the richest men in the United States. He was independent of partnerships, and could dictate his own terms to the iron-manufacturers of Pennsylvania, where alone anthracite coal is used in the process of smelting.

He had worked all night, not without distractions. Besides the anxiety he felt in regard to the safety of the threatened houses, the one with fire, the other with the abduction of its mistress, his mind was occupied with the thought that in the morning he should know whether or not it was possible that Alana Honeywood would ever be his wife.

He had determined that there should be no more suspense ; that he would go to her, frankly tell her that he loved her, and ask her to marry him. He would do this, not as the prospective partner in a large and flourishing establishment, not as the possessor of a method of manufacturing iron, that was in itself a source of great wealth, but simply in the capacity in which she had always known him, the superintendent of her works, her hired servant. How she would receive his declaration he did not know ; he could not even conjecture, with any satisfaction to himself, what her answer would be. Sometimes he had been bold enough to think that she loved him. But these occasions were rare ; for generally he had, when submitting the question to his heart, received rather discouraging replies. She was always considerate for him, always kind, always reliant upon him ; but then she was his employer, and he had been a faithful servant, and it was right that she should treat him with kindness and respect and confidence, even if she did not entertain the slightest glimmer of love for him.

But after his contest, if such it could be called, with Alec Todd, and his signal discomfiture of that unpleasant person, there had been a few moments during which he was sure she loved him. There was a softening of her manner toward him that she had never before exhibited, a tremulousness, a depth of feeling in her voice that had never been yet there for him, a look from her dark-gray eyes that never, since he had known her, had she given to him. Still, even these, he thought, after a short delirium of happiness, might have been nothing more than manifestations of the gratitude she would naturally feel toward her deliverer.

After two hours of sound sleep he was up, but he felt unrefreshed, for the rest had not been sufficient. It was a cool morning ; but he left the house without disturbing any one, and went down to the river, to a quiet little nook, resolved to take his morning's bath in the Susquehanna.

The water was colder than he had thought for, but he swam around in it till the bodily reaction that, with him, always betokened mental exhilaration, began to make its appearance. The stuffy feeling about his head was gone, his skin was in a glow, and, by the time he had walked briskly home, he had the appetite of a cart-horse for his breakfast, and a frame of mind that was fit for any effort in any direction that was likely to be demanded of him.

He finished his breakfast without the usual conversation with his mother relative to the work and other doings of the day. She forbore to ask questions, or to offer suggestions, for she knew what was on his mind, to the exclusion of every other subject, and she did not desire to run the risk of disturbing any course of thought upon which he might have entered. On his meeting with her at the breakfast-table he had told her that at last his experiment had succeeded, and had hinted at the prospect of wealth and influence thereby opened to him. Then, after her congratulations, a few words had been said in regard to the quiet night they had passed, notwithstanding the conspiracy that had been formed to injure them—an immunity that, as Benham laughingly suggested, was mainly, if not altogether, due to the fact that the two chief conspirators were in jail.

He was just about to make his usual morning tour of the works, his horse being at the door, when Mr. Wade was announced. He was a little put out by the visit, for it deranged his plans, and might even altogether suspend their execution for that day at least. The round of inspection that he made every day, immediately after breakfast, extended to all the departments of the business: forge, iron-mines, coal-mines, building operations—all were embraced within the range of his visits. Then he generally went to meet Alana in her office, prepared to give her a complete idea of the state of the works in all their ramifications,

Now, he had heard her say that she intended going to Harrisburg that day, and as the train that she would probably take left the works at 10.5, and as it was now half-past eight, there was very little time to devote to Mr. Wade. Indeed, unless his business was connected with the works, in which case he should feel bound to attend to it, he would not do much more than to wish Mr. Wade a good-morning, before excusing himself from further conversation.

But Mr. Wade's business was important. He had heard of Benham's second adventure, and he had come to the fountain-head for the knowledge of it that he desired to get.

"I am afraid," said Benham, looking nervously at his watch, "that I have not time to tell you the particulars as fully as I would like. I must go at once to the Colerain iron-mine, for there's been an irruption of water there that the foreman tells me will be a source of great trouble and delay ; and then I have the Paxton coal-mine to look at, and then the forge to go through, and then the several foremen to confer with, and—"

"Say no more," exclaimed Mr. Wade, laughing. "I won't keep you a minute. I have my horse, and if you've no objection I'll ride with you and we can carry on our conversation while we are going from one place to the other. By the by," as the two gentlemen left the house, and were about mounting their horses, "what do you think of my iron-mine ? I wish you would make a thorough inspection of it. You—that is, Miss Honeywood—ought to have it, for it's worth more to her than it is to any one else."

"We were talking about it yesterday," said Benham, as he swung himself into the saddle. "I have already advised her to purchase it._ I took the opportunity a few days ago of examining it thoroughly. It is not a purchaser's business," he continued, laughing, "to enhance the value of property offered him; but I agree with you, that it naturally belongs to the Susquehanna Iron-Works."

"There is only one way by which I can do business of this kind with Miss Honeywood, and that is to have the mine appraised by three disinterested but competent persons. My relations with her are such as to prevent bargaining. Let her appoint an appraiser, I will appoint another, and these two will select a third. They shall fix the price, and for that sum I will sell it."

"That is fair, and I have no doubt that she will accept your proposition."

"Very well! Now, tell me all about this adventure of yours last evening. It interests me more than you suppose. You have had it in your power twice to be of great service to Miss Honeywood; for I am inclined to think that this scheme that you appear to have disarranged concerned her much more than it did any of the rest of us. Besides, I had a visit this morning from Miss Pink, who gave me what information she picked up yesterday in Harrisburg."

Benham smiled at this last piece of intelligence. It was, however, no more than was to have been expected. Miss Pink was not only the village postmistress, but she was the circulator of intelligence on her own account as well. He said nothing, however, about that lady, not even telling Mr. Wade that she had previously retailed her news to him. He did not care to talk about Alana with anybody just then more than could be helped. However, he saw the advantage to the cause of justice of placing before Mr. Wade all that he had acquired relative to the conspiracy that he believed existed to abduct Miss Honeywood, and therefore he gave him all the details of his adventure of the evening before.

During the recital Mr. Wade asked no questions, preferring to let Benham—who was a very direct and concise speaker, never using an unnecessary word, or wandering from the point—to communicate his knowledge in his own way. When the story was ended, with the announcement that the man was in the Dauphin County Jail, Mr. Wade gave a sigh, which was probably meant to be expressive of the satisfaction he experienced at this happy termination, for the present at least, of the affair that had come so near ending in a much more deplorable way.

"Do you think," he said, after he had reflected several minutes upon the situation—"do you think that you would know that woman again?"

"That would depend upon how she was dressed. I have a very clear mental impression of her appearance, as she looked yesterday. But, if I were to see her without a bonnet, her hair arranged differently, and her clothing otherwise changed, I might not know her. The variations in women's dresses are so great that it is easier for them than for men to escape recognition."

"Did she speak properly—use good English, I mean?"

"Yes, I think so."

"And the man?"

"Yes."

"Now tell me, Mr. Benham, does the woman resemble any person you have ever seen?"

"Yes. She looks like Todd. She is a refined likeness of Todd. She held herself like a lady, and spoke like one."

"Looks like Todd! That's just what I thought. Now, try and recall all the other faces you have ever seen. Of course you can't do that, but put your whole mental force on the subject. Did you ever see any other person that this woman resembled?"

"Yes, I think so; but I am not so sure on this point as I am on the other."

"Who is that person?"

"That," said Benham, "I do not think I ought to tell.

It is, perhaps, more a suspicion than a fact with me, and therefore I do not feel as though I ought to express myself more decidedly."

"Well, I suppose you are right. You're a sensible fellow, Benham. Your head is always level. I wish I could take you into my confidence in this matter. There's a great deal in it, and I have no doubt that, if we felt equally free to talk to each other, we should find that we are thinking in the same direction. I really feel as though I wanted advice. I should like, of all things, to confer with you, but as things now are I do not feel at liberty to do so. Perhaps, however, in a day or two, I may have more freedom. On one point I am sure you are with me. You would not like any harm to come to Miss Honeywood."

"I would rather it should come to me," answered Benham, quietly.

"I believe you! There's no mistaking you, Benham; you're as true as steel. I wish she'd get married; then she'd have a natural protector."

Benham made no reply to this last remark of his companion. They were then approaching the Colerain mine, which was situated at the upper end of the ravine in which Todd's house stood. As they came near, they saw that many of the men that ought to have been at work were lounging about the mouth of the mine, and occasionally uttering derisive cries when a car-load of ore was brought up to the surface, or when the foreman made his appearance. Benham at once suspected that a strike was in process of organization, and his mind at once jumped to the conclusion that Todd had been meddling with these men in like manner as he had with the brick-layers. When they were within fifty yards of the mine, the foreman saw them, and at once came forward to meet them.

"What's the matter, Mr. Schettler?" inquired Benham; "why are not these men at work?"

"Well, sir, the fact is, that they refuse to obey my orders.   It's all on account of me, sir."

"How many of them are in this?"

"Only about twenty out of the seventy-five."

"Who is the leader?"

"A Welshman, named Jones."

Benham at once rode up to where the strikers were con-
gregated, some of them sitting on logs, others lolling on
the ground, but the majority of them walking about, and
talking with the men not in the strike, that came up from
the mine with the loads of ore.

"Jones," said Benham, "I want to speak with you."

There was no answer.

"Is Jones here?"

"Yes," said a gruff voice, "Jones is here, but if you
want to speak to him you can come to him as well as he
can come to you, and a dom sight better!"

"That's easily done!" said Benham, dismounting, and
approaching the man, who stood a little apart from the
rest, talking energetically to a man that had just come out
of the mine.   "Now," he continued, as he stood in front of
Jones, a big, burly, red-headed fellow, "what's the meaning of this?"

"The meaning of it is that we won't work under a
dommed Dutchman no longer—that's what it means, Mr.
Benham."

"Very well, you are your own judges of the matter, but
you can't stay here to interfere with these men that will
work.—Now, men," he went on, addressing the loiterers,
"those of you that wish to quit work, come down at once to
my office and be paid off.—Mr. Schettler, give me these
men's names.   They are discharged, unless they go to work
again within five minutes."

"Well," said Jones, "that's spunky talk, Mr. Benham,
and I think you'll find that you're going further than your

rope will allow. As for me, I'm going to stay here as long as I like, and not one of us is going to work till Alec Todd's made foreman."

"Alec Todd is in jail, and he's likely to stay there till he goes to the penitentiary."

"Todd in jail! And what put him in jail?"

"His own crimes. He nearly killed his wife, and he tried to injure the mistress."

"When was all that? You see we don't know, till the next day, and sometimes not then, what takes place at the forge."

"It was yesterday afternoon. Now, Jones, you have a wife and children. Have you forgotten the time that your baby fell into the wash-kettle, and nearly got scalded to death, and how the mistress came here, and took your little one in her arms to her own home, and nursed it, night and day, till it was well? Are you the man to want to work under the scoundrel who threatened to cut off one of her fingers, unless she put him in charge of this mine? Where would your baby have been but for her? Jones, I'm ashamed of you. I thought you were a man."

"And so I am a mon, Mr. Benham," cried Jones, sobbing like a child. "I didn't know that the mistress was in it. My God, Mr. Benham! I wouldn't do anything to hurt 'the mistress'; ond if ever I lay my hands on Todd it'll be a bod day for him—yes, a verra bod day! You're right, Mr. Benham: if it hadn't been for the mistress, God bless her, my little Ally would have been in her grave. —Come, men!" he continued, turning to the strikers, who were gathered together at a little distance, awaiting the result of the interview; "Todd's in jail for licking his wife, and trying to lick the mistress. You wouldn't work under a mon that would hurt the mistress? No, not a dom one of ye!" as the men responded in emphatic negatives; "then go back to work, the strike's over."

"Thank you, Jones," said Benham, holding out his hand, which the big, lumbering fellow grasped and shook with a will; "I thought you wouldn't go against the mistress. Now, can you tell me what started this affair?"

"Well, sir, Todd was here yesterday morning, and he said you were going to get rid of us as soon as you could, and put in a lot of Dutchmen at lower wages, He told us that if he was made foreman, he could stop it, and that all we had to do was to strike, and you'd give in at once."

"I thought he was the instigator. Of course he lied. There has never been the slightest intention of discharging any one of you, or of lowering your wages. If you have any cause of complaint against Mr. Schettler, all you have to do is to come to me with it frankly, and I'll inquire into it; and if you are right I'll make matters straight."

"I say, Mr. Benham," said the man, coming up close to Benham and speaking in as low a tone of voice as he was capable of producing from a vocal apparatus unaccustomed to such an exercise, "I hope you won't say aught of this to the mistress. I wouldn't like her to know that —that—after all she did for my little Ally, that I was bad enough to go against her. You see, sir, I never thought it was against her I was going. I only thought of Mr. Schettler, and the story that Todd told."

"I'll not tell her that you were in it, Jones. It would hurt her feelings very much if she thought you would do anything to injure her. I know she regards you as a friend. Now get to work. You'll not hear of this again to your disadvantage.—Come, Mr. Schettler, I'm ready to talk with you about opening that north gallery a little further, and getting that water out."

After his conference with the foreman, Benham rejoined Mr. Wade, who had remained an attentive observer of what had taken place, and whose admiration of the superintendent's method of dealing with the men was unbounded.

"You must have a good deal of knowledge of human nature, my friend," he said. "You could twist those fellows, any one of whom could make mince-meat of you in a minute, around your finger if you wished to. I don't know what Miss Honeywood would do without you."

"I know them pretty well," said Benham, with a smile. "They're a good lot, but horribly ignorant, and easily imposed upon by such a scoundrel as Todd. Now, Mr. Wade," he continued, after they had turned off to the north on their way to the Paxton mine, only a few hundred yards distant, "what is the meaning of all this? I must tell you that I too have had a visit from Miss Pink, and that she spoke of things that, taken in conjunction with what I already know, have caused me a good deal of anxious thought."

"Ah! Miss Pink saw you also, and told you doubtless all that she told me. By this time, she's told everybody that has called at the post-office."

"Yes, and she told me among other matters that this fellow, Todd, declared to Mr. McClure that he was Miss Honeywood's uncle."

"Yes, so I understand," remarked Mr. Wade, dryly.

"Of course, the rascal lied."

"I don't know; I am not sufficiently acquainted with Miss Honeywood's family to be enabled to express an opinion. He may be, however. Families get awfully scattered and run down in this country."

"Why should there be this conspiracy to abduct Miss Honeywood, and who are the man and the woman I disturbed hatching their plans at 'Washington's Throne'?"

"Now, my dear Benham, be reasonable! Surely you know more of that matter than I do. You heard them talk, you saw them both, you dragged the man all the way to the village. If you couldn't find out who they are, how the devil can I?"

"True, but it appears to me that we ought to be doing something to circumvent these scoundrels. It will not do for us to remain quiet while they carry out their vile schemes."

"My dear boy, it appears to me that we can, for the present at least, be satisfied with what has been done ; with what you have done, in fact. You have put two of them in jail, and while they are there the Susquehanna Iron-Works and its inhabitants are safe from their depredations."

"They may have accomplices who are not yet caught."

"I think not. If there had been others, you would have heard some mention of them. No, depend upon it, there are only Todd, the other fellow, and the woman."

"I suppose I shall have to go to Harrisburg, to-day or to-morrow, to appear as a witness."

"Yes, I suppose they will have their examination to-morrow morning, and that they will then be committed for trial, or released on bail. It would be an outrage to release them on bail."

"That is a matter that may safely be left to Judge Mierson. It is entirely discretionary with him, and he is not disposed to show undue leniency to such fellows. I shall go down myself this morning and try to have an interview with them."

Everything was found in order at the Paxton mine, and then the two gentlemen turned toward the forge. They rode the rest of the way in comparative silence, and at a fork in the road Mr. Wade turned off to go to his tower. Benham inspected the furnace, and was then ready to make his report to Alana. His hour had come—in a few minutes he would know his fate. What would he not have given if those minutes had passed, and he knew that Alana was his promised wife! With a firm step, but with a heart that beat many pulses quicker than was natural to it even in times of great excitement, he crossed the lawn and was about to open the door that led into Miss Honeywood's office, when a sudden thought struck him, and he retraced his steps to his office.

There he wrote a letter to Messrs. Cummings, Jansen and Jones, thanking them for their offer, but respectfully declining it, giving as his reason that he had made a discovery that would, he thought, revolutionize the process of iron-manufacture, and that he desired to devote all his time to this matter.

"Now," he said, "I feel more comfortable."

CHAPTER X.

ALANA was seated at her usual place at the desk, the top of which was covered with papers. She had passed a restless night, and her face gave evidence of the fact. She rose, as Benham entered the room, and, advancing toward him, held out her hand.

"My friend," she said, "I was too much overcome yesterday to thank you properly for your timely kindness to me. I shall never forget what you did for me. It would have been a good deal had your interference been accidental, but it showed such thoughtfulness for my welfare that it has sunk deeply into my heart."

Alana was an emotional woman. She showed what she felt, and the tears started to her eyes, as in these few words she thanked her rescuer.

As for Benham, he was quite unprepared for this demonstration. He had entered the room with his note-book in his hand, and with his thoughts at the moment on the subjects he would have to bring to Miss Honeywood's attention. Her words, and actions, and exhibition of passion, caused a revulsion of feeling, and immediately determined him to drop the business part of his visit, and to plunge at once into the matter that was nearest his heart. He held her hand in his for a moment, and then, with his eyes fixed on hers, he raised it to his lips. The action did not appear to astonish her. She made a feeble effort to withdraw her hand, but he held it firmly in his, and she allowed it to remain. She knew instinctively what was coming;

she had seen it in the look he had given her; she felt
already the sweet ties of the happy bondage that every
right-minded woman feels when she really loves. For one
delicious moment she gave herself up to the thoughts that
flashed like lightning through her mind, and then, forcibly
withdrawing her hand, she turned away, and, going to the
window, looked out at the frowning wall of mountains that
faced her.

Benham stood for a moment undecided. He was not
skilled in the ways of women, but he had seen enough of
Alana, since he had come into the room, to give him some
hope that she loved him. For a moment, but only for a
moment, he was undecided what to do; then, with the
consciousness that his love gave him that all inequality between him and her was gone, he walked to the window and
gently laid his hand on her shoulder. She did not move
or even turn her face toward him, but he felt her form
tremble, and he saw a tear fall on the window-sill before him.

"Alana," he said—it was the first time in all his life
that he had ever called her by her first name—"I have loved
you a long while, dear; ever since I came here, I think.
I have tried to bury the feeling in my heart, but I can do
so no longer. I am not so strong as I thought; it has got
the better of me, and for weal or for woe I must speak
now. Will you hear me?"

She did not answer, but she covered her face with her
hands, while the tears that she did her utmost to restrain,
but could not, trickled through her fingers. What was she
to say to him? She loved him, loved him with all her
heart and soul; but how could she permit herself, she a
nameless woman, to become the promised wife of a man
like John Benham? No, she loved him too well to bring
dishonor into his house, and every moment that she allowed him to be deceived was an injury to him. Still, he
was not blind, he was not a fool, he must see that she loved

him. How, then, could she reconcile the words she felt she must speak, with the evidences of her emotion, so clear and distinct that he could not fail to perceive and to understand them ? It was impossible. If she told him that she did not love him, it would be a lie. She could not utter it; she felt that the falsehood would stick in her throat. And yet to say that she loved him, but could not marry him, would be to make him call for an explanation that she was certain she could not give. Not now, at least. She caught at the hope that there might be a time when she could explain. It might be, too, that his love was so strong that he would be willing to take her to his heart notwithstanding the stain upon her birth. She would live on that hope. Yes, he might speak, and she would speak too, and he should know that if she could not promise to be his wife the fault was not hers. It would be hard if she, an innocent person, should have to suffer to that extent for the sins of others. She had tried to do her duty in all the relations of life in which she had been placed, and yet this load of shame that others had incurred fell upon her shoulders, oh ! so heavily, that she felt as though she could not bear it all through her life. Yes, he should, if he pleased, tell her that he loved her, and she would listen with eager ears to the gracious words that might fall from his lips. There might be happiness for them both in the consciousness that they loved each other ; happiness, too, in the increased freedom of association that the knowledge would give, and then, after a while, when she knew his inmost soul better than she knew it now, she would tell him all. She was timid ; she had ever since her father's death been disposed to brood over the position in which she found herself, and to magnify the effect that a knowledge of it would cause in others, till she had become morbid and fearful to a degree that interfered with the force and the correctness of her judgment.

He loved her! He had told her that. All her doubts, all her fears, on that point, were at an end. There was a world of thought for her in the few words he had spoken; and yet, he had asked her if he might say more, and she had not answered him, but had stood there, with her back turned to him, and her hands covering her face. Still, he must know what her answer would be if she could speak. He must know that, if she did not love him, she would have spoken long ago, with a coldness and decision that would have told him what she thought. Still, it was not kind for her to give him only silence for an answer, when her heart was overflowing with love for him.

A woman with a declaration of love ringing in her ears is, in one respect, like a drowning person. Thoughts go through her brain with marvelous rapidity, just as the man who has gone down for the third and last time, never to come up again alive, unless pulled up by some power not his own, has all the events of his life pass as though in procession before his mental vision. All this, that it has taken the reader several minutes to go through with, flashed through her brain in a tenth part of the time, and then, when she arrived at the conclusion that she ought to give him an answer, she dropped her hands from before her face, and, turning round, looked at him for an instant only; and then she was in his arms, and clasped to his heart.

"I did not know that you loved me," she said, smiling through the tears that John Benham kissed from her eyes. "How should I? You were always so cold and formal with me."

"And yet I loved you all the time," said Benham, still holding her head pressed to his breast. "You might have known, dear, from that very coldness, that I had something to conceal."

"But why should you wish to conceal it? Think how

happy we might have been, all these years, in the knowledge that we loved each other!"

"I thought you might misunderstand me. I was in a
subordinate position. It might have seemed to you impertinent for the superintendent of the Susquehanna Iron-
Works to fall in love with their mistress."

"And what," she inquired, raising her large gray eyes
to his, and with a grave smile on her face—"what made
you think that I had changed?"

"I don't know; something, I can not tell what. It
may have been a look, it may have been a word, it may
only have been an inflection of your voice, it may only have
been an inspiration, an instinct, with nothing at all for
its foundation but the promptings of my own heart. Yesterday I was in despair; to-day I had hope, and then, when
you spoke to me just now and thanked me with tears in
your dear eyes for the work of yesterday, I felt sure that
the time had come for me to unburden my heart."

"You would have got the same answer if you had spoken
years ago. I have loved you as long as you have loved
me, only I could not tell you what was in my heart. You
might have seen it, though; sometimes I thought you did
see it; but then you at once became so reserved and formal,
that I came to the conclusion that after all you were simply
trying to do your duty as the superintendent, and that love
for me never entered your mind."

"Ah, dear, you will find out, when you know me better,
what a proud man I am! But, now tell me, don't put me
off with what has been. I want to know that you love me
now; that you love me as fondly as I love you; that I am
henceforth to be first in your heart for evermore; that you
are my own dear Alana, soon, very soon, to be my wife;
that—"

A loud knock at the door interrupted him. It does not
take long under such a circumstance for lovers to separate.

I have known a young man to be sitting on a sofa with his Dulcinea's head resting on his manly breast, his arms around her, and words of the most devoted affection, that one would have thought must have required the concentrated effort of his whole mind, flowing from his lips, and yet, on the sudden opening of the door, the young woman would be found to be reading a book, and the young man would be seen to be critically studying a picture hanging on the opposite wall. The movements were not quite so rapid as these, in the case of Benham and Alana; but when, in answer to the knock, she said, "Come in," Mr. Wade found her seated at her desk, and John Benham standing at one end of it, with his note-book in his hand, looking as impassive as though the whole of his visit had been devoted to the giving of statistics of the iron-product for the past month. Alana's face, had it been carefully studied, would have shown signs of emotional disturbance, but no one apparently could have listened more attentively to the reading of the superintendent's notes than she was listening when Mr. Wade opened the door.

"I came," he said, not noticing that anything unusual had occurred, "to say that I have just received a telegram from Harrisburg, which requires me to leave here on the next train. If you are going down, Alana, we might go together. I have a little business with you which we could go through with in the twenty minutes we shall be on the train. It will be here in ten minutes, and we've no time to spare."

"Then, Mr. Benham," said Alana, turning to the superintendent; "I shall have to defer hearing your report till I come back. Will you kindly come over this evening? I shall be quite alone." She gave him a look, as she spoke, which John thoroughly understood.

"Yes," he answered; "I will come over after tea."

"Won't you take tea with me?" inquired Alana. She

felt that she wanted him now to be always with her. "You have not sat at my table since your mother left me, and only once the whole time she was here," she added, with a smile.

"Thanks! I will come to tea."

"Then we will finish our business. Now I am afraid I shall have to ask you to excuse me while I get ready to go to Harrisburg. Good-by." She held out her hand to him as she spoke, while a happy smile played over her face, and then she was gone.

"She feels grateful to you, Benham," said Mr. Wade, "for your rescue of her from that scoundrel Todd, yesterday. I have never known her so gracious. She's a lovely woman, but she's out of place here; or rather I should say wasted. She ought to be married. She's just the woman to make a good man happy."

"Yes, I think she is."

"There's Mr. Trevor; he's dead in love with her. But, though she likes him as a friend, she would not marry him, I'm sure."

"No, I don't think she would."

"Well, if such an unobservant man of women as you are can see that, she must have made it very apparent."

"She's so kind to everybody that she's liable to be misunderstood, perhaps. But I think she makes it very clear that, though she likes Mr. Trevor as a friend, she does not love him."

"Yes, you're right. Then there's the doctor. Now, I have sometimes thought that she liked him better than any one else, but latterly I have changed my mind. He worships the ground that she walks on."

"He's a good fellow."

"Yes, he's a good fellow; but she'd never marry a man because he's a good fellow. She's a woman, Benham, who is prepared to go through fire and water for the man she

may love, but she would demand just as great a degree of
devotion from him. Now, as you must have seen, there's
nothing heroic about either Mr. Trevor or Dr. Arndell,
and therefore, however much she may like them, she'd
never marry either. I'll tell you what it is, Benham : if
you were a marrying man, you'd be the one for her ; but
you'll die an old bachelor, I suppose."

"You think I am heroic?" said Benham, interrogatively, and smiling at the same time.

"I think you have the stuff in you of which heroes are
made, and that, if you had the chance, you'd be a hero.
You've come pretty near it already."

"Come, Mr. Wade," said Alana, entering the room at-
tired for her journey. "We have only three minutes in
which to reach the train." She looked very pretty in the
little round hat with its eagle-feather that she had on her
head, and that did not hide the luxuriant tresses of her
dark-brown hair. Again she held out her hand to Benham.
This time it was daintily gloved, and he pressed it lovingly
in his. "I shall expect you to tea this evening. Good-by."

"Good-by, my darling," he whispered, as Mr. Wade
went out of the room before her. "God bless you !"

She was gone, and he went over to the forge to his daily
duties, his head in a whirl of delight that made him feel
as though he was walking on air. He tried to attend to
the work before him ; he apparently heard the statements
of the foremen of the several gangs of men, and he made
answers that seemed to them to be correct ; but, if they were,
he did not know it at the time. The force of routine, he
thought, as the matter afterward came into his mind, was
so strong that he gave the proper directions automatically,
and without his consciousness participating in the acts.
How could he do otherwise when his whole mind was filled
with the sense of the great happiness that had come to
him !

7

At dinner he informed his mother of what he had done, and the result thereof.

"I told you how it would be!" said Mrs. Benham, kissing him in her enthusiasm and self-satisfaction with the realization of her prediction. "I knew she liked you. Now, my dear boy, you will be very happy. Of course, you will not now accept the partnership offered you."

"No, I declined it this morning before I saw Alana. I did not want to go to her in any other capacity than as the superintendent of her works. As such she has known me for many years, and as such I wanted her to accept or reject me."

"What a chivalrous fellow you are, John!" said his mother, looking at him fondly.

"I don't know about that. I am as well off now in this world's goods as she, but then I gained that while in her service. I intend to give her a half-interest in my discovery, for it was to a great extent through the facilities her works afforded me, and during time that belonged to her, that I was able to conduct my experiments. It will give us all the wealth we shall need."

"Of course, you have as yet come to no understanding as to the time when you will be married?"

"No, she had to go to Harrisburg," he answered, with a smile, "and there was not sufficient time for us to discuss that point. I am going to take tea with her this evening, and I shall urge a speedy marriage. I am alarmed for her, after the doings of yesterday, and I think I can protect her better if I am her husband as well as the superintendent of her works. I haven't told you that there was the beginning of a strike this morning at the Colerain mine, set on foot by that villain Todd, and that I arrived there just in time to stop it."

Then he informed his mother of what had occurred at the mine, and how the incipient disturbance had been subdued by the mere mention of Alana's name.

"I am sure," he continued, after his mother had expressed her sense of his conduct on the occasion in question, "that there is a conspiracy composed of at least three persons, the object of which is to do harm to Alana, probably for the ultimate purpose of pecuniary gain. Todd, and the woman who was at the rock on the mountain yesterday, and of whom unfortunately we have not succeeded in finding a trace, are apparently the tools of the fellow whom I captured. As you will remember, he would not give his name to me, nor supply any information of himself whatever. I believe he told Squire McElroy that his name was 'Thomas Johnson,' but this is probably assumed. Now, it appears to me that it would be a monstrous error to keep Alana in ignorance of the scheme against her. Hitherto I have had no right to interfere. Mr. Wade is her counsel, and in some sense her guardian, being the co-executor with herself of her father's will. He is fully acquainted with all that I know, except the one fact that the woman bears some resemblance to Alana—a circumstance that I have not before mentioned to you."

"The woman looks like Alana! How is that?"

"Ah! that I do not know. Probably it is accidental. For a time I did not recognize the resemblance, but last night, while I was at work, it came to me. It is not a strong likeness, and her features are coarser than Alana's, but there is a similarity in form and in expression. The woman is very much like Todd—like enough to be his sister; probably she is his sister. Now, you will recollect that Miss Pink told us last night that Todd declared that he is Alana's uncle. If this is true, and the woman is Todd's sister, then this same woman is either Alana's aunt or her mother."

"She can not be her mother!"

"No, for, as I have always understood, her mother died when Alana was an infant."

"Yet you remember that, for a long time after Mr. Honeywood's death, advertisements were kept in the newspapers asking for information in regard to a woman, named Sarah Mullin, who in the year 1855 made, in Philadelphia, the acquaintance of Mr. Francis Honeywood. I have the paper here," continued Mrs. Benham, going to a desk and taking from it a newspaper carefully folded. "Yes," as she looked through the columns, and after a little time found what she wanted, "here it is. She is requested to communicate, without delay, with Mr. William Wade, attorney-at-law, Susquehanna Iron-Works, Dauphin County, Pennsylvania. My dear John, this may be the woman."

"Yes, but that advertisement I have always understood refers to a woman who had been in the family, and in regard to whom Mr. Honeywood desired to make some provision in his will, but forgot it. And so Alana, knowing his wishes, sought for the woman, in order to carry them out."

"How did you hear all that?"

"I don't know, now. I never paid much attention to the circumstance, and, indeed, never heard the advertisement read till this moment."

"My dear John, that is very absurd. People don't advertise for women after that fashion. Let me see," opening the paper and proceeding to read:

"'Sarah Mullin, who, in the year 1855 or thereabout, in the city of Philadelphia, made the acquaintance of Mr. Francis Honeywood, is requested,' etc. Now, does that read like an advertisement for a nurse? Not a bit of it!" and Mrs. Benham replaced the newspaper in the desk, with the air of a person who had made a statement that was incontrovertible.

John Benham was silent. He was thinking deeply of the circumstances that had been brought to his mind, and was endeavoring to deduce from them a conclusion that would satisfactorily account for them. Mrs. Benham, however, had her own ideas on the subject, and that they were plausible the reader will doubtless admit.

"I'll tell you what I think, John," she said, resuming her seat, and showing by her manner the extraordinary interest that had been aroused within her. "This Sarah Mullin is a woman with whom Mr. Honeywood had formed illicit relations. She is no relative of Alana, but her father on his death-bed requested her to seek the woman out, and to make provision for her. Likely enough he had treated her badly, as men often treat women under such circumstances. Todd is her brother, and the two are in league to force all they can out of Alana, by first getting her into their power. As to Todd being Alana's uncle, that is a lie. She is not like him in the slightest respect, is she?"

"No, I should say not: and yet there is sometimes a certain faint resemblance between them. Still, it is nothing—accidental, perhaps, just as is the woman's to her. I shouldn't be at all surprised if your solution of the matter is correct. But who, then, is the other man—the one that I dragged over the road very much to his damage, I am happy to say?"

"That I can not tell you. Does he resemble anybody you ever saw?"

"No, I never saw a face like his. Of one thing, however, I am certain—he is the leader; the others are his tools. Now, let us see how the matter stands:

"1. The woman looks something like Alana, but not much. Alana, as you know, resembles her father greatly.

"2. Todd bears a still less resemblance to her; that, I think, may be considered to be accidental.

"3. But Todd and the woman are very much alike; in features, in expression, in voice, in manner. They may certainly be regarded as brother and sister, and the woman's language relative to him showed that she was intimate with him.

"4. Todd declares that he is Alana's uncle. It is of prime importance that the truth or falsity of this statement should be at once established, and I propose to devote myself to the question.

"5. The woman showed that she had an affection for Alana that was at times superior to all other considerations, and that would probably, if she could be separated from her two confederates, come to be a ruling passion with her. The woman must be found, and taken into our service against the others.

"6. Conference should at once be had with Alana. She will be able to give data that can not fail to be of service, in the warfare that is going to be waged against this vile gang.

"I think," he added, after a moment's reflection, "that these are the chief points. Do you think of anything else?"

"No, you seem to have covered the whole ground; but what are you going to do?"

"First of all I'm going to Harrisburg, to see Todd. The other fellow will probably tell me nothing, but Todd I have reason to believe, can, by a mild degree of bribery, be got to disclose the whole plot so far as he knows it. I shall this evening reveal all to Alana, and seek to obtain her confidence. I shall take her advice in regard to further taking Mr. Wade into partnership. He can, I think, be of great service: in the first place, he is a very sensible man; and, in the next, he is a good lawyer."

"Do you think she knows yet that Todd claims to be her uncle?"

"No, I am quite sure she does not yet suspect such a thing. But she can not long remain in ignorance, for Miss Pink will make it her special business to tell her at the first opportunity. It will, therefore, be much better that she should hear it either from Mr. Wade, or me; and, if he has not told her by this evening, she shall hear it from me. No one in this world can have a greater interest in her than I."

"She may be able to tell you something of this woman."

"No, I think not. Mr. Wade probably knows more than any one else about her."

"Am I to speak of your engagement?" inquired Mrs. Benham, suddenly changing the conversation.

"No, certainly not, till Alana gives her consent. I will tell you a good deal more to-morrow morning than I can tell you now."

He looked at his watch, and found it was time for him to be at his office. Alana was expected back in the train that arrived at five o'clock. He would have gone to the station to meet her but for the fact that, as he never before had done so, he thought it might attract attention were he to do so now, and thus give rise to surmises for which Alana might not yet be ready. At six o'clock he would see her, and he impatiently awaited the arrival of that hour.

In the mean time the train came in, and a few minutes afterward he saw, from his office-window, Alana entering the house with her veil drawn closely over her face. The distance from the station to her house was less than a hundred yards, and she had as usual walked it. John Benham was not a romantic man nor one given to effusive demonstrations, but he kissed his hand to her as she walked past without seeing him; the first time in all his life that he had ever perpetrated such an act.

CHAPTER XI

It took about twenty minutes for the train to go from the Susquehanna Iron-Works to the station at Harrisburg. Mr. Wade and Alana were fortunate enough to find a compartment of a parlor-car empty, and into this they went at Mr. Wade's suggestion, he desiring, as he said, to have a little conversation with her. She would, however, greatly have preferred to be alone. She had ample food for thought without having other topics brought to her attention, but she had always acted upon the principle that disagreeable subjects caused less trouble if they were faced and at once disposed of; so she resigned herself to Mr. Wade and his communication.

"There is very little time at my disposal," he said, as soon as they were seated, "but what I have to say will not take long, and it is too important to be deferred. I have to ask that you will not, under any circumstances, go to the jail to-day to visit Todd. I have reason to believe that he will send for you as soon as he knows that you are in town, and he will know that a few minutes after you get there."

"How should he know, and what will he want with me?"

"He will know from a person whom he has hired to tell him when you leave the works, and who is now on this train; that person will go at once to the jail and will tell him. As to what he will want with you, I am not sure, but there is very little doubt that his object is to extort money."

"Are prisoners allowed to see whom they please?"

"Under certain restrictions, persons who have not been convicted and are simply detained for trial, are allowed to see whom they please. A person is deemed innocent till he has been proved guilty."

"And they can send out messengers and receive messages?"

"Yes, if they can afford to pay for them, and there is nothing objectionable in the communications they send or receive."

"I certainly have no desire to see the man, and yet there are some matters about which I would like to talk with him. He is certainly the one that came to see my father many years ago."

"I hope soon to put you in possession of all the information in regard to him that has been obtained. I defer doing so now because a good deal of it I do not believe, and it would merely be causing you distress for nothing to tell it to you. Be patient and hopeful; I think everything will come right."

"I try to be patient, and I try still harder to be hopeful. There is so much to make life pleasant that I try to shake off all the troubles that come to me."

"Yes, you are brave; you were always brave. Do you recollect the time, it must be sixteen or seventeen years ago, that I took you with me to fish in the Conodoguinet? We had to cross the Susquehanna, and coming back you accidentally let go the string of fish we had caught, and which you were trailing in the water over the stern of the boat. Without a word, you at once jumped overboard and began to wade down the stream after the fish. Of course, I went after you, but, before I could reach you, you had got into deep water, and down you went over your head. I grabbed you as you came up and pulled you into the boat, half drowned. The first words you said were, 'Oh, the

fish, I've lost the fish !' And so you had. They had been
carried down the river toward the sea to be eaten by the
cat-fish and eels before they had gone far on the way."

"Yes, I recollect," said Alana, laughing. "I got very
wet, and got a good scolding when I reached home, besides
being laid up with a cold for a week or more. I owe my
life to you. Sometimes I think it would have been better
if you had let me drown."

"Why, just now you were saying that there was so
much to make your life happy !"

"So there is, but, oh, so much to make it miserable !
How can I be sure of a moment's happiness when there is
a sword suspended over my head that may fall at any moment ? "

"I shall try not only to keep it from falling, but to take
it away altogether."

"Yes, and you will not succeed. How can you ?" she
added, bitterly. "It belongs to me, and in due time it
will fall. You might as well try to change the course of
that river. But, Mr. Wade," she went on, "you have
knowledge in your possession in regard to my mother and
perhaps of other relatives that you are keeping back from
me. I do not think this is wise, nor is it kind. I am the
person most interested, and I ought to know of all that is
going on."

"That is right," rejoined Mr. Wade, with emphasis,
"and you shall know. I am obliged to stay in Harrisburg
till to-morrow, and to-morrow evening I will give you all
the information I now have, and will, I believe, be able to
ease your mind of the burdens that now weigh so heavily
on it. But here we are at the station. I suppose you will
go to Mrs. Priestley's ? "

"Yes, I shall dine with her. Will you get me a carriage, please ? "

They left the train, and then, when Mr. Wade had put

her into a carriage, they parted, he to call on the district attorney, with the view of conferring with him relative to the prisoners in the jail and as to the means to be pursued to find the woman of the party, and Alana to visit her friends Mrs. Priestley and her daughters.

As she drove up Market Street to the River Bank, on which Mrs. Priestley had her handsome residence. she thought that, after all, she might as well have been allowed to come to Harrisburg without the company of Mr. Wade, as the only matter that he had had to bring to her notice was a request that she should not go to the jail to visit Todd, even if he should send for her, as she had been given to understand he probably would. Well, if he were. as seemed likely, her uncle, why should she not go to see him? Indeed, why should she not take the initiative in the whole business, and direct its course? She was not a child, to be kept in ignorance of important matters that concerned her. And then there was now John Benham. Who could be a wiser counselor to her than the man she loved, and whose wife she would one day be? "His wife!" she exclaimed. "No, I can not be his wife till this mystery that surrounds me is cleared up, and then, perhaps, when he knows who and what I am, he will not want me. He told me to-day that he was a proud man.

"But, no," she continued, "it can not be that that man is my uncle. I'll not believe it till there is better proof of it than the fact that my father said he is my mother's brother. My poor father! He was very weak when he told me all that. His mind had been wandering at times for several days. My God! what if it should be all a mistake? What if there were no Sarah Mullin? What if my mother were a good woman, and I not—"

She did not speak the word, for the carriage had stopped at Mrs. Priestley's door, and the course of her thoughts was interrupted. But, just as she was entering the house, a woman, closely veiled, approached her from around the corner, near which the building was situated.

"Are you Miss Honeywood?" inquired the woman in a tremulous voice, hurrying forward, so as to reach Alana before she got into the house.

"Yes."

"I have a note for you," taking as she spoke a letter from under her shawl and giving it to Alana.

"I will read it and send an answer."

"Please to read it now. It will require but a moment, and I will take back your answer."

Alana, still standing on the steps, opened the envelope, and read the note:

"DAUPHIN COUNTY JAIL, *Friday.*

"Alexander Todd would like to see Miss Honeywood as soon as possible. He wishes to apologize for his conduct yesterday, and to communicate important information. Do not fail to come."

For a moment Alana hesitated. Then she spoke:

"Did you say you would take my answer?"

"Yes."

"Then tell him I will come."

"At what time shall he expect you?"

Alana took out her watch. It was then a quarter to eleven. "Tell him," she said, "that I will be there at three o'clock." Then a sudden impulse moved her.

"Are you a relative of his?" she asked.

"It doesn't matter who I am," answered the woman, working her ungloved fingers nervously. "I'm nobody that you know."

"Will you raise your veil and let me see your face?"

"No."

"Why not?"

"Because I do not choose to do so. That is sufficient

reason, I suppose, in a free country. Besides, perhaps I am afraid of shocking you with my ugly face. It isn't every one that's as beautiful as you." Then, in a changed tone, and as though fearful that she had annoyed or hurt her interrogator by her rudeness, she said : "I can not tell you now who I am. Perhaps some day not far distant I may do so. Give me your hand a moment—your right hand."

Alana held out her hand.

"Take off your glove, please."

Alana removed the glove.

The woman took the hand that was again outstretched, and looked at it through her veil, as though studying its form and the lines that indented the rosy palm. It was a shapely hand, not especially small, for Alana was not a small woman, but beautifully proportioned and kept. The woman held it in hers for a few moments while she gazed at it, and Alana thought she heard a smothered sob. Then she raised it to her lips under her veil, and then Alana was sure that a tear dropped upon it.

"Who are you ?" she said, a vague feeling of hope and fear filling her breast. "You must tell me who you are." She withdrew her hand, and tried to raise the woman's veil ; but she was not quick enough, for her visitor descended the steps and was thus beyond her reach.

"At three o'clock," she said, "he will expect you. Farewell ! Be patient, and in time you will know all." Then, with a quickened pace that was almost a run, she disappeared around the corner. Alana followed her, determined, if possible, not to lose sight of her ; but, when she arrived at the corner, there was no one like the woman in sight.

Slowly she retraced her steps to Mrs. Priestley's, not doubting that the woman who had exhibited so much emotion in her presence was her mother, and blaming herself for not having more determinedly persisted in trying to make her reveal her identity. At first she thought she would not go into Mrs. Priestley's. The incident had entirely unfitted her for the society of this lady and her daughters, filling her mind with quite different thoughts from those that she knew would be prompted by the brilliant women she had come to visit. But, upon reflection, she deemed it advisable to try her utmost to act as though there were nothing to trouble her, at least till the time came when the crisis should be reached. She was aware that this would be a difficult task, for she was not good at concealing her emotions, and she was not quite sure that she would not break down in the attempt. But certainly there was no place that she knew of where such an effort could be made with greater chances of success than in Mrs. Priestley's house, and no persons so capable of diverting her mind as this lady and her daughters. So she again ascended the steps leading to the front door, and this time she rang the bell.

If Harrisburg society could be said to have any leader, Mrs. Priestley was the leader, and her two pretty daughters were her lieutenants. The fact was, however, that Harrisburg society did not have a leader. Not because it was too large or too small, but because it was cut up into numerous factions that took their origin from the religious predilections of the members. Thus there was a Methodist, a Lutheran, a German Reformed, a Roman Catholic, a Presbyterian, and an Episcopalian circle, each as rigid in its lines as if they were made of cast-iron. The two latter, however, were the most prominent, and in fact the only ones in which fashionable people were to be found. What there was about the others that cut them off from their Presbyterian and Episcopalian brothers and sisters it would be difficult to define, but that they were cut off there is no doubt. They dressed as well, they knew as much, they followed similar occupations, they were among the oldest settlers, but, for all that, the others were the *élite*, and their right so to be was not seriously questioned.

But if the Methodist, the Lutheran, the German Reformed, and the Roman Catholic cliques gave way before the Presbyterians and the Episcopalians, the fight for supremacy between the latter was severe and bitter, and had been going on ever since "the Church" was established in the town. At first, the Presbyterians had carried matters with a high hand. That was when the little establishment on the River Bank was weak in numbers; but latterly the Episcopalians had received several noted accessions from Philadelphia, Boston, and other large cities, and, although not yet so numerous as their religious rivals, were, in their own estimation at least, infinitely more select; and head and front among them was Mrs. Priestley.

She was a handsome woman, intelligent, sprightly, vivacious, quick at repartee, with just sufficient impudence in her composition to prompt her to say sharp though good-natured things to her friends, and still sharper things without the good nature to and of her enemies. She preferred to let herself out to their faces, for the element of fear of the consequences was not one of her characteristics; but if they were not present she was not thereby prevented expressing her mind in regard to any acts of which she suspected them to be guilty, or of any disagreeable personal peculiarities that she imagined them to possess.

Of course, such a woman was certain to have many enemies as well as friends, as is the case with all aggressive people, and while the one category hated her as she herself used to say "like fury," the other loved her very dearly.

Her daughters, Rubina and Colletta, were like her in all essential respects, except, of course, in the one matter of age, and in the one other feature that they were not quite so aggressive. They were emphatically what is called

"sweet girls"; were very pretty and accomplished, well
dressed, and, above all, intelligent. They possessed, also,
that happy faculty which their mother was still able to
share with them, of making their home delightful to the
young men of the city, and they were almost always certain to have two or three distinguished-looking gentlemen
in their retinue when they went to church or received their
friends at their own home, that had apparently just arrived
from Philadelphia or New York or Carlisle Barracks—
the latter, army officers. As a consequence, they were at
once the admiration and the envy of all other society women in Harrisburg, and especially of those belonging to the
Presbyterian persuasion.

Alana had known the Priestleys ever since she could
recollect. There had been some basis for the rumor which,
however, had never reached her ears, that, if her father had
lived a few months longer, Mrs. Priestley would have been
her step-mother. The prevailing belief was that Mr. Honeywood was a widower, and he had taken no pains to correct
the impression. Latterly Alana had at times suspected
that Mrs. Priestley was acquainted with the circumstances
of her father's early life, as he had told them to her, but
she was never quite sure on this point. Certain it is, however, that Mr. Honeywood greatly admired Mrs. Priestley,
and that the lady was equally fond of him. Alana, however, saw nothing in the intimacy beyond friendship, but
there were many Harrisburgers that predicted a marriage
between the two as soon as the lady had mourned the con-
ventional period for the departed Mr. Priestley. Mr.
Honeywood's death, before the probationary time had
elapsed, gave a quietus to all this gossip.

"Is that you, Alana?" were the words that greeted
Miss Honeywood, as she was asking the servant whether or
not the ladies were at home. "I thought it might be that
hateful Mrs. Boggs, and I was looking over the stairs to see

if John had the sense to tell her we were not at home. She has been here for five successive mornings at this very hour, and has always been told that we were not at home. She'll find out if she keeps it up for a year that I'm just as determined as she is! How are you, my dear?" kissing Alana as she spoke. "It's good for sore eyes to see you, and how sweet you look!—Rubina! Collie! here's Alana Honeywood. Drop all that nasty embroidery and come down to my sitting-room. They're making cushions for the church fair. Well, why don't you tell me how you are? Have you lost your tongue? Now I know what you're going to say," as Alana smiled, "so you needn't say it. I know I'm a garrulous old woman. That antiquated old maid, Flora McFlimmer, who believes that there are babies in hell a span long, told me so to my face a week ago. But didn't she catch it? It's my private belief that she went home, committed suicide, and has been secretly buried. She hasn't been seen since, that's certain. Now I'm done. Not another word will I utter till you have told me all about yourself. You've come to stay with us a week at least?"

"No, I must go back this evening. I have an engagement that is imperative.—Ah, here are the girls! How are you, my dear?" to each, as she kissed them. "Don't let me stop your work for the church."

"Oh, we are glad to have it stopped for a while," said Miss Priestley.

"Yes, and I'm sorry I ever began it," exclaimed Colletta, the younger. "It's stupid work, and church fairs are stupid things."

"You ought to have been here last night," said Mrs. Priestley. "We had Mr. Gargoyle, from New York, and Mr. Manly, from Philadelphia, and George Galland, of course; he's always here, and Lieutenants Frisbie and Fairfax from Carlisle."

"Don't forget Stickney Grammout, mamma," interrupted Rubina.

"I should have mentioned him next, if you hadn't taken the words out of my mouth. We danced till twelve o'clock, and then we had a nice little supper. Miss Saunders was here. She dropped in accidentally, of course, though Abram told me, this morning, that she poked her head out of the window and stopped him as he was returning with the musicians I sent him for, and asked what was going on. Did you ever hear of such deceit? She asked me if I'd go to the Presbyterian church with her, next Sunday, to hear the Rev. John Sniggs preach, and I'm glad I gave her the answer I did."

"What did you reply?" inquired Alana, with a smile, knowing well that something sharp was coming.

"I told her I'd as soon go to a circus on Sunday as to a Presbyterian meeting-house!"

"And what did she say to that?"

"Say! what could she say? She merely went through the entirely superfluous work of turning up her nose higher than Providence has turned it for her, and walked off. Now, tell me the news. I'm dying to know how you are getting along."

Of course, the most important piece of intelligence that Alana had to communicate, was relative to the affair in which Mr. Alexander Todd had been engaged, and which had terminated so disastrously for that person. Of her engagement to John Benham she was not yet prepared to speak, but she had been nothing loath to mention him as her defender, and had not been stinted in her praise of his thoughtfulness and gallantry.

"Mr. Benham is one of my friends," remarked Mrs. Priestley, after she and her daughters had expressed their thankfulness at Alana's escape. "He used to be very fond of Rubina, and at one time I thought they would make a match of it."

"O mamma, how can you say such a thing! Mr. Benham never spoke ten words to me in his life. He was always too busy over his studies to care for society."

Alana smiled. She knew Mrs. Priestley's way of talking. Rubina was a nice, pretty girl, but she was not the one John Benham would have married.

"Well," rejoined the elder lady, "he came here more frequently than he went anywhere else."

"Yes, but that was because Uncle Tom was a scientific man, and took great interest in John Benham while he was yet a boy. He came here to see Uncle Tom, and to talk chemistry with him, not to see me."

"Well, well, my dear, have it your own way. He's not a marrying man, that I admit.—Of course, Alana, you feel very grateful to him for his courageous defense of you. But what became of the villain Todd?"

"Todd is in jail here." Then the idea occurred to her that it would be well to reveal her intentions relative to the visit she was going to make the man. "I'm going to see him this afternoon, and I would like you to go with me."

"Going to the jail, to visit the fellow!" cried Mrs. Priestley, in astonishment; "Alana Honeywood, what do you mean?"

"I am not sure that I know," answered Alana, a little wearily; "as I was coming in here, a woman overtook me and gave me this note," handing it, as she spoke, to Mrs. Priestley.

The lady took the note and read it.

"I would not go, unless I had a policeman in the room with me," she said. "It may all be a scheme to get you into his hands, and to cut off one of your fingers, the brute, after all! You surely wouldn't see this wretch alone?"

"Yes, I must see him alone. I am not afraid. It will be easy enough to take the precaution of having an officer

in the next room, who will come in should I call for assistance."

"My dear, you don't know these fellows. He might
stuff a handkerchief into your mouth as soon as you are
alone with him, so that you could not call, and then cut
off your fingers at his leisure. What does he care if he is
discovered, after he has committed the act? It's only a
year or two in the penitentiary. And if his wife dies, he'll
get a life-sentence anyhow."

"I shall have to go," answered Alana. "I have promised to be there at three o'clock to-day."

"I would not go for a million dollars!" exclaimed Colletta, with energy; "I believe it's a decoy letter."

"I'm sure it is," said Rubina. "It's just the kind of
a note Amelia Williams got, last winter, from a man who
said he had cheated her father out of a thousand dollars,
and asked her to meet him on the bridge half-way to the
island on the next day at three o'clock in the afternoon, so
that he could return it. She said nothing about the matter to any one, but went to the rendezvous, expecting to
come back with a thousand dollars. You know what a
lonesome, dismal place the bridge is. Well, she got there,
and there was the man, sure enough, waiting for her. Instantly she was seized by two other men that sprang out
from behind the timbers, gagged and thrown into a covered
wagon that drove off rapidly back to town. She was blindfolded so that she could not see where she was being taken
to. A week afterward she was carried back in the same
manner to the bridge at the same hour and left there.
Where she had been all the time she could never discover,
and the family naturally don't care to talk about it. She
has never been outside of the house since."

"Well, my dear, Mr. Todd is so peculiarly situated at
this time that he can't very well abduct me," said Alana.
"I shall take proper precautions, but I shall have to go

and see him. Mr. Wade came down with me this morning,
and he seemed to think that Todd would want to see me.
He asked me also not to go. I didn't promise him, fortunately, so that I shall not be breaking my word. I may say
to you that I have especial reasons for wishing to hear what
the man has to say."

"Very well, then," said Mrs. Priestley, with a little
irritation in her voice; "if you are bent on it, I'll go with
you, but a more foolish undertaking I never knew of in all
my life!"

"Don't be cross with me, dear," said Alana, putting
her arms around Mrs. Priestley's neck and kissing her. "I
am not easy in my mind just now. There are several
things that trouble me, and that prevent me being very
happy. If you are unkind, I shall break down altogether."

"Unkind!" exclaimed Mrs. Priestley, returning Alana's
embrace. "If I could be unkind to you, I ought to be
squeezed flat in a rolling-mill! Never mind me. You
know I love you dearly. Of course, I'll go to the jail with
you."

"You may trust her now," said Colletta. "Whenever
she makes that speech about the rolling-mill, she's in earnest. She has a great horror of being thin."

"Come, miss," exclaimed Mrs. Priestley, "you must
treat your mother with more respect!—About this Todd,"
she continued, turning to Alana, "is he at all presentable?
His note isn't so bad, except that he changes you from the
third to the second person."

"No, he is a ruffian of the worst type. He looks and
acts like a ruffian."

"What could have been his object in attacking you?"

"He wanted me to promise to make him foreman of
one of the mines."

"What can be the nature of the information he speaks
of in his note? Have you an idea of it?"

"Yes, I have, but I would rather not mention it now, for I may be wrong. I hope to be able ere very long to take you into my confidence."

Then they talked of various events that Mrs. Priestley and her daughters brought up for discussion, most of which were more or less mild forms of scandal; and then, after dinner, Mrs. Priestley ordered her carriage, and in it she and Alana drove to the Dauphin County Jail.

CHAPTER XII

THE Dauphin County Jail is a strong and handsome structure, built some forty or more years ago, according to the modern system of prison architecture. When Mrs. Priestley's carriage drove up to the door, and the two well-dressed ladies got out and entered the building, the passers-by wondered what could be the cause of the visit. Both Mrs. Priestley and Miss Honeywood were known by sight to most of the inhabitants of the city. It was not the fashion in Harrisburg for ladies to visit prisoners for religious or charitable purposes; there was no remarkably distinguished criminal in jail at the time who might be the subject of curiosity; so the wise men marveled, and told their wives that night, when they went home to tea, that Mrs. Priestley and Miss Honeywood had been seen going into the jail.

"Perhaps they were arrested, and were allowed to go there of their own accord, so as not to mortify them too much," said pretty Mrs. Layton, who led the Presbyterian opposition. "I always knew that Mrs. Priestley's arrogance would have a fall, and, as to Miss Honeywood, what can you expect of a woman, brought up a Protestant, and who encourages idolatry by building a Roman Catholic church at her own expense?"

"Has she done that?" inquired Mr. Layton, who, though a terrible antagonist at the bar, was a veritable sucking-dove in the presence of his wife. "I think—and I say it with great diffidence, my dear, in view of your superior knowledge of such matters—that there must be some mistake about that."

"There is no mistake, Mr. Layton, for I had it from Miss Pink, who has just this moment left the house. Miss Honeywood announced it to the workmen, who came to congratulate her on her escape from a man who tried to force her to make him foreman of one of her mines."

"Oh! yes, Todd—as precious a scoundrel as there is outside of Moyamensing. I hope to have the satisfaction of sending him there."

"Why, what have you to do with him?"

"He's in jail, my love, and will be tried at the next term of the court; and, as I am the district attorney, I shall have the pleasure of conducting the prosecution. I have just had a long conversation with Mr. Wade about the fellow."

"And why, pray, couldn't you tell me all that, Mr. Layton, instead of allowing me to go on and make all kinds of surmises? Of course, Miss Honeywood has gone to see Todd, and Mrs. Priestley is chaperoning her."

"Yes, I suppose so."

"Really, Mr. Layton, you are an exceedingly aggravating man. You come home with a mystery which is no mystery at all. Why couldn't you have told me the whole story in the first place?"

"Professional secret, my dear."

"Then why did you tell it at all?"

"You forced it out of me, my dear. That is, you attributed an erroneous cause to Miss Honeywood's visit, and—"

"And you felt called upon to defend her," interrupted Mrs. Layton. "I don't see why you should set yourself up as the defender of Miss Honeywood. A rival to Mr. Benham! I don't see what there is in Miss Honeywood that *all* the men should be rushing forward in her defense."

"My dear, you are worth—"

"Yes, I know what I'm worth. If it hadn't been for what I was worth, I'd have been Mary Maxwell yet, as far as you are concerned."

"I was going to say that you are worth all the Miss Honeywoods in the world for me."

"And, as there's only one, I appreciate the force of the compliment. No, no, Henry, I am forced to the conclusion that you married me for my money." Mrs. Layton shook her head sadly as the full force of her conviction struck her, and her eyes filled with tears. But, as she had, ever since a week after her marriage, daily expressed a like opinion, the announcement had lost a good deal of its original influence, so that now Mr. Layton merely stroked his mustache and looked sad. Leaving him and his wife to settle their little matrimonial difficulty after their own fashion, let us return to Mrs. Priestley and Alana Honeywood, whom we left just as they had entered the jail.

Like the greater number of jailers, Mr. Justus Schwanger was a kind-hearted man. Probably in no class of men has there been a greater revolution through the progress of civilization than in that of the keepers of prisons. According to tradition, they were formerly a cruel set of men, always doing everything in their power to make the lot of those under their charge as hard as possible. Now, however, the captive finds in his keeper his kindest and most sympathizing friend—one who, from the instant of his incarceration, throws off all the stiffness of official etiquette, and treats the unhappy creature with a familiarity that looks as though it were born of years of friendly social intercourse.

Mr. Schwanger, whose grandfather was a Hessian soldier captured by Washington at Trenton, and who declined to be exchanged, received the ladies with his customary politeness, and ushered them into a large, plainly furnished

8

room, the windows of which were mere slits in the stone wall, and which were further protected by stout perpendicular and horizontal iron bars, the interstices between which would not have admitted the passage of a pigeon.

"Is there any one you'd like to see?" he inquired, addressing Mrs. Priestley.

"It is I who wish to see Alexander Todd," said Alana.

"He's not been tried yet, and so he is allowed to receive visitors. What name, please?"

"Miss Honeywood. He wrote to me requesting an interview."

"Oh, yes! excuse me, I didn't know that you were Miss Honeywood," and he looked at her as though to make himself acquainted with the features of the woman that Todd had attacked. "I'll bring him here in a moment; but," he added, "he's a bad fellow, I'm afraid."

"Yes, I know that, and I don't feel altogether safe with him, especially as it is necessary that I shall see him alone."

Mr. Schwanger thought for a moment, and then, looking kindly at Alana, said:

"By opening that grating in the door I can see into the room from the gallery there, a distance of at least twenty feet, and too far for me to hear your conversation. Now, if you will sit here"—placing a chair as he spoke—"and not move, I will watch you as carefully as if you were my own daughter, and, at the least offensive demonstration from Todd, I'll be down on him with my revolver. He has nothing in the way of a weapon about him, and I'll make him sit there in that chair, and if he moves it will be bad for him."

"You are very kind. I shall now feel perfectly safe."

"And I," said Mrs. Priestley, "will sit with Mr. Schwanger, so that you will have two pairs of sharp eyes watching you."

The jailer left the room, and in a few minutes returned with his prisoner. Then he again retired, accompanied by Mrs. Priestley, and Alana was left alone with the man who had expressed his intention of cutting off one of her fingers.

Confinement in jail had certainly improved his personal appearance, whatever may have been the effect upon his morals. He was clean—externally, at least—his hair was brushed, his face shaved, and his clothes were in order. Alana looked at him closely. Yes, he surely was the man that had visited her father many years ago, and who had met with such a rough reception.

"I'm to sit in this chair, and not to move from it," he said, with a surly tone, "unless I want to run the risk of getting a pistol-bullet in me. As I never take chances of that sort, I'll stick to this seat. I've too much to live for, I guess," he added, ironically, "and I want to stay here and enjoy it."

He took the seat that had been placed for him by the jailer.

"I'm sorry I frightened you the other day," he resumed. "I had taken too much whisky, and when I do I get playful. Of course, I wouldn't have done you any harm, and it was confounded mean in Mr. Benham to handle me as he did. I'll try to be even with him for it some day!"

"We will not discuss that matter," said Alana, quietly. "I shall always feel that Mr. Benham rendered me a great service."

"Of course, that's the way you look at it; but I think you ought to give me credit for having some natural affection. A man isn't likely to want to hurt his own niece."

"Your niece! No, I will not believe it!"

"Well, whether you believe it or not, it's true. You're the daughter of my favorite sister, Sarah Mullin."

"Then how," inquired Alana, displaying no emotion, though she felt a little pang through her heart at the announcement—"how does it come that your name is Todd?"

"My name is Todd simply because I choose at present to call myself so; but I am your uncle, Alexander Mullin."

"You will have to prove your claim before I will admit it. It's an easy thing for you to say that you are my uncle. When you prove the fact I'll acknowledge you."

"Thanks! It's just as easy to prove it as to say it. Do you recollect ever to have seen me before you came to my house the other day?"

"Yes, I saw you in my father's library."

"Did he tell you who I am?"

"He told me on his death-bed that you are my mother's brother, but there are circumstances that lead me to believe that this is not correct."

"And what may these be?" inquired Todd, looking sharply at Alana, while his face became a shade paler.

"They are chiefly two," she answered, not shrinking from his gaze. "First, he was very weak, his mind had been wandering at times for several days, and even that morning had been confused. It may have been, therefore, that he made a statement that was not true, and that had he been in health he would not have made. Second, inquiries instituted shortly after his death led to the discovery that Sarah Mullin's only brother was killed by a policeman in the city of Philadelphia, in November, 1864."

"I see you are tolerably well informed," he rejoined, apparently more at his ease after hearing what she had to say, "but your investigations have not led you to the whole truth. Listen to me, and I think I shall be able to convince you that I am your mother's brother, and consequently your uncle.

"Your father," he went on, after a moment's pause, as though to collect his thoughts and put them in order, "boarded with my mother in Sansom Street, Philadelphia, near the Academy of Natural Sciences. She had a daughter Sarah and two sons, William and Alexander. I am Alexander."

"Two sons?" inquired Alana, while her heart sank within her.

"Yes, two. William lived at home, and, as you say, was killed by a policeman. I did not live at home, but at that time resided in Baltimore, where I was a master bricklayer. I had received a pretty fair education, as you can tell from the way I talk, and had made some money. I got into a bad habit of drinking too much whisky, however, and I came down several pegs. It was while I was in Baltimore that your father behaved badly to my sister, and—"

"Stop!" cried Alana, raising her hand as though to emphasize her words. "My father never wronged man or woman. If there was any wrong done, it was your sister who did it, and not my father."

"Do you not call it a wrong to seduce a woman, and then to refuse to marry her?"

"Yes, but my father committed no such crimes. He may have sinned, but he did no wrong to your sister. It was she, if indeed the whole story is not a delusion of my father's and a falsehood of yours, who refused marriage when he offered it, who deserted her infant, and who entered upon a career of vice, from which all his efforts could not withdraw her. If she is alive, and if she is my mother, I am ready, willing—yes, anxious—to own her before all the world, and to do my utmost to comfort and protect her. God knows I have been unceasing in my efforts to find her; and God knows that, were she lying in the gutter, I would take her to my heart and try to reclaim her! Bring her to me, or tell me where she is, and I will make good my words this very day, if possible."

"I see you know the story, but it has been tinted to suit the particular light that illuminates your surround-

ings.   However, we will not talk about that part of the subject; my object in asking for this interview was somewhat
different.   It is about myself that I wish to confer with
you at present.   Your mother may come later, but now my
personality is of more importance."

"Not to me !"

"Well, if not to you, certainly to me.   There is no
doubt about my being your uncle.   Your father's statement to that effect is true.   I have told you the story of
his affair, or whatever you choose to call it, with my sister
and your mother, exactly as you have heard it from him,
except that the coloring is different, as would naturally be
the case.   The Mullin side is white to the Mullins and
black to the Honeywoods, and *vice versa*, but there are
certain facts in regard to which both parties agree.   Besides that, you have only to look at me to be convinced
that we are relations."

"If your sister is my mother, why was not the advertisement answered that was kept in the newspapers for
many months ?   And why were all the inquiries that I instituted without success ? "

"There are reasons for both those facts that may be revealed to you in due time," said Todd, a little hesitatingly.
"At present, however, I desire to confine our conversation
to myself.   Now please, my dear niece, give me your attention."

Alana shrank at the word "niece" as though some
poisonous reptile had stung her.   He saw the movement,
and the expression of disgust that came to her face.

"You don't like the idea, I see, but it's one that you
will have to become reconciled to.   But to business.   Sentiment is all very well in its place, but it has nothing to
do with our affairs just now, except to the extent that
policy warrants.   I don't like being in jail, I don't want to
be tried.   One of my friends is also here, I understand, and

Benham is the man who put him here. He wants to get out too, I've no doubt. You can get us both discharged. You have only to say the word to Mr. Wade, and he'll speak to the district attorney, and that will be the end of it. Now, for this good work for us we'll engage never to trouble you either with ourselves or your mother, provided you will give her enough to live on for the remaining years she may have to stay in this sorrowful world—say fifty thousand dollars."

"If my mother wishes to share all I have in the world, she has only to come to me or reveal herself so that I can go to her. With you I will make no terms."

"You had better think well before you decide adversely. If I am tried, there will be a great deal concerning your father and mother and you brought to the full light of day for the world to consider, that you would not wish to have revealed. There will be no mercy shown. Your origin, your mother's career in sin, as you were pleased to call it just now, will be exposed. The secret that your father guarded so carefully all his life will be divulged, and, as we shall present it, it will make a bad showing for him whose greatest pride it was to pass for a man of honor. If you value his reputation you will think twice before you refuse my requests, and, thinking twice, will grant them."

Alana was for the moment staggered with what the man said. He had played his cards, and it was just as Mr. Wade thought. He wanted money. But he offered what some persons would have thought a fair equivalent for the sum asked, and she had to admit that his demand was not, under the circumstances, an extravagant one. She believed now that he was her uncle. The facts, so far as she knew them, all went to establish the relationship except the one of his supposed death, and it was more than probable that his statement that there were two sons was correct. But who was the other of whom he spoke as also being a prisoner, and made so by Benham? Had her lover again interfered for her protection? And why, if so, had nothing been said to her of the circumstance? She would like to be free from Todd. She was willing to pay him to keep out of her sight, but she would not interfere to effect his release, and, as to buying immunity from the presence of her mother, that was not to be thought of. She had her duty to do to the woman that had brought her into the world, and please God she meant to do it, if it ever came within her power, though all the world witnessed what some might think her degradation. No, she would not purchase immunity from her mother.

In the mean time Todd had been closely watching Alana's face, and seemed to divine intuitively what was passing through her mind. He began to feel that, in offering to free her from all fear of association with her mother, he had gone too far. He saw that the girl was resolved, no matter how degraded a criminal or how vile her mother might be, to claim her and to give her whole heart to the work of reformation that might be required. In an instant, therefore, he changed his tactics. He was a sharp man, as the reader has doubtless already perceived, and this was by no means the first contest of the kind he had had. For years he had lived on his wits, and they had, from his standpoint, done him good service, and he hoped to get still further benefit from them. Before Alana could answer his propositions he announced his improved plan.

"I see," he said, "that you are not pleased with the idea of being separated from your mother. I honor you for the sentiment, though I said just now that it has nothing to do with business. I was mistaken; it has a good deal to do with it. Very few young ladies in your position would care to be hampered with a mother like yours. You know something in general about her, but you can't know much of the particulars. If they were known, they could not help but be disagreeable to you. I don't suppose they'd bring you down to her level, but they'd shock your fine friends pretty badly, and I guess Mr. John Benham, who seems to have started up as your champion, would feel small when he found out that you have a mother that led —well, we won't say anything about that, just now. You shall have your mother if you want her. Get me out of here, and give me the fifty thousand dollars, and I'll promise to keep out of your way all the rest of my life."

"Very well," she said, her face as pale as a sheet, for she felt that she was speaking the death-sentence of her new-found love; "bring my mother to me, and I will give you the money. But what assurance have I that you will keep your word with me, and never let me see or hear of you again?"

"That's a proper question, and one that shows you to be a good business woman, even if you are a little sentimental. Unfortunately, the case is one that does not admit of my giving bonds for my continued disappearance. All I can do is to give you my word, and, as it happens, you won't be likely to put much confidence in that, for you'll think, and you're doing it now, that, after I get the fifty thousand, I'll come back, in a year or so, for fifty thousand more, and so on. Well, now, think a moment: suppose I did, what difference would it make to you? You are not the woman that can be blackmailed. You wouldn't pay a cent, and if I got troublesome you'd call in the police. Don't you see? I couldn't do you any harm; all the harm that can be done, you will have done by taking your mother home with you and owning her. Her whole story will come out at once. There isn't a policeman in Philadelphia that isn't looking for her, under one or the other of her names; for you see, out of respect for the family, she don't go by the name of Sarah Mullin, and it might be that you wouldn't keep her long, for they've got detectives all around,

and they'd be sure to spot her and carry her off. That," he
continued, warming with the subject, as he saw the shudder
that Alana gave, while she covered her face with her hands,
to hide the shame even from this wretch, that his revelations caused—"that's the reason I thought you'd rather
pay to have her kept out of your way. You'd find it a
deal sight more comfortable, and she isn't used to the sort
of life you'd give her, either."

It was a struggle with Alana. She believed that the
man was speaking the truth ; she was sure her mother was
even worse than she, in her most despondent moods, had
ever imagined her to be. On the one hand, she was offered
immunity from all association with the woman, and with it
the retention of her position in the social world, the continuance of her newly found relation with John Benham,
and, ere long, the certainty of becoming his wife. On the
other hand, were the shame of being known as the illegitimate daughter of an infamous woman ; the sense of humiliation she should feel, at being compelled to call by the holy
name of mother, one who had outraged all social laws, and
in whom even the maternal instinct had probably never existed ; and, above all, the impossibility of ever marrying
the man she loved. "I can never disgrace him," she
thought, as she sat there in the jail, pondering over what
Todd had said, "by becoming his wife, and the mother of
his children. No, no, it is impossible ! I love him too
dearly for that ! I shall gain a mother—my God, what a
mother !—and I shall lose the noblest, the best, the bravest
man I ever knew. But it is my duty. God give me
strength to perform it !"

Her decision was made once and for all.

"No," she said, "I wish to find my mother. I will
give you the money. I will try to get you released from
prison. I shall do these things as compensation to you for
bringing my mother to me. You can go, or stay, just as

you please. If you annoy me, I shall appeal to the law for protection, and perhaps," speaking very slowly and deliberately, "if you were to trouble me very much, and there were no other way of getting rid of you, I should become desperate and then I should have you killed. There is Mullin blood enough in me," she added, bitterly, "to make me unscrupulous in dealing with people like you."

"Yes, you would have Mr. Benham put a bullet into me, I have no doubt," said Todd, with a sardonic smile. "There's some of your mother's blood in you, as you say, and it shows itself every now and then. However, we won't quarrel. I'm a man of peace when I'm sober, and you need never fear that I'll ever show myself to you, or let you hear of me. So far as you are concerned, from the moment you pay me the money, I shall be dead. Now, I want to show you that I haven't deceived you. I have kept back my documents just to give you a chance to believe me on my word, and without written proofs. Now see here":

With these words, he took from the breast-pocket of his coat a package of letters, which he proceeded to open.

"There," he resumed, after he had spread them all out on his knees, "are all the letters from your father to your mother that were written during the last fifteen years of his life. Four every year; sixty letters. They accompanied the checks that he sent to her every quarter. If he did not destroy them, you will find among his papers the answers conveying the receipts. As you see," handing several of them to Alana, "they are in his own handwriting, and they are, most of them, addressed to Montreal, Canada; and the checks were all drawn upon the banking-house of Campbell, Scott & Glasgow, of that city, with whom he kept funds for that purpose. But the last remittance was in United States Treasury notes, seven hundred and fifty dollars, and went by express. Here is the letter transmitting the money."

Alana took the letters and ran her eye over them. It was true; just as he had said. This, then, was the reason why no information had been obtained in regard to the bank upon which Mr. Honeywood's checks in favor of Sarah Mullin were drawn. This man, then, was her uncle; her mother was within reach, her life was henceforth to be an isolated one, her young dream of love was over. She closed her eyes, for she felt her head swim, and heard a soft musical murmur in her ears, while an indescribable sensation of weakness swept through her. She knew that she was about to faint, but, by a powerful effort of the will, she sustained her sinking forces. Todd was again speaking:

"That's not all I have to tell you," he was saying; "the most important part is yet to come, and it's the part you'll like best, I guess. Your father—"

A slight noise, as if of some conversation outside, interrupted him, and assisted her to rouse herself from the state of semi-torpor into which she had fallen. She opened her eyes, for she heard the voice of some one calling, " Alexander Todd!" and looked around her. Mr. Schwanger, the jailer, had entered the room, and was coming toward the man whose name he had just spoken. She heard very distinctly every word he said, but for the life of her she could not have moved a limb.

"Alexander Todd," repeated the jailer, "I am sorry to be obliged to change your quarters and to restrict your liberty. I have just heard that your wife is dead, and I am ordered to hold you on the charge of murder."

Then Alana heard no more. A feeling as though she were in the midst of a vast, void space impressed itself upon her, and she fell senseless to the floor.

CHAPTER XIII.

WHEN Alana recovered consciousness she found herself lying on a sofa in the jailer's parlor, with Mrs. Priestley, Mrs. Schwanger, and Dr. Worth bending over her, and all three entreating her to take just one swallow of the draught that the physician was holding to her lips. She possessed the excellent virtue of being obedient to the medical authority set over her, so that, as soon as she had regained sufficient intelligence to comprehend what was desired of her, she complied without a question. Then she closed her eyes again, and dropped off into a quiet slumber from which she did not awake for half an hour. The doctor had taken his departure as soon as she had swallowed the mild mixture of brandy and water that he had given her, saying that her pulse was all right, and that, when she awoke, she would probably be as well as she ever had been in her life —physically, he meant, of course ; of her mental distress he knew nothing.

"Do you feel better, dear ?" inquired Mrs. Priestley, tenderly. "I could see that you were having an awful time with that man, who, if he gets his deserts, will hang for the murder of his wife !"

"Don't speak of it, please," said Alana, with a shudder. "It is horrible ! It was that that turned the scale against me. I should not have fainted but for the announcement that Mrs. Todd is dead. Poor woman !—and yet sometimes it is better to die than to live !" She spoke these last words in a voice inexpressibly sad, and then closed her eyes while tear after tear rolled down her cheeks.

"Take a little more of this brandy and water," said Mrs. Schwanger, a pretty, good-natured dame. "The doctor said that I should give you the rest of it as soon as you awoke."

"No; I really do not require it. If he were here to see how hot my skin is, and how rapid is my pulse, he would not wish me to take it."

"Yes, I see that you are quite feverish," said Mrs. Priestley, passing her hand over Alana's forehead. "Do you feel well enough to come with me, and to be put into a nice bed, and to stay there until you are quite well? The carriage is at the door."

"What time is it?"

"Half-past four."

"And the train that I am to take leaves at five!"

"You surely will not think of going home to-night!"

"Yes, I must go. As I told you when I came this morning, I have an engagement that can't be deferred."

"You will kill yourself!"

"No"—with a sad smile—"I am tougher than you think for. I am not easily killed. No"—under her breath —"not easily killed!"

Then she rose from the sofa, and, going into an adjoining room, bathed her face and hands in cold water, into which the good Mrs. Schwanger emptied a bottle of bay-rum. This refreshed her greatly, so that, at the end of a few minutes, she expressed herself as ready to go to the railway-station, and, after warmly thanking Mrs. Schwanger, and inwardly resolving to show her appreciation of that lady's kindness in some more substantial manner, she entered Mrs. Priestley's carriage, and was driven to the station. All the way, however, her friend continued to insist that it was the most foolhardy act that Alana had ever done in her life, and that it would not be a matter for surprise were she to hear to-morrow that it had terminated in a brain-fever.

"Then I shall send for you to come and nurse me," said Alana, throwing her arms around Mrs. Priestley's neck and kissing her. "You have been ever so kind to me to-day. I feel as though you were entitled to my confidence; but I can not give it yet. I must ask you to bear with me a little longer; you will soon know all."

"Whenever it suits you, my dear, it will suit me. You know, Alana, that you are one of the very few women I believe in. You are such a sincere woman, and sincerity is the rarest of the feminine virtues. I know that there is something troubling you, and, when you think I can help you to bear it better, tell me of it. Now, here we are, and there's your train, as I'm a living sinner, just coming in! A minute more and we should have missed it."

The ladies got out, Mrs. Priestley going with Alana to the cars, and seeing her safely in a section of a palace-car where she could lie down.

"Give my love to the girls," said Alana, "and don't think badly of me, whatever you may hear."

"Think badly of you? I'd as soon think badly of the Virgin Mary! Good-by, dear; telegraph me to-morrow how you are."

Arrived at home, Alana, as we have seen, had walked the few yards from the station to her house with her veil down, and was, as she entered the door, the unconscious recipient of John Benham's wafted kisses.

After inquiring into the circumstances attending Mrs. Todd's death, and discovering that the poor woman had died from a fracture of the skull, as the doctor had feared would be the case, Alana sat down in the library to think as calmly as she could of the course that she had to pursue. The matter that required immediate consideration and ac-

tion was her newly formed relation with John Benham.
She had invited him to take tea with her, and in an hour,
unless she countermanded the invitation, he would be in
her presence as her accepted lover—her future husband.

What was she to do ? She felt that she, the illegitimate
daughter of a woman, a great part of whose life she did not
doubt had been passed in prison, and who was even now
hidden from the sight of the officers of the law, and the
niece of a ruffian who had killed his wife, and who, in all
probability, would end his life on the gallows, could not
present herself before this honorable man who had told her
of his love and tell him she would be his wife. To do so
without informing him of the whole degrading truth, would
be a fraud upon him that she was absolutely incapable of
perpetrating, and for which she felt he would be fully justified in never forgiving her. To let him come, and to tell
him who and what she was, though she had now no doubt
that he would, notwithstanding her associations, take her
to his heart, would be exacting a sacrifice of him that she
conceived she ought not to ask, and that she loved him too
much to allow him to make.

And yet she knew that to give him up would be the
greatest trial of her life, and one to which she felt that she
could not, with all her strength of character, with all her
knowledge of what was her duty, subject herself. Was not
he, she asked, as she sat in the library wringing her hands
in her extremity, the judge of what was his happiness ? If
he were willing to take her as she was, why could they not
go together to some out-of-the-way place where they were
unknown, and live in each other's love ? She was wealthy,
he was a man full of resources. What if she should tell
him all and leave the decision with him ? Would she not
in her heart despise him if he should, with all the odium
that clung to her skirts, turn from her coldly and say :
"My wife must, at any rate, have a decent origin. I can

not wed the bastard of a strumpet, the niece of a murderer!"
That was what she was : the bastard of a strumpet, the niece
of a murderer. "My God!" she exclaimed, "why should
there be such vile things in the world, and such vile words
to call them by?"

She could not hold the same opinion five minutes. As
new phases of the situation presented themselves before her,
she changed her views, and thus, after half an hour's rambling and painful thought, she was no nearer the solution
of the question that so intimately concerned her than she
was when she began to think. One thing she did, however,
decide upon. She would not countermand the invitation.
He should come, she would see him once more, and, if the
separation were inevitable, it should be unaccompanied by
shifts and evasions and subterfuges. He should come, and
the rest should be left to chance or to the course of
events, as the evening might develop them. She looked
at the clock on the mantel-piece. It was ten minutes
after six. In less than half an hour she might expect
him. She went to her room, changed her dress, bathed
her face and hands in iced water, smoothed her hair, sending away her maid, for she wished to be alone, and at half-
past six descended to the drawing-room to await her lover's arrival.

She was very calm when she entered the room, and yet
she had not been seated longer than two or three minutes,
when a strange inclination to follow whither her emotions
might lead her, seemed to fill her whole being. She rose
from the chair, and, going to the large mirror that filled the
space over the mantel-piece, looked at herself critically in
the glass. She felt afraid of herself, she did not know what
to think, and yet, as she looked, she could not perceive that
any change had ensued in her countenance. She could not
but admit that she was comely, and she could not say that
she had ever looked better in her life. "He thinks I am

beautiful," she said, with a smile. "I care not what all the rest of the world thinks. I care for him, and for him alone. He loves me and I love him. What else is there worth considering? I will tell him all. He will remember his words of love, he will kiss me, he will clasp me in his arms, for he loves me, and he will think of nothing but that. I have power over him to bend him as I will. I will be his if he will take me, and he will take me, for he loves me. There is nothing to be said after that. If his father were a criminal, if his uncle were a murderer, if his birth were as infamous as mine, I should love him all the same; yes, more than if the blood of all the Howards ran in his veins. For he would be the same, and I should pity him for his misfortunes. To-night I shall be his affianced wife; to-night I shall be happy, whatever the morrow may bring forth. I shall never marry him; I can never disgrace him by becoming his wife, but this night he shall tell me of his love, and I shall say 'no' to nothing he may ask. It may be a crime," she continued, walking away from the mirror and clasping her hands together, "but to commit crime is natural to me. My mother is a criminal; she loves crime for its own sake; she voluntarily rejected a virtuous life; she has lived in prisons and worked at prison-labor. My uncle, while stealing, was killed by an officer of the law; another killed his wife, and is in jail for the murder. What is there in me to make me better than they? I am Alana Mullin, the bastard. Yes, that is what I am. What right have I to the virtuous love of a good man? What right have I to set myself up as a respectable member of society, and to associate with good people? How I hate that word 'good,'" she exclaimed, bitterly. "What has it to do with me? I belong to the criminal class. My place is among the dregs of society, not here among honorable people. Well, I shall put myself there, and I shall begin by deceiving the man who loves me and whom I love. That will be a fair start, and it will not take long to bring me down to the level of my mother!"

She turned as she spoke, and saw John Benham standing before her.

"Oh, my love, my love!" she cried, as the blood seemed to rush in torrents to her head till she reeled like a drunken woman, and fell into the arms that were held out toward her. "Save me! save me!" and then she wept and sobbed as though her heart would break.

"My darling!" he said, with infinite tenderness in his voice, "what is the matter? You are ill. Look up; it is I. You are not afraid of me?"

"No, no, not of you; I am afraid of myself!"

"What is it, dear?"

"I do not know," she sobbed. "It seemed to me as though I were on the verge of some great crime. I feel safe now, for you will protect me."

"Yes; but you are nervous. You have overtasked yourself to-day, and you are feeling the effects; come, sit down and tell me all about it. What have you been doing? If you are like me, you ought to feel very happy." He led her to the sofa, and placed himself by her side.

"Now," he said, smiling, "if there is anything on your mind, out with it."

"Yes, I ought to be happy, I know. You and your love are all the world to me now, and yet I think I am the most miserable of women!—no, no, I do not mean that. While you are with me, I am happy. See, do I not look so?"

She raised her eyes to his, while her face was irradiated with a smile that, if it did not mean happiness, could not have been interpreted by the most skillful physiognomist.

"Yes, I think you are happy," he said, after he had feasted his eyes with a long look at her beautiful face.

"I am going to forget everything to-night but you. You asked me this morning to tell you that I loved you.

No, no!"—as he looked down at her hand and took it in his—"you must look me straight in the face. I want your eyes as well as your ears, and your whole attention. Yes, that will do. Now for my confession :

"I have loved you," she said, speaking very slowly and deliberately, but evidently with a calmness that she did not feel, "since long before my poor father died. It has not been a sluggish passion, but has grown with every hour of my life, till now it fills my whole heart and soul. It has, till this day, been an unhappy love, for I thought, most of the time, that it met with no response from you, and—"

"Ah, but, my darling, you know better now," said Benham, interrupting her.

"Yes, I know better now. But is it not strange—almost wicked—that we two should have lived within a stone's throw of each other, should have met every day, should have loved with our whole hearts, and yet should have persistently tried to conceal it one from the other, and with success, too, through all these years? It was not through the instrumentality of others that this was done, for there was no one to interfere between us. You and I could have done what we liked. It was not from the want of opportunity, for we might have been as intimate as brother and sister, had we so pleased. It was not that there would have been anything wrong in our love, for we had both, so far as our own lives were concerned, lived them in soberness and truth."

"Why was it, then, my darling?" said Benham, smiling at her earnestness.

"I'm coming to that. It was because we doubted each other's love though sure of our own, and through that doubt we have lost years of happiness that we can never make up; they are gone, however sweet those to come may be."

"Yes," he answered, "they are gone; but the future will more than atone for them."

"But you must never doubt me again, for I love you, and I could tell you so every minute of my life, it seems to me, and each time the utterance of the words would be a happiness to me. Come," she continued, actuated by a sudden impulse after he had kissed her lips, and sworn eternal faith in her love, and constancy in his own, "tell me why you love me?"

"Why do I love you?—because you are Alana Honeywood, and the embodiment of all that I hold beautiful, and pure, and lovely."

"Ah, how sweetly you answer me! May I question you again, and, perhaps, again and again?"

"You may ask me any question you like."

"And you will answer truly, without regard to anything but the truth?"

"Yes, I will speak the truth"; and his tone and look showed her that he would.

"Then tell me. Suppose—and I shall put a strong case—suppose my father had been a bad man, a thief, a burglar, a murderer—anything you like that is infamous; that he had been repeatedly tried for his crimes and sent to prison, and that, instead of reforming when the opportunity was offered to him, he continued to pursue his evil ways from pure love of sin and crime—would you, if I were the daughter of such a man, would you love me, and speak to me as sweetly as you did just now?" She paused and waited for his answer, as though her life depended on what he should say.

Again Benham smiled at the gravity of her voice and manner, and was about to answer her to the effect that if all her relatives had been as bad as her supposititious father, and had all passed the greater portion of their lives in prisons, she would be the same; that he loved her for what she was, not for what her father, mother, and brothers and sisters might have been, and much more to the same effect, when the noise caused by some one at the door interrupted him, and he had hardly time to make such a change in the relative situations of himself and Alana as the presence of a third party rendered necessary, when the door opened and Mrs. Winebrenner entered the room.

"So you're home, Miss Honeywood"—she always in presence of others spoke to Alana as Miss Honeywood—she said. "I've been up to see about that poor woman, and have given directions for her burial such as I knew you would approve. She never recovered consciousness."

"To whom do you refer?" inquired Benham; "not to Mrs. Todd, surely!"

"Yes, to Mrs. Todd. Haven't you heard that she died at about two o'clock to-day?"

"No. I have been in my office all the afternoon. It will go hafd with her husband, but not hard enough, I am afraid."

"Can they hang him for the crime?" inquired Alana.

"No, I think not. It would be impossible to prove malice, or intent to kill. Evidently he only meant to push or pull her out of the way. Are there any children?"

"No," answered Mrs. Winebrenner, "there are no children, thank Heaven!"

"Yes, you may well say, thank Heaven! both for the sake of the children and of society," said Benham, warmly. "The sooner such stock as Todd's runs out, the better for the world."

"Do you believe that the tendency to commit crime is hereditary?" inquired Alana—"that the children of criminals are necessarily criminals?"

She spoke with a little tremor in her voice, which Benham noticed, but which he supposed was due to the interest she felt in Mrs. Todd, and the recollections evoked of her narrow escape from Todd's effort to maim her.

"I certainly believe in the hereditary transmission of a

tendency to crime," answered Benham. "To say that the children of criminals must necessarily be criminals would probably be too strong a statement, but undoubtedly the tendency exists, and, if overcome, it is only through persistent education in right directions, and absolute separation from all vicious influences."

"You believe, then, in a possible good child from criminal parents?"

"Oh, yes," he replied, smiling and wondering at her interest in the subject. "All things are possible outside the pale of mathematics; but I have recently been reading a work which goes far to show the great difficulty of changing hereditary tendencies of the kind in question, for it proves that the skull and the brains of criminals are different from those of other people."

"And if the brains are different, the characters must certainly be in accordance with them?" said Alana, interrogatively.

"Yes, it would seem so. Probably, however, or at least possibly, if the child be subjected to good influences at a very early age, the form of the brain would be changed, and the tendency to criminality overcome."

"Then we are not what we make ourselves, but what our parents and early associations make us? It's very interesting. But, come, there is Abram, to tell us that tea is ready."

She spoke with an indifference that she did not feel. Benham's remarks, evidently based as they were upon his real opinions, had disturbed her, and brought back all her old fears and morbid feelings. What he had been going to say, when Mrs. Winebrenner interrupted him, would have been spoken with special reference to her and his love, and his passion, not his intellect, would have dictated his opinions. Now they were given without the disturbing influence of his emotion, calmly, coldly, as he really believed them, and as he had formed them after study and reflection. It was the death-blow to all her hopes! The blood of a race of criminals ran in her veins; the tendency to crime existed in her, and only required the proper exciting cause to bring it into activity. And yet she loved him so dearly! He was so tender and sweet with her, that to lose him now, just as the vista of happiness was opening to her gaze, would be more than she could bear. Still, there was no alternative. The cup was at her lips, and she must drink the draught that carried with it the destruction of her new-born love. No, not that, though it were better if it could be so, and if, from this night on, there should be an entire oblivion of the passion that had sprung up in her heart, and the full fruition of which she was never to taste. That mercy was to be denied her, for she should love, and— what could be worse in this world?—love hopelessly, despairingly.

It was a tremendous struggle that was going on within her, and the evidence of which she was obliged, so far as she could, to conceal from Benham and Mrs. Winebrenner. And, as many emotional women are prone to do, she exerted herself more than she intended, and in consequence appeared to be in excessively high spirits, an incongruity that struck a little harshly on Mrs. Winebrenner, though Benham, while noticing it at first, considered it to be nothing more than the natural reaction from the state of mental depression in which he had found her.

But as the evening wore on, and Alana laughed and joked over subjects that well-ordered people would have regarded as more calculated to excite tears than mirth, and she gave utterance to opinions that he was quite sure were not her real ones, Benham began to think that there was an abnormal element in her exuberance. He watched her, therefore, more closely, and ere long became convinced that she was acting a part that was in reality painful to her.

The discovery disturbed him beyond measure. He was quite certain, taking into consideration her state when he had entered the room, and she had fallen into his arms, imploring him to save her, that she had had something occur to her while in Harrisburg that had greatly distressed her and had disturbed the usual regular working of her mind. He was sure that she was not well, and he longed for tea to be over, and for Mrs. Winebrenner to leave them to themselves, in order that he might implore Alana to give him her confidence.

At last tea *was* over. Mrs. Winebrenner, whose face had all along expressed the astonishment she felt at the evident familiarity that existed between Alana and Benham, pleaded that business, connected with Mrs. Todd's funeral, required her to visit the carpenter, who combined the work of an undertaker with that strictly appertaining to his trade when his services for the dead were required.

Alana and Benham were therefore again alone. He had a great deal to say to her, but was this the proper time to say it? First, he would obtain her confidence, and then he would determine how further to act. That was what he finally decided upon.

9

CHAPTER XIV.

Mr. ALEXANDER MULLIN, or Todd, as he now preferred to call himself, was more than surprised at the announcement made by Mr. Schwanger, the jailer. He was astonished. The possibility that any serious injury had resulted to his wife, from the swing into the corner that he had given her, had never entered into his mind ; and now to be told that she was dead as the result of the wounds he had inflicted, was, from every point of view, distressing to him. In the first place, he rather liked the woman. She had stuck to him faithfully for many years, and she had rendered him good service in several of the little scrapes into which his disregard for the law had led him. Moreover, she had been endowed with excellent common sense, and had, by her prudential counsels, kept him out of several difficulties into which his associates would otherwise have drawn him, or into which his own enterprising but rash spirit would have prompted him to enter.

To be sure, she had opposed the scheme in which he was now engaged, and had altogether disapproved of his coming to the Susquehanna Iron-Works. It might be, he thought, that, before dying, she had spoken of matters that it was for his interest should not now be known, but this he conceived, after having considered the subject in all its bearings, was not, after all, very likely. She had always been true to him, notwithstanding that he had at times treated her badly ; and besides, as he understood the matter, she had not emerged from the state of unconsciousness into which she had passed soon after the attack that he had made upon her. So that, even had she been so disposed, she would not have been able to talk about him.

But still more was he distressed on his own account. He knew enough of the law to be aware of the fact that he could not, when all the circumstances were known, be convicted of murder in the first degree. Doubtless the grand jury would indict him for that grade of murder, but an indictment and a conviction were, as he had had several times in his career good reason to know, very different things. He had not intended to injure his wife, much less to kill her. He had meant only to pull her from between Miss Honeywood and himself, and her head striking against a piece of furniture, the fracture of her skull, and her subsequent death, were results that he had not contemplated. He knew this very well, but how was he to prove it to the satisfaction of a jury? No one had, so far as he knew, witnessed the affair, at that stage, but Alana. Doubtless she would tell the truth, for she must know, as well as he did, all the circumstances of the event, and she, although a Mullin, was not likely to lie. Still, it was humiliating to him to have to depend upon her for the integrity of his neck. Some women that he knew, and relatives of hers, too, would not, in a like state of affairs, hesitate a moment in giving such false evidence as would effectually secure them from any further attacks of an enemy. He was sure, however, that she was not one of that kind.

But even if not murder in the first degree, it was bad enough. At the very best, he could not expect to escape confinement in the penitentiary for many years, and perhaps for life. He had been engaged in the act of perpetrating an assault upon Miss Honeywood, had robbed her, and had announced to her his intention of cutting off her fingers. He had had the knife in his hand, and he had been stopped, midway in the attempt, by John Benham.

His wife had lost her life while endeavoring to prevent him
committing a felony, and she had lost it at his hands.
Yes, it was bad enough.

All his schemes were now at an end. He was no longer
in a position to exact terms from his niece. She was effectually protected from him, and as to her mother—here he
rose from the only chair in his contracted cell, and walked
as far as he could several times over the stone floor—as to
the mother, well, he supposed he should be obliged to let
that part of the affair settle itself. It had passed beyond
his control.

Then, again, there was another complication. His confederate was also in prison, put there, too, by John Benham,
and, as he had reason to believe, from the account given
him by the woman, after his captor had obtained information of importance in regard to the schemes in which they
had been engaged. Benham's house had not been set on fire,
Alana had not been abducted. Everything so far had failed.

It was very clear to him, however, that at the time of
her visit Alana had known nothing of the proposed arson
and abduction. If she had, she would have made her
knowledge manifest in some way. Benham had not told
her. Doubtless he, too, had his schemes, and he did not
think it advisable to frighten her by taking her into his
confidence. Clearly his enemies, at that particular period,
had the advantage of him.

His quarters in the jail were much less comfortable than
those he had previously occupied. He was now regarded
as a dangerous character, with much greater inducements
to attempt an escape than when he was merely held on the
charge of assault and battery, with intent to maim. He
was, therefore, put into a cell, and was not allowed to leave
it, except upon stated occasions, and then only when accompanied by a keeper. Moreover, he had been told by
Mr. Schwanger that he would not be allowed to see all the

people that might desire to communicate with him, or to send messages over the city. He had expressed a wish to say a few words to the man that had been brought in on the previous day, and it had been arranged that he should do so, but now he was told that it could not be allowed. This disgusted him very much, and caused him to inveigh bitterly against the system that, as he said, treated an innocent man as though he were guilty. But Mr. Schwanger only shrugged his shoulders and replied that he had his orders, and that he intended to carry them out.

"But," rejoined Todd, "the man has property of mine under his control that I want to inquire about. It may be a great loss to me if I don't see him at once. There isn't any serious charge against him, I suppose, and he'll be out in a day or two on bail."

"I don't know about that," said the phlegmatic jailer. "There may be more against him than you think for. Still, I don't know that there'd be any objection to your seeing him in my presence. I'll bring him up now, if you like, and you can talk to him from your cell, while he stands outside on the gallery."

"As if I wanted to speak about my private affairs before you or anybody else! No, I thank you! Not if I know myself! However," he continued, "bring him up. I suppose I'll have to submit, but it's hard lines. Of course you know I didn't mean to kill my wife. I was too fond of her for that. You'll see that Miss Honeywood, who isn't prejudiced in my favor, will say that it was a pure accident. Bring up the man. I only want to say half a dozen words to him."

Mr. Schwanger, who had been conversing with Todd through the grating in the door of his cell, made no reply to the prisoner's somewhat rambling speech, but went at once to another part of the jail where the person calling himself Johnson was confined.

"How are you, Johnson?" he said, as soon as he came in sight of the man. "I suppose you haven't heard what's happened to poor Alec Todd?"

"Heard! How could I hear, I'd like to know?" growled the man. "This is the most high-handed out-rage that ever occurred in the State of Pennsylvania. I'll make some one smart for it when I get out! Conspiring to commit arson! That is the charge, and on the testimony of a man who, by his own admission, was listening to private conversation. No, I'm in for another reason, and I'm smart enough to understand the whole matter, too. I've nothing to conceal. My real name is Johnson, Thomas Henry Johnson. And you can make the most of it. As to Alec Todd, as you call him, I never heard of him in my life."

"Never heard of Alec Todd! Why, he says you've got property of his, and I've come now to take you up to him!"

"He's a fraud. I never heard of the man before."

"Then you don't want to talk with him?"

"No, why should I? What are your jail-birds to me? I'm a gentleman, and I never was in such a position as this in all my life. I went up to a big rock on Peter's Mountain with a lady, a friend of mine, in whom I'm free to admit I'm interested. I wanted to show her the view, for she has artistic tastes, just as I have; and then this man Benham pounced upon us, frightened her to death, I suppose, for I haven't seen her since, and dragged me over a rough road before a justice of the peace, and then made a charge of conspiracy against me!"

"The lady that you speak of has been here several times to see Alec. *She* seems to know him, anyhow, for she says she's his sister."

"Well, she may be his sister, for all I know. I'm not supposed to know all the relatives of the women I'm acquainted with, am I ? Because he's her brother, it doesn't go for granted that I know him, does it ? Now, Mr. Jailer, I think you're unreasonable. Ask the lady when she comes again if she ever saw me in company with Todd, and I guess you'll get an answer in accordance with what I tell you. I never knew that she was a Todd. She's Mrs. Sarah L'Estrange now, and a widow. It's possible she may at some future time be Mrs. Johnson."

"L'Estrange!" exclaimed Mr. Schwanger. "Why, she gave her name as Mobley this morning!"

"Oh, well!" said Johnson, laughing, "she goes by many names. It's a whim of hers. She's fond of mystery. The fact is," he continued, lowering his voice to almost a whisper, "her name's neither L'Estrange nor Mobley. You keep your ears open, and you'll hear something in a few days that will astonish you. You'll find out then what her real name is, and so will some other people, too."

"Well, it's nothing to me what her name is, so long as it isn't Sarah Lansing, better known to the New York and Philadelphia police as 'Confidence Sal.' There's a handsome reward offered for her. She's wanted in Philadelphia for a jewelry robbery, and if I could lay my hands on her it would be five hundred dollars in my pocket; and more, too, if I got some of the stolen property back."

If Mr. Schwanger had been a particularly observant man, he might have noticed a change in Johnson's countenance, as this information was being communicated. As it was, he saw nothing more than that, as it seemed to him, the man was not interested in "Confidence Sal," or in the reward offered for her apprehension. Receiving no response to his communication, he prepared to take his departure.

"So you don't want to see Alec ?" he said, rising from the chair he had occupied. "He'll be disappointed."

"No, I don't want to see him, and, what's more, I won't see him. He has mistaken me for somebody else."

"Well, I'll tell him what you say. Good-evening. Are you quite comfortable?"

"Comfortable!—that's a pretty question to ask a man situated as I am. Look at these hands with the skin scraped off the knuckles down to the bones! Mr. John Benham did that, and I'm going to pay him in full for it, if it takes me all my life!"

"That was because you wouldn't walk, wasn't it?"

"Yes, of course it was. Why should I walk when he had no business to arrest me?"

"Oh, no, of course not! But then, you see, as you wouldn't go like a good citizen, why, he just had to take you in his own way. It was pretty hard on you, I admit, pulling you along as if you were a sled; but John Benham, unless he's changed mightily since he lived here, isn't the one to consider the feelings of a man that he thought was engaged in perpetrating a crime."

"But I wasn't, I tell you!" exclaimed Johnson, angrily. "However, I don't want to talk about it. You're kind enough, anyhow. I suppose I can have anything to eat or drink that I want?"

"Yes, if you pay for it. You're not convicted yet. Anything but liquor. No liquor allowed to any prisoner without the order of the doctor."

"That doesn't hurt me, for I'm not a drinking man. Now there's Todd—"

"I thought you didn't know Todd?" interrupted the jailer, quickly.

"Well, can't I speak of a man without knowing him, and without being snapped up like that? It seems to me that you're always on the watch to catch me in some slip or other. You might as well save yourself the trouble, for I'm one of those men that don't make slips."

"Not even when caught by John Benham?" said the jailer, interrogatively, and with a playful smile.

"No, not even then. No man's safe if he can't go up a mountain when he pleases, and talk with the woman he's in love with, without being followed and seized as if he were a jail-bird. Now, let's drop all that. Here's five dollars; get me good meals every day till that runs out, and, if I'm here then, I'll give you more. If I get out to-morrow you can keep what remains, or give it to the poor. And there's another thing," he continued, as Mr. Schwanger took the five-dollar gold-piece that Johnson held out to him. "If Mrs. L'Estrange comes here this evening tell her I'd like to see her. Does she know I'm here?"

"Yes, she knows. You see all the Harrisburg police were looking for her last night when you were brought in, and they couldn't find her. Between you and me, they're not half so sharp as they think they are. She came here this morning, and I was going to keep her, but the district attorney, who had had an interview with Mr. Wade, our great lawyer, told me to let her alone, and it seems the police have been instructed not to arrest her. I guess they're waiting to see what she'll do about Todd."

Again Johnson's face expressed interest in the communication of the garrulous jailer, who was unthinkingly betraying the secrets of his superiors. Was there anything more that he could get out of him? If there was, doubtless Mr. Schwanger would reveal it of his own accord. All he wanted was a listener.

"Well," said Johnson, "if Todd's her brother, of coarse she's interested. But what they wanted her for last night is a mystery to me. She's as innocent of the crime of conspiracy as I am, and that's just as much so as an un-born child."

"You couldn't make it stronger, Thomas," said the jailer, getting more friendly even than he had been, "not if you were to try for a million of years. It isn't much in the way of conspiracy that such an innocent can go into."

"No; and another thing: when my lawyer, Mr. Staggers, calls, please show him up at once, or come for me to go down to him."

"All right. Anything more?"

"Yes, there's one thing more. Perhaps, now that we've settled all our little affairs satisfactorily, you'll tell me what's happened to 'poor Todd,' as you call him."

"Oh, yes, of course! To think I should have forgotten that! Well, you know he was brought here, just a little while before you were, for robbing and assaulting Miss Honeywood, and threatening to cut off her finger; also for knocking his wife down. Poor fellow! I'm sorry for him. He's had bad luck, for this afternoon his wife died, and Alec is in now for murder."

"You don't tell me that! That's bad—very bad! Was she conscious when she died?" He asked the question with a greater degree of anxiety than would have been altogether justified by the non-acquaintance of the husband—and presumably with the wife—that he had professed; but the circumstance was not noticed by Mr. Schwanger.

"No; I know she never recovered consciousness from the moment she fell."

Johnson gave a sigh of relief.

"Well, I'm sorry for her, and I'm sorry for him, too. I don't suppose it will go so very hard with him. I guess it isn't more than manslaughter, or something of the kind. I suppose he was drunk at the time."

"Yes, I believe he was."

"If ever I have anything to do with a drunken man again, I hope the devil will carry me off to the lowest pit in the infernal regions!"

"Again! Why, you didn't have anything to do with Alec, did you?"

"Anything to do with Alec! Didn't I tell you I don't know him?"

"I thought you said 'again.'"

"Your hearing's bad—too bad for a jailer. You'd better look out. Next year the Democrats will carry the county, and your deafness will be a good excuse for giving your place to another fellow."

"I'm not afraid. What would you like for supper?"

"Oh, anything. A half a dozen nice little cat-fish would do as well as anything : little ones, mind you ! Not much bigger than your finger, and from the river, not the canal."

"Why not from the canal?"

"Why, don't you know that Bill Fleming was drowned in the canal last week, and that they haven't yet found his body? Of course, all the cat-fish between this and the Five-mile Lock are feeding on it, and I don't care to take Bill at second hand."

Mr. Schwanger laughed, and then finally succeeded in tearing himself away from his facetious prisoner.

When he arrived at Todd's cell, he found him anxiously awaiting his coming, and when he reported that Mr. Johnson not only declined to make the desired visit, but had stoutly asseverated that he did not have the honor of Mr. Todd's acquaintance, the anger of that gentleman began to rise. But this was only for a moment. He seemed to recollect himself, and muttered that there must be a mistake somewhere.

"What did you say his name is?" he inquired, with a sudden brightening of his manner and voice.

"Thomas Henry Johnson is what he calls himself now."

"A stout, thick-set man, over six feet high, with coal-black hair and beard?"

"No," answered the jailer, laughing. "He's a short, thin man, with red hair and beard."

"Oh, well, he's not the man I thought he was. He's

right, I guess. I don't know him, and, what's more, I don't want to know him. My friend's name is Regis."

"That's the ticket, is it?" he remarked to himself, as the jailer walked away. "We're not to know each other. Well, he's smarter than I am, and it's safe to follow where he leads. Now, if Sarah would only come and give me the news, I'd be ready to turn in on that tombstone there that they call a bed." He waited a half an hour, during which he ate the frugal repast—for, having no money, he was reduced to the jail-fare—supplied by the people of Dauphin County, and then, as he had slept very little the night before, he lay down on the not over-luxurious bed and was soon in a state of obliviousness of all passing events.

But, although Mrs. L'Estrange, or Miss Mobley, did not put in an appearance to Mr. Todd, she came to the jail like a faithful woman-adherent, and asked to see him. This request Mr. Schwanger declared he could not grant without authority from the district attorney. Circumstances had changed since the lady's last visit; persons accused of murder were not allowed to receive visitors from without, except by special permit, and in the presence of a keeper, save always the legal counsel.

"I didn't know she was dead," she replied. "It must have been a great shock to Alec. Did he go on much?"

"Well, I can't say that he went on unreasonably," replied Mr. Schwanger, with the caution of a "Pennsylvania Dutchman." "He was disturbed, of course."

"He never meant to do it. It was all an accident. I must see about bail for him at once, although I scarcely know a person in the place."

"I guess it isn't bailable. You see, they draw the line at murder. They'll bail them for almost everything else, but there's a prejudice against the shedder of blood, and I guess Alec will have to stay here till he's tried."

"He's got no lawyer, either. He sent for Mr. Wade

last night, but he refused to assist him. I'll go up to-morrow and see what I can do with him."

"If you can get Mr. Wade, you'll have the strongest lawyer about here. Why, a jury generally takes things just as he tells them! But, Miss Mobley," he continued, "although I can't let you see Alec, there's another gentleman here that's dying to see you, and there isn't any restriction on him, except such as I choose to impose, and on this occasion you're free to go to him."

"Don't call me Mobley, please. Alec always gives me that name, because he didn't like my changing it for L'Estrange."

"A widow, I suppose?" said Mr. Schwanger, interrogatively.

"Yes, a widow. But you said there is a man that wants to see me. Is it Mr. Johnson?"

"Right you are, Mrs. L'Estrange. Follow me, please. I'll take you to his room. It's twice as big as a cell, and therefore we call it a room. Half an hour, Mrs. L'Estrange. That's all I'll be able to allow you this evening. But if you set yourselves to it you two can get through an awful amount of talk in half an hour."

"O Thomas!" exclaimed the woman, as soon as she was in the presence of her friend. "This is a bad thing for poor Alec."

"Yes, he's your brother, I hear. Family ties were always strong with you, Sarah. Now, don't go to crying!" as she put her handkerchief to her eyes, and sobbed a little. "I guess if Miss Honeywood can be got to come out pretty strong, it won't go so very badly with him. What sort of a man is your brother?" looking at her with a peculiar expression which she seemed by her look to understand. "You know I never saw him."

"Yes, I know," she answered; "I never talked to you about him. He's not very strong-minded, and then he drinks too much. That's the cause of this trouble. He wouldn't have been in this scrape if he hadn't been drunk."

"Ah!" joined in Mr. Schwanger, "liquor is the cause of more scrapes than all the other things put together. I'll come for you in half an hour, Mrs. L'Estrange, and," he continued, turning to Johnson, "if Mr. Staggers should come while Mrs. L'Estrange is here, shall I show him up?"

"Yes, I've no secrets from Sarah, or from any one else, for that matter."

"All right!" and with this ejaculation Mr. Schwanger went on his way along the iron gallery, and the man and the woman had the room to themselves.

CHAPTER XV.

"Now," said Mr. Johnson, as soon as he found himself alone with Mrs. L'Estrange, "don't talk above a whisper, for prison-walls have ears, and don't do anything that you wouldn't care to have all the world see, for they have eyes."

"Things couldn't be worse than they are, it seems to me," said the lady, sitting down on the one chair in the apartment, while Johnson sat on the edge of the bed. "You in prison for conspiracy, Alec in prison for murder, and the whole plan, laid with such care, absolutely destroyed."

"Yes, and you watched, and liable to be arrested at any moment."

"I watched! How do you know that?"

"From the old fool that's just gone. He let out that there's a policeman here, from Philadelphia, looking for you; and a reward of five hundred dollars offered for your apprehension. If he knew who you were, you wouldn't get out of this jail till you went to Moyamensing for ten years."

"I am pretty well disguised, ain't I?" said the woman. "I don't think even you could recognize me as the woman you saw a week ago in Philadelphia."

"No, I don't think I could," he answered, looking at her critically. "You certainly can change your features more completely than any person I ever saw, man or woman. But you're known as the woman that was talking with me yesterday on the mountain."

"Am I ?"

"Yes ; and there's some scheme on foot to trap us, for special orders have been given that you are not to be arrested. They wouldn't do that unless they thought they would gain something by letting you alone. Of course you're followed and watched, every step you take."

"I'll tell you what it is, Thomas," said the woman, rising from her chair and approaching him. "I'm frightened ! If I should be caught now, I shall end my days in the penitentiary. I've got enough to live on, and I'm going away. Yes," she continued, as the man made a deprecatory gesture, "I am going away, and this very night, too ; I'm tired of the whole affair. I've lost heart in it since I saw her this afternoon, with her fair, honest face, so different from mine. I could scarcely believe, as I looked at her, that the same blood runs in our veins."

"You go away, and leave your friends in the lurch ! It's the first time you ever did such a thing. I wouldn't have thought it of you."

"I've more at stake than you have. They can't do anything with you, whereas, if I'm caught, it will be ten or fifteen years, and I shall not live that long."

"I don't think you ought to go. You have it in your power to get us all out, and to get the money too. What did Todd settle with the girl this afternoon ?"

"I don't know, for I'm not allowed to see him. She spent an hour or more with him, and fainted at the end of the interview. I can't stand anything of that kind. If I had known that she was as good and as beautiful as she is, I could never have gone into the scheme."

"Well, you've gone too far now to back out."

"No, I'll back out whenever I choose. I'm my own mistress yet, thank God !"

"You know," said Johnson, without losing his temper, "that I can stop you whenever I please."

"No, I don't know anything of the kind."

"I've only got to tell Mr. Schwanger, when he comes for you, that he can make five hundred dollars very easily by taking you into custody, for that you are 'Confidence Sal,' that committed the great sneak jewelry robbery in Philadelphia."

"Oh!" she exclaimed, with intense passion, though still speaking in a voice not much louder than a whisper. "You can! True, so you can; and I, in my turn, can turn round and say, 'Here is Mr. Tony Rackett, otherwise known as "Tony the Lifter," who committed the great Chalmers Bank robbery two years ago, and by arresting whom you can put another five hundred dollars into your pocket.' What would you say then, Tony, my dear?"

"I'd say," answered the man, with a low laugh, "that I had lost all confidence in women. But come, my dear, it won't do for you and me to quarrel. We've too much at stake. Sit down, and I'll soon convince you that you've nothing to fear from the police, and that by going on with the campaign you can achieve a victory all by yourself, and get Alec and me out of this hole."

"I'll listen to you," she said, resuming her seat, "but I shall not change my mind."

"Well, all I ask is, that you hear what I've got to say. If, then, you decide that you will look after your own safety, and leave your friends in the lurch, why, I'll say nothing more. You know as well as I do that, when I said I'd denounce you, I was joking."

"I'm not so sure of that. However, I'll take your word for it. Go on!"

"What I have to say can be said in a very few words. It is this. Go at once, this night if you can, to Miss Honeywood, and declare yourself. Take your proofs with you. They are strong enough to convince Mr. Honeywood himself, if he were alive. They will establish your identity

beyond all question. You will be immediately acknowledged ; you will then have all the Honeywood interest on
our side, Mr. Wade, the district attorney, and all, to say
nothing of the sinews of war, money. You will accomplish
all that we have been driving at, and without the necessity
of resorting to arson, or abduction, or force of any kind.
After all, the straightforward way is the best, especially
when you can pursue it without risk."

The woman thought for some minutes without saying a
word. Evidently the idea struck her favorably.

"It looks well," she said at last, "and I don't think I
would hesitate, were it not that I am afraid for that affair
in Philadelphia. The police, as you say, are looking for
me, and I might be taken at any moment."

"You are safer in Miss Honeywood's house than any-
where else on the face of this earth. You're not such a
fool as not to see that, are you ? "

"I suppose I should be comparatively secure there,"
she said, musingly. "But there's another thing. Alec has
all the letters, and I'm not allowed to see him."

"That's bad, but even that may be overcome. Old
Schwanger will be along directly to escort you down. Tell
him that Alec has some letters belonging to you, and ask
him to get them. He'll go up and see the letters, and he'll
find that they're addressed to Miss Sarah Mullin, one of
your names, you can say, and are of old dates, and he'll
bring them to you."

"Yes, I suppose he would. But didn't you say that
the Harrisburg police were watching me ? "

"Yes, but they're set on by the Honeywood interest,
and, as soon as they find you safe in the Honeywood man-
sion at the Susquehanna Iron-Works, they'll abandon the
scent."

"I shouldn't be surprised if Alec made some sort of an
arrangement with her this afternoon. She was a long while

with him in the jailer's room, and they must have talked over the whole affair. She wouldn't have fainted unless he had told her the story."

"Well, you'll find out as soon as you see her again. She's been trying to get track of her mother these two years past."

"Yes, I know, and if it hadn't been for that bad luck in Montreal, I'd have been installed at the Susquehanna Iron-Works two years ago."

"You didn't even know he was dead till you got out, did you?"

"No, and then I only discovered the fact by accident. I might have written while I was in the reformatory prison at Penetanguishene, but I was afraid that, if he knew I was in the penitentiary, he would stop the allowance."

"And all that time you were being sought for all over the United States, and a standing advertisement kept in the newspapers."

"Yes, but I was advertised for as Miss Sarah Mullin, whereas, except for getting my letters and checks, I was known as Sarah Mobley. There was a misunderstanding all around."

"And Miss Honeywood could not have known anything of the real state of affairs."

"There you are mistaken. She has known a good deal ever since her father died, but not all. He probably told her something, and his pride prevented him telling the rest. Some of it he himself didn't know."

"It's a strange and very complicated piece of business, but I think you're the woman to straighten it all out. Just think, too, what a splendid position you'll be in!"

"Yes, it will be very good. I'll take good care of you and Alec."

"You'll be sure to succeed. Your resemblance to her would of itself be sufficient to establish the relationship, and when that is backed up by the documents you'll be irresistible."

"Am I, then, so very much like her?"

"So Todd says. I've never had the pleasure of seeing her, for, owing to the ruffian Benham, I was nabbed the very day I got there, and you frightened to death. By the by, how did you get off? This urgency of our affair has made me forget your special trouble for the moment."

"No one interfered with me. In fact, I met no one till I had gone several miles on the way. I took a road that led into the Jonestown road, and entered Harrisburg by that way after the search was over. I left the buggy at the livery-stable and walked to Mrs. Klinger's, in Raspberry Alley, where I am still staying."

"You won't forget your old friends when you come into part ownership of the Susquehanna Iron-Works, will you, Sarah? And you won't feel that you can do better than to marry me?"

"No, I'll not forget my promise; I'll marry you inside of three months, as I said I would."

"And then we'll settle down into a quiet life and live according to law and gospel?"

"Yes, I'm tired of the way I have lived for the last twenty-five years or more. You know I'm not far from sixty years of age—fifty-seven last birthday."

"You don't look a day over forty."

"You'll think differently after we're married," she said, with a smile. "Every year will show then. I'm almost old enough to be your mother."

"A woman's as old as she looks, and no older. I am forty-one, and you look forty. What's the objection to that, I'd like to know?"

"Oh, I've no objection, if you're satisfied."

"Then you've decided to stay and carry the thing through?"

"Yes," hesitatingly, "I suppose so."

"Then go at once. It's now," taking out his watch, "a quarter past eight. There's a train at 9.10; you can be there by half-past nine. The rest may safely be left to you. The woman that got ahead of the father so successfully may well be trusted to manage the daughter."

"Yes, there would be no trouble on that score. It would be easy enough to do it. Everything is in my favor; but, Tom "—it was the first time in her life that she had called him "Tom "—" I hate to do it. Should she ever find out what I am, it would be the death of her, and though she has taken every means to find her mother, she has acted from a sense of duty. She can not have any love for such a mother as hers, and when I go to her and say 'I am your mother,' knowing as I do—"

"Now, Sarah," interrupted Johnson, "you are getting sentimental again. Now, in my experience, business and sentiment are absolutely incompatible. If you can't go about the affair in a rather cold-blooded sort of a way, you'd better give it up."

"I can't help liking the girl, Tom; she's my—"

"Well, what if she is? Can't you disregard the ties of blood when you've got so much depending on it as rests on this matter? After it's all settled, and you're fixed in your position, it will be time enough for you to feel sentiment. Of course, you should show it as soon as you meet, but keep the upper hand of it, for, if it gets the upper hand of you, we're gone!"

"What difference does it make whether or not I control my feeling for her?"

"It makes this difference: If you let your sentiment run away with you, you'd just as likely as not cry and sob, and go down on your knees to her and confess the whole affair. Then, where would we all be? Now hush, for here comes old Schwanger!"

"Well, Mrs. L'Estrange, here I am, punctual to the minute," said the jailer, good-naturedly, as he entered the room. "I hope I don't cut short your conversation."

"No, we have got through," she answered. "But I think," putting on a pleasant smile—and, as she was still a handsome woman and had brought all the resources of art to make herself look younger than she really was, she could smile pleasantly when she chose—"I think you have treated me very cruelly."

"How so?" inquired Mr. Schwanger, reciprocating the smile. "I never treat ladies cruelly if I can help it. Sometimes I have to do things that go against the grain; but then, you know, Mrs. L'Estrange, duty comes before pleasure."

"It certainly could have done no harm to allow me to say a word to my poor brother."

"No, I don't suppose it would, but you see I have my orders, and when a thing is put down for me in black and white by my official superiors, I've got to go by it. Lord! if I had my way, you might talk to Alec all night if you wanted to."

"I'd have to give up talking to him to-night, even if your heart were as soft as mine, for I'm in a hurry. But you can do something for me that will save me a great deal of trouble. Alec has a lot of letters belonging to me. They are old letters addressed to me as Miss Sarah Mullin. Get them for me. This you can surely do without breaking your rules."

"Old letters, and addressed to you? Well, I don't see any objection to that. You'd better get them, too, for to-morrow the district attorney will take possession of everything, and then you'd have to go to him for them. Wait here till I come back. I guess, however, you'd better write a line, and then he'll know that I ain't fooling him."

Mrs. L'Estrange took a card from her pocket-book and

hastily wrote a request to Todd to deliver the letters to Mr. Schwanger, adding the words, "I'm sorry for you."

The jailer looked at the writing long and closely. "This is a little more than we bargained for," he said. "However, I'll let it go; but of course he knows you're sorry for him."

"Now," said Johnson, as soon as the man was out of hearing, "go at once. Do your best. I know what you can do when your heart's in your work. You'll find her at home, alone. Mr. Wade's in the city, and Benham doesn't go out at night, so I hear. I can't tell you how to do it, for you know better than I do. How do you think you'll work it?"

"How do I know?" said the woman, moodily. "Don't ask me anything more about it, as I may give it up. It's the worst piece of work I ever undertook. My heart's not in it, Tom, and it's no use for me to deceive you or to try to deceive myself. If I hadn't seen her to-day with the troubled look on her face, and the tears glistening in her sweet eyes, I could go to the business with more spirit; but, as it is, I'm afraid I'll break down and spoil the whole thing, and then you'll be sorry that you made me go."

"It won't go wrong if you'll keep your sentiment down, and, when it comes to the pinch, I'm not afraid that you won't do it. You're not a fool, and when you find that there's danger if you give way to all that nonsense that you've got in you, you'll manage to master it as sure as—"

"Hush! here comes Schwanger.—Well"—to the jailer, as he approached—"and you got the letters? Yes, I see you did. That's very kind of you, and I'll forgive you for not letting me see my brother. You didn't bring me any message, did you?"

"Only," said the jailer, handing her the package of letters, the same that Todd had exhibited to Alana—"only that he wants you to get him a first-class lawyer at once."

"Yes, I'll attend to it. Good-night, Mr. Schwanger. Many thanks.—Good-night, Mr. Johnson. I'll try and see you to-morrow."

She had still a quarter of an hour to spare before the train that was to take her to the Susquehanna Iron-Works was due. She would have liked to go to her lodgings and make some little alteration in her dress, but there was not time for that; and, moreover, upon reflection, she concluded that any great degree of neatness or of elegance about her attire would not be in consonance with the part she had to play. As she stepped out of the jail she looked around for a cab, but not finding one in sight—and if she had been fully acquainted with Harrisburg she would have saved herself the trouble of looking—she descended to the sidewalk, and, turning to the right, went toward Third Street. Down Third Street she walked—not rapidly, for there was plenty of time—to Market, and then, turning to her left, soon reached the railway-station. A solitary policeman was walking up and down in front of the entrance, but he took no notice of her, and she went in and bought her ticket. In less than five minutes the train came rolling into the station, and in five more minutes she was on her way to the Susquehanna Iron-Works.

She tried to arrange in her mind a plan of procedure as the train dashed on, but she found it a difficult undertaking. Indeed, in all the affairs in which she had heretofore been engaged she had found it better to leave the details of her operations to be spontaneously evolved out of the circumstances of the events, rather than to plan them beforehand from insufficient data. In the present instance she knew absolutely nothing of Alana's surroundings, of her habits, her mode of life, her character even. She had reason to believe that she was gentle, and anxious from a sense of duty to find her mother, and she had still greater reason for believing that the realization of her wish in this respect would be a great shock to her. Evidently the case was a difficult one, no matter from what standpoint she viewed it ; but then she was a woman of infinite resources and of strong dramatic instincts. She had softened many obdurate hearts in her day by a look, a gesture, or a tone, employed at exactly the right time, and in the right way. She had been repeatedly acquitted of offenses of which she was clearly guilty, by a mute appeal to the twelve men in the jury-box, that, in spite of the evidence against her, carried with it something that induced them to give a verdict in her favor, or else to do what was almost as good for her—disagree.

Again, she had, when ordered to stand up and to say what she pleased in her own behalf, previously to receiving the sentence that was to consign her to the State's prison, risen to her feet, and, with streaming eyes, bowed head, and clasped hands, stood the very personification of repentance, and had so acted upon the heart of the judge that he had lessened by one half the term of confinement that he had intended to give her. It would be strange, she thought, as these and many similar instances of her power came to her mind, if she could not move the heart of Alana Honeywood to regard her with favor.

It was half-past nine when she arrived at the Susquehanna Iron-Works. There were no persons on the platform but the station-master and a couple of other railway officials, and they were too busy attending to their own affairs to trouble themselves with hers. The night was dark, and there were no street-lamps ; but she knew where the main street was, and she had a correct idea of the situation of the house that she intended to make the scene of her demonstrations. All the little shops were closed, but the lights were still burning in the tavern. She paused as she came opposite to this, the only public lodging-place for strangers in the village, and at first thought

10

that she would go in and secure a room for the night ere
the doors were closed ; but reflection told her that such an
act could only be justified by an anticipation of failure,
and she did not mean to fail. Finally, she reached the
grounds in which Alana's house stood. The gate was
open. She entered, and, following the flagged path that
led to the front door, stood at last on the broad veranda
that entirely surrounded the building.

There was still a light in the hall, as there was also in
the room on the right of the entrance. The curtains,
however, were drawn close, so that, though she tried her
utmost, she could not obtain the slightest view of the interior. Then she put her ear close to the window and listened. At times she thought she detected the soft hum of
conversation, and once was sure she heard a woman's sob
or suppressed moan, but she could not distinguish a word
of what was being said. Then she went round to the back
of the house. The servants were still up, for there were
loud voices and laughing in the kitchen and other rooms
devoted to household purposes, but the doors and heavy,
solid shutters, so generally used in that part of Pennsylvania, were closed, and again she was prevented seeing
anything of the occupants. Retracing her steps, she arrived a second time at the front of the house. Even yet
she had formed no clear conception of what she was going
to do. Obviously, however, the first thing to do was to
get into the house. She felt for the knob of the door-bell
and was just about to pull it, when she heard a voice inside, as if of some one walking in the hall. She had
barely time to shrink back against the wall so as to be in
almost complete darkness when the door opened and a man
passed out, and, crossing the veranda, descended the steps
and was soon lost in the blackness of the night. She
waited until his footsteps on the flagging were no longer
to be heard, then she boldly turned again toward the door,

and seizing the bell-handle gave it a vigorous pull. She could hear the sound of the bell in the distance, and then the steps of some one approaching over the tiled floor of the hall. Then the door was opened and a flood of light from a hanging lamp fell full in her face.

"Is Miss Honeywood at home?" she inquired.

"Yes," answered the man, evidently taking her for the wife of one of the workmen; "but she can't see you to-night. You'll have to call in the morning."

"But I must see her to-night, for I have business of great importance with her."

"I don't believe she'll see you, but you can step into the reception-room, and I'll see. Will you give me your name?"

"No, it's of no consequence now. Tell her that an old friend wishes to see her."

He ushered her into a room on the side of the hall opposite to that of the one in which she had seen the light and heard the sounds. A lamp on a table burned low. She had hardly more than seated herself, when the man returned.

"Miss Honeywood," he said, "is not very well to-night, and begs that you will excuse her till morning."

"Did you tell her that my business was of importance?"

"Yes, I told her that you said you had important business with her, and she says that, if you can not wait till morning, to go to Mr. Benham about it."

"Please go back and say to her that my business is with her personally, and that it is indispensable that I should see her to-night."

The man departed on his errand, and it was some minutes before he came back. When he returned he said:

"Miss Honeywood will see you. Walk this way, please."

She followed him across the hall, and he, throwing open the wide door, she found herself in a large room, with Alana Honeywood standing in the center of the floor. The man shut the door and hastily left the house, going in the direction of Benham's dwelling.

CHAPTER XVI.

THERE was a directness about John Benham's methods of dealing with serious matters that had served him well all through his life, and that he now intended to bring to his aid in the effort to get at the secret of Alma's emotional disturbance. He was certain that something of importance had occurred to her during her visit to Harrisburg, and that since her return she had been endeavoring to overcome or to conceal its effects, but with the usual result in such cases of still more decidedly deranging her mental equilibrium. He knew that she was the object of the nefarious designs of several unprincipled persons. He had seen the evidence of this fact in the conduct of Todd, and in the revelations that had been unconsciously made to him on Peter's Mountain. Two of the conspirators were in jail in Harrisburg, the other was still at large, and was the one that he suspected had met Alma in Harrisburg, and had said or done something that had either frightened her or caused her a painful degree of anxiety.

That some of these people were relatives of Alma's there were strong reasons for believing, but as yet he had not by any means made up his mind that any family ties existed between her and them. He was not one to jump at conclusions. His mind had been well trained in scientific pursuits, that required absolute proof of the correctness of propositions submitted to it before they could be accepted. The mere facts of personal resemblance, and that one of the men had declared himself to be her uncle, were not sufficient to decide the question. The claim, to be established, must have stronger grounds to rest upon than these. At any rate, relatives or not, they were enemies, and it was necessary for the well-being of the woman he loved that their machinations should be prevented. To effect this object, with the utmost possible efficiency and dispatch, she and her friends must act in concert, and of course before they could do this there must be perfect confidence among them. This was his reasoning, as he walked by Alana's side from the tea-room to the drawing-room, and that caused him to resolve to take the decisive step of asking her to unburden her mind to him.

But Alana had also been thinking. To live on, meeting Benham day after day, and yet withholding from him all knowledge of a secret that she now felt he ought to know, was no longer to be thought of. She had definitely determined, during the last few minutes that she had sat at the tea-table, that it was her duty to refuse to marry him. She would not announce this decision to him without giving him the full story of her shameful origin and connections. Then he would know, no matter how much he might love her, that one coming as she did, bearing a load of infamy that others had placed upon her, but which for all that was none the less hers, was not the woman to be his wife. No, no, he would not know this. He would plead with her; she felt sure he would tell her that she was the same to him whether she owed her origin to the highest or the lowest of mankind; whether her relatives were saints or sinners; but she would be firm. She knew where his honor was to be found, and she would see that no act of hers should tarnish its brightness.

We have seen how she had been first of one mind, and then of another, like all persons whose hearts and intellects are at variance. In the beginning, she had thought that she could enjoy her new relations with the man she loved,

for a while at least, without making revelations that might
part her from him forever. Then she had wavered, at one
time resolving to tell him all before he had spoken another
word of love, and at another deciding to postpone the recital till she had, as it were, got deeper into his affections,
and had thus become a necessity to him. Now, she was
convinced that there was but one course for an honorable
woman to pursue. She had considered the subject in all
its bearings and in all its possibilities. Longer delay
would be an outrage upon him, and disgrace to her. Her
decision had been made, and the story should be told.

It would not be necessary, at this time, for her to go
into all the details of her family history. These could be
given him at any time, should he decide to know them.
The essential facts could be stated in few words. They
were sufficiently striking to impress themselves, with all
requisite force, on his mind, and he should know them before he left the house that night.

That he would be shocked, she knew very well : that he
would turn from her in disgust, she did not believe. For
all that she had resolved to refuse to be his wife, she
craved his love with a degree of intensity that was painful
to her. If he should—it was not to be thought of—but if
he should accept her decision, without making an effort to
change it, then her anguish and humiliation would be complete. Death itself would be preferable to that.

They stood in front of the coal-fire that burned brightly
in the grate. She meant to tell him her story with as
much calmness as she could command, and certainly without making any appeal to his love or his pity. The day's
experience had given her strength, or rather it had sufficed
to blunt her emotional nature to such an extent as to render
it less susceptible to such impressions as those to which it
was about to be exposed. When burning water has scalded
the skin, even a red-hot coal is not felt.

Ah, now that the time had come for her to speak, how hard it was for her to begin a recital that would bring the blood of shame to her cheeks, and put an end to the career of happiness, upon which, for a little while, she had thought she had entered! It had to be done. There was no escape. What would he say and do? She asked herself this question for the hundredth time. Well, she would know, before she had half finished, what his thoughts were, and whether or not he loved her for herself, with all her imperfections, and with all the shame that clung to her.

"There is something," she said, "that intimately concerns me, and that you ought to know. It is a sad and a shameful story, but it is one that I must tell you, for it is my only justification for what I am about to do. Perhaps I should have told you this, when you first spoke to me of your love, but I did not know as much of it as I know now; and, besides, your words were so sweet to my ears, that for a while I fancied that I might not have to tell you at all. I shrank from doing aught that might make me lose your affection. You can understand that—that—"

He had fixed his eyes on hers from the moment that she had begun to speak, and when she hesitated for a moment, and lowered her eyes from his, he took her head between his hands and, bending forward, kissed her lips.

"There is nothing you can tell me," he said, with all his strong feeling, "that can lessen my love for you, or shake my confidence in *your* truth or *your* honor. There may be others not so true and not so honorable, but what is that to you and me?"

"God bless you, my love, for those words!" she said, still by a wonderful effort preserving her calmness, for she felt as though she would like to throw herself into his arms and sob out her emotion on his breast. But she would not, even then, tell him that there was no crime or sin for her to reproach herself with. He must find that out for himself, as he heard her story.

"My father, on his death-bed," she continued, while her face became crimson, as she told the story of what she thought was her shame, "revealed to me the fact that I was not born in wedlock. Before he could acquaint me with my mother's address, he was dead. He said enough, ere he left this world, to make it very certain to my mind that my mother was a wicked woman, one whose life had been impure, and shameful, and criminal. It was through no fault of his that he was not married. She refused to be his wife, in order that she might plunge still deeper into the depths of the infamous course upon which she had entered."

"Alana, my darling!" cried Benham, while every fiber of his being thrilled with emotion. "Purity itself is not purer than you. What is all—?"

"For God's sake do not speak to me yet!" she exclaimed, as she stepped backward, for he would have taken her in his arms and pressed her to his heart—"or—or I shall never have the strength to tell it through to the end. No, no!" as he followed her with outstretched arms, and the love-light in his eyes. "Do not touch me! Wait till you hear all. Then perhaps you will hide your face from me and flee in horror from the house."

"Alana!"

It was only one word, but he had put into it a world of reproach. He turned from her, and, going to the mantelpiece, bowed his head upon it, while his whole frame trembled with the emotions that held him in bondage.

But the words were no sooner out of her mouth than she comprehended the wrong they did to him, and she could have torn her tongue out for having spoken them.

"John!" she said, approaching him but not touching him, and still speaking with the forced calmness that seemed to have become automatic with her, "I did not know what I was saying. O John!" she continued, clasping her hands together, "pardon me those cruel words. Look at me once again. I dare not trust myself to say what is in my heart. But I am not myself. You must know that. There has been so much to bear that not even the happiness that came to me this morning when you told me you loved me has sufficed to make me quite myself. John," coming still nearer to him, and now the tears streaming from her eyes, and her voice becoming low and husky, "for the love of God let me see your face once more, or I think I shall die here at your feet!"

"No," he cried, turning, and this time clasping her unresistingly in his arms, while he kissed her lips, her eyes, her hair—"no, you shall not die. You shall live to be my sweet, my honored wife. Oh, my darling, my darling, did you think for one moment that my love was so frail a thing that it would go down in any storm that others could raise? What is it all to you and to me? You are mine. You gave yourself to me this morning, and mine you shall be, please God, till the sod covers one of us!"

"But you have not heard all yet. The rest is just as bad, perhaps worse than what I have told you." She smiled as she spoke, and, throwing her arms around his neck, drew his head down and kissed him.

"Well, you shall tell me all, and then I will tell you some things that have come to my knowledge, and then we will advise together what we shall do."

"Ah! how can I hold out against you? I had resolved that I would relate the whole sad story of my origin, and of the ties that still hold me down far below the plane on which you stand, and make no sign of my love for you, but I had miscalculated my strength. I could not do it. Now I shall stand here with your arms around me, and tell you the rest.

"My father," she went on, after a little pause, "would have married my mother on his death-bed had she been present, but, as I said, he died before he could reveal her address to me. But her name he told me. It is Sarah Mullin. For many years he had sent her money, but when, after his death, I tried to discover her, all my efforts were in vain. Not a trace of her could be found. Once she came to the village, several years ago, accompanied by her brother. I saw him, at the time, in this house. I have seen him to-day. I saw him yesterday. He is the man from whose violence you saved me.

"This morning he sent for me to visit him in the jail. There is no doubt that he is my uncle. He knows where my mother is. She has been in prison; has probably just been released. He is to arrange for her coming to me—at least, that was the agreement between us; but now that he is held on the charge of murder, I do not know how it will be. But I have seen her, I am quite sure, though I did not get a sight of her face. She brought the letter from—from—the man in jail, and took back my answer.

"Now you know all. I am, as you perceive, the illegitimate daughter of a convict woman, and the niece of a murderer. Now you can understand how I have suffered since I knew you loved me, and how unworthy of that love I feel." She bowed her head as she spoke these words, and, with her hands clasped, stood before him in an attitude of profound humiliation.

"That you should suffer, and suffer keenly, is a matter of course," he said, taking both her hands in his, and laying them over his heart; "but I shall help you to forget your sorrow. The stain that rests on others has not passed to your pure soul, which, white as that of an angel, shall yet enjoy the happiness that life has to offer. Come, look up! Here in my heart is your home. I will stand between you and all harm. Give me that right at once. Be my wife to-morrow, and together we will fight our enemies, and, with God's help, we shall conquer them."

"Yes, if I could rest here forever," she said, in a voice broken by emotion, as she laid her head on his breast, "I should ask for no greater happiness. But you do not think of what you are saying. Your love, dear, makes you blind. You forget that my mother lives, that at any moment she may come to me; that if I marry you, you would have her as an inmate of your house, and be subjected to all the association that her relationship to me implies. There may be crimes that she has committed, and for which the officers of the law are seeking to arrest her. She might be dragged to a prison from under your eyes. Your love is sweeter to me—yes, I will say it, for it is true —sweeter than the love of God. It breaks my heart to say what it is my duty to say, but I love you too much to disgrace you. I can not be your wife."

"But you must be my wife! I knew, before you told me, that the ruffian Todd claimed to be your uncle; I knew that a woman, his confederate, whom I have seen and heard confessing her designs upon you, was probably your mother. I knew these things before I asked you to be my wife. What if their blood does run in your veins? It has not poisoned you. You are proof against its venom. I told you just now, when you questioned me as to what I would do if your father had been an infamous man, that the fact would not change my love, for that you are good and true, and I say the same now, when it is your mother who is bad. You will do your duty to her, and I shall help you to do it. Who knows but that in time she may become worthy to have you for her daughter?"

"I can not disgrace you before the world as I should were I to marry you. Love you I always shall, and, when I tell you, as I do now, of my irrevocable decision, I know that I am speaking words that will break my heart, if—if—it is not already broken."

"No, dear, your heart shall not break; and you shall marry me. But you are pale, and you are trembling like a leaf. Sit here, or rather, lie down on the sofa, and give me a little time to think."

He led her to the sofa, and, making her lie down, placed a soft cushion under her head. "Now," he said, "stay there quietly till I come back. I'm going to breathe a little cold air." He left the room, and she could hear his steps as he paced up and down the veranda in front of the house. In five minutes he was with her again.

"I did not want any more light as to how I should act," he said, as he took a chair and, drawing it to the sofa, sat down by her side. "I wanted to clear my brain so as to be enabled to place the matter before you as it should be placed. I am the best judge of what will disgrace me, and I think I know the world better than you do, and that it will not—the better part of it, and that is all you or I need care for—consider you disgraced if you acknowledge an erring mother, and seek to bring her back to a moral life. It would be much more of a disgrace to me if I could be so base as to let you go from my heart because you have unworthy relatives, than for me to comfort you in your sorrow, and to aid you in your efforts to reclaim them.

"And," he continued, speaking with more and more firmness, "I can not allow an erroneous notion, like the one you entertain, to wreck forever your happiness and mine, to come into our new-born love and part us just as we are united. Besides, you do not yet know that this man Todd is your uncle, or that your mother is yet alive."

"Yes," she said, "there is no doubt that he is my uncle. I have seen him, talked with him, and he has shown me some of his proofs. Moreover, he has promised to bring my mother to me."

"This was in the jail yesterday?"

"Yes, I spent more than an hour with him, and then he was charged with the murder of his wife, and then—then I think I must have fainted."

"My poor darling! You have indeed had enough to trouble you. Now," he continued, "let us face this matter together, like brave and honest people, anxious to do our full duty, and at the same time to secure our happiness. As I said just now, I have some knowledge of what you have told me."

Then, in as few words as possible, he informed her of what he had discovered on Peter's Mountain, of the incarceration of the man and the escape of the woman—doubtless, as he said, the one that had brought her the message from Todd, and that would put in a claim to being her mother. Then he told her of Miss Pink's contributions to a knowledge of the subject, of Todd's attempt to excite a strike among the workmen in the Colerain mine, of his conversation with Mr. Wade, and of his intention to confer with him further.

"We can not," he continued, "allow these people to make good their claims merely by their assertions, and by personal resemblances that may only be accidental. They must establish them in the most irrefutable manner. They must account for every day since your father knew them; they must show why they began their operations here by entering into a conspiracy to abduct you, and what the man I caught on Peter's Mountain has to do with the matter. Who knows but that they are three swindlers, three criminals, whose only object is money? Did Todd ask you for money?"

"Yes, I am to give him fifty thousand dollars, and he is to produce my mother, and forever after keep out of my way."

"My poor child, you have put yourself into the hands

of a villain ; or, rather, you would have placed yourself in
his hands, if the law had not, by detaining him for murder, put it out of his power to carry out his part of the bar-
gain. You will be safe enough from him now, for he will
probably pass the rest of his life in the State's prison.
You ought not to have gone to the jail. You are not fit
to cope single-handed with such people."

"Mr. Wade asked me not to go."

"Mr. Wade was right. He suspected that they would
try to entrap you into some arrangement by which they
could get money."

"I am sure the man is my uncle. He showed me many
letters that had contained checks sent by my father to my
mother. I know the handwriting."

"To whom were they addressed ?"

"To Miss Sarah Mullin, although she was at the time
going by another name. My father told me that."

"You did not see the face of the woman that brought
the letter from Todd ?"

"No, she kept her veil down."

"I saw it, and I would know her again among thou-
sands."

"She is like me ?"

"Yes, she resembles you, and she is still more like
Todd."

"I am sure she is my mother."

"Well, we shall see. It is possible that they are both
vile impostors engaged in a bold attempt at fraud. Now,
will you make me a promise ?"

"I will promise anything you ask except to marry you.
I can not bring you down to my level. My love for you is
too great for that. I see my degrading associations too
vividly yet. If you were to ask me to inflict horrible tor-
tures upon you, and to stand by and witness your agonies,
you would not expect me to comply. How much less,

then, should I obey you when you command that I should
torture your soul, and in all the years that we should live
together, be a spectator of your suffering, and feel that
your anguish is my doing! No, no, I can not!"

"Suppose," he said, stroking her hair with one hand,
while the other held hers fast in its clasp—"suppose I
were to say to you, 'Let us leave this place for some other
where we are not known, and where as man and wife we
can live together safe from the scandal-mongers who might
if we remained here make us the subjects of their venom-
ous tattle,' would you go with me?"

"Yes," she exclaimed, while she threw her arms
around his neck and drew his head to her breast. "I
would go this night, this very instant! I would leave all
the rest behind, so that I had but you; but I can not disgrace you and your children by making it possible for man
or woman to say, 'There goes the man who married Alana
Honeywood, her real name being Mullin, whose father was
never married to her mother, whose mother—was—was a
harlot—I might as well speak the word that they would
speak—and a convict; whose uncle murdered his wife, and
is now in the penitentiary for the crime'—or to point to
your children and mine, honorably born of our lawful and
sinless love, to say those things of them, and perhaps even
to taunt them with their shameful origin. No, no, I can
not do it!"

"Well, my darling," he said, gravely but tenderly, "if
I do not, in ten days, unmask these people, and show them
to you as the impostors I believe them to be, I shall hold
you to the pledge you have just made, and we will depart
to some distant spot, where we can live in the consciousness of our own rectitude, and bring up the children that
God may give us without the fear of a stigma resting upon
them, or of their being subjected to cruel insults. Remember, however, that I shall do this for your sake, at the same

time feeling that you are wrong to demand it. If I do expose them, I shall expect you to interpose no further objections to becoming my wife, no matter how wicked or degraded your mother may have been, or ruffianly your uncle is. No," seeing that she was about to speak, "do not answer now. We have at last arrived at an understanding, and we will let the matter rest till the time comes for acting upon it. What I was going to ask of you is not what you supposed. It is likely that some one, or more, of these people will visit you, or attempt to have an interview with you. The man whom I caught on Peter's Mountain appears to me to be the leader of the conspirators, and the most cunning and dangerous. It is not probable that he can be detained in prison just now for any considerable time, as he will doubtless get bail, and it would be difficult to prove the existence of the conspiracy. Now, promise me by the love that you bear me, that you will not, so far as you can exert any power, allow any one of these people to converse with you without either Mr. Wade or myself being present."

"That I do, most heartily. I will not allow any one of them to converse with me unless you are present. I confide in you, and in you alone."

"Thanks, dear!" He kissed her, and rose to his feet. "Good-night!" he continued, holding out his hand to her. "You have had a troublous day, and you are weary. You need rest. Go and take it, and leave your sorrows to me."

"Yes, for you are strong and masterful. Good-night, my love! my own! and do not think hardly of me for making your honor dearer to me than my own happiness."

"Ah, but you forget that in sacrificing your happiness you are also destroying mine, and I don't intend that you shall do either!"

"John !" she cried, rising and following him, as he
went toward the door.

"No," he answered, perhaps divining what she was
about to say.   "Not now ; wait till I have exposed these
people or have failed in the attempt.   I have pushed you
too hard.   You shall give me your answer in ten days, and
then your intellect will agree with your heart.   In ten days
you shall be my promised wife, and our home shall be here
with our friends around us, or in some place where we are
strangers."

He turned and left the room, while she stood with her
hands covering her face, and the tears streaming through
her white fingers.

CHAPTER XVII

WHEN Mrs. L'Estrange, as for the present we shall continue to call her, entered the drawing-room, Alana was standing almost in the place that she had occupied when Benham had left the room only a few minutes before. She had, on his departure, thrown herself on the sofa, and had given way to a paroxysm of weeping: but, at the sound of the door-bell, she had recovered herself, and had begun to assume an appearance of calmness. When Abram announced a visitor, she sent word that she was not well, and had referred her to Benham, under the supposition that the business, alleged as an excuse for so late a visit, related either to the approaching funeral of Mrs. Todd, or to some matter connected with the dwelling of one of the workmen. But the persistency of the woman had to some extent roused her suspicions, and she had accordingly, while directing her to be admitted, sent Abram for Benham, in fulfillment of the promise she had just made to him.

Mrs. L'Estrange gave one glance around the apartment, for the purpose, apparently, of making sure that they were alone, and then, clasping her hands before her, she stood with bowed head, as she had several times stood before the judge on the bench, to receive his sentence, and, as she had had good reason to believe, not without exciting his compassion.

One look was sufficient to reveal to Alana the fact that, in the humble and apparently contrite woman that stood before her, she saw the one that had brought her Todd's letter, and the one that was probably her mother.

"I can not speak with you now," she said ; "I have sent for a friend to be present at this interview. Sit down, please ; he will be here in a moment." John Benham's words to her had served to put her on her guard. She did not intend to give way to any filial feeling till all doubt in her mind relative to the woman's identity with her mother was removed. She was hardening her heart to the utmost of her ability.

"Alana," said the woman, without noticing the words addressed to her, and speaking in a singularly soft and musical voice, "my child, I have come to atone, if I can, in your sweet presence, for all the sins of a wicked life, for —for—I am your mother."

"I do not know. How should I know ? If you are my mother, it seems to me that I should be the last one to whom you should come. You deserted me in my infancy, you wrecked my dear father's life, you have passed your days in sin and shame ; and now, after the lapse of a quarter of a century, when your hair has grown gray in vice, and when you have just been released from prison, you come to me and speak of atoning for your infamous life ! If, on the other hand, you are not my mother, what are you, then, but an impostor, to be put out of my house ? "

"My God," cried the woman, throwing up her hands, as though in horror at what she had heard, "this from a daughter to her mother ! Now I know that you are in very truth my child. The Mullin blood runs through every vein of your body."

"Yes," answered Alana, bitterly, " it does. I have you, or one equally depraved, to thank for that, and, thank God, too, I am able to stand here to-night and tell you so ! You say you are my mother. I do not believe it. The Almighty Father, who is just to his creatures, would

not have permitted my mother to live and to come here to
taunt me with the shame of being her daughter!"

"I am your mother, Alana!" dropping on her knees
and raising her hands piteously. "For the love of God,
give me a chance! See! I am on my knees before you.
A mother kneels to her daughter and implores mercy!
Oh, my child, my child, look at me," tearing off her bonnet and brushing back the hair from her face, "look at me
and see your own image. Your father loved me once. He
was kind, but you are as cruel as the grave!"

Alana clasped her hands and looked imploringly toward
the door. Why did he not come? What was she to do?
She felt that she was yielding. Her heart was beginning
to soften; the first thrills of filial love were springing up in
her breast. She looked closely into the countenance of the
pleading woman who still knelt upon the floor. Yes, it
was so. She must be her mother, or why the wonderful
resemblance to herself that she saw in every feature of the
face before her? She was about to yield, to rush forward,
and, raising the woman from her knees, clasp her to her
heart, when something in the expression of the suppliant
caused her to restrain herself, and again raised her doubts.
What it was that she saw she could not then or ever afterward exactly determine. It might have been a look of tri-
umph, or of cunning, or of insincerity, something that had
at any rate struck her with overpowering force.

"No," she said, assuming the hard and pitiless tone
that had characterized all that she had heretofore said—
"no, you are not my mother. My mother left me an
infant in the poor-house to be brought up as a pauper.
But for her I should this moment be the promised wife
of a man whose shoe-strings you, whether mother or impostor, are not worthy to loosen. She would not even at
this late day desire to lead a virtuous life. The taint of
sin was too deeply implanted in her soul for repentance

ever to spring up within her. She even refused the honorable marriage that my father offered her. She had begun life as a harlot, and as a harlot she preferred to remain."

"That is false!" cried the woman, springing to her feet and looking defiance at the girl, who had covered her face with her hands for very shame at the words she had uttered. "That is false!" she repeated. "I was married to him, lawfully married, and, if he was too drunk at the time to know what he was doing, it was none the less a legal marriage, and I am here as his widow to claim my lawful rights. I have appealed to your heart in vain. I hoped, fondly hoped, that there might be a spark of a daughter's love in your breast for an erring mother, desirous of leading a new life, but in the place of such a child as I thought to find, I discover to my horror that I have given birth to a monster that God in his infinite mercy separated from me when she was too young to exhibit the callousness of her stony heart, but that for some wise purpose of his own he has permitted to insult me in my old age."

"My father married, did you say? Married to you?"

"Ah, then, there is something that can rouse you! Yes, married to me, your mother! Since I have failed to touch your heart, perhaps your mind may be interested in the proofs I have here that all that I have alleged is true."

Alana sprang forward at the words, while the woman as she was speaking took from the pockets of her frock two bundles of letters and papers which she proceeded to undo.

But before she was able to do much in that direction, Benham had entered the room, and seeing at a glance the relative situations of the parties, and the effort that the woman was making to open her packages of documents, at once took in all the points of the occasion, and was advancing to take part in the discussion, when Alana saw him.

"I tried to keep my promise," she said to him. "I sent for you as soon as this woman came."

"Yes, I know. I was not at home. I went to the forge for a few minutes, and have just this moment got your message. Still, I perceive that I am in time, unless it may be that my absence has caused you some annoyance."

"And who are you, sir," inquired Mrs. L'Estrange, surveying him superciliously from head to foot, while she drew herself up to her full height, and assumed all the dignity of appearance and manner of which she was capable—"who are you that come here to interrupt a private conversation between a mother and her daughter—unbidden, too, by the mistress of the house ? "

"I am the superintendent of these works," replied Benham, "and I am here at the request of this lady," taking the hand that Alana held out to him, "the mistress of this house and of all that pertains to it."

"I think not. As the widow of Mr. Francis Honeywood, the late owner of this property, and as that young woman's mother, my rights should go for something."

"His widow !"

"Yes, his widow. Is there anything strange in the fact that, being dead, he should have left a widow ? "

"And may I ask where you have been all these years ? "

"You may ask what you please. But I shall certainly answer no questions put in a hostile spirit. I was about to convince this young lady, whom I will not yet designate by the name of daughter, since she declines to regard me as her mother—I was about to exhibit to her the evidence that her mother is a married woman, and then to show her that I am her mother. Perhaps you will not venture to prevent my so doing."

"Yes, I certainly shall. I am here, in fact, for that very purpose. She is fatigued, and requires rest. Besides, she evidently does not believe that you are her mother, nor," he added, looking her fixedly in the face, "do I."

"I am sure she is not my mother," said Alana. "I can not tell you why I think so, but I am as certain of it as I am of anything else in the world. For a moment I thought she was speaking the truth, but now I know that she is an impostor."

"Some secret light, I suppose," said Mrs. L'Estrange, sneeringly, "that illumines Miss Honeywood's mind, and enables her to perceive what she wishes to perceive. After all her pretended efforts to find her mother, she rejects and insults that mother when she comes, heart-broken, into her daughter's presence. What am I to do? I am ready to exhibit my proofs, and yet you refuse to allow me to do so. Is that just? Is it kind to an old woman, who *may* be that girl's mother, even though you both believe, or affect to believe, that she is not?"

"I think I had better see the papers," said Alana. "I would rather examine them to-night than defer the duty to another time. I should feel easier if I saw them now, although I do not feel that they would shake my conviction that she is not my mother."

"Very well," said Benham; "perhaps it would be better to end the matter at once.—Produce your evidence, madam, if you please," turning to Mrs. L'Estrange, who still had her papers in her hand. "Will you sit here at this table? You will find it more convenient."

"Thanks. You are very kind. It will be more convenient for us all."

She sat down in the chair that Benham drew up to the table for her, while he and Alana sat opposite.

While she was getting her papers in order he took the opportunity of studying her face more closely than he had yet done, and he was, in consequence, convinced beyond a doubt that she was the woman that had been with the man

on Peter's Mountain, and that had succeeded in making
her escape. How was it possible, then, that she should be
Alana's mother ? He called to mind all that he had heard
the two say relative to the abduction and the confinement
in the house on Berry's Mountain, and the firing of his
own house in order that attention might be diverted from
the prime object—the securing of Alana's person. If this
woman was the widow of Francis Honeywood, it was incon-
ceivable that she should consort with criminals like Johnson and Todd, even though the latter was her brother, and
enter into a conspiracy with them to abduct her own
daughter for the purpose of extorting money. No, the
thing was out of the question. The woman was certainly
an impostor.

And yet, as he looked at her, he could not but admit
that she was wonderfully like Alana. A coarse likeness,
but nevertheless a startling one. To what was the fact
due ? Was it possible that the features of a person could
so exactly resemble those of another without there being
some blood relationship ? He tried to call to mind all the
resemblances between unrelated people that had ever come
under his observation, but there was not one in which the
similitude of features was so marked as in this instance.
And yet there was a difference of thirty years or more in
their ages.

One circumstance astonished him, and that was the fact
that she did not appear to recognize him as the man who
on the previous day had surprised her with Johnson hatching their conspiracy to commit arson and abduction. She
must have seen his face as she looked up and saw her companion dangling in the air and being lifted up to the top
of the rock by Benham's strong arm. He had seen her
face then, and was conscious of catching her eye, though
she had at once dropped her veil and hurried frightened
from the spot. Besides, she had probably visited Johnson

11

in prison as she had visited Todd, and he must certainly have told her of the way in which he had been treated, and mentioned the name of his captor. But for all this she seemed to be absolutely unaware of the fact that she had seen him before or that he had seen her.

"If you are ready now," she said, interrupting his meditations, "I will begin with the exposition of the evidence upon which I rest my claim.

"In the first place, it gives me great pleasure to be the means of removing one serious blot from that young lady's escutcheon. However bad a woman her mother may have been—and I call you both to witness that I have in no way endeavored to extenuate her wickedness—she was legally married to Francis Honeywood. Here"—she continued, taking one of the papers from the table—"is the marriage certificate, which shows that the marriage took place on the 11th of March, 1854, nearly a year before you were born. To be sure," smiling as she spoke, "he was only a boy, and I was a woman of mature age, but neither fact invalidates the marriage; neither does the one that he had taken too much champagne just before the ceremony to fully comprehend what he was doing, or to recollect it afterward. The clergyman and witnesses, however, saw nothing amiss about him."

She handed the paper to Benham, and he and Alana read it carefully through from beginning to end. It was to the effect that, on the 11th day of March, 1854, in the city of Philadelphia, Francis Honeywood and Sarah Mullin, being of lawful age, were duly united in the holy bonds of matrimony by the Rev. Melanchthon Jenkins, a minister of the gospel, authorized by law to perform the marriage ceremony. It was witnessed by Jonathan Smart and Lewis Eaton.

"I know both those gentlemen," said Benham. "Mr. Smart is general manager of the Truesdell and Stone

Mountain Railroad, and Mr. Exton is the superintendent of the Grayquill coal-mines. They can both be easily communicated with in a day or two. I am not acquainted with the handwriting of either of them, but the certificate looks as though it might be authentic."

"It *is* authentic!" exclaimed Mrs. L'Estrange, with energy. "And, if you thank me for nothing else—and I admit that my appearance and claims are not matters for which you should offer thanksgiving—you ought to be rejoiced, Miss Honeywood, that a stain is removed from your name and your mother's!"

"Yes," said Alana, "it is a cause for thankfulness, and I am very grateful. But my father was very positive that he was not married."

"Yes, for he regarded the whole matter as a trick, and refused always to believe that a marriage had taken place. I am honest enough now," continued Mrs. L'Estrange, dropping her eyes as though in shame, "to admit that I took an advantage of him that was altogether inexcusable. I was much older than he. I and the young men whose names are signed as witnesses to that certificate entered into a plot to make your father drunk, and then, while he was in that condition, I was to marry him. It was begun as a joke, but it ended in earnest. They all boarded with my mother, and one afternoon we went on an excursion to the Falls of Schuylkill, where we had a cat-fish dinner, and drank a good deal of wine. Then one of the gentlemen, Mr. Smart I think it was, went for the clergyman, a respectable but ignorant and simple-minded man, and in the parlor of the tavern, at the Falls of Schuylkill, we were married. The next day and ever afterward your father refused to admit the validity of the marriage, and even declared that the whole story was false, and that no ceremony had ever been performed. Several years ago I came here with my brother, the same who is now in jail in Harris-

burg. Mr. Honeywood would not even see me, and again
denied that there had been a marriage. He appears to
have died either in the same belief, or in the same spirit of
obstinacy."

Certainly, so far as Benham could determine, the ap-
pearances were in favor of the woman's truthfulness. The
certificate bore the names of persons he knew, and who
could be appealed to within the next day or two. It was,
he thought, scarcely probable that a false certificate could
have been concocted when the fraud could be so readily
detected. And the woman's frankness in telling of her
own misdeeds in connection with the marriage, was calculated to prepossess him in her favor. He was astonished,
too, at the admirable way in which she expressed herself,
and which was clearly that of an educated person. He had
understood, perhaps, only by inference, that the Mullins
were all coarse and ignorant people. Todd evidently was
of this stamp, but this woman, his sister, spoke in excellent English, and with a quiet reserve of manner under
what, to her, if she was not an impostor, must have been
trying circumstances. Still, while admitting the genuineness of the certificate, he was not prepared to believe that
the holder of it was the woman that had married Francis
Honeywood, and was consequently Alana's mother. The
facts within his knowledge that militated against her identity were too strong to be overcome without much more
direct evidence than any she had yet offered, which, in
reality, did not extend beyond the facts that the certificate
was in her possession, and her own unsupported declaration that she was the woman that had contracted the marriage.

Resolving that not a day should elapse before he communicated with Messrs. Smart and Eaton, he handed back
the certificate.

During all this time Alana had of course been intensely

interested. The belief that Benham expressed in regard to
the genuineness of the marriage certificate, and her own
conviction of its validity, removed from her mind one of
its greatest loads. At any rate, she was legally the daughter of her father, entitled to bear his name, and to inherit
his estate even without the formality of a will. She was
not a bastard, whatever else she might be. The one personal stain was therefore removed.

And she was disposed to go further than Benham, and
to admit that the woman was her mother. She could not
conceive how otherwise she should present so plausible a
case and bear herself with such entire confidence of the
success of her claim. She had detailed the circumstances
of the marriage with such circumstantiality, and with such
an air of truth, without attempting to gloss over or to excuse her own participation in the victimization of the
young student, that Alana could not see how she could be
lying. She was calm, self-possessed, confident, not attempting to enforce belief in her statements, but simply
allowing them to make their own way to the sense of justice and truth of her judges.

As a natural consequence of this phase of mind, she
began to reproach herself for the hard manner in which
she had acted, and for the cruel, if truthful, words she had
used. "If she is my mother," she thought, "nothing
can justify my brutal conduct. I must have been mad to
have acted as I did."

She would have given utterance to her thoughts, but
for the fact that Benham, by a look, warned her to be
silent.

Mrs. L'Estrange took the paper that Benham returned
to her, and, laying it on the table, proceeded to unfold the
other documents in her possession. These she arranged in
chronological order, and finally, taking up the first one of
the series, she resumed her remarks :

"I arrived here with my brother on the 18th of August, 1866, remaining at the tavern while he came to this house to see my husband, and to induce him, if possible, to do me the justice of acknowledging the marriage and of making provision for my support. Of course I knew that I could enforce my claims by law, but I was indisposed for several reasons, some of them based upon facts not at all creditable to me, to appeal to the courts. I found, however, that he was still obdurate. He would not admit that a marriage had taken place. Then, in order to intimidate him, my brother threatened him with exposure and the law. At this he became very angry, so my brother informed me, and forcibly ejected him from the house. However, he subsequently wrote to me, proposing a compromise. By the terms of this arrangement he was to pay me three thousand dollars a year, and I was not to annoy him in any manner. He kept to the agreement, as did I also."

"My father declared on his death-bed," said Alana, "that he had before and after my birth offered to marry my mother, but that she had persistently refused to be his wife."

"Yes, he did several times. But I refused, because I was already married ; and, besides, I did not at that period of my life desire to be regarded as his wife." And again she hung her head as if ashamed to look Alana in the face.

Benham gazed at the woman in surprise, not unmixed with admiration of her surpassing shrewdness in the new *rôle* of honesty upon which she had entered. Apparently she was willing to reveal all the acts, no matter how sinful or criminal or dishonorable, of her past life. Such frankness he had never met before in a depraved character such as he believed her to be. No more effective method of disarming suspicion and bringing honest opponents over to her side could have been devised, and she had used it with a skill that could scarcely be surpassed. A more consummate actress he had never come across, although he had, like most men of his age, met with many designing women. That she was acting, that she was a false wretch who ought to be in the cell of a prison if she had justice done her, he was more and more convinced, every moment, in spite of the apparent ingenuousness that characterized every word she spoke. He saw, too, how easily Alana would have fallen a prey to the woman's wiles had she been left alone, as Mrs. L'Estrange had evidently expected would have been the case. However, his time had not yet come.

"As you perceive," resumed Mrs. L'Estrange, seeing that she had made a decided impression upon her listeners, though unaware of the character of that produced upon Benham—"as you perceive, I am familiar with the facts connected with my unhappy relation with Mr. Honeywood, and that I have no disposition to deny them, or to diminish their odiousness. I admit at once, and for all, that I was a wicked woman, but for all that I am Francis Honeywood's widow, and am entitled to all the rights pertaining to that relation.

"These letters, of which this is the first, are from Mr. Honeywood to me. They are addressed to me as Miss Sarah Mullin, at Montreal, the city in which I had determined to reside, though for a good reason I called myself Sarah Mobley, and was known by that name throughout the city." .

"Why," inquired Benham, quickly, "did you change your name?"

"Out of regard for my mother, who was a respectable woman. The only one of the family, so far as I know; for my occupation was a shameful one." Actually, as she spoke these words, a blush suffused her cheeks. "Can this woman," thought Benham, "bring the blood to her face at will ?"   Apparently, she colored just as some emotional actresses can bring tears from their eyes.

"You can read this letter, and all the others, if you choose," she continued, handing it to Benham.   "It's one of a number that came quarterly from the time that we made the arrangement, until Mr. Honeywood's death. Each one contained a check for seven hundred and fifty dollars."

Benham read the letter.   It was just as she had said. He looked over the others, as Alana had done, and found them to be almost exact copies of the first.

"Now," she said, folding up the letters and tying them into a package, "there is one thing more.   Doubtless you have in your possession, Miss Honeywood, specimens of my handwriting, the checks, for instance, with my indorse-ments, or my letters transmitting them.   They must have been found among your father's papers at his death.   Take any one of the letters in question and read it to me, with-out letting me see a word of it, and I will make you an exact copy.   That will be an additional piece of evidence of the honesty of my claim."

"There are no checks, and no letters of the kind, to be found," answered Alana.   "Not even the check-book can be discovered.   Neither is there anything to show where my mother lived, or upon whom the checks were drawn. I knew nothing on the subject till I talked with the man in the jail this morning."

"Ah, you talked with him !   He is your Uncle Alexan-der.   Did he tell you anything different from what I have told you ?"

"He told me some things that you have not mentioned. And he was about to tell me of something that he said would please me, the marriage of my father, I suppose, when—"

"When he was charged with the murder of his wife. Of course you know that it was an accident.   But," not waiting for a confirmation of this assertion, "what did he tell you that I have not told you?"

"Before that question is answered," said Benham, who saw that his time had now come, "and before expressing an opinion on the genuineness of your claim to be Mr. Honeywood's widow, I have a few questions to ask. My object, and the object of Miss Honeywood, is to get at the truth. If you are her mother, you will of course be received as such, and treated with the consideration to which you are entitled. If you are an impostor, it is proper that you should be exposed."

"Very well," she said, though her face became a little paler than it had been, and a slight twitching occurred about the angles of her mouth. "I am ready."

CHAPTER XVIII

"You are now Mrs. L'Estrange, I believe?" said Benham interrogatively.

"Yes."

"Is that an assumed name?"

"No. I was married to a French Canadian two years ago."

"Is your husband living?"

"He died a week after our marriage. He was a hunter, in the employ of the Hudson Bay Company, and was drowned in the St. Lawrence while attempting to cross the river on the ice. Here," taking a newspaper from her pocket, "is an account of the accident. It is a weekly newspaper, and the announcement of my marriage, and his death, are in adjoining columns."

Benham glanced at the newspaper that she handed him. She had spoken the truth.

"Why did you make no demand for your quarterly allowance after Mr. Honeywood's death?"

"Because I was in prison and could not. I was committed at about the time he died, and just before the payment was due. I did not know of his death till my release. I had inquiries made of the bankers, but the answer was that there were no funds. The last payment was made in United States notes, and sent to me by express."

"That is exactly as the man in the jail told it to me," said Alana to Benham.

"Doubtless it is correct," he answered.—"Now," again

addressing Mrs. L'Estrange, "for what were you imprisoned ?"

"Is it necessary to go into that matter?" she inquired, with a somewhat weary air. "And before my own daughter, too ? You might spare me further humiliation and shame."

"Thus far you have not spared yourself. I must insist on the question."

"For what reason ? What good can you gain by the answer ?"

"That I do not yet know. It may be of importance in the determination of your character."

"Well, have it as you wish ! I was convicted of fraud, and of obtaining money under false pretenses."

"You have been in prison many times ?"

"Oh, yes."

"And are now being sought for by the police ?"

"No."

Here Alana whispered something to Benham.

"Todd, whom you admit to be your brother, says that detectives from Philadelphia are now in search of you."

"If Alexander Todd said that," she exclaimed, in a louder tone of voice than she had yet employed, "he lied !"

"Very well; we will not further discuss the matter. It will be very easily settled by a telegram to the Philadelphia chief of police to-morrow morning."

A deadly pallor overspread her countenance at these words. Benham noticed it, but, without referring to the circumstance, went on with his examination.

"Did you ever see me before to-night ?"

"Never to my knowledge."

"But I have seen you."

"That may be. I am not expected to see all the people that see me."

"True, but you have seen me before."

"Oh, well, if I have, I didn't notice you."

"I saw you on Peter's Mountain yesterday afternoon ?" interrogatively.

Now, Mrs. L'Estrange knew of course what the previous questions were leading to, and she had therefore ample opportunity for reflection as to what she should answer when the inevitable came. She was fully conscious of the fact that, if she admitted that she was the woman Benham had seen at Washington's Throne, on Peter's Mountain, in conference with Johnson, and engaged in a conspiracy to burn Benham's house and to abduct Miss Honeywood for the purpose of extorting money from her, it would be a fatal blow to her pretensions. She knew, also, that it would be almost impossible to prove that she was the woman. Johnson, of course, would swear point-blank that she had never, to his knowledge, been on the mountain ; the failure of the searchers sent out by Benham, and of the Harrisburg police to obtain even so much as a trace of the woman, was in her favor. Her tracks, she believed, were so fully covered up that the identification of the Peter's Mountain woman with herself would be a matter of great difficulty, if not an impossibility. There would be no one to testify against her but Benham, and Johnson would positively contradict him by swearing that not only was she not on Peter's Mountain, but that no woman was with him.

Besides, in all her controversies with policemen, judges, juries, and prosecuting attorneys, she had derived more benefit from boldness even than from apparent frankness. Long experience in devious paths had made her an expert at evasion, and she knew just when to confess and when to deny, and, denying, to stick to her assertions with an obstinacy that showed no variation or relaxation. When, therefore, Benham's question came, there was no hesitation.

"I was not on Peter's Mountain yesterday afternoon," she said, calmly, as though entirely unaware of the importance of the question and answer. "In fact, I was never on Peter's Mountain in my life."

For a moment Benham was astounded at the brazen effrontery of the woman; but before he could return to the assault, Mr. Wade was ushered into the room, and, in consequence, the order of proceeding was for the moment interrupted. In a few words Benham explained the situation, and then the examination was renewed.

"You deny explicitly that you were on Peter's Mountain yesterday afternoon in company with a man?"

"Most explicitly," answered the woman, closing her lips tightly, and laying her folded hands on the table before her.

"Let me state fully what I know, and then perhaps we shall understand each other better.

"Yesterday afternoon I went up to near the summit of Peter's Mountain, to a place called Washington's Throne, a large rock overlooking the valley and the river. I approached from the north, and when I arrived at the top I heard voices. I looked over the edge and saw below me a man and a woman. They were engaged in earnest conversation, the purport of which was that they were members of a band of conspirators—three in number—whose object it was to abduct Miss Honeywood, to carry her to a house on Berry's Mountain, and then, when she was in their power, force her to agree to certain outrageous propositions tending to the advantage of the conspirators. The man was captured by me, and is now in jail. The woman escaped. You are that woman! I saw your face distinctly, and there is no doubt that I am correct."

While Benham was speaking, Mrs. L'Estrange's face assumed an expression of the greatest astonishment. She heard him through to the end, and, when he had finished, she raised her hands and eyes as if appealing to Heaven, and ejaculated :

"My God ! that I should be charged with a conspiracy to abduct my own daughter ! The man is either insane or—or—drunk."

"Are you acquainted with Johnson, now in the jail at Harrisburg ?" inquired Benham, quietly, without noticing the implied charge made by the woman.

Now, it was Mrs. L'Estrange's policy, and, in fact, her uniform system of procedure, in such cases as that in which she was now concerned, to admit all charges that could be readily proved, no matter how damaging they might be to her interests. She knew, of course, that the fact of her acquaintance with Johnson, and her visit to him in the jail, could be readily established. She therefore promptly answered :

"Yes."

"He is a friend of yours, I suppose ?"

"Yes, Mr. Johnson is a friend of mine. He is a very superior man, and has been badly treated."

"That remains to be seen. Being a friend of yours, he would not be likely to manufacture a falsehood in regard to you, especially one that might be the means of getting you into trouble. Last night, in his examination before the justice of the peace, he declared that he had gone with a friend, Mrs. L'Estrange, to Peter's Mountain, in order to let her enjoy the fine landscape."

While Benham was speaking, the woman's face again became pallid, and she looked as though she were about to faint. Large drops of perspiration stood out on her forehead, and her voice, which had all along been clear and ringing, now became husky and faint.

"It is impossible !" she muttered. "He could not have made such a statement."

"Yes," said Mr. Wade, "he did, for I have read the record in Squire McElroy's office."

"I do not know why he should make such an assertion. It is none the less false."

"As I came down the mountain-side," resumed Benham, pitilessly, although he perceived that the game was already over, "I saw a piece of a blue veil, such as that you now wear, that had been torn off by an overhanging branch. I secured it, and have it now in my pocket. Will you allow me to see if yours is torn, and if the piece corresponds with the lost portion, if there is any ?"

She could not refuse. To do so would only make mat. ters worse. She did not know that her veil was torn, and there was, therefore, a chance that the fragment was not hers, and then it would be sure evidence in her favor. She therefore removed her veil and laid it on the table. Benham took the piece from his pocket, and, spreading out the veil, found that the fragment exactly fitted a torn place at one corner. He then handed the veil back to its owner and returned the piece to his pocket.

Mrs. L'Estrange was a picture for the physiognomist. At first, as Benham began to speak of the veil, she put on a faint smile, that was nothing more than the contraction of certain facial muscles, such as might be produced by the galvanic current without the element of mirth or pleasure entering into it. Then, as she saw that the piece in Benham's possession exactly corresponded with the rent in her veil, the sardonic smile disappeared, and a look of stolid defiance took its place. She saw that she had been convicted of a series of falsehoods, and that therefore increased doubt was thrown upon her statement that she was the widow of Francis Honeywood, but she did not for all that intend to renounce her pretensions. She had, however, tried one plan and it had not succeeded. Something might still be effected by threats and intimidation, although she knew that, if these were resisted, her position was such as to absolutely preclude the possibility of her resorting to legal measures. Before, however, she could say a word, Mr. Wade, who had listened with the utmost attention to the examination, and had been observing her closely, said :

"Probably no additional evidence touching Mrs. L'Estrange's association with Johnson yesterday afternoon is necessary, but I may say that I have ascertained that she, and a man answering to Johnson's description, and who in hiring the vehicle gave her name and his, left Harrisburg yesterday afternoon in a buggy that they hired at Sanger's livery-stable, and that late in the evening it was returned by the lady without her companion being with her."

"All this amounts to nothing," said the woman, rising from her chair and preparing to depart. "You are not disposed to receive me as Mr. Honeywood's widow. Of course, then, I shall be obliged to obtain my rights by an appeal to the law. I shall at once take legal advice, and you will hear from me very soon through my counsel. I hoped to save trouble and ill-feeling, but in this I have been disappointed. In the mean time I shall remain in Harrisburg." She bowed formally to Alana and the gentlemen, and was preparing to leave the room.

"Stop, please," said Mr. Wade ; "you can not be allowed to go. I took the trouble while in Harrisburg to inquire into your antecedents to a somewhat greater extent than you have chosen to reveal them. I telegraphed this morning to Philadelphia for an officer who, I am disposed to think, knows something about you. He is in the hall, waiting the signal from me to enter, and see if you are the woman you are suspected to be. Should my suspicions be confirmed, he has a warrant for your arrest that he obtained this afternoon. I do not wish to be harsh with you. If there is anything you would like to say you can speak."

While Mr. Wade was making these remarks the woman

gasped for breath, and clasped the back of a chair apparently to save herself from falling. Alana, seeing her distress, went to her, and would have supported her to the sofa ; but, rousing herself, Mrs. L'Estrange kept her off with a motion of her hand, while she turned to Mr. Wade even yet with a remnant of her defiant manner.

"You may cause me a great deal of annoyance," she said. "I have admitted that my life has been an evil one, and I do not deny that I am at this moment justly liable to arrest and imprisonment."

"You did deny it, just now," said Benham.

"The matter, however, which it concerns you all to investigate is not, it appears to me, my misdeeds, but whether or not I am the widow of Francis Honeywood. I have presented evidence to-night that ought to be sufficient to satisfy any reasonable minds that I am the woman I claim to be. Admitting that I have only partially succeeded, admitting that I have barely raised the slightest presumption in your minds that I am that girl's mother, is it prudent, is it kind, not to me, but to her, to injure her through me by raising scandals about the woman who may be her mother? I appeal to you, as a man of experience and a lawyer, to say if I have not at least established a possibility in my favor." She sat down as she finished speaking, and looked with something of an imploring expression on her face at Mr. Wade.

"You are certainly mistaken," answered that gentleman, "in supposing that you have in the slightest degree convinced us that you are Mr. Honeywood's widow. We are prepared to admit that you have established certain points relative to this young lady's mother, but you have failed altogether to make us believe that you are her mother. Who you are, I do not know—I have not even a suspicion ; but I have no doubt that we shall unravel the mystery, and exhibit you and your confederates in your true colors. As one means of effecting this object I am going to have a detective officer take a look at you." He went to the door as he spoke these last words, and opened it.—"Come in, Mr. Josephs," he continued.

At the name, Mrs. L'Estrange covered her face with her hands, while Alana, feeling that this was a critical moment in her existence, watched the proceedings with pale face and bated breath.

Entering the room, Mr. Josephs made a bow, and then his eyes roamed round the apartment for a moment, till they rested upon the cowering woman who was trembling with apprehension, and who still kept her face covered. Walking to where she sat, he looked at her fixedly for a moment, and then gently laid his hand on her shoulder, while he gave a significant glance at Mr. Wade.

"Sarah Lammy," he said, very quietly, "I have a warrant for your arrest on the charge of robbery. Get ready to go with me. There is a train for Philadelphia at 12.20."

"You are mistaken," she exclaimed, though with a shaky voice, while she dropped her hands from her face and looked squarely at the officer. "My name is L'Estrange, and I am not guilty of any robbery for which I have not already been punished."

"Oh, come, now!" said Mr. Josephs, losing his hitherto quiet and respectful tone, "don't try that game with me. You're Sarah Lammy, *alias* 'Confidence Sal,' and you are the principal in the big diamond robbery at Smith, Lukens & Werton's in Philadelphia, a little over a month ago. Why, Lord bless you! you and I are old friends. I'll treat you kindly, as you know. I'll telegraph for a section of a sleeping-car for you, and you'll wake up in Philadelphia none the worse for your journey."

"Can't you stay here in the village till morning? I'm very tired. Yes, worse than tired; I'm ill. There's a tavern near here at which I can get a room."

"I'm afraid to trust you, Sarah—upon my life I am! You got away from me once before just by abusing my kindness. While I sat all night and watched the door of your room, you got out of the window. No, you'll have to go to Philadelphia to-night."

"Can't you let her stay?" interposed Alma. "She looks faint and weary. Surely she can not escape from you!"

"All of which goes to show, miss, that you don't know 'Confidence Sal!' Why, Lord bless you, she ain't tired a bit! She can make herself look as if she was just fagged out and ready to drop into the first grave that she might come across, when all the time she's as fresh as a four-year-old colt. She ain't done any hard work to-day: she never did any in her life; and, as to being made sick by what's happened to her here to-night, she ain't the kind to take on about such a thing. She'd tell you just as straightforward a story to-morrow, and with just as many particulars, all fitting into one another like a first-class piece of cabinet-work, and never feel any more tired than if she had just waked up out of a nine-hour nap. She's the sharpest one we've got—ain't you, Sal?"

Not deigning to reply, the woman rose, and without a word prepared to follow the detective from the room.

"I won't put the bracelets on you, Sarah," said the officer; "I guess I can manage without them, and it always goes against my grain to iron a woman. You mustn't think hard of me," he continued, in a lower voice, but still loud enough for all in the room to hear, "for not letting you stay at the tavern, but that business is business no one knows better than yourself."

He turned when he had finished speaking, and with his prisoner left the room.

"She is well named," said Mr. Wade, emphatically, "'Confidence Sal!' The atmosphere seems to be clearer now that she is out of it."

"And yet I am sorry for her," said Alana, in a low tone. "I know that she is not my mother, but at one time my feelings got the better of my judgment, and I was very near yielding my belief in spite of the strong light that in the beginning shone upon her in some incomprehensible way, and revealed to me that she was an impostor. I seemed then to see her in all her inborn depravity and to perceive the falsity of her claim. But, for all that, I think I should have accepted her statements had I been alone."

"Yes," rejoined Mr. Wade, "an emotion has more influence with a woman than a reason, and I, for one, am glad that it is so. Women who are in all things governed by their intellects are rather dreary creatures, to my mind."

"But who can she be?" inquired Alana. "She has in her possession papers that must at one time at least have belonged to my mother; and then her knowledge of circumstances that I know to be true, and her remarkable likeness to me, are facts that it is difficult for us to explain."

"I shall make it my business to unravel the mystery," said Benham. "I shall start for Montreal to-morrow. I shall telegraph this night to Messrs. Smart and Eaton, and I hope to follow up the clews I shall receive till the whole affair is made as plain as day. I shall go to the jail to-morrow and see what can be got out of our two prisoners."

While he was speaking, Mr. Wade sat stroking his mustache, and looking from one to the other of his two companions in a knowing way, as though he had succeeded in solving a question that had been causing him some disturbance. When Benham had finished his remarks the old gentleman threw himself back in his chair, while a pleasant smile passed over his countenance.

"I think I comprehend how matters stand," he said, in a reflective sort of a way, and without addressing any one in particular. "But I think, Alana, that you ought to have taken me into your confidence. Surely I am an old enough friend for that!"

"Yes!" she exclaimed, "you are my second father." She came round to where he sat and, putting her arms around his neck, kissed his forehead. "I should have told you all very soon, but there has not been time. It only happened this morning, and matters are still unsettled between us."

"How unsettled? I don't understand."

"John is an honorable man, and sprung from an honorable lineage, while I—"

"Tut, tut, tut!" interrupted Mr. Wade. "What nonsense! What difference does it make to him whether his lineage is honorable or not, or whether yours is base or not? Would he be any worse a man if his grandfather had stolen a sheep? Would you, my dear, be any better if your mother had been a paragon of all the virtues? I admit that the world in its narrow-mindedness would be very apt for a while to put on an air of virtuous indignation, but the moment it discovered that you did not care for its opinion, and, above all, that you were successful, it would turn round and worship you—all of it, at least, except the envious. They would never forgive you. If John Benham loves you, as I suppose he does—and he's a bigger fool than I take him to be if he doesn't—you have no right to make him unhappy, provided you love him."

Alana had gone back to her place at the table, and for a moment, after Mr. Wade had ceased speaking, she remained silent, apparently thinking profoundly of some engrossing subject. Then she rose, and, going to where Benham sat, she laid her hand on his shoulder.

"John," she said, "I will be your wife if you will take me."

"God bless you, dear!" he said, with emotion. "I felt sure I should get you some day; but for all that I shall not give up my efforts to solve the mystery connected with that woman—"

"Good-night, Alana!" interrupted Mr. Wade. "Good-night, Benham. You are right; stick to that. Fathom the whole iniquitous scheme to its utmost depths."

He was gone, and the two lovers were again alone.

"You are going away," said Alana; "and from me," laying her head on his breast as she spoke.

"Yes; I shall go long before you are up." He placed his hands on her head, and pressed it against his heart. "There is much to be done, but with God's help I shall do it, and so effectually, that you will never after have anything to fear from those wretches."

"Do not go," she pleaded; "stay with me. Let them go their own way. They can not harm us."

He smiled, remembering how differently she had spoken only a couple of hours previously.

"No, dear," he replied; "I shall have to go. This specter must not have a chance of reappearing to trouble you. I shall try to lay it forever, and then—"

"Well, then," she said, looking up into his face, and smiling happily—"then I shall be your wife."

He bade her good-night, and going to his office, which had a telegraphic connection, he sent dispatches to Messrs. Smart and Eaton, hoping to get answers before his departure in the 8.30 train for Harrisburg, but requesting that replies might be also sent to him at his hotel in that city. He then paid a final visit to the forge, waked up his assistant, and gave him instructions relative to his duties during the ensuing ten days, and then went to bed, in the hope of getting an hour or two of sleep before it was necessary for him to be up. He did not sleep much, but at nine o'clock he was in Harrisburg, on his way to the Dauphin County Jail.

CHAPTER XIX

ARRIVING at the jail, Benham's first object was to have an interview with the man who could be most benefited by his influence. There was not much that he could do for Todd, who would certainly have to stand his trial for the homicide of his wife, and who would surely receive a sentence of several years in the penitentiary. But against Johnson it would be difficult to prove any very serious offense, though he had no doubt that some punishment would be awarded on the evidence that he should give. If, however, Johnson should exhibit a disposition to expose the conspiracy with which he was evidently connected, there was reason to believe that the district attorney would be disposed to deal gently with him. It was to him, therefore, that Benham decided to address himself more particularly, reserving Todd for any subsequent manipulation that might appear to be necessary.

Mr. Schwanger was not in an especially good humor when Benham sought an interview, for the purpose of getting authority to visit the prisoner. A man confined for some trifling offense had the night before committed suicide, under circumstances that ought not to have existed in a well-governed institution, such as was the Dauphin County Jail. As a consequence, Mr. Schwanger felt that he would be blamed by his superiors, and perhaps even deprived of his office. He was well acquainted with Benham, and ordinarily would have been delighted to oblige his visitor in the manner desired, but now he felt that it

was necessary to be unusually strict; so, notwithstanding
Benham's entreaties, he refused to allow him to see either
Todd or Johnson without an order from the district attorney, or one of the county commissioners. It was in vain
that Benham pleaded urgency, and want of time to hunt
up any one of the officials named. Mr. Schwanger was
obdurate. All his Pennsylvania German blood was roused
into obstinacy by the catastrophe that had occurred, and
reason was for the time being dethroned.

"It's no use talking, Mr. Benham," he said; "I know
very well that you won't kill either of the men, but who
knows that one or both of them might not commit suicide
the moment they saw you?"

"How can they?" asked Benham, angrily. "I shall
not give either of them a knife, or a pistol, or a dose of poi-
son, and it is to be supposed that they are not allowed to
retain a stock of those articles in their possession."

"No, I'll take my oath they haven't anything that
would kill a mouse, much less a man."

"Then, how in the world are they going to commit suicide?"

"I'll tell you: they might do it just by holding their
breath, out of pure spite. I knew a man do that once.
Todd's a desperate fellow, and I wouldn't trust him a minute; and as to Johnson, he's the smartest fellow that was
ever in this jail. I shouldn't be surprised if he could swallow his tongue."

"Swallow his tongue! What are you talking about?"

"Exactly what I say, Mr. Benham. I'm not a fool.
When I say 'swallow his tongue,' that's exactly what I
mean, and if you don't understand how a man, when he
wants to kill himself, swallows his tongue, so that it chokes
him, it's your fault, not mine."

"Well, never mind. I don't care anything about it.
Where does Mr. Dayton live?"

"He lives on Front Street, just above Market, but he's not in town. He went to Carlisle this morning, early, and won't be back till this afternoon."

"Where will I find one of the county commissioners?"

"You'll find one of them in Hummelstown, one in Highspire, and the other would be at his residence in Chestnut Street, if he hadn't gone to his brother's funeral, at Heckert's Gap. You didn't know that Christ. Mumma was dead, did you?"

"No."

"Well, I thought you didn't, else you wouldn't have asked where you could find Conrad. However, they'll be here with the coroner at eleven o'clock, and then you can see all three of them."

"And, in the mean time, I'll miss the train for Philadelphia at 11.30. I thought to find you a reasonable man; on the contrary, a more blindly obstinate person it has never been my misfortune to encounter. Here are all three of the conspirators in custody, and you doing your utmost to—"

"All three!" exclaimed Mr. Schwanger, interrupting Benham. "Who's the other?"

"Why, the woman, of course, who was here with them yesterday afternoon. You allowed her, a notorious criminal, to see these men; and you refuse me, whose only object is the furtherance of the ends of justice."

"What! Mrs. L'Estrange?"

"Yes, Mrs. L'Estrange."

"Who arrested her, and what for?"

"An officer from Philadelphia took her through here early this morning from the Susquehanna Iron-Works, as she happens to be the leading operator in the great diamond robbery at Philadelphia."

"Sarah Lammy?"

"Yes; otherwise 'Confidence Sal.'"

12

"And I had her here right in my very hands, and missed the chance of making five hundred dollars by arresting her! And then one of my prisoners hangs himself, and with a rope, too. If he had done it with his shirt cut into strips, it wouldn't have been so bad, for a jailer can't be expected to know that a man means to kill himself, and forthwith take away his shirt, and towel, and sheets, and so on. But, of course, the commissioners will want to know how he got a rope."

"How did he get it?"

"How the devil should I know? I suppose he brought it in with him. I had him searched, but no rope was found on him. Perhaps he had it sewed into the lining of his coat. They're up to all sorts of tricks; and now, to think that I should have missed the reward for Sarah Lammy! That sticks in my craw; and, if it gets out that she was here and I didn't know her when there's a full description of her hanging up in my office, I guess I'll never hear the end of it."

"No, I don't think you ever will, especially when it is known that you allowed her to communicate freely with her fellow-conspirators."

"I'll tell you what it is, Mr. Benham. I'll let you see them. You might make it unpleasant for me before the commissioners, but I'll trust to your generosity, and you may go up. Which one do you want to see first?"

"Thanks. I'll have a little conversation with Johnson first. I may not care to see Todd at all."

"Very well; follow me."

Mr. Schwanger led the way from the front building to the long extension in which the cells for prisoners were situated. Arriving at the one that had been assigned to Johnson, and which was on the lower tier, he opened the iron grating in the door and looked within.

"Johnson!" he called.

There was no answer.

"Johnson!" in a louder voice.

Still there was no response.

"I suppose he's gone to sleep," he said, taking his key and inserting it into the lock. "It's astonishing how these fellows do sleep. Making up for lost time. I guess." He turned the key as he spoke, but something in the result appeared to disturb him, for he suddenly gave the door a push and opened it.

"That's strange," he said, in a low voice. "I certainly locked it last night, and now I find it unlocked."

Hastily entering the cell, he looked around the narrow confines. There was no one in it but himself. "By Heavens!" he exclaimed, excitedly, "he's gone, and I'm a ruined man!"

He sat down on the one chair that the cell contained, and, covering his face with his hands, burst into tears.

"Everything's gone wrong," he sobbed, "and now this thing finishes me for good."

"Cheer up," said Benham, laying his hand on the man's shoulder. "I don't think this is your fault. He couldn't have got out without collusion with one of the keepers, and therefore I can't see that you are to blame. You are not expected to watch individually every prisoner under your charge."

"That's true, but I'll be held responsible. By George! I'll find out how he escaped, anyhow."

He went out of the cell and blew a whistle, the sound of which resounded all through the prison, and in an instant the guards were assembled on the gallery in front of the cell that Johnson had occupied.

"Who had charge of this division last night and this morning?" he inquired, surveying with no very pleasant look the half a dozen men that stood in a row before him.

"I had charge," answered one of them, "until five o'clock this morning."

"Did you examine the cells before you were relieved?"

"Yes, sir. Everything was right when I turned over the charge to Bell."

"Well, everything's wrong now. The prisoner in No. 11 has escaped, and either you or Bell let him out. Where is Bell?" But already the others had discovered that Bell was not present, and no one knew where he was. Inquiry revealed the fact that he had not been seen since he relieved his predecessor at five o'clock.

"Search the jail!" ordered Mr. Schwanger, at last thoroughly aroused, although knowing that it was too late for any good to be accomplished by seeking inside the prison. "Search the jail from top to bottom. They may not yet have left the building.—And you, Williams," addressing one of the men, "go at once and notify the chief of police. Request him to telegraph to all the neighboring towns, above all to Philadelphia, and then come back here at once so as to be ready to make your report in writing, in time for me to submit it to the commissioners. I don't think they can blame me for this affair, anyway," turning to Benham, who had all along remained a silent spectator and listener of what was going on, and apparently expecting a consolatory answer.

"No, Mr. Schwanger," said Benham, good-naturedly, "so far as I can see, you are not to blame for the treachery of one of your subordinates, and the consequent escape of one of your prisoners. I don't know anything, however, at present, that could be more unfortunate. He is a dangerous man—the most so of the whole gang."

"And that gang consists of Todd, 'Confidence Sal,' and himself?"

"Yes, so far as we know definitely; but I am afraid some of the men employed at the Susquehanna Iron-Works have been influenced by Johnson and Todd. They are both very specious rascals, and fully capable of imposing on the average workmen in forges and mines. You see how readily he succeeded in corrupting your keeper."

"He's one of the best talkers I ever knew, but he's nothing to 'Confidence Sal,' or Mrs. L'Estrange, as she called herself yesterday. You never met her, did you?"

"Yes, I spent the evening with her, and was present when she was arrested by the Philadelphia detective."

Without appearing to notice the look of astonishment on the jailer's face, he continued:

"I suppose you have no objection to my seeing the other worthy?"

"You can see him certainly, if he also hasn't escaped. I'm not sure of anything just now. I've trusted these scoundrels too much, and, as to the keepers, the most of them are only a degree better than the prisoners, and some of them are worse. I set out to teach myself, and as a consequence I had a fool for my pupil. I'll turn over a new leaf from this time on. I'll go down to Cherry Hill and get some lessons, and when I come back I'll rule this jail with a rod of iron as sure as my name's Schwanger— if," he added in a low voice, "the commissioners don't turn me out."

Again he led the way, Benham following, and ascended a steep flight of iron steps that connected the lower with the upper tier of cells. Stopping in front of one of the doors that opened upon a narrow gallery, from which one could look up to the skylight and down to the first tier of cells, he opened the grating and looked in.

"Well, what's up now?" inquired the occupant, coming to the grating and looking through it at his visitors.

"Nothing, only here's a gentleman that wants to see you for a few minutes."

"All right; but he can see me a good deal better if

you'll open the door and let me come out into the light.
A nice opinion he's likely to form of me, looking at me
through this hole ! "

" I guess his opinion of you is pretty much made up
already, and he's not likely to change it to your favor if
you had all the electric lights between this and Halifax
turned on to your face."

" Oh ! " exclaimed Todd, for the first time getting a
good look at his visitor and recognizing him, " it's you, is
it ? I don't see what you want with me," he added, sulk-
ily. " If it hadn't been for you, I wouldn't be here now."

" I am not so sure about that," replied Benham. " I
don't think you would have got away, and if I hadn't
stopped you when I did you might not have been here, but
you would quite certainly have been dangling by the neck
from a tree on Peter's Mountain."

" Oh, you think so ! Well, it's some satisfaction for me
to be able to inform you that I've more friends about the
Susquehanna Iron-Works than you think for, and that if
anybody dangled from a tree it might have been you and
not me."

Benham looked around him, and discovering that the
jailer had gone off, doubtless to continue his demonstrations against the fugitives, he said :

" I've not time to quarrel with you. You may find it
to your advantage to be honest with me. You are in a
tight place. You'll be tried for robbery from the person,
and for murder. Your best witnesses, your only ones, in
fact, on the latter charge, will be Miss Honeywood and
myself."

" And you both know that I didn't intend to kill my
wife."

" Yes, I think we do. Still, you'll get severe enough
punishment, although you may not swing. Judge Wilkins
has no mercy on fellows like you, and will give you the

full extent of the law. But I think, for all that, I can help you. I think if you will give me certain information that I have reason to believe is in your possession, the district attorney will consent to ignore the charge of robbery on which you would get at least five years in addition to your other sentence."

"If that's all you got to offer I'll hold my tongue. I'm one of those lamps that don't burn unless you fill it pretty full of oil. It doesn't make much difference to a man of my age whether he gets twenty or twenty-five years. If you want me to tell you anything, you've got to get me out of this place."

"That I can't do, and I'm free to admit that if I could I wouldn't. You're a great rascal, and you stand a good chance now of getting your deserts—you and your sister also."

"Who are you talking about?"

"About your sister, Sarah Lammy. You didn't know that she was arrested last night at Miss Honeywood's house, and that she is by this time safe in Moyamensing Prison?"

"You don't mean to tell me that!"

"Yes, I do. She made the attempt, and a very determined and shrewd one it was, too, to pass herself off as Miss Honeywood's mother. She was exposed, and Josephs the detective, recognizing her as 'Confidence Sal,' who perpetrated the late great diamond robbery in Philadelphia, arrested her."

"So that job's done for! Well, it will disgrace Miss Honeywood more than it will any one else, for my sister is her mother, and Sarah Lammy, as you call her, is my sister. Now you won't get anything more out of me. So you might as well take yourself off. You've got three of us in jail. That ought to satisfy you, though you aint' safe yet by a long shot!"

"No, I don't feel quite safe, now that Johnson is out."

"Johnson out!"

"Yes, he escaped early this morning."

"Escaped, and left me here?"

"He went off with one of the keepers; bribed him, I suppose."

"And left me here when he might just as well have taken me along!" He disappeared from the grating, and Benham could see him walking up and down his narrow cell, and hear him muttering words indicative of his anger at the neglect shown him.

"I'll tell you what it is," said Todd, at last, coming again to the grating, "he's served me a dirty trick, and I'll tell you all I know about him, at any rate. Now, come close. He's Tony Rackett," he continued, whispering into Benham's ear. "He's an escaped convict from Sing Sing, and has fifteen years to serve there yet for robbing a bank, and they're looking for him for another bank-robbery, too. All he cares for is money, and he'll risk his life or liberty for that any day. It's my opinion that he's gone back to your part of the country, and that you'd better go back too if you want to protect your own, and catch him."

"You think he has returned to the Works?"

"Yes, I'm sure he has. Now, you'll do me a good turn on my trial—you and Miss Honeywood—by telling the truth, when you might, by a very small lie, get my neck stretched; and there's strong temptation, I know, for you to tell it and finish me at once. Many a one in your place would so fix things as to hang me, and not damage his conscience much either. But you ain't that sort. I'll do what I can for you to bring Tony to grief, for he's served me a scurvy trick. I knew it was his plan to go right back to the Works and pick up what he could. There's good pickings in Miss Honeywood's house, and in yours, too, besides the safe in your office, where you keep the money for the payment of the men. Then he's bound to be revenged on you for bringing him here and preventing the first plan; so he'll set fire to your house just as like as not. He don't want to be bothered with women, so you needn't be afraid for Miss Honeywood. That was my idea about carrying her off, you know; and that's nipped in the bud, I guess. I think you'd better go just as fast as you can back to the Works, for it's my opinion he'll make things brisk up there by to-morrow if he has his way. I won't tell you anything about my sister. She's always been square with me, but Tony's a dirty dog, and I'll be even with him if I can."

Benham listened to this speech with rapt attention. What was he to do? To go to Montreal, with all that he held dear on earth exposed to the attacks of a ruffian, was not to be thought of; and yet he was by no means certain that Todd was not lying for the purpose of preventing further inquiries being made in the direction of his sister and her schemes. Apparently his better plan would be to return to the Works, and, preparing for Mr. Tony Rackett and his associates, await further developments. Or, better still, if the necessary information could be obtained from Todd, prevent them. One thing was clear to him, and that was that there was sufficient danger to make it inexpedient for him to go to Montreal.

"I guess I can tell you just about where Tony is now," said Todd, resuming his revelations after having observed the interest they had excited in Benham, "and if you choose you can nab him before he has a chance to start things. He's mighty sharp, though, and you've got to work against him with all the sense you've got, for he calculates exactly how his adversary will act in every possible case. The only way you can beat him is by not letting him know that you're about. Get him off the track as far as you're concerned, for you're the only one he's afraid of."

Benham again thought of what the man had told him. Apparently he was sincere; but, then, much observation had taught him that such scoundrels as Todd were always apparently sincere when they have an end to accomplish by hypocrisy. He could not quite make up his mind whether the fellow's obvious desire to have him return to the Works was due to the wish to save his sister from further investigation, or to a feeling of revenge against Rackett, and a consequent solicitude to secure the destruction of that person. He reasoned, however, that no great delay could ensue from the postponement of his visit to Philadelphia and Montreal for a few days, whereas, if he were absent, and Rackett should make a foray on the Works, the consequences would be in the highest degree direful.

"I'll trust you, Todd," he said, at last. "Give me all the information you can, and I'll act upon it, believing you to have told me the truth."

"I suppose, when it suits me, I can lie like other people," answered Todd, with a smile, intended to express frankness, "but this time it suits me to tell the truth. I know the country between Peter's and Berry's Mountains as well as if I had been born there and lived there all my life, for you see I made it my business, having little plans of my own, to study it. You'd better make notes of what I'm going to tell you, for, if you were to forget a single point, you'd miss the place."

"Haven't you pretty nearly got through with your talk?" broke in Mr. Schwanger, coming up the steps and beginning to speak ere he had got to the top. "I'm expecting the commissioners here now in half an hour, and I wouldn't like them to see you talking to a prisoner."

Benham went forward to meet him.

"Todd is going to give me some very important information," he said, "that is entirely in the interest of law and order. I have no objections to the commissioners being made acquainted with the fact. However, it is not likely that it will take him more than a few minutes to finish."

"Very well, I'll leave you alone. There's nothing to be found of Johnson or Bell. Williams reports that two men like them were seen by a policeman at half-past five this morning going toward the railroad. I've telegraphed to Philadelphia, but they probably took the Chicago express that passes here at 5.45, in which case they were in Philadelphia before we discovered their escape. I'd have given a thousand dollars rather than have had that fellow get away."

"So would I," said Benham, returning to the cell, "and ten times that and again ten times if I had it."

"Now," resumed Todd, "to find Tony, all you've got to do is to return to the Works, but to go back at night, and let no one—not a soul, if you can help it—know that you're there. Tony will have assistance, and his spies will tell him all your movements. I shouldn't wonder if they are on your track now. His place is not the one on Berry's Mountain. We took that for a special purpose that fell through. It's on the south fork of Powell's Creek, just where it makes a bend to the north to empty into the main stream, and not more than two hundred yards from the junction on the east bank. There's something of a hill there, and the creek winds round it, hugging it pretty close. Half-way up this hill is Tony's house, or rather, hut. It's built of stones and logs, and I guess was put up by the lime or charcoal burners when they were working at that place. You can't see it from the creek, for it's well concealed by a big spur that comes out of the hill right there. The best way for you to catch Tony would be for you to come down on him from the top of the hill rather than up from the creek. You'd better, if you follow this plan, stick to the road that, coming from

Dauphin, crosses Peter's Mountain, and reaches the valley just to the west of the Big Swamp. Then keep on the road, crossing Powell's Creek at Hoffman's, and keeping along the north bank till you come to a road that starts from a grist-mill. Don't take that road, but continue on along the creek till you reach a saw-mill. There you will find a road running almost due east. Follow it till you strike the south edge of the hill. Then you will be not far from Tony's place. You can go up the hill and strike him from above."

"That's all clear and very precise," said Benham. "I've got it all down here, and I shall act upon it within forty-eight hours. I know the country thoroughly, and shall have no trouble in catching your friend if he is where you think he is. I need not say," he continued, "that if you are true in this matter it shall not be to your disadvantage. I am not able to promise anything beyond my good will, and I think that of my friends, and that it will be exerted to obtain such an amelioration of your punishment as may not be inconsistent with the demands of justice."

With these words he left the gallery, and after a word of thanks to Mr. Schwanger repaired to his hotel. Here he found dispatches awaiting him from Messrs. Smart and Eaton. Both gentlemen confirmed the statements of Mrs. L'Estrange, or Sarah Lammy, relative to the late Mr. Honeywood's marriage, and informed him that affidavits to that effect would be immediately forwarded to Mr. Wade, as Benham had requested.

CHAPTER XX.

BENHAM was strongly impressed with the truth of Todd's statements, and of the value of the information he had received from that worthy, and an incident that occurred while he was in the act of reading the telegrams sent by Messrs. Smart and Eaton tended still further to increase his confidence in Todd's good faith. He was standing at the counter of the hotel-office with the telegrams in his hand, having just had them given to him by the clerk, when, happening to raise his eyes, he saw a man standing at the other end of the counter and regarding him very attentively. At ordinary times the circumstance would not have attracted his attention. He knew a great many people, and a still greater number knew him by sight at least. Besides, Benham was a striking-looking man, and was sure to be stared at more or less wherever he might go. But now his mind was so fully occupied with what Todd had told him that he determined to keep his eyes on the man. The idea that he might be watched by spies in the interest of the escaped prisoner, that had been suggested by Todd, occurred to him very forcibly. He therefore gave the man a good, steady look so as to get a notion of his appearance that would not be likely to fade out of his memory, and then he proceeded to read the telegrams. Each was long for a telegram, and of course of great interest to him, establishing the fact as it did that Mr. Honeywood had been lawfully although perhaps fraudulently married. For himself personally he cared nothing about the matter. Indeed, his love and admiration for Alana were so great that no extent of parental degradation would have diminished those emotions in the slightest degree. In fact, so far as he could determine from the analysis of his thoughts, imperfect as it was that he could make under the circumstances, he was inclined to think that he should, if possible, love her all the more for any ignoble origin that she might have had, and that he would feel happier in his love.

He was engaged with his telegrams, and had forgotten all about the man that had stared at him so fixedly from the other end of the counter, when suddenly he felt a slight cooling sensation on the back of his neck as though some one was breathing on it. Without moving his head he turned his eyes in the direction of a mirror that was nearly opposite to him, and there saw that the man was very calmly looking over his shoulder while pretending to light a cigar with a match, and was endeavoring to read the writing on the paper before him.

Benham's first impulse was to turn and seize the man, and to give him a lesson in decency in the shape of a good shaking or a sound box on the side of his head, but a moment's reflection was sufficient to convince him that policy required that a different course should be followed. Without, therefore, letting the fellow see that he had been observed, he folded up the dispatches and putting them into his pocket inquired of the clerk in a loud voice when the next train started for Philadelphia.

"The accommodation-train goes in half an hour," he answered. "It's made up here. It's as tiresome almost as a canal-boat, for it stops at every station."

"Yes, but I'm in a hurry to get to Philadelphia. It's now eleven o'clock. I'll have time to see a gentleman on business, and I'll be in Philadelphia by five o'clock this evening."

While this conversation was going on, Benham had

glanced every now and then at the man who he was now sure was a spy, and perceived with satisfaction that he was eagerly listening to what was being said. He congratulated himself on his forbearance in not having given him a castigation, and then went a short distance to the office of a prominent coal-dealer, with whom he had a business transaction to consummate, leaving directions with the clerk for his valise to be sent to the station in time for the 11.30 train.

Promptly at five minutes before the time for the starting of the train, Benham was at the station. He glanced around him as he entered the ticket-office, and was not at all surprised to discover, looking over the piles of books kept by the newsman, the identical person who had already shown so marked a desire to pry into his affairs. Benham stepped up to the little window out of which the ticket agent was looking, and in a loud voice, intended to reach the spy, asked for a ticket for Philadelphia. Then he entered the car of the train that was standing on the track, and, seating himself at a window, looked out. The man was there, on the platform, having evidently kept Benham in sight till he had seen him on the train and apparently bound for Philadelphia. As the train moved out of the station, Benham saw that the man turned and walked rapidly away in the direction of Market Street.

Benham had selected an accommodation-train purposely, with the object of leaving it at Middletown, the first station after Highspire, at which it stopped, and the nearest one at which he would be able to hire a conveyance to take him, by a somewhat roundabout road, back to the Susquehanna Iron-Works. He was well acquainted with the country, and it was his intention to drive through the roads to the east of Harrisburg, to Dauphin, a station on the Northern Central Railroad, and then, taking a late train, arrive at the Works somewhere in the middle of the night, trusting to chance and good management to escape observation.

Arriving at Middletown, he had no difficulty in hiring a buggy, a pair of horses, and a driver; and, in less than one hour, was on his way to Linglestown, at which place he proposed to take dinner, and to stop till the day was so far advanced as to allow of his reaching Dauphin, where he was well known, after nightfall.

As a boy, he had frequently traversed the fertile fields in the southern and eastern parts of Dauphin County, shooting quails—or partridges, as they are there called—and had many a time eaten and drunk at Mrs. Schupp's tavern. The good woman had known him well ten years ago, but he hoped that, with the lapse of time, he had become so changed, and her eyes so old, that she would not recognize him. For she was a famous gossip, and Linglestown was very near the base of the First Mountain, one of the ranges of which Peter's Mountain was another of the group, and it was not at all improbable that Johnson, or some of his gang, might be prowling about the vicinity, and likely at any moment to take advantage of Mrs. Schupp's hospitality. Besides, the rich farmers in the vicinity offered tempting baits for marauders such as they, and had already suffered from masked desperadoes, who, now that his attention was directed to the matter, Benham had no doubt were under Johnson's command. They could very easily make their headquarters on the north side of Peter's Mountain, and, coming down through Heckert's Gap and Manada Gap, prey on the inhabitants of the country between the mountains and the Swatara Creek, without any great fear of being caught.

It was near two o'clock when Benham drove up in front of the "Hoofnagle House," by which name Mrs. Schupp's hostelry was known. While the driver took the horses round to the stable behind the house, Benham entered the large apartment that served as sitting-room, bar-room, and office, and inquired of the young woman sitting there, and knitting a stocking, whether or not he could obtain refreshment for men and horses.

"Dinner's over two hours ago," answered the damsel, without raising her eyes or ceasing her occupation, "and mother's gone down to Schwenkfelder's."

"I'd just as soon you'd get me and my driver something to eat as have your mother get it."

"Would you? But you see it isn't as you like," still not stopping her task, or looking at him.

"No, it's as you like. Now, I know you've got a nice chicken, and some new-laid eggs, and fresh bread and butter, and some big potatoes in the spring-house, and in that cupboard."

"Sakes alive! how did you know all that?" exclaimed the girl, dropping her work, and for the first time condescending to look at her visitor.

"Oh! I guessed as much," answered Benham, smiling. "Perhaps," he added, with a view of getting as far as possible into the good graces of the young woman, "I've been here before."

"I shouldn't wonder. That's what frightened me. How do I know that you ain't one of those masked robbers that drive round the country in the daytime to hunt for good places to rob, and then come down at night and do the work?"

"I don't look like a robber, do I?"

"Well, I don't know about that," answered the girl, still looking somewhat frightened, but evidently acquiring confidence. "They say they're just as good-looking as other men. Mrs. Schwenkfelder saw one of them last night, though she was half dead with the scare."

"Was Mrs. Schwenkfelder robbed last night?"

"Why, goodness gracious! Didn't you know that?

Of course she was. All the spoons that her great-grand-
mother brought from Germany more than a hundred years
ago, and a cream-jug, that she wouldn't have taken a thousand dollars for. For it had once belonged to Martin
Luther's wife's mother, so they say; though," with a con-
temptuous toss of the head, "I don't believe them stories
much. Two hundred dollars in gold," going on with her
recital, "that they'd had ever since long before the war,
and that they kept when they might have got more than
two for one for it, and a thousand-dollar bond, to say nothing of a piece of silk, that she meant to have made up next
week, in time for the meeting of the classis in Harrisburg."

"How she did talk, after being fairly roused!" thought
Benham. Evidently she was a chip of the old block. He
recollected her as a yellow-haired child running about the
one long street in bare legs and feet through week-days,
and on Sundays appearing in all the glory of sky-blue
mousseline de laine trimmed with red bows, and a hat that
shone with all the colors of the rainbow. But that was ten
years ago, when she was eight years old, and answered to
the name of "Very," which was short for Veronica.

"You'll let me have that chicken and the other things
now, won't you, Miss Schupp?" he said, taking a seat as
though he intended to stay whether she did or not. "If I
were a robber, it isn't likely I'd ask you for anything. I'd
tie your feet to that chair and help myself."

"O Lord!" she exclaimed, jumping up from the
rocking-chair that she had kept vigorously in motion all
through the interview. "That's just what they did to
Mrs. Schwenkfelder, and old Mrs. Sloterbach who was in
the house, having come over from Wormelsdorf on a visit.
She's eighty-nine, and she goes all around the country
visiting her friends just as if she might be only nineteen.
Mrs. Schwenkfelder saw the face of one of the men as he
bent over her to tie her. He was a tall man, about your

height, I guess, and as broad-shouldered as you, only he wore dark clothes while yours are light, rather. He had a piece of black cloth over his face with holes cut for his eyes. While he was tying her, the cloth slipped off, and then she saw his face, all covered with a thick black beard, and with only two front teeth, one on each side of his mouth, just like, as old Mrs. Sloterbach said, as though they were mile-stones. Yes, I'll give you something to eat," proceeding as she spoke to set the table, "and she says she'd know him again if she was to see him a hundred years from now."

"I'm quite sure of it. That's a good girl. Now, Very, my dear, be as quick as you can, please, and—"

"How do you know my name is Very?" she asked, smiling at last, and showing a pretty set of teeth. "Are you acquainted about here?"

"I used to come out here to hunt. Many a partridge I've killed in Jake Hoofnagle's fields over there by Paxton Creek, and your mother has cooked them for me, too."

"I wonder who you are? May be you're one of them Albright boys from Manada Furnace. Only they're more stuck up than you are. If you wouldn't mind a cold snack, there's a nice cold roast chicken in the spring-house, and a bit of hog's-head cheese that George Kraus, who took tea with us last night, said couldn't be beat in Lebanon County. He's from Myerstown, in Lebanon County, and he just thinks we people in Dauphin don't know any-thing about housekeeping. But I guess we took him down a peg or two before he left, for he had to admit that our apple-butter was better than what his own mother could make, and she took the prize at the agricultural fair at Lancaster last year."

"By all means give us the cold chicken and the hog's-head cheese," said Benham, as soon as Miss Veronica's breath had given out, and she was forced to stop to give her lungs a chance to recuperate.

"Yes, it will save you half an hour's time, I guess, and then I'll make you some tea or coffee, whichever you like. There's a cold apple-pie, too."

"I shall dine like a king, and I'll take tea instead of coffee. I say, Very!"

"Well, what is it? I don't mind your calling me Very, because you began ten years ago," she went on, not waiting for an answer. "But when I was at school at Lititz—and I've only been home since June—everybody called me Veronica. The sisters thought Very was undignified."

"I wish you'd tell me something more about the robbery last night."

"Oh, I'll tell you all I know, and that's as much as any one knows, I guess. It was about one o'clock this morning when it took place. Four men were in it, all with their faces covered with black cloth just like the one that Mrs. Schwenkfelder saw. They didn't do any harm to any one except to tie them to chairs. Mr. Schwenkfelder is in Philadelphia; at least he was, but I guess he came back by the first train after he got his wife's telegram. Mother went down there as soon as she heard about it, and she hasn't got back yet, but Mr. Heydecker, our pastor, came by here an hour ago and gave me all the particulars."

"Did he tell you what kind of looking men they were?"

"Yes, one, the one that had the cloth fall from his face, was very tall, six feet five at least, so Mr. Heydecker said, but the others were rather undersized. The tall one was the leader, and one of the men he called George; by mistake, I guess, for he swore awfully just after he did it. After they had got all the silver and money and bonds they could lay their hands on, they went for something to eat, and sat down at the table and had a good supper. Then they went away, and this morning, when the hired man came to the house, he found the two ladies still tied to their chairs."

"Is that the only robbery that's been committed about here?"

"Oh, no! There have been half a dozen more during the last two weeks, and there are several detectives at work trying to find the robbers. But so far they haven't discovered a trace of them. One thing's very certain—they don't live near here. All the country this side of the mountain's been gone over."

By this time the table was set and the eatables placed on it in tempting array, and Miss Veronica, going to the back door, called the driver to come in and partake, which he did with an appetite almost as great as that that Benham was exhibiting. Never had chicken and hog's-head cheese tasted better than they did now; the bread was fresh and light, the butter sweet, and, if the tea might have been better, the delicious cream that Miss Schupp poured into it with a lavish hand gave it a flavor of its own that more than compensated for original deficiencies.

Then the horses were again hitched into the buggy, and Benham prepared to resume his journey. It was then about three o'clock, and he had at least ten miles to go, the greater part of the distance being over two ranges of mountains, and by not a very good road. However, he did not desire to get to Dauphin much before the passage of the train that was due at the works at 11.30. That was a freight-train, but there was always a passenger-car attached to the rear end of it, and it rarely carried more than two or three persons.

"I do wonder who you are," said Miss Schupp, in her most insinuating voice. "Ma'll be here now in half an hour, and she'll ask me who's been here, and I won't be able to tell her."

"Well, tell me," said Benham, smiling, "how much I

am indebted for the delicious repast you've given us, and the feed for the horses, and anything else that comes under the heading of food for man and beast, and then, if you'll promise not to tell anybody but your mother, I'll send you word this day week who I am."

"I suppose two dollars will cover everything; but it's ridiculous, the idea of waiting a week to know who you are!' I sha'n't care anything about it by that time. I suspect you're one of them detectives looking for the robbers. Yes, that's it! Oh, I'm sure, from your face! Well, to think that I was such a fool as not to see it the moment you came in."

"You're a good guesser, Very. Yes, you've hit it. I'm looking for the robbers. Give my love to your mother"—he handed her a two-dollar note as he spoke—"and tell her that she couldn't have treated me better than you have. The Hoofnagle House has never been better kept than it is now, not even when your father was alive. Good-by! I'll let you know when I find the robbers."

The buggy drove up to the door as he spoke, and he got into it.

"I half believe you're fooling me," she said, with a little laugh. "There's to be an apple-butter boiling here to-night, and there'll be lots of fun. You'd better stay, and then you can give your messages to ma yourself. Miss Maclay and her brother are coming from Harrisburg, and lots of ladies and gentlemen from Hummelstown and Manadaville. May be, if you'll stay, you'll get a chance to catch the robbers."

"No, the inducements are strong, but I shall have to tear myself away. Good-by!" The driver touched the horses with his whip, they sprang forward, and Miss Schupp, watching the retreating vehicle till it had passed the Winebrennarian church, re-entered the house, and be-look herself to the occupation of knitting, that Benham's arrival had interrupted.

As to Benham, the intelligence given him by Miss Schupp was well calculated to fill his mind with anxiety and fear. He had now no doubt whatever that Todd's story was not only true, but that that worthy had not revealed the one half of what he knew. He had told enough to lead, if prudently acted upon, to the discomfiture of Johnson, or Rackett, as he should now be called, but nothing more. A regularly organized gang of desperadoes existed, and the headquarters were in the immediate vicinity of the Susquehanna Iron-Works. As usual with such bands, they had not attacked the homes or property of those living near them, but had confined their depredations to the residents of more distant localities. Doubtless, however, as they exhausted the revenues of the well-to-do people living on the fertile plains south of the mountains, they would turn their attention to the no less wealthy inhabitants of the valleys, and especially to the Susquehanna Iron-Works, upon which they had no doubt long been casting covetous eyes.

It was not likely, he thought, that they would come down on the Works that night, and even if they did, highly improbable that their attempt would be made before midnight, by which time he would be at home, and in a measure prepared for them. Still, the idea of the danger to which his mother and Alana were exposed caused him a greater degree of uneasiness than he had experienced for many a long day.

As they drove along over the country road that ran almost due north from Linglestown, and that had almost from the start begun to rise in its ascent of the First Mountain, he began to lay out his plans for effecting the capture or destruction of Rackett's band. In the first place, his presence at the Works must be known to none but those upon whom he could depend, with absolute confidence in their integrity and efficiency. In his own house he intended that he would, if possible, let no one except his mother know of his return. He did not know to what extent, if any, the workmen had been tampered with, and, as the two women-servants of his establishment had acquaintances among them, he deemed it expedient to keep them in ignorance of his whereabouts.

As to Alana, he was in doubt, for a long time, how to act toward her in the matter. At first he thought he would take her into his confidence ; then, as some weighty objection to that procedure suggested itself to him, he determined not to reveal his return to her. Then, again, his inclinations would get the better of him, and he would decide that it would be unkind to her and to himself not to acquaint her with the fact of his presence at the Works. Besides, he argued, she was endowed with good sense, of the kind generally known as "common"—though why it should be called so is a mystery, seeing that it is comparatively rarely met with—and that her advice as to the methods to be adopted for defense and attack would be valuable. Finally, however, he arrived at the conclusion that it would be better, upon the whole, to keep her in ignorance of his return. The circumstances that turned the scale in favor of this conclusion were the facts that she had already suffered great anxiety and distress through these people ; that she now believed that her trials, so far as they were concerned, were nearly at an end ; and that to re-excite her fears would be to run the risk of making her seriously ill, especially as the matter was one that it might take several days to bring to a satisfactory termination.

Scarcely of less importance was the consideration of the effect that the knowledge that she was suffering would produce upon him, and the disturbance in his natural equilibrium that would thereby be produced. In dealing with such scoundrels as Rackett, it was indispensable that he should have all his wits about him, for there was no doubt that he would have to use them. Now, if he were to be subjected to the influence of the knowledge that Alana was alarmed for his or her own safety, he knew himself well enough to be conscious of the fact that his mind would not work with that degree of dispassionateness that was requisite for the success of the campaign upon which he was about to enter. No, she must know nothing of his arrival and stay at the Works till there was no doubt of the discomfiture of his and her antagonists.

This question settled, he gave himself no further anxiety on the subject of the detailed plan of procedure, except that he determined that he would, the first thing in the morning, send for Dr. Arndell and discuss with him the tactics to be employed. There were several employés whom he intended to take into his confidence, and who would constitute his attacking and defensive parties. This much he could settle now ; the rest must be arranged after a fuller knowledge of the circumstances than was now in his possession.

Up to this time he had made no effort to engage his driver in conversation. The man was a big, lumbering fellow, with the peculiar Pennsylvania-German build and cast of features constantly encountered in the middle part of the State, and with a like degree of mental stolidity to that possessed by his type in general. Like the rest of his kind he talked English, and without any notable peculiarity. Forty years before it was very different. Then there were many, even among the young of those living in the region in question, who either did not speak any other language than their peculiar *patois*, or, if they did speak English, did it with an accent that at once revealed their origin. At that time a large edition of the laws passed by the Legislature was printed in the German language.

Even high offices were filled by persons whose knowledge of the predominant language of the country was so imperfect that they were unable to obtain a clear idea, even if they had not been naturally stupid, of the matters submitted for their official action.

Thus, upon one occasion, a case of great importance was being argued at Harrisburg before a full bench, composed of the chief judge and two associate judges, who, strange to say, were not required to be lawyers. Indeed, if I am not mistaken, it was expressly provided by law that they should not be lawyers. The chief judge gave great attention to the case, and at the conclusion of the speeches of the lawyers announced his decision. It was observed that one of the associates, an old Dauphin County Pennsylvania German, was very diligently, apparently, taking voluminous notes upon sheet after sheet of paper, and the chief judge, a recent appointment, thinking to find a confirmation of the views he had expressed, turned to him and said:

"I should like to hear my learned brother's opinion upon the points involved."

"Vat vas dat?"

"Observing that you have taken full notes of the case, it would be a satisfaction to receive your views."

"Vat, dem?" pointing to the sheets of paper.

"Yes, your notes."

"Ah, mein Gott! dem ist nicht notes. I vas only drawing a cow."

Whether the driver, whose name was originally Schneider, but who was now called Snyder, was mentally "drawing a cow" or not, Benham soon discovered that he apparently had no idea on any subject, for he found it impossible to get a word out of him except "yes" or "no," and even those monosyllables he generally dispensed with by substituting for them a nod or a shake of his head. He therefore ceased trying to draw him into conversation, and, trusting to his own knowledge of the region of country through which they were passing, lighted a cigar, and allowed his taciturn companion to indulge in such reflections as his dull brain was able to suggest.

They had now reached the summit of the First Mountain without meeting a living soul. The road was rocky and ran through a dense growth of timber; but Mr. Snyder, whatever his degree of sociability, was a good driver, and gave his attention to his horses with an efficiency that argued strongly in favor of his faithfulness to the duties of the position in life to which he had been called. Descending the north side of the mountain, they crossed Fishing Creek, and then the valley between the First and Second Mountains, and then the ascent of the Second Mountain was begun. The road over the First Mountain had not been a bad one, although sufficiently rugged, but now they found that there was no road except such as had been made by wood-cutters, and that some care was required to keep in the right direction. Occasionally a wrong turn was made, but Snyder very soon detected the error and got back to the road that was a little better marked than any other, and that led almost due north over the ridge. The descent of the Second Mountain was not a matter of much difficulty, and ere long Stony Creek was reached. Here there was a well-kept country road that ran along the creek, crossing and recrossing it almost every hundred yards. It was well that the difficulties of the journey were in the main surmounted, for when they struck the creek it was quite dark, and travel over such a road as the one they had followed over the Second Mountain would have been impossible. Turning to the west, they skirted along the base of the mountain and on the banks of Stony Creek, till at about nine o'clock Benham found himself entering the precincts of the borough of Dauphin. It would be two hours and a

half before the train that he had contemplated taking
would be due.   What to do with himself in the interval he
did not know.   Suddenly an idea struck him.

"Are your horses fresh ?" he asked the driver.

"Yes."

"It's about six miles farther to where I want to go.
Can you drive me there ?"

"Yes."

"How much more shall I give you ?"

"Three dollars."

"Very well, then ; go on through Dauphin. Follow the
road along the Susquehanna till you turn the point of
Peter's Mountain.   Then take the right-hand fork, and in
five minutes afterward you will be at the Works.   You can
do it in an hour."

No reply was made to this, and, without further conversation, within the hour the light at the railway-station was
in sight.

"Now," said Benham, when they had arrived within a
hundred yards of the station, the road here running close
to the railway, "stop here, for I prefer to do the rest of
the distance on foot.   Here's your hire," handing him as
he spoke the sum agreed upon, "and here are five dollars
for yourself."

The man took the money, but said not a word in acknowledgment of the gift, except something that sounded
like "All right."   Then, Benham having descended from
the vehicle, he drove off rapidly in the opposite direction,
and was soon lost to sight and hearing.

For a moment Benham stood, undecided what course to
take.   By going to the right, he would be obliged to pass
near the forge, and run the risk of being observed by some
of the workmen.   By keeping to the left, he would have
to pass through the village street, and would be equally
liable to notice.   He could take a course midway between

these two roads, and one that would lead him in almost a direct line to his home, but it was through fields, and over ditches and ponds, and, as the night was dark, was not a very comfortable or even safe one. Nevertheless, he decided to follow it; so, climbing the fence that bounded the road on the farther side from the river, and with the flames pouring from the forge-chimneys to guide him, he plunged forward. Several times he stumbled and fell over big stones, and once got into a ditch that was half full of stagnant water; but, in less than a quarter of an hour, he was at his own door, without having been observed, so far as he knew, by a living soul.

CHAPTER XXI

AND then, just as he was about to let himself in with his latch-key, and make his arrival known to his mother, an idea occurred to him, which appeared to be so extremely natural, that the only wonder was that he had not conceived it before, and -that was, to go and stay with Dr. Arndell, and, making his headquarters with his friend, direct his campaign with a much greater likelihood of keeping his presence a secret than would be the case were he to stay in his own house. The doctor kept but one servant, and he was a man ; he took his meals at the tavern, and it could easily be arranged that food should be sent from that place, ostensibly for a sick friend under medical treatment. He looked at his watch, and, by the lurid light of the flames rising from the forge-chimneys, he saw that it wanted a quarter to eleven. The doctor, he knew, sat up late, and he had no doubt that he should find him, in utter disregard of the principles of sanitary science, smoking his tenth cigar for the evening, and looking forward with pleasing anticipations to the oyster-supper that it was his custom to cook for himself when the bivalves were in season, and to eat just before going to bed. He therefore descended the steps, and, turning sharply to the right, proceeded in the direction of Dr. Arndell's residence. On his way he had to pass directly in front of Alana's house. He stopped for a moment. All was still, and below all was dark. In an upper room, the one immediately over the drawing-room, and occupying the southeast corner, a light was burning. The blinds were down, and against one of them the shadow of a woman was projected, its outlines sharp and clean, as though she were sitting directly in a line between the lamp and the window. She was motionless, her hands resting in her lap, and her head bent forward, as though she were deep in thought. He kissed his hand to her. "God bless you, my darling!" he exclaimed, passionately. "Your dear heart is torn with fears and sorrows, but, with God's help, it shall ere long be filled with joy." He gazed fondly at the figure on the window-blind a moment longer, and was turning away, to resume his walk to the doctor's house, when he saw the hands of the shadow raised to the face, and held there as though their prototype were suffering an agony of grief. For an instant he was tempted to ring the bell, and reveal his presence to her, but, as he looked, the light was extinguished, and then he could see no more. In a few moments he was at Dr. Arndell's door.

Here he did not hesitate. He knew that the doctor's man slept over the stable, and that, when the physician was obliged to go out at night to any considerable distance, he was notified of the fact by a loud bell, the cord of which hung from the ceiling, near the head of his master's bed. The house-bell, after dark, was always answered by the doctor in person. Benham gave it a vigorous pull, and, in a moment or two, the door was opened, as he had supposed it would be, by Dr. Arndell himself.

"Good heavens, Benham!" exclaimed the doctor, a look of astonishment overspreading his face. "I thought you went to Philadelphia this morning. Has anything happened? Come in."

"Yes, a good deal has happened," answered Benham, as the two entered the doctor's cozy sitting-room, adjoining his office. "I started to go to Philadelphia this morning, but, in consequence of what I heard, I have come back, and one object I had in returning was to get your assistance in a matter of vital importance to us all here at the Works."

"Well, sit down and take a pipe, or a cigar, and a bottle of Bass, and tell me all about it. You know me well enough to have no doubt that I am at your service for any kind of aid I can give you. So that point is settled. Now, in order that I may be enabled to act intelligently, tell me the whole story."

"You're a good fellow, and I thank you with all my heart. The gist of the whole matter can be told in a few words. There is a band of robbers occupying a hut on Powell's Creek, a short distance east of the Big Swamp. I know the exact place. They have already committed several robberies in Lower Paxton and in East and West Hanover Townships. It is their design to attack us here at the Works, either to-morrow night or the night after. Their leader is the man Johnson, *alias* Tony Rackett, whom I captured and had sent to jail on a charge of conspiracy to burn my house, and, what you have not yet heard, to abduct Miss Honeywood and hold her for a ransom or to extract money from her. This morning he escaped from jail, taking one of the keepers with him, and is now doubtless with his gang. Todd, who was also a member of the band, gave me the most of these facts in revenge for Rackett going off without him. A spy was set to watch my movements, but I think I have succeeded in leading him astray. He thinks I am by this time in Philadelphia. I left the train at Middletown and drove here by way of Linglestown and over the mountains. No one in the world but you and my driver knows I am here, and he does not know who I am. I want you to keep me here in absolute secrecy while we plan and execute a campaign against the rascals, and I want you to take charge of one division of our forces, while I look after the other."

While Benham was speaking, Dr. Arndell's face, as the several pieces of information were given him, went through many different expressions. He had a warm-hearted and sympathizing nature, and was capable of forming strong attachments. He liked Benham, and he loved Alana, and the proposition therefore that was made to him at once found a ready response. Besides, he was of a decidedly adventurous disposition. Immediately after receiving his degree of Doctor of Medicine he had entered the United States Army as an assistant surgeon, and had passed the first five years of his professional life west of the Mississippi River, in almost continual warfare with the nomadic Indians of that part of the country.

Benham had made his acquaintance while both were in attendance on the course of instruction in the University of Pennsylvania, the one in the scientific and the other in the medical department. When, therefore, old Dr. Simpson, who had been the physician to the Works ever since Mr. Honeywood had founded them, took it into his head to marry a rich Boston widow and to go to that city to reside, Benham wrote to Dr. Arndell and offered him the vacant position. It was a good one, as those things go. The Works paid him twenty-five hundred dollars a year for attending the workmen, and he made a similar sum by his general practice. His expenses were not great, so that he was gradually accumulating money. To be sure, he had at first met with the strenuous hostility of his less fortunate rivals, through the spirit of trades-unionism that exists to a small but powerful extent in the medical profession, and that if it had its way would degrade a noble calling to the level of bricklaying and shoemaking. But he was an aggressive man, and when attacked he not only defended himself but attacked in return ; so that, ere long, it got to be regarded as a dangerous thing to throw stones at Dr. Arndell, for he was very likely to find the weak spots in his assailant's armor, and to direct his blows at them with a vigor that made itself felt.

It was the most natural thing in the world that a man with his mental organization should have great confidence in himself, but in his case this feeling was carried to an extent that reached the verge of absurdity. There was scarcely anything within the range of possibility that he did not think he could accomplish, and, as it often happened that his performance fell far short of his anticipations, he was somewhat in danger of getting an unenviable reputation for unreliability. Nevertheless, he did so much more than most other men with his opportunities would have accomplished, that those who knew him were very willing to excuse his failures in view of his actual accomplishments.

For several years he had been in love with Alana Honeywood, and, though she had never gone further with him than to treat him with politeness, he felt very sure in his own mind that he had only to ask her to be his wife in order to have her fall into his arms. He had not, for various reasons, asked her yet. The recent death of her father was one of these, and his love for his profession another. He could not yet quite make up his mind to retire from its active duties, as he probably would have to do if he married the mistress of the Works. But he had almost brought himself to view this step with complacency, if not with satisfaction, and he had determined that in the course of a month at the farthest he would request her to become Mrs. Arndell. As regarded Benham, he had not the slightest idea that there was anything to fear from that quarter. Benham, he had said to himself many times, was not a marrying man. Besides, he was so confident of his own powers to fascinate any woman to whom he should pay attention, with the view of matrimony, that he would have felt very little apprehension even if he had known that Benham was

also in the lists as a suitor for Alana's hand. He had at times
a little fear of Mr. Trevor. Clergymen, he admitted, had
great advantages, so far as subduing the average woman's
heart is concerned, over men in general. He had never
been called to see Alana professionally, whereas Mr. Trevor
had not only ministered to her on Sundays, and often on
week-days, at his church, but had also repeatedly called at
her house to offer her such consolation and strength as religion affords.

Still, for all that, Dr. Arndell had had opportunities
for becoming intimately acquainted with Alana far superior
to those afforded by ordinary social intercourse. Mr.
Honeywood's illness had been of long duration, and during
its continuance he had been thrown into very close and
even confidential relations with her. She had thus learned
to respect and like him for his ability, and for his kindness
to her and her father. And the doctor, on his part, was
quite sure that he had placed himself deep in her affections. Moreover, there had been repeated occasions like
that of Mrs. Todd, in which he and Alana had met at the
bedside of suffering humanity, and which had still further
served the purpose of causing them to like each other. He
had, therefore, entertained far less fear of Mr. Trevor as a
possible rival in Alana's affections than would otherwise
have been the case. He was quite sure that the clergyman
was madly in love with her, but he had after much observation convinced himself that her heart was untouched.
Like the generality of people, his judgment was better
when brought to bear on others than when it concerned
himself and his interests.

It did not take him long, notwithstanding the astonishment that Benham's communication gave him, to decide
how to act in the emergency that had come upon him.
He was ready to give his aid to the utmost of his ability,
and to act in accordance with Benham's suggestions. It

was not often that he was disposed to follow the leadership
of another, but in this case his friend's interests were so
much greater than his own, that he yielded to him the
direction of the details of the undertaking upon which
they were about to enter.

"Of course you can stay here," he said, "and no one
will be any the wiser. You can cook your own meals, or
they can be sent from the tavern. The latter will be perfectly safe, for I shall cause it to be understood that I have
a sick friend staying with me for medical treatment, and
no one will suspect who he is. I don't know that I ever
told you, Benham, but I am very much attached to Miss
Honeywood, and I am going to ask her to marry me. Of
course, therefore, I have an immense interest in trying to
get the upper hand of these scoundrels."

Benham reflected for a moment over these last words of
his friend. What was he to do? He had not, he conceived, any right to speak to a third party of his relations
to Alana without her consent. The engagement had not
been announced, and could not properly be by him till she
gave the word. And yet, unless he told the doctor how he
was situated in regard to her, he would feel as though he
were entrapping a man under false colors into a scheme
different from that that it appeared to be. He knew perfectly well that Alana would not marry Dr. Arndell. Was
it not his duty to say so? If he placed the matter frankly
before his friend, there might be immediate disappointment, but it could not be said hereafter that there had
been any false pretenses, or that he had acted in a disin-
genuous manner by allowing a self-deception that a word
from him would have prevented. The alternatives made
an embarrassing situation from which there was no escape.
Dr. Arndell had stated that the strongest inducement that
he had for assisting to defeat the machinations of Rackett
and his gang was his attachment to Alana, and his inten-

tion of asking her to marry him. He (Benham) knew that there was not the remotest prospect that such a marriage could take place. He knew that Alana had not the faintest spark of affection for Dr. Arndell. He knew that she loved *him*, and that she would be *his* wife ere many days had passed. Well, at any rate, so much of the truth as was necessary to undeceive his friend must be told him, and then he should decide anew whether or not he would assist in bringing the robbers to grief.

"Yes," he said, "you and all of us have an interest in defeating them, independently of any affection we may entertain for Miss Honeywood. No one who knows her can help loving her, I suppose."

"Oh, yes, but I love her very differently. I shall ask her to be my wife, and I have every hope that she will not refuse."

"But, my friend, she will refuse."

"You don't know her as well as I do. I know her inner life. I have been with her when her heart has been moved. I have condoled with her, have wept with her, and the man who has looked into a woman's heart as I have looked into hers, has gone far toward sounding still greater depths."

"I don't believe such things go for much when one of the parties is a woman whose father has just died, and the other is the family physician."

"My dear fellow, you don't know what you are talking about! I suppose that a physician, if of suitable age, and unobjectionable in other respects, can marry, if he chooses, any woman that comes under his professional charge. Miss Honeywood has never, however, been my patient. If she had ever occupied that relation to me, I should not think of marrying her. It's a low thing for a physician to do—fall in love with a patient. But there are bonds of sympathy between Miss Honeywood and me that can readily be

changed into bonds of love. On my part they are so
changed already, and on hers they will readily strengthen
when I speak to her of the affection I have for her."

"What an egregious ass the man is!" thought Ben-
ham; "consideration for his feelings would be wasted.
He never appeared to me before in such a ridiculous light.
I am almost sorry I came to him."

"I suppose," he said, aloud, "that if you were to hear
that Miss Honeywood is engaged to be married to another
man, you would be very much disappointed."

For an instant the doctor looked at his questioner as
though in doubt whether to be serious or amused. There
was something about Benham's way of putting the question that disturbed him, and yet the idea impliedly con-
veyed seemed to him so utterly preposterous that he could
scarcely restrain a smile. It did not take him long to recover his equanimity. His vanity was proof against such
an assault as this. He curled his mustache, which was
long and silken, while he answered :

"There is only one man that I have at times been ap-
prehensive might pass me in the race, and that is Mr.
Wade. Like you, however, he is not a marrying man.
Both of you will die old bachelors. But he has had excellent chances. As executor of her father's will, and her
lawyer, he has, of course, been thrown into very intimate
association with her. I am satisfied, however, that although he may be a little touched, she does not care for
him."

Was it not time to bring the man to his senses? Benham thought it was. At any rate, he would spare Alana
the annoyance of a declaration of love from a fellow whose
self-assurance and inordinate vanity would probably prevent his taking "No" for an answer.

And yet, notwithstanding this one disagreeable feature
in his character—one that Benham had never before ob-

served to be manifested to the like extent as on this night—Dr. Arndell was a man whom most people liked, for he possessed many sterling qualities that more than compensated for the single weakness. It was proper, therefore, that he should be dealt with gently, and be undeceived to just the extent necessary to free Benham from all suspicion of double-dealing, and at the same time show him that there was nothing more hopeless than the passion he might feel for Alana. To accomplish this last end would be a difficult piece of work, for, like other men in whom vanity is the predominating factor of their lives, he would not be likely to credit any assertion that tended to wound his self-love. However, that, after all, was a matter with which Benham need not greatly concern himself. He would do his duty when he told the truth.

"I don't think you need be afraid of Mr. Wade," he said, quietly. "My dear fellow," he continued, more earnestly, "I feel uncomfortable to hear you talk so confidently of winning Miss Honeywood's hand, when I know that there is not the remotest chance of your doing anything of the kind. Miss Honeywood is already engaged to be married."

"Impossible! There is no one here but you, the parson, and Mr. Wade, and I have already shown that any one of you three is out of the question. I don't think she knows a man in Harrisburg that she would be willing to marry."

"She is engaged to be married."

"You know that to be a fact?"

"Yes, I know it to be so, and I will tell you more, of course with the understanding that the information goes no further, at present—until, in fact, she chooses to speak of the matter."

"Very well," said the doctor, rather lugubriously, at the same time eying Benham rather sharply. "I shall say nothing about it, but I think I can decide who is the favored man."

"Yes, I am sure you can, and therefore it will not be necessary for me to say anything further on the subject."

For a few minutes there was complete silence. The doctor got ready a chafing-dish, and a great bowl full of raw oysters, and busied himself in making, with milk, butter, pepper, salt, and cracker-dust, a compound which, having brought almost to a boil in his dish, he proceeded to amplify by the addition to it of the juice of the oysters. Then, when the mixture was again near the boiling-point, he put in the oysters, and then, placing on the cover, allowed the contents to look after themselves, while he got a couple of big goblets, and opened a like number of bottles of his favorite ale.

During the entire course of his procedures neither of the two friends had spoken a word. The doctor's whole attention was apparently engaged with his cooking operations, and Benham was smoking a cigar, and watching the rings of smoke that he formed with great artistic skill, as they whirled round on their own axes and rose gracefully to the ceiling.

"Come," at last said the doctor, "you must be awfully hungry after your long drive. Sit up here, at the table, and give me your opinion of my culinary powers. As to this ale, if you don't like *it*, I shall think your gustatory sense has become paralyzed. Now," he continued, as Benham drew up at the table, "there's no time to be lost in dealing with these scoundrels up the valley. It's my opinion that we should make a reconnaissance this very night. What do you say?"

"What do I say? I say that you are one of the best fellows and truest men that ever lived!" exclaimed Benham, rising and grasping the doctor's hand.

They looked each other in the face for a moment. It

was evident that now there was no danger of a misunderstanding.

"That may be," replied Arndell, "but I will add 'and one of the damnedest fools!' Now sit down. This stew is perfection, if I can judge by the look of it and by the odor, and, when we have refreshed the inner man sufficiently, we'll go out on our little tramp, unless you have some better plan to suggest."

Evidently the doctor had not been so deeply in love as he thought, or else he had got out of it very effectually: or, again, was managing to conceal in a thorough manner any chagrin or disappointment he might feel. Benham was disposed to think that all three of these conditions existed. At any rate, his friend had not apparently been seriously wounded by the announcement that had been made to him. He had undoubtedly been profoundly astonished, in fact almost stunned, by the reception of information that was so totally at variance with his preconceived ideas. He had not spoken, because he could not speak: but he had disposed of his accumulated nervous force by busying himself with the preparation of the supper. Under like circumstances a man will take a run around the block, a semi-hysterical woman will twitch her fingers, or beat a tattoo on the floor with her heels. In each instance the balance is restored, and an explosion is prevented.

"I have a barrel of oysters sent to me from Baltimore every week," said the doctor, after Benham had begun to eat of the stew, and had pronounced it the best he had ever taken. "I'm writing a paper on 'Brain-Work in its Relations to Food,' and so far, it appears to me from my experiments, that more and better thoughts are produced from oysters than from any other article of diet. I eat two hundred and fifty a day, and take nothing else, except three small bottles of Bass's ale."

"Very well," said Benham, smiling at the idea of such

rank materialism as that announced by the doctor, though
for all he knew it might be entirely correct. "I am glad
you are in such fine condition for elaborating a plan of
operations for to-night. Now, suppose you enlighten me
as to how we ought to proceed against the enemy?"

"I would do nothing to-night," answered the doctor,
evidently much pleased with the confidence that Benham
appeared to place in him, "but to go up there very quietly,
and find out exactly how the land lies, and get some idea
of the number of rascals we shall have to fight. Of course,
whenever we make our onslaught, we should have enough
force to crush out all resistance. This is not to be a contest for glory. We don't want to get hurt, and we do want
to kill or capture the whole crew."

"We had better act under the authority of the law,"
said Benham. "I shall go to-morrow and make a deposi-
tion before Squire McElroy, and get him to send Spriggs
the constable with me, and to appoint our whole party
special constables. In this way we shall be sure to be right.
Otherwise we shall be, I am inclined to think, a band of
marauders."

"Does Miss Honeywood know anything of this?"

"Nothing."

"Does she know that you are here?"

"No; she supposes me to be in Philadelphia."

"Are you going to tell her anything about it?"

"No. I do not wish to cause her anxiety."

"She's a brave woman. She does not know what fear
is. I have seen her with small-pox and scarlet fever, and
typhoid fever, yes, and typhus all around her, and she moving as calmly about the room as though she were at a ball
or a Sunday-school. My God, what a woman she is! I
wonder if you know her as well as I do, if you have watched
her windows all night only to feel that you were looking at
the place where she was sleeping; if you have dreamed of

her night after night, and then, unable to sleep, have got
up in the dead of winter and walked all over the mountain
till daylight came, and all because you found she did not
love you! I have done all this, and yet she does not know
it; and while I, like a fool, rested in fancied security, you
have stepped in and, without an effort, have carried her
away from me forever. My God, it is hard!"

It had come at last. He had kept back the torrent of
his passion till, in an unguarded moment, he had mentioned her name, and then recollections had been evoked
that had broken through all the barriers he had raised, and
let loose a flood of emotion that carried everything before it.

Benham was astounded. It was a revelation to him,
and one for which he was altogether unprepared. What
was he to do? He could not speak of his love and devotion, as Arndell had done. His whole soul revolted at the
idea. He could not cite feeling for feeling, and act for
act, in a contest to determine who loved her the most. He
could not speak of his wakeful nights, his hopes, his fears,
his battles with himself, and of his final victory. To do so
would be a sacrilege that, rather than commit, he would
tear the tongue out of his mouth!

He was sorry for the man that had loved and lost, and
he respected the honest passion that showed itself in every
word and action, and that had so grandly assumed the
mastery. The man that could feel as Arndell evidently felt,
could not be deliberately false. He was worth keeping as a
friend at almost any cost, and Benham determined to keep
him if possible.

"Ah! my friend," he said, "I know now that you suffer. I can say nothing to comfort you. Your own manly
nature will bring you the solace that you need." He arose
from his chair and held out his hand to Arndell. "Good-
night," he continued. "I—"

"Sit down, Benham," said Arndell, taking the hand that was offered him and clasping it warmly; "I will take your hand, but not to bid you good-night. Forgive me, forget all that I said just now in a moment of insanity. You are the best friend I have in the world, and I don't mean to give you up. We have work to do for her, and it is kind in you to let me have a share in it. Of course, she never cared for me, or she would not have consented to marry you. That's common sense. You are not the man to be satisfied with a half-love, and she is not the woman to give you anything less than her whole heart and soul. If she had loved me, I could have made her happy; but she did not, and now you will make her happy. I think I must be of a very badly balanced mind, and certainly a very unobservant one. I shall continue to love her all my life, but I shall love her loyally and honestly, and none the less for her being your wife. That's all. Don't say anything more, please, but put on your hat and overcoat, and let us go on our tramp up the valley."

CHAPTER XXII.

It was nearly twelve o'clock when the two friends left the doctor's house on their tour of observation. The distance that they had to traverse was about six miles, and it would probably take them something over two hours to accomplish it. The night was a dark one, thick clouds obscuring the sky, and taken in conjunction with the north-east wind that was blowing, and the coldness and dampness of the atmosphere, betokening a snow-storm. They had passed by the forge and all the outlying buildings, without either Benham or Arndell venturing to speak. Each seemed to be fearful that, if a word were spoken, it might lead to the introduction of a topic that each deemed it safer to avoid. The road ran along the northern base of the mountain, past the little hamlet called Matamoras and the somewhat large one known as Enterline, and generally following the line of Powell's Creek. They had not met a single person, and all the houses that they passed were dark. Occasionally, a dog barked as they went by a farm-house, or a country store, but the noise did not suffice to disturb the sleepers in the dwellings. They could not have been more alone if they had been walking on the great Western prairie, instead of through the center of one of the most populous counties in the State of Pennsylvania.

At length they arrived at the little stream that emptied into Powell's Creek, and that is known as the South Fork. They crossed it easily, by stepping from stone to stone, for there was but little water in it; and then they found themselves in the triangular piece of ground between the two creeks, and in face of the hill, upon which, according to Todd, Rackett and his gang had their habitation. Here they stood for a moment or two, each endeavoring to determine in his own mind the course of procedure, and thus, if possible, to avoid any lengthened discussion of the plan of operations.

But they were not allowed much time for reflection, for, while they were cogitating on the matter before them, they heard the sound of voices, coming apparently from their right, as though of persons descending the mountain. There was no road at this point, but there was a foot-path that had been made by a family, that had several years previously inhabited a house, that stood on a plateau half-way up the mountain, and which they used when they had occasion to descend into the valley. The house had been allowed to go to ruin after the people had moved away. In fact, it was never anything more than the flimsiest kind of a structure, and the elements had played sad havoc with it from its foundation to its roof.

From this house, south, over the mountain, there was a good wagon-road leading into the valley between Peter's and the Third Mountains, and therefore constituting the main thoroughfare by which the dwellers kept up their communications with the world at large. Benham, who was well acquainted with the building and its surroundings, at once came to the conclusion that it was probably used by Rackett and his band as a stable for their horses, and this opinion was confirmed by the remarks that were made by the people who were approaching, and that also served to reveal their identity as members of the gang. He and his friend had barely time to step aside behind a large bowlder, before the parties were near enough for their conversation to be distinguished.

"I thought the gray horse went a little lame coming

up the mountain," said one of the men. Benham started, for he recognized Johnson's or Rackett's voice.

"Yes," was the answer, "he cast a shoe going down, and the road's so devilish stony that I suppose it made his foot tender."

"Well, be sure and have him shod the first thing in the morning, for to-morrow night there will be some hard work for him and the other horse, as well as for us."

"All right, captain ; and, while I'm at it, I guess I'd better have the harness looked to. It's likely to be strained, for we may have to travel pretty fast."

"Yes, only be careful not to excite suspicion. What do the people around here take us for ?"

"Why, they don't think much about us, I guess. You know there's only four of us, including you and Bell, and you only came to-day. Before that there was only Jinks and me, and we passed for a couple of hunters from Balti-more, come up to shoot partridges and wild turkeys. We didn't have any trouble in getting all the people about on our side, for we paid 'em well for everything, and hired this place, and the house up the mountain, for twice as much as they're worth. They're an awful stupid lot, these Pennsylvania Dutchmen."

"Yes, they haven't sense enough to come in when it rains. If they had, they'd have bounced us long ago. I shouldn't be surprised if Jinks was sound asleep."

"He's pretty tired, for you see he was up all last night, and that pain in his face kept him from sleeping to-day. But he said Davis, Fox, and McCaffrey were coming up to-night to divide the swag they got at Linglestown. That was a pretty good haul, captain."

By this time the three men had passed the bowlder, be-hind which Benham and Arndell were hid, and had as-cended so far up the hill that their conversation was no longer distinguishable. Benham had, however, obtained

some information that astonished him, the chief of which
was the statement, made by one of the gang, that men
named Davis, Fox, and McCaffrey belonged to their organization, for these were three of his best workmen.

From what had been said, the two friends were led to
the conclusion that there were four men that lived in the
house on the hill, two of them being Rackett and the one
who, with him, had just gone up the hill, and the other
two being the one named Jinks, and the jail-keeper who
had assisted Rackett to escape. Besides these four were
the three forge-men, making seven in all as the probable
number that would constitute the attacking party on the
Works, if they got the opportunity of making their contemplated foray. Evidently, from the remarks made in
regard to the horses, it was intended to make the attempt
on the following night.

They might have returned home, content with the
knowledge that had been so easily obtained, but Benham
was of the opinion that the men from the forge were in the
house on the hill, and that not only was it desirable to settle the question of their identity, but that still more valuable information would be obtained were they to ascend
the hill, and, if possible, get a peep into the interior of the
building occupied by the marauders. Arndell was at first
disposed to think that the result would not be worth the
risk. "We have no arms," he said, "and those fellows
are walking arsenals. I am ready to fight them if there is
anything to be gained by doing so, but then I want something to fight with."

"Yes, we ought to have brought pistols with us; but,
although we are unarmed, there is so much to be gained
by seeing something of those fellows in their den, by hearing something more of their talk, that I think we should
make the attempt to observe them a little more closely. If
we can get a good sight of their faces, we shall be able to

swear to them, for I suppose we shall arrest them to-morrow some time before they make their contemplated onslaught. An ounce of prevention is worth a pound of cure."

"How do you propose to get at them?"

"Go round the hill and ascend it from the other side. There may be others of the party out who will probably come up by this path, and who would, if we were on it, come across us. There is a good path by which we can reach a point considerably above them, and then we can descend to the house. If we should be surprised, we can get away with ease, for the night is dark, and we know the country; and, besides, they would be very careful not to alarm the neighborhood."

"Very well, I am with you. I think you are right. It would certainly be a great satisfaction to get a good look at their faces. Come along!"

Slowly, and with the utmost care, to avoid making a noise, Benham and Arndell passed round by the left so as to get on the north side of the hill, and then taking the path that led up to the top, they still more carefully began the ascent. Neither spoke a word, for each was impressed with a sense of the necessity of taking every possible pre-caution to avoid detection by men whose senses were, from the nature of their lives, always on the alert against dan-ger. Arndell was especially cautious. His experience of army-life on the frontier in Indian hostilities had furnished him with many valuable lessons. So very careful were the two amateur detectives, that fully half an hour elapsed before they reached the point above the house from which the descent was to be made. The distance now was short, not over a hundred yards. It was even more necessary, however, than it was before, to be vigilant, for the slightest noise, such as that caused by stepping on a dry branch, or by a loose stone rolling down the hill, would certainly give

14

the alarm, and put a stop to further investigation. All, however, went well, and in a few minutes they found themselves on a narrow platform, with the log hut not ten feet distant from where they stood.

The door was on the opposite side, but on that facing them were two windows in each of which a pane of glass had been broken, and the opening closed with some old rags stuffed into it loosely. Through these windows the light from a large fire, and from several candles, came out, as did also the subdued sound of voices. Making a sign to Arndell to approach one of the windows, Benham went to the other, and standing back a short distance so that his face could not be seen by the inmates of the room, he looked in.

Yes, there were seven men, and to his great regret, for the fact caused a shock to his confidence in human nature, three of them were workmen from the forge. He knew them well. They were as good artisans as he had under him, and, if he had been making up a party with which to attack the robbers, he would probably have selected these three to be of the number—Davis, Fox, and McCaffrey, married men, men with children, who had a good stake in society, and who had over and over again been the recipients of Alana's bountiful kindness. The doctor had also recognized them. He did not speak, but Benham saw him shake his fist at the men, and could see the flash of anger on his face.

The three forge-men sat together in front of the fire, smoking their clay pipes, and watching attentively the four others who were seated around a rough table playing cards. One of the four was Rackett; the others, Benham took it for granted, were Jinks, Bell, the late keeper, and the man who had just returned with Rackett. On the table were various articles of silver-ware, such as forks, spoons, knives, napkin-rings, and cups of different kinds, for which the men were gambling. A candle stood at each corner, and in the middle a big jug, from which they drank in rotation, and which was passed to the three forge-men who sat by the fire.

So far the conversation, which each of the observers could hear with distinctness, related to the game that was being played. Apparently Rackett had been most successful, for the largest pile of silver lay at his place, and he seemed to be in a better humor than the others. At last they all threw down their cards, and Rackett gathered all the remaining articles into a heap, and added them to the already large pile at his side.

"Now, boys," he said, "to-morrow night you'll have a chance to win all this back, and I'm pretty sure you'll do it. I ought to have some reward for my sufferings during the last few days. Look at these hands!" holding them out as he spoke, and exhibiting the abraded knuckles to his sympathizing friends. "If I only had the fellow here that did that, I'd take the skin off of his whole body! You know him, Jinks, don't you?"

"Oh, yes!" answered the man addressed, rising as he spoke, and showing himself to be a remarkably tall person, probably, thought Benham, the one who had led the band that had robbed Mrs. Schwenkfelder—"oh, yes, I know him by sight."

"Well, don't forget that I want to catch him alive! I want to pay him up for these knuckles. Besides, if we follow the plan I've thought of, we'll not only catch him, but we'll get him out of the way; and he's more to be feared than any one else at the Works."

"That he is!" exclaimed one of the forge-men, Davis. "I seen him once knock a man down for striking at him, and the cove never got up on his feet for over an hour."

"Very well, we'll take care that he doesn't knock any one of us down. Now, men," he continued, "this is the

last time we'll all be together till we meet to-morrow night
to strike our blow. So listen to what I've got to say. You
—Davis, Fox, and McCaffrey—will remain at work at the
forge till the clock strikes twelve. You will then go to
Benham's house ; two of you remaining hid behind the
bushes to the left of the path that leads to the door, while
the other knocks and tells Benham that he is wanted at
the forge."

"I'll go to the door," interrupted McCaffrey. "I'll
tell him that the blast-pipe has fallen down. That'll fetch
him out mighty quick !"

"Very well," said Rackett, approvingly ; "that will do
first rate. Then, while he's going to the furnace with you,
Davis and Fox will jump on him from behind, and each will
give him a whack on the head hard enough to knock him
senseless. Leave him there, and he will be properly taken
care of by Bell, who will pitch him into a wagon that will
be ready and drive off like the devil. Then you will go to
the office and serve the watchman there in a like manner.
You will be joined there by Jinks, Hopkins, and me, and
you will then receive further orders."

"All right, captain !" said Davis. "You'll find us
true blue. Will you want any tools ? You know we work
in the blacksmith's shop, and if you want anything in our
line we can fetch it along."

Rackett looked contemptuously at the man. "Tools !"
he exclaimed, at last, "as if such clumsy things as you
work with would be of any use in opening a burglar-proof
safe ! No, I've got my own tools, and, what's more, I know
how to use them, too, and so do Jinks and Hopkins.
And—"

He stopped and appeared to be listening, while a look
of apprehension passed over his face. "Boys," he said, in
a voice too low for either Benham or Arndell to hear
"there's somebody outside watching us. Don't let on that

I've said so, but keep up the talk. When I lay my hand on the table, do you, Jinks, say in a loud voice, 'The fire's going out.' Then I'll say, 'I'll go for an armful of wood.' Leave the rest to me, but, if you hear me call, rush out as fast as the devil will let you and seize the spy!"

"Yes," he continued, in a loud tone, "I think we've got things laid for a very successful job to-morrow night. Then we'll be off to the Alleghanies. There's lot of good picking about Cresson and Altoona, and we'll leave a light behind us that will show us the way!

"There are two of them," he went on, in a voice not much above a whisper, while at a motion from him that no one not in his confidence would have perceived, Jinks went on talking in a loud key—"one at each window! I heard them breathing. Our lives depend on prompt action." As he spoke these words, he laid his hand across the corner of the table nearest to him.

"Hello!" exclaimed Jinks, "we've let the fire go out," rising at the same time as though to go out for wood.

"I'll get the wood," said Rackett; "I want a little fresh air. This room's as full of smoke as a smoke-house."

"Keep quiet," whispered Benham to Arndell, as he heard those words, and saw Rackett move toward the door. "The wood-pile is at the front of the house. He's not likely to come round here. There's more of their plot yet to be revealed."

But the words were scarcely out of his mouth before, with a yell, a man dashed around the corner of the house, and, throwing his arms around him, held him in a grip that prevented him exerting his strength, while almost at the same moment a half-dozen men were on the spot, and he was seized and held so securely that resistance was out of the question.

"Run!" he exclaimed to Arndell, as soon as he perceived the situation of affairs. "Never mind me; get off as soon as you can!"

Arndell gave one look at the struggling mass of humanity about Benham. Somehow or other he had been overlooked, every man rushing to the assistance of their leader. He saw that he could do nothing, but it was still possible to thwart their schemes, so he dashed down the hill at the top of his speed, and in a few moments was out of reach.

"Damnation!" cried Rackett, "why didn't you seize the other man? Now everything's spoiled, and we'll have the whole country at our heels in an hour!" He looked around him as he spoke. "I thought so," he continued; "those forge-men have taken themselves off already. We'll probably find them leading our pursuers. That was Todd's work, getting them in. Damn him! I'm glad I left him in jail."

"Well, we've got this fellow safe enough, anyhow," said Jinks, with a laugh.

"What use is he, I'd like to know, when the other one has got off scot-free, and is half-way to the Works by this time, and stopping at every farm-house to give the alarm? We'll get away at once. You, Hopkins, go up as fast as you can to the stable and hitch in the horses. Wait there till we join you. You, Jinks, put away all the plunder, except the money, in the place we agreed upon; and you, Bell, if you've tied that eavesdropping rascal tight enough, drag him into the house till I take a look at him."

Bell, who had wound a rope around Benham's body, while Jinks and Hopkins held him, thereby fastening his arms securely to his sides, seized his prisoner by the legs, and dragged him into the room.

"By George!" exclaimed Rackett, with a laugh, "that reminds me of the way a fellow served me the other day. Hand me that candle and let us see who he is."

Benham lay on his back, and Rackett, taking the candle stuck into an empty bottle for a candle-stick that Bell gave him, bent over and held it close to the captive's face.

He started, as he recognized the man who had made him a prisoner a few days ago.

"So, my good master!" he exclaimed, "I've got you, then, have I? Now my time's come, and, if I don't get even with you, may I never have a moment's happiness in this world, or in the world to come!—Here, Bell, gag him so that he can't make a sound. Then you and I will carry him up the hill to the wagon, for I'm going to take him along, to deal with at my convenience.—Hurry up, Jinks!" to that worthy, who had taken up the floor in a corner of the room, and was filling a large hole with silver-ware and other valuables. "Cover those things over with a bushel or two of earth before you put down the floor again. We can come for them at any time. Hurry, for God's sake! we haven't a moment to lose! Now," as Bell, having fastened with a broad leathern strap a thick pad of raw cotton over Benham's mouth, rose to his feet, "catch hold of this gentleman's legs. I'll take care of his arms, and we'll walk away with him easily enough.—Damn you!" he continued, shaking his fist in his enemy's face, "I'd drag you all the way up the mountain if I wasn't just now in a hurry. I'll begin with you to-night, though. Oh, you may laugh!" as a smile passed over Benham's face. "You won't feel much like laughing when I begin on you, I guess.—Now, Jinks, if you're ready, come along!"

He and Bell took hold of Benham, the one by the legs and the other by the shoulders, while Jinks, gathering together a lot of wraps of various kinds, took the lead up the path to the house that they had converted into a stable. The ascent was not very steep, but Benham was not a light weight, and before they reached their destination Rackett was obliged to give up, and to call for Hopkins and Jinks to take a hand. In a few minutes the natural terrace on which the stable stood was reached. The wagon was ready, Benham was incontinently pitched into it, where he lay upon the bottom, and then the men entering, with Hopkins as driver, the vehicle, drawn by a pair of stout though perhaps tired horses, was pulled up the mountain as rapidly as the circumstances permitted. Arrived at the summit, the road turned sharply to the east, and the wagon followed it, going, now that the ground was more favorable for rapid traveling, at a greatly increased rate of speed.

"We shall have to give up all idea of going to Cresson and Altoona now," said Rackett. "What we have to do is to strike for the upper part of the county as fast as possible. There we have friends who will look after us, and there we shall be safe from any pursuit that may be made."

"I suppose," remarked Jinks, in a whisper, not intended for Benham to hear, "that we'd better go to Sykes's on the Big Lick Mountain. We'd never be looked for there."

"That's what I mean to do," answered Rackett, also in a low voice. "I wonder," he added in a louder tone, "who the other fellow was? He," jerking his head toward Benham, "wouldn't tell, even if the gag was off of his mouth."

"We're pretty safe from any rumpus he can raise. Before he gets back to the Works we'll be ten miles on our way, and not far from twenty from where he'll be. And he can't have an idea of the direction we have taken."

"Oh, we're safe enough now. We're four miners going to Pottsville. As to our friend here, he'll keep silent enough, I guess, till I do something to him that will make him speak. It's damned hard, though, that we've got to give up, for the present at least, the best prospect that we've had for many a day!"

"Yes, and to run for our lives like a lot of—"

"Oh, well," exclaimed Rackett, resignedly, "the good dog, if he does not hunt to-day, will hunt to-morrow; and, though the wolf may lose his teeth, he doesn't change his nature. We'll come to the top some of these days."

"You're a philosopher, captain."

"So was my father before me. In fact, Jinks, to use a common expression, I've seen better days. But I've had all the chance I want for studying philosophy, and not out of books, either, though I could once hold my own even there with the best of them. There's a matter now on my mind that's enough to start all the thinking power a man's got. You told me this afternoon that Squibb had come in and reported that that man lying there had gone to Philadelphia. If he went to Philadelphia, how does it happen that he is here now? And how did he know where we were? Evidently he fooled Squibb somehow or other."

"That's clear enough. Now, how did he find out anything about us?"

"We don't have to go far to settle that point. Either Squibb is a traitor—and he's just as likely to be as not, for I've suspected him for some time—or Todd has told on us. Neither of them is to be trusted, but I'd rather pin my faith to Todd than to Squibb. The name's enough for me. By George! I'm so anxious to know who the traitor is, that I've half a notion to let the man go, if he'll tell me who gave him his information."

"I'm clearly in favor of letting him go anyhow. We're sure to find him troublesome, and, as to killing him, you know we never take life unless in the most absolute self-defense."

"I don't mean to kill him, but I'm going to give him something to remember me by. Look at my hands! That's his work, damn him!"

"If you were to throw him out of the wagon, tied and gagged as he is, you'd punish him enough and save us a good deal of trouble. It's dangerous having him along.

He has to be watched all the time, and we want all our attention for ourselves."

"Well, I'll think about it. As you say, it's dangerous keeping him. We've got to stop at the first blacksmith's and have the gray horse shod, and, if any one was to look into the wagon, it might start the devil after us. Wait till sunrise. There's no danger now, at any rate."

"He couldn't do us any harm, now, if we should leave him here on the mountain. If you want to revenge yourself on him, tie him to a tree and give him a hundred lashes on his bare back. He'd be sure to remember you for that as long as he lived, and, in my experience, these fellows like him hate of all things to get a blow with a whip."

"That might do," said Rackett, reflecting. "I must do the best I can. Where the devil can't put his head, he must put his tail."

CHAPTER XXIII.

THE one glance that Dr. Arndell gave at the men who had seized Benham, and the words that his friend spoke to him, were sufficient to show him that nothing was to be gained by remaining a moment longer in a place where his capture would certainly be the next incident, and with it the loss of all hope of defeating the elaborate plans that had been revealed to him and his companion. He cursed the forgetfulness that had permitted him to come on such an expedition without arms of any description. The next best thing, however, to killing every one of the band, was to get back as soon as possible to the Works, and to organize a party to go in pursuit of the villains. Down the hill he went at the top of his speed, when, finding that there was no pursuit, he went on the remainder of the way not slowly, by any means, but with more composure than had characterized the first hundred yards of his flight. At first he thought he would alarm the dwellers along the road, but he reflected that they were a torpid-brained set of people, into whose sluggish minds it would take him more time than he had to spare to get an idea of what had happened, and then twice as long for them to determine what to do.

As he hurried along the road he had ample opportunity to grasp the details of the situation, and to determine what course to take in order to secure the apprehension of the robbers. That they would at once decamp he felt very certain, but as to what direction they would take he had

not the slightest idea.   Probably they would seek the
mountains in the northern part of the county, or the still
more rugged regions of Schuylkill County, where there
was already a sufficient degree of lawlessness to keep them
company.   Benham was a prisoner in their hands.   That
was the first point to be considered, and at once an effort
must be made for his release.   That they would do him
serious injury, if not put him to death, was quite within
the range of possibility.   Outrages of the kind had before
that time been perpetrated by bands of marauders, who,
living in the seclusion of the mountains, and sustained by
many of the miners, had had things pretty much their own
way for several years past.

Then, as he walked rapidly along the road, passing
house after house on his way, he began to perceive the
difficulties that surrounded him, and the probability that
ere he could arrive at the Works, organize a body of
pursuers, go back to the house on the South Fork, and
take up the trail, the outlaws would be far on their way to
some retreat in the mountains that would afford them immunity from all efforts at discovery.   At the same time it
was necessary that he should return to the Works, see the
assistant superintendent and Mr. Wade, and advise them
of the contemplated attack, which it was possible the band
might not have renounced.   Had it not been for this obligation he would have stopped at a farm-house, procured a
horse, and started back for the purpose of discovering the
route taken by the robbers.   This done, it would not be a
difficult matter to head them off before they had arrived at
their lair.

He had gone only about a fourth of the distance to be
traversed before he would arrive at the Works, and was beginning to feel tired.   His walk had been almost a run,
and for several years past he had not been accustomed to
much physical exercise.   Already his exhausted muscles

were becoming incapable of doing the work to which he was forcing them, and he perceived that he should have to stop and rest, when he heard the sound of approaching footsteps behind him. He had barely time to turn aside and hide himself behind a bush when three men, going very fast, went by him. They passed so close to him that he could have touched them with his outstretched hand, and he at once recognized them as the three forge-men whom he had seen in the house with Rackett and his associates. Here was another source of perplexity. What were they doing there? The idea struck him that they had been sent back to carry out a part of the plan, the details of which he had heard stated, perhaps even to set fire to Benham's house, out of revenge for what had happened.

Now, therefore, it appeared still more necessary for him to reach the Works at the earliest possible moment, and, in order to do so, he would be obliged to overcome his prejudices, and appeal to one of the neighboring farmers for assistance. On his right, across the creek, dwelt old Simon Schnetter, who he knew had several good horses, and whom he determined to let so far into his confidence as to induce him to loan or hire him one of the animals. He turned off from the road, and was about crossing the creek, when he saw in front of him a horse standing quietly in the pasture. Going forward, he perceived that there was a halter on the animal. Why not take the horse, improvise a bridle, mount him, and hurry on to the Works? The thought was no sooner conceived, than he proceeded to put it into execution. The animal allowed itself to be approached, and Arndell, taking the rope that hung from the head-piece of the halter, gave it a twist through the beast's mouth, and then, with a spring, he was on its back. Re-entering the road, he dug his heels into the horse's flanks, and at a break-neck pace hurried on toward

his destination. So swiftly did his steed carry him, that
the four miles he had to go were traversed in less than half
an hour. He saw nothing of the three forge-men. Doubtless at the sound of horse's hoofs behind them, they had,
fearing they were being pursued, turned aside from the
road till the supposed danger had passed.

It was now nearly five o'clock, and day was beginning
to break. He had, at last, finally decided upon the course
to be pursued, and there was no time to lose if he meant
to do all in his power to liberate his friend, and capture
the robbers. First he went to his own house, and ordered
his man to put him up something to eat and to saddle his best
horse. Then, still on the animal that he had appropriated
to his own use, and without satisfying the curiosity that
Terry's face as well as several covert observations expressed,
he rode to Mr. Wade's tower, and, after a series of thunder-
ing knocks on the door, caused that gentleman to put his
head out of the window and to inquire in no gentle tone
what was the matter.

"I want to see you immediately. It is Dr. Arndell."

"In the name of Heaven, what's the matter?"

"There's a good deal the matter. Come down at once,
for I have no time to lose."

Mr. Wade did not stop to consider the order of his coming, for, in less time than it has taken to write these lines,
he had opened the door. In slippered feet, and with a
blanket thrown over his shoulders, he stood there, while
Arndell rapidly gave him an account of what had occurred.

"Of course," said Mr. Wade, "the first thing for me
to do is to at once secure the arrest of the three forge-men.
Doubtless they will tell all they know. Then I shall acquaint Mr. Coleman, the assistant superintendent, with
what you have told me, and we shall be prepared for defense, and attack, too, if we are visited by the villains. I
had information from Todd yesterday that they might be

expected to-night, and I should have got ready for them
to-day. If Benham had only telegraphed me of his intentions, a good deal of trouble would have been avoided."

"Will you say anything to Miss Honeywood?"

"I think not. There are circumstances that render it
inexpedient to cause her the alarm that she would experience if the whole truth were told her, and she would never
be satisfied with anything less than the whole."

"You are right. I think that for the present, at least,
she had better know nothing whatever about the matter."

"She thinks Benham is in Philadelphia, on his way to
Montreal."

"Then let her continue to think so. Now, my friend,
I must be off. Explain my absence by saying that I have
been called to a distant patient. I shall instruct Terry
accordingly. Leave to me the capture or destruction of
the villains, and the liberation of Benham. If I require
anything in the way of assistance, or if I shall have any
news to communicate, I shall telegraph."

"Poor Benham! it may go hard with him. That rascal Rackett owes him a grudge, and he's likely to revenge
himself now."

"Don't speak of it, please. It makes my blood run
cold, and I'm not squeamish, to think of what devilish
ideas may come into their minds. They will not probably,
however, execute any designs they may have formed while
they are on the road. They will postpone action till they
reach a place of safety. But now I must be off. Leave it
all to me. I shall save Benham, I think, and capture or
kill the robbers. Good-by! I feel that everything here
is safe now."

"Good-by, Arndell. God bless you, and grant you
success!"

The two friends shook hands; the eyes of both of them
moistened with tears that, man-like, they tried to repress,

and then Arndell rode back to his own house, and Mr.
Wade, hastily dressing himself, prepared to perform that
part of the programme laid down for him.

Arndell found his horse ready for him.   He told Terry
that a case of importance required his immediate attention
in a distant part of the county ; directed him to return the
horse that had served him so well to its master, and to pay
whatever sum might be demanded for the use of the animal; and then, putting two revolvers into his coat-pockets,
and seeing that his saddle-bags, containing something to
eat and drink, were properly adjusted, he started off on his
expedition.

It was his intention to go back to the house on the
South Fork, and follow the men till he had positively assured himself of the route they had taken.   Then he proposed to go around them by shorter roads, that, although
not admitting of the passage of a wagon, were, nevertheless, practicable for a horse.   Having got in front of them,
he intended to gather together half a dozen courageous
men, and then either to attack the robbers openly, or to lie
in ambush for them, as the circumstances of the situation
might seem to require.   He had taken the precaution to
take a folding map of Dauphin County with him—one
on which every road and water-course and mill and dwell-
ing-house was indicated—so that he would at all times
know exactly where he was, and, as he galloped along over
the road that he had just traveled, he took this guide from
his pocket, and (for it was now broad daylight) began to
study the points that appeared to him to be of most importance.

It did not take him long to reach the foot of the hill
upon which stood the house that the robbers had occupied.
Dismounting and hitching his house to a sapling, and with
a pistol in his hand, he climbed the mount.   It was just
possible that some one or more of the gang might have

been left behind, so that it was necessary for him to proceed with caution. His care was, however, as we know,
unnecessary. The place was deserted. He did not stop to
inspect it, but, returning to where his horse was fastened,
he unhitched the animal, and, leading him up the hill, kept
on following the path till he arrived at the hut that had
been used as a stable. Here he found all the evidences of a
hurried departure. Pieces of harness were scattered about,
a horse-blanket lay in a corner, and a hat, probably one
that had been stolen, hung on a peg. There was but the
one road that they could have taken from this point, and
that led directly up the mountain. Arndell now mounted
his horse. The ascent was not very steep, and he was accordingly able to get over the ground with considerable
rapidity. At last he arrived at the summit of the ridge,
and here some deliberation was necessary. The main road
kept straight on to the south, and led to the valley below,
in which Linglestown was situated, or rather, it led to that
valley, after three other ranges of mountains were crossed.
The other turned suddenly to the left, and led along the
crest of Peter's Mountain, the two making as nearly as possible a right angle with each other. A mistake now would
lead to failure, for, if he took the wrong road, Rackett and
his gang would be far out of his reach before he could re-
trace his way. He went first over the one road and then
over the other, inspecting each foot of the way carefully,
and endeavoring to ascertain which showed recent marks
of horseshoes and wagon-wheels. He made up his mind
that the road along the ridge was the one the men had
taken, for he thought he discovered the indications mentioned, but he was not sure. The ground was hard and
stony, and neither the horse's shoes nor the wagon-wheels
made any very marked impression. Still, he thought he
detected in several places fresh marks of both, and his decision was made accordingly.

But, he had not gone more than a mile from the fork
of the roads, when he saw something white, like a letter-
envelope, lying on the ground. To dismount and to pick
it up was the work of an instant. It was the envelope of
a letter, and, turning it over, he read to his great delight
the direction :

> "JOHN BENHAM, Esq.,
> *Susquehanna Iron-Works,*
> *Dauphin County, Pa."*

There was no doubt now. He was on the right track.
Benham was alive, and probably still unhurt, and had managed to throw the paper out of the wagon, with the object
of its acting as a guide to those who might be in pursuit of
his captors. Arndell hurried on, therefore, with renewed
hope and vigor.

He had never once faltered in his idea of where his
duty lay. Once or twice the thought had flashed through
his mind that, by leaving Benham to his fate, his own suit
with Alana might possibly be advanced, but the notion
had not been entertained for a single moment. He was an
honorable man, his instincts were those of a true-hearted
gentleman, but, even with such, the suggestion of a shameful act will sometimes rise in the mind, to be at once, of
course, buried deep in the limbo of rejected temptations.
It is only the weak and dishonorable that nurse these despicable thoughts. Men like Arndell make short work of
them.

Still they *did* come, and, now that he knew he was on
the track of Rackett and his villainous crew, and that it
was probable that he would be the means of restoring his
successful rival unharmed to the woman he loved, they
rose in his mind more rapidly, and with still greater vivid-
ness, than when he was comparatively doubtful of the result.

"What more likely," ran the seductive suggestion, "than that Alana, after she had recovered from the shock and grief at Benham's death, as she is sure to do in time, will turn with love and admiration to the man who had the reputation of having risked his life to save that of his friend ? You will have shown your loyalty and courage. You have not spared yourself. She will know all that, and she will feel grateful. A woman's gratitude is the first step toward love. Your studies in comparative psychology have taught you that, and, besides, you feel sure that already she holds you high in her regard. During her father's illness you and she clasped hands often over the bed of a dying man. Your nerves have thrilled at her touch. Have hers, when she has felt your fingers close over her own, been stirred out of their usual calmness ? Probably not, but they would have been moved, doubtless, if you had made any effort to win her love. You have rested supinely, secure in the vain thought that you could win her at any time that you chose to honor her with a declaration of your love. Well," he exclaimed aloud, "you have been a fool ; now take the consequences of your folly like a man, and act as a loyal gentleman should toward the friend to whom he owes almost everything that he is and has."

He had not diminished his rate of speed while the short contest referred to was going on in his mind, but, with its termination, he touched his horse lightly with the spurs, and went on still more rapidly. So far as he could judge, the fugitives had nearly three hours the start of him. But he was quite sure that he had been gaining rapidly on them ever since he left the abandoned house. His horse was a splendid animal, that thought nothing of an all-day gallop ; whereas, one of those driven by the men of whom he was in pursuit was lame, and in no event could a wagon travel over the mountain-road as swiftly as could a man on horse-back. Probably the lame animal would give out altogether,

in which event Rackett would certainly be in bad straits
with a man on his hands, a hostile man at that, whom he
would find it difficult to dispose of with safety to himself
and his band.

He looked at his watch as he reached a point of the road
where it turned squarely to the north, It was seven o'clock.
The morning was a dark and gloomy one, and the wind
was still from the northeast. A few flakes of snow were
falling, evidently the begining of a snow-storm. He was
looking at the ground, watching the big flakes as they fell,
when suddenly his eyes rested on something white, that
looked like a snow-flake, but was larger than any he had
ever seen. He had passed it in his rapid course over the
road, but something urged him to go back and to examine
it, although the loss of time incident to such an act was an
unpleasant feature. Returning to the place where the object lay, he discovered that it was a piece of white paper.
Dismounting and picking it up, he saw that it was a piece
of the nib of an envelope, and probably also thrown out
by Benham. He took from his pocket the envelope he had
found near the fork of the roads ; the fragment fitted perfectly to a place in the nib, from which a piece had been
torn. So far, then, all was going well.

He was now crossing the elevated plateau known as
Broad Mountain, at the foot of which lies the village of
Lykens, at which place he expected to hear something of
the party of which he was in pursuit. So far as he knew,
he was unknown to every one of them, but of this he could
not be sure, for it was not improbable that they had at various times visited the Works, under one pretense or another,
for the purpose of becoming acquainted with the principal
features of the place, and that they were well acquainted
with him by sight. It was the custom of such rascals as
he had to deal with, to neglect nothing that might be of
service to them in their nefarious schemes. It was not

likely that they had contemplated robbing him, for the
game would not have been worth the candle; but, in ascertaining this fact, they had doubtless familiarized themselves
with him and his surroundings. It would certainly be a
great advantage if he were not known to them, for ignorance on their part of his personality would enable him to
approach them, and perhaps even to travel with them, till
such time as he should deem it advisable to spring the
mine that he might have prepared. The risk, however,
was too great, and so he decided to keep himself out of
their sight till he was ready to strike a blow that should
prove overwhelming.

But, in such matters as the one that he had on hand,
it is rarely possible to form a plan of operations, and to ad-
here to it without variation. He had already begun to
descend the north side of the Broad Mountain, when the
snow, that had for half an hour or more been falling thick
and fast, began to cover the earth to such an extent as to
show the marks of the horse's hoofs and the wagon-wheels
of the party in front of him. He knew, from this fact,
that he was close upon the fugitives, and, almost as this
knowledge came to him, he heard voices on the road before
him, coming apparently from no greater distance than a
hundred yards. He stopped, in order that he might hear
more distinctly. Yes, there were two voices, both of men,
who were urging horses to greater speed. He could also
hear the rattling of the wagon-wheels over the stony and
frozen ground.

He was now within two miles of Lykens. He was acquainted with several people of the village, and especially
with the physician, Dr. Green, whom he had attended during a severe illness a couple of months ago, and upon whom
he was certain he could rely, not only for advice, but for
material aid. Dr. Green and he had stuck together in several medical quarrels, and any one who has been in a squab-

ble of the kind knows that it is highly conducive to warm friendships and keen enmities. For nowhere are generosity and illiberality, magnanimity and meanness, probity and misrepresentation more distinctly manifested than in the ranks of that profession whose members are engaged in caring for the welfare of human bodies. Dr. Green was a man of courage and reliability. It would be worth a good deal to Arndell to get to Lykens before Rackett and his gang drove into its precincts. It would mean the rescue of his friend, and the capture or death of the robbers.

While he was thinking the matter over, he was still keeping his horse moving, but only at a walk, for he found that that pace was sufficient to maintain desirable distance between him and the enemy. He had all along heard the rattling of the wheels, but suddenly this noise ceased, and then no other sounds reached his ears but that of men's voices. A turn in the road prevented his seeing farther than twenty or thirty yards. He dismounted, hitched his horse to a tree, and then, turning into the forest for a short distance, moved cautiously in the direction of the wagon. At times he walked upright, at others he crawled through the thick underbrush, but at last he came upon the road which, at the point at which he struck it, was some ten feet below the plain upon which he stood. Effectually screened by dense bushes, he crept up to the edge of the elevation, and looked down at the group below him. There he saw a wagon with two horses, and four men standing around it, engaged in earnest, yes, angry, conversation. The distance from him to them was not over twenty feet, so that every word they spoke was heard as distinctly as though it had been addressed directly to him. There was no other sound to break the silence of that cold, snowy morning on the northern slope of Broad Mountain.

CHAPTER XXIV

THE first thought that occurred to Arndell was expressed by the words that his mind conceived, though his organs of articulation did not speak them: "Where is Benham?" There were Rackett, Jinks, Hopkins, and Bell, but his friend was nowhere to be seen. His mental question was not long unanswered, for the first few words of the men's conversation sufficed to give him a clear idea of the situation.

"There's no use trying to take him along," said one of the fellows, whom he recognized as Jinks. "We're broke down, and it's as much as we can do to look after ourselves, much less a man who any moment may get us into trouble."

"That's so!" exclaimed Hopkins, emphatically. "I vote for leaving him. We can barely get to Lykens, and there we may have to stop till we can get another horse. What would we do, I'd like to know, with a red-hot enemy in the wagon? Why, any little boy or girl, playing in the street, might find him there."

"I think we'd better leave him," said Bell, who appeared to Arndell to be more terrified than the others, for he was shaking, probably with fear, though possibly with cold. "I guess the fellow that got away will bring the country down on us, and it would go mighty hard with me if I was caught."

"Pshaw!" exclaimed Rackett. "You haven't done anything yet but help me to get off, and that little job last night, and no one knows you were in that. I see, however, that you're all scared, and so, if it will help you to get back your courage, I'm willing to leave the fellow here in the woods. Yes, I'm willing to leave him," holding up his hands and exhibiting the scars that they bore, "but not till I've paid him for these, and, when I get through with him, I don't believe he'll be good for much except to feed those crows sitting on that tree."

"You don't mean to kill him, do you?" inquired Jinks, anxiously.

"Yes, I do. I'm bound to pay him for his treatment of me; and then, dead men tell no tales. He's heard every word we've said while he's been lying in that wagon, and I know him well enough to be sure that if he gets off he'll pursue us to the last day of his life but that he'll catch every one of us."

"I'm opposed, tooth and nail, to any killing," rejoined Jinks. "We've done nothing yet, at least not since I've been with the party, to cause us to swing, and I don't mean to risk my neck just to give you your revenge. Take him out of the wagon, strip him, tie him to a tree, and give him as many lashes as you like, and then leave him here; but, as to killing him, I'm dead against it."

Arndell had listened to this dispute with the most painful anxiety. He saw that he had it in his power to save his friend, and he determined at all hazards to do so. He had in each of the side-pockets of his overcoat a large-sized army revolver that was good to kill a man at a hundred paces. He was a good shot, and he felt sure that he could kill or disable two of the robbers before his presence should be discovered, if the other two should stay to find out who was their adversary. One man firing from an ambush half a dozen shots quickly, one after the other, always leads to the idea of a larger attacking force than really exists. He took out his pistols, looked at them carefully in order to see that they were in good condition, and then calmly awaited the development of events.

"Take him out, anyhow," said Hopkins, "and let's see what he looks like. We've all agreed that we've got to leave him, dead or alive. For my part, I'm in favor of ending him here on the spot."

"Not on this spot," said Bell, "not on the road. We'd better drive off to one side if we're going to do anything with him."

"Well," observed Rackett, composedly, "that depends altogether on what you're going to do. If you're only going to give him a flogging, we'd better drive off the road; but, if we're going to finish him, here's as good a place as any, for there's a ditch that will hold him, and plenty of stones and loose earth to throw over him. Take him out!"

At this order, Hopkins and Bell got into the wagon, and, letting down the tail-board, shoved Benham out till his feet projected, and then Jinks caught hold, and, by their united strength, the body was laid, not very gently, on the snow-covered ground.

Arndell could scarcely restrain himself from at once delivering his fire on the miscreants who had so grossly maltreated his friend, for Benham was tied hand and foot, and the gag was still over his mouth. As he lay, motionless, with the snow falling on him, he looked more dead than alive. His feelings, while the wretches were discussing the question of how further to dispose of him, may possibly be imagined by those of my readers that have been in similar situations, if any such there be—and Heaven grant that there is not one!—but they can scarcely be conceived by others.

"Now," said Rackett, "this matter has got to be settled at once, for we've no time to lose. I don't want to do anything against the wish of the majority, and by the vote

15

of the majority I'll be guided. There's no use in talking about it any longer. We all know how the thing stands, so we'll take a vote at once. What do you say, Jinks, on the question of death to the fellow?"

"I say no!" answered the man, firmly.

"And you, Hopkins?"

"Yes."

"Now, Bell, it's your turn."

"Yes," said the man, in a feeble voice. "I guess it's safer to end him. Dead dogs don't bite."

"That's good sense," continued Rackett. "So the thing's settled without my vote; but, for form's sake, and as we're all in the one boat, I'll vote 'yes.'"

"I won't have anything to do with murder," said Jinks, emphatically. "You'll have to count me out."

"What do you mean?"

"I mean that, if you're going to kill that man, I'm going away."

"You'll desert us?"

"I don't call it deserting you. I don't mean to leave you for good. When I came into this crowd, it was with the clear understanding that there was to be no killing except in self-defense. Now, if you've made up your minds to kill that man, you'll have to do it, I suppose, but you'll do it without me." With these words Jinks fumbled about in the wagon for a comforter that belonged to him, and, having found it, he wrapped it about his neck and prepared to leave, by holding out his hand to Rackett to bid him good-by.

"I can't shake hands with a man that leaves his friends in the lurch," said Rackett, folding his arms across his chest. "Some of these days you'll be sorry for this."

"No, I won't be sorry for it, Tony Rackett!" exclaimed Jinks, for the first time showing any anger; "and it won't do either for you to threaten me. There's nothing of the traitor about me. It's you that's breaking the agreement by killing that man. As to shaking hands with you, I guess, as things go, my hand's cleaner than yours in more ways than one. But don't you threaten me, for it isn't safe for you, and men don't die of threats."

"Where are you going?" inquired Rackett, not noticing Jinks's remarks.

"I'm going to Lykens first, and then I'm going to take the railroad to Millersburg. From there I'll go to Philadelphia, I guess."

"If you don't go to the house on Powell's Creek, and help yourself to the stuff that's there," said Rackett, sneeringly.

"Perhaps I may. There's no one got a better right, for more than three fourths of it came from my work."

"Well, go. Help yourself. For one, I'm glad to get rid of you."

"And the next time we meet, Mr. Tony Rackett, you and I'll settle our little affair!"

Jinks walked off without saying another word. He turned a bend of the road and was almost at once lost to the sight of his companions, though, from his superior elevation, Arndell could see him rapidly making his way down the slope of the mountain.

"Now that we're rid of Mr. Jinks and his cowardly notions, we'll settle with our friend," said Rackett, as he kicked Benham's prostrate body. "There's only one way to do a thing of this kind so as to show no favoritism. We'll each give him a shot. Get your pistols ready, boys, and at the word from me fire at his heart. I think you'd better set him up against that bank; then, when he falls, he'll go into the ditch, and it will be easy work covering him over with stones and earth. We can topple a ton of earth on him from that bank."

Arndell would have fired at this moment, but for the fact that the three men were too widely separated to admit of his getting in three shots before one or more of them would have a chance of shooting Benham. The arrangement proposed by Rackett was calculated to do away with this condition. By it Benham would be placed against the opposite bank to that on which he (Arndell) stood, and his would-be executioners, standing with their faces turned toward their victim, would be unaware of what was going on behind them till he had discharged his shots, and, if God gave him full force, they would not know much about the matter afterward.

"Take off his gag," commanded Rackett. "I want to give him a chance to talk back a little."

In an instant, Bell had loosed the strap and removed the great wad of cotton that, since leaving the house, had been fastened tightly over Benham's mouth.

"Now sit him up on that rock, with his back against the bank, and then come here to me."

This order was also quickly executed, and now, for the first time, Arndell had a good look at his friend's face. The lower part of it was swollen and discolored from the constriction to which it had been subjected, but the eyes were still bright, and his whole expression was that of a man who, though he had made up his mind that his last hour had come, was prepared to die with unflinching courage. Never before had Arndell loved his friend as he loved him at that moment.

"Mr. John Benham," said Rackett, taking a position some five or six feet in front of his prisoner, "do you see these hands?" holding out his hands, and touching the knuckles of first one and then the other.

"Certainly, I see them."

"It's your work."

"Yes, it's my work. I gave you the opportunity of

walking, and you would not; so I dragged you over the ground till you consented to be more obliging."

"Yes, that's exactly what you did, and now you're going to get your pay. I'm going to kill you! You are sitting now on the brink of your grave, and in less than five minutes you'll be lying in it with a ton or more of stones and earth over your dead body!"

"Yes, I suppose that is what you intend to do. I heard you discussing it just now."

"I think this is the happiest moment of my life. There's nothing sweeter than dearly bought revenge. Its sweet to kill you, but I want to add to the joy of this moment, and at the same time heap a few coals of fire on your head, by doing you a favor. Is there any message you'd like to be given to any one? If there is, you may trust me to give it."

Benham was silent. He appeared to be thinking.

"No," he said, at last, "I have no message to send by you."

"Think a moment. You're in love with Miss Honeywood. I've seen and heard enough to know that. Don't you want to send her word that you died thinking of her?"

"No, God forbid! Not by your foul lips. She will know what my thoughts are."

"Then, by God, say a prayer for the safety of your soul, for your hour has come!—Hopkins, stand here on my right. Bell, stand on my left. Cock your pistols, and when I finish counting three, fire at his heart! We'll not bandage his eyes. I, for one, am not afraid to look him in the face. Besides, I want to see whether he winks or not when I say 'three.'"

The men arranged themselves as Rackett directed, and stood with their pistols in their hands ready for the word. At that instant Arndell, who was not more than ten feet distant from the line that they made as they stood in the road, raised his right hand, and, taking deliberate aim at Rackett, fired. Without looking to see the effect of his shot, he aimed again, and this time at Hopkins, and fired. Both men fell instantly, while Bell, panic-stricken, could not move a limb for fear, and, receiving Arndell's third shot, leaped a foot or more into the air and fell dead. With a bound Arndell was down the bank and over to the opposite side before Benham had recovered from his astonishment at not being shot. He had shut his eyes, and was murmuring a prayer, more for Alana than for himself, and had thought that the shots were directed at him by the three robbers, never for an instant dreaming that his three foes were stretched bleeding upon the earth. Without stopping to look at them, Arndell hurried to cut the cords that bound his friend, when the sound of another shot broke upon his ear, and Benham fell over to one side with the blood gushing in torrents from his mouth. Rackett's last earthly act was to fire that shot.

Dr. Arndell was a good surgeon, and he knew instantly what had happened. Benham had been shot in the right lung. He tore off the clothing from the chest of the wounded man, and discovered that the bullet had not gone through the lung. It was a bad enough wound, but not necessarily a fatal one. At home, and with good nursing, he would have expected recovery to result, especially in a man with such a good constitution as that possessed by Benham ; but here, in a snow-storm on a mountain, two miles distant from shelter, and without the requisite facilities for properly dressing the wound, he felt that the chances were adverse. Nevertheless, he was a man of ready resources in cases of emergency such as the one before him. He lifted the wounded man in his arms and carried him to as level and smooth a piece of the road as he could find. Then he took off the overcoats of the dead robbers and placed them under him, using his own for a covering. Examining the wound more carefully than he had yet done, he found some small pieces of clothing sticking in it, and these he removed. The ball had not broken a rib, but had gone between two at the upper part of the chest, leaving a few small fragments of bone near the surface, and these he also took away.

Benham had not lost consciousness, but he was very faint. He would several times have spoken, but for the fact that Arndell had told him not to say a word, for that speaking was likely to bring on a renewal of the hemorrhage, and that meant death. Leaving him for a moment, the doctor hurried back to where his horse was hitched, and led the animal forward to where Benham was lying. Then from his saddle-bags he took the cold meat and bread and butter, and, most important of all, a flask containing some old brandy that his man had placed there. He broke the ice over a little puddle at the side of the road, and, mixing some of the water with a small portion of brandy, held the silver cup from the bottom of his flask to Benham's lips till he had swallowed the contents.

The doctor knew that his friend had eaten nothing since the night before, and his army experience with gunshot-wounds of the lungs had taught him that the best results were obtained by keeping up the strength of the patient and by good nursing. He had no facilities for making those excellent preparations of food that modern science has devised for the sick and wounded, but he could do something to meet the immediate necessities of the case, while he thought of what it would be best to do with a view to the future welfare of the wounded man.

Searching in the wagon, he found that the former occupants had laid in a good store of provisions, and, among other things, he discovered a dozen or more eggs. Two of these would be as good food and as much of it as Benham now required. He found that the brandy had acted well, and that there had been no return of the hemorrhage. He gave him the eggs raw, and then, seeing that his patient was comparatively comfortable, he took his own breakfast while he looked around him for the first time, and studied the features of the situation. The marauders were dead. Bell was shot through the heart, and Hopkins right through the center of the chest. Both had died instantly. Rackett had, like Benham, been shot in the lung, but the bullet giving him his wound was twice as large as that in Benham's body, and the result had thus been much more decided. He had held on to his pistol, and had been able, with his last strength, to shoot the man for whom he entertained so great a hatred. Instantly afterward he had fallen back dead.

Arndell took hold of the dead bodies and laid them in a row by the side of the road. Then he examined the wagon and horses. Of the latter, one was entirely broken down, and would probably be unable to go half a mile farther. He therefore unhitched it and put his own horse in its place. He now had a team that was equal to the work of going to Lykens, where his friend Dr. Green lived, and with whom he did not doubt he could place Benham till he was well enough to admit of his being removed to his own home. Or, upon consideration of the actual state of the wounded man, it might be advisable to place him in a railway-car specially prepared for him, transport him over the Summit Branch Railroad to Millersburg, and thence, without change of car, on the Northern Central to the Susquehanna Iron-Works. That was a matter, however, to be determined by circumstances as they might be developed.

He was fearful of the consequences of moving Benham from the ground into the wagon, for he knew how greatly absolute rest is conducive to the recovery of a person with a bullet in his lung. There was, however, no escape. The snow was falling faster than ever, and the temperature was getting lower. Longer delay might be fatal.

First of all he took the woolen comforters from the necks of the dead robbers, and bound them around Benham's chest so as to make it as immobile as possible. After he got to Lykens he meant to attend to this point more effectually still.

"Now," he said, to his friend, "I'm going to put you into the wagon and drive you over to Lykens. If you stand the journey well, I'll have a car of some kind fitted up for you, and you can go straight on to the Works; but, if you are much exhausted, I'll take you to Dr. Green's. You know Green, of course? You mustn't answer. I don't want you to speak a word or to move a muscle more than you can help. Just let your body be perfectly passive, and leave it all to me."

He had already, with several articles of clothing and a blanket that he had found under the front seat of the wagon, extemporized a bed, and on that he now proceeded to place his friend. It was hard work to do this without more or less exciting the circulation and thus running the risk of renewing the hemorrhage; but he did finally succeed, and Benham lay as comfortably as was possible on the bed of the wagon, with sufficient soft materials between him and it to lessen the hardness of the roads.

"I must speak," he said, in a whisper, "if I die the next moment. God bless you! I shall never forget you." He held out his hand as he uttered the words, and then closed his eyes, as though from very weakness.

"Hush!" said Arndell, greatly moved, grasping the proffered hand. "Any doctor would have done as much."

Benham smiled faintly and shook his head.

"Now," resumed Arndell, "not another word. You may think as much as you wish, but no talking. Revenge in cold blood is the devil's own work," he continued, as he gave a last look at the bodies of the robbers. "A more diabolical scoundrel than Rackett it has never been my bad luck to encounter.—When you are stronger," turning to Benham as he drove off, "I'll tell you my adventures, but not now."

Slowly, almost painfully slowly, he drove down the side of the mountain over the road that led to Lykens. Not a soul did he meet till, after an hour and a half had elapsed, he reached the first house of the village. This was a tavern. He stopped here, for he thought it best to make an early report of what he had done, in order that the legal authorities might take cognizance of his acts. Entering the bar-room, he called the landlord, a big, burly fellow named Jacob Krause, aside, and, in as few words as possible, gave him the chief points of the affair, very much to that worthy's astonishment. But what was his surprise, on looking around the room, to see, sitting in front of the red-hot stove, Jinks, the very man who had left Rackett and his gang rather than countenance the murder of Benham!

Evidently he had not taken notice of Arndell's arrival, or, if he had, he did not consider it a matter of any importance, not being aware that the doctor was in any way connected with Benham. Doubtless, he had heard the shots on the mountain, but had taken it for granted that they were leaden messengers that took the death-sentence to Benham.

Krause, however, like many of his class, was gossipy, and liked to feel the importance attached in country towns to the possessor of great news. As soon, therefore, as Arndell had finished his recital, the innkeeper cried out:

"Well, boys, Dr. Arndell has done the biggest thing that's been done in Dauphin County since I've known anything about it! He's killed three robbers back here a couple of miles on Broad Mountain, and saved Mr. Benham's life, but not till the devils had put a bullet into his body."

Arndell had his eye on Jinks while Krause was speaking. At the first words, the man raised his head and listened ; but, before the innkeeper had finished, he was on his feet and moving rapidly toward the door.

"Stop !" cried Arndell, springing in front of him and drawing one of his pistols. "Another step, and you're a dead man !—This is one of the robbers," he continued, addressing the half-dozen men who were in the bar-room. "He left them because he was opposed to the killing of Benham. Seize him !"

The man made an effort to take a pistol from his pocket, but, before he could accomplish his purpose, several pairs of strong hands had grasped him, and he was soon overpowered and bound.

Of course, no such exciting incidents having ever before occurred in the borough of Lykens, or in its vicinity, the little village was at once thrown into a state of great agitation. Many persons, men and women, gathered around the wagon, so as to get a sight of Benham ; and when the doctor drove off toward his friend's residence, the vehicle was followed by a crowd of people, anxious to get a sight of the sufferer when he should be carried into Dr. Green's house. Others started ahead, to notify the physician of the coming wounded man, and others, again, with the high constable of the borough, Peter Zeigler, as their leader, hurried off on horseback, in wagons, and on foot, to the place on Broad Mountain where lay the dead bodies of the three robbers. It was a great day for Lykens, and the memory of it will endure from generation to generation.

Arndell had not gone far on his way when he was met by Dr. Green, coming toward him as fast as his not very long legs would carry him. He was a precise little fellow, well up in his profession, and devotedly attached to Arndell, and, as often happens in country towns in which the physician is the best-educated man, the most important

person in the place. He had been several times chief bur-
gess of Lykens, and had once been sent to the Legislature.
He might have continued to hold either office, or both,
had he so chosen. But office-holding interfered with his
practice, so he had given it up.

"What's all this I hear!" he exclaimed, as Arndell
stopped the wagon to speak to him. "Mr. Benham
wounded, and in that wagon! Bring him to my house at
once, and keep him there till he gets well. How did it
happen? Where is he shot? Is it a bad wound?"

"I want you to see him," answered Arndell, "before I
decide whether to take him home at once or not. He has
a wound in the apex of the right lung. There's been some
external hemorrhage, as well as coughing of blood. He's
doing pretty well. I'd like to get him home, if possible,
because—because—his mother is there, and all his belong-
ings; but if it should prove to be unadvisable to make the
attempt, I shall ask you to let him stay with you till he is
well enough to be moved."

"All I have is at his and your disposal. I think you
had better make up your mind to leave him here. He
must be very much exhausted. I'll go ahead and open
the gate, so that you can drive right into my garden, and
then we'll shut out these people, while we examine him."
So saying, the little doctor was off again, while Arndell
resumed his slow journey.

Arrived at the doctor's house, he drove into the garden,
as had been arranged. Then the gate was shut, and, getting into the wagon, Dr. Green joined his friend in making an inspection of the patient.

It was apparent to both of these medical men that Benham was thoroughly worn out. His pulse was feeble and
very frequent, his face pale, his hands and feet cold. Further fatigue was not to be thought of. Besides, taking
him home would involve three liftings—once into the car,

and once from it at the Works, to a vehicle of some kind, and again at Benham's home ; whereas, by staying with Dr. Green, only one—into his house—would be required. So it was decided that he should remain, and that Arndell, after he had seen that his friend was as well situated as was possible under the circumstances, should return to the Works, and break the news of what had happened to those most interested. It was thought better that this should be done in person than by telegram, as less likely to lead to misunderstandings of Benham's actual condition.

It did not take long, with the aid of a couple of strong men and a hair mattress, to transfer the wounded man from the wagon to the comfortable bedroom that Dr. and Mrs. Green placed at his disposal. The lady was as kind as her husband, and nothing was left undone that could tend to insure the sufferer's welfare. It was Arndell's intention to return that night, probably bringing with him Mrs. Benham and Alana, both of whom he was sure would insist upon seeing his friend, and, perhaps, even of staying and nursing him through the worst part of his illness. But before he left, he received notice to attend before Squire Garman, and make the necessary affidavit relative to Jinks. He obeyed the summons, and was then informed that an inquest on the bodies of the robbers would probably be held on the following day. Jinks had nothing to say in his defense, and was committed to stand his trial. Arndell felt somewhat kindly disposed toward the man, but he did not forget that he had suggested to Rackett to give Benham a hundred lashes on his bare back, and that his opposition to murder was probably based more on considerations for his own safety than on any other motive. It was with satisfaction, therefore, that Arndell saw him going with him on the same train, bound for the jail at Harrisburg, and heavily ironed.

CHAPTER XXV

It was with somewhat mixed feelings that Alana went to her bedroom after the departure of Benham and Mr. Wade, following that of Mrs. L'Estrange in the custody of officer Josephs. She had reason to believe that she was not the illegitimate daughter of her father, but born in lawful wedlock; but this knowledge was more than offset by the renewed evidence that had been presented relative to the evil courses of her mother. She would rather have had the stain on her birth remain, if she could have received assurance that her mother had not been the depraved woman that all the signs that had thus far come to her showed her to have been.

And then, the questions—Who was her mother? Where was she? Was she alive or dead?—came uppermost in her mind and gave her ample food for thought during the greater part of the night that she lay awake, unable to sleep from the state of excitement into which her nervous system had been thrown. Who, also, was the woman that had attempted to pass herself off as her mother? That she was an impostor was very evident; but who was she, that knew so much about her mother's family, who so strongly resembled Todd—who was certainly her uncle, her father had admitted that—and who had her mother's marriage certificate in her possession? All these were questions that must be solved before she could be mentally at rest.

Yet she would have been almost willing to let them go

without further seeking to unravel their mysteries, if she could have felt quite certain that she had done right in accepting Benham as her lover and future husband. True, he had promised to come back with the proof that the woman calling herself her mother was an impostor; but what of that? Was it not quite probable, ay, even certain, that her real mother had been equally bad with this false one? Had not her own mother been in prison, living under false names, and leading a life of impurity and criminality all her life? What difference did it make which of them was her mother?

The next day, soon after the assistant superintendent had made his report, she went to Benham's house to pay a visit to his mother. He had been gone several hours. He had told Mrs. Benham the general purport of his journey, and had also given her the essential points of the visit made by Mrs. L'Estrange to Alana, so that after the ice was broken between the two ladies—and it took some little time to do this, for neither was quite sure how far she should venture upon giving and receiving confidence—the conversation turned upon the subjects that were uppermost in the heart of each. Mrs. Benham was a sensible woman, one who was more likely than not to take a practical view of any matter submitted to her judgment, and the opinions that she expressed relative to the existing condition of affairs were calculated to do away with a good deal of the morbidness, or hypersensitiveness, that Alana was experiencing.

"My dear child," she said—"I surely may call you so now—I do not suppose that I can adduce a single fact or argument beyond those that John has already brought forward. He has, you may depend upon it, given it all the thought at his command. He is honest in everything, and though I can not venture to say that in the present instance he is disinterested, I am quite sure that he would not urge you to do an act that could be considered unworthy of a good woman. He loves you for yourself. He believes that he can make you happy, and that you will be to him that greatest of all earthly treasures that a man can possess, a good wife. I think that, after what he has said to you, you are bound to dismiss your scruples. It is not at all likely that the world at large will ever know your family history, and, if it should be exposed, what of it? For a little while it may cause some talk, but mankind is on the whole just in its treatment of its fellows. It will take you for what you are, it will see how true a woman you are, it will recall the goodness of your father, and the whispers against your mother will soon cease to be uttered, and in a short time will have been forgotten. Take an old woman's advice, my dear, and leave it all to take care of itself. Don't risk your own and John's happiness by looking back at unpleasant things that are not of your making, and which, therefore, do not detract from your goodness."

"I will try to see the matter as you do," answered Alana. "I feel that you are right, but it would have added much to my happiness, and to his too, I am sure, if I could have come to him with an unsullied name."

"Ah, my dear, our names are sullied or unsullied as we ourselves make them! What is a noble ancestry worth if the descendants are unworthy; and who that is himself good and true bears in mind an ignoble descent against the man or woman whose life has been pure and lovely? And as to the wicked and the malignant, those despicable creatures who are always on the lookout for something to allege against those who are better than they, what matters it what they say? You should be glad that they can not charge you with aught of which you need be ashamed."

"You are very good to me. I shall know you now better than I have known you before. You and John have not been very sociable with me."

"No, dear, for we were fearful of being misunderstood."

"You should have known me better. I am sorry when I look back and see what I have lost all these years."

"We shall make up for it, now," said Mrs. Benham, embracing Alana; "and I promise to give you all of my company that you wish if you will not object to letting me see your brave, sweet face very often—often, that is, until you are married. Then I shall take myself off."

"No!" cried Alana, returning her caress. "You shall not leave us."

"Yes, dear, I must. I don't suppose I should be a bad mother-in-law as mothers-in-law go, but the best are better still when they don't live with their married children. Now—"

"May I come in and join the love-feast?" said Miss Pink, appearing at the half-open door. "I knocked twice, but, receiving no reply, I ventured to open the door. I give you my word that I have not heard a word of the conversation, but I couldn't help seeing! Of course, it's nothing for either of you to be ashamed of."

"You should have knocked louder, Miss Pink—but come in. I am very fond of Miss Honeywood, and I am sure she is fond of me."

Alana said nothing, and remained standing as though about going away.

"Yes," exclaimed the irrepressible Miss Pink, "and you're likely to be still fonder of each other, if what a little bird told me this morning should prove to be true. I had just opened the window to air my bedroom, when a little bird hopped on to the sill and said, 'Althea, there's something going to take place at the Works that will make your heart swell with joy—that heart that always swells when your friends and neighbors are made happy.' Was the little bird speaking the truth, or was it a naughty little bird that told lies?"

"You will have to ask it, Miss Pink," said Mrs. Benham, severely.

"I did ask it, my dear friend, and it answered that all the little birds around the Works were singing with joy over the happy event that is to occur, let me hope, very soon. But I won't press you too closely. I know, yes, I know from my own experience," she went on, simperingly, "how embarrassing certain matters are to the unsophisticated woman's mind. You see how disinterested I am. Now that there is no danger that I shall be misunderstood, may I not take you into my confidence and tell you that if I had been a little older, I should probably have taken your place in—in—in the affections of—of—well, you know who?"

"Do you refer to my son?" inquired Mrs. Benham, with all the austerity that she was capable of putting into her voice. "Because, if you do, I must insist upon saying that you never could, under any circumstances, have been his wife."

"Do you think so?" asked Miss Pink, quite unabashed by the rebuke. "It only shows how often we are ignorant of what is passing under our very noses. However, I am a peaceable girl, one that never wants to make a disturbance or to cause ill-feeling. Therefore, if you please, we will let the matter drop."

"Good-by," said Alana, holding out her hand to Mrs. Benham. "Won't you come over this evening and take tea with me? I shall be quite alone. You like *bézique*, and so do I."

"Yes, I will come with pleasure. Good-by, dear."

"Good-morning, Miss Pink," said Alana.

"Good-morning, Miss Honeywood. I'm sure you're not jealous of me." But Alana did not hear the last words. She had gone before they were spoken.

"Now, Miss Pink," said Mrs. Benham, "I think it is

my duty to tell you that you are a prying, meddlesome,
and impertinent woman, and that you need never set your
foot inside of my house again! There is a proverb to the
effect that 'he that pryeth into every cloud may be stricken
with a thunderbolt.' I hope you will think of it, and change
your ways; and there is another that teaches that 'he who
touches pitch will be defiled,' and *I* intend to profit by that
one. I am very busy this morning. and I beg. therefore,
that you will allow me to attend to what I have to do."

"My dear Mrs. Benham! You surely don't mean
what you say. What have I done?—I, who am so careful,
so reticent, so indisposed to hurt even a fly! Think of
what I might have said, under the circumstances, had I
wished to hurt Miss Honeywood's feelings! And this is
my return! *My* feelings are nothing! Oh. no!" taking
out her handkerchief, not as clean as it might have been,
and pressing it to each eye in turn. "I came here to do a
kind—kindness—and this—this—is my re—reward!"

"How dare you say that you might have married my
son?"

"So—so—I might," answered Miss Pink. continuing
to sob, and to superfluously dab her eyes with her handkerchief. "If—if—you knew as much as I do, you—you'd
treat me dif—differ—er—ently."

"What do you mean, woman? Do you mean to tell
me that my son ever proposed marriage to you?"

"No, no—not exactly that," answered Miss Pink, re-
gaining in a measure her composure, though she still continued the make-believe sopping-up process with her handkerchief. "I could see that he admired me. I have
watched him from my window, when he did not know that
I was looking at him, and he has often looked up and
kissed his hand."

"It is impossible! I don't believe one word of it.
Kissing his hand to you! You must be crazy."

"I admit that I may have misinterpreted his actions. He might have been stroking his beard. But it looked very much to me as though he were kissing his hand."

"Ridiculous!"

"Perhaps so, but there were other things much more decided. I can tell when a gentleman admires me, I think. I never gave him any encouragement, for I felt that I was too young to marry. But I did not come to talk about this matter. I have found something that may be of importance, and I hoped that you would tell me what to do with it."

"You have been very foolish, and I don't believe I can ever forgive you for saying that you might have married my son if you had chosen."

"You are too good a Christian, Mrs. Benham, to harbor unkind feelings against one who, at the worst, has only been mistaken. We are none of us perfect. To err is human, and I am very human. To forgive is divine, and you are very divine. Let us drop the subject. I shall try to bear my cross with meekness and humility."

"Pshaw!"

"Well! well! if all the world were agreed, it would be a very stupid place. But let me tell you the errand on which I came. Do you believe in dreams?"

"No."

"I do, and I believe that the soul of a human being can leave its earthly tenement and visit other people. I had such a visit last night."

"You mean that you had a dream."

"Call it what you please. It happened during my sleep, but it was none the less real, for it awoke me, and continued for nearly a minute after I had ceased to be asleep. I saw your son, Mr. John Benham, standing in the middle of the room and regarding me with an affectionate expression on his face. Therefore I know what his real feelings are, even though circumstances may stand in the way of his open avowal of them."

"You seem determined to make me uncomfortable to-day, if you can," rejoined Mrs. Benham with increased asperity. "I suppose no one can prevent your dreaming of my son, but you are very foolish to come to his mother with your absurd fancies. You had a most improbable dream, and that is all there is about it."

"Yes, I know he has gone away. I met Lucille, Miss Honeywood's maid, this morning, and she told me he had gone, but I think she mentioned Montreal."

"Oh! and I suppose it was from Lucille that you obtained information of the other matter to which you had the indelicacy to refer. You ought to be above gossiping with people's servants. I shall warn Miss Honeywood to be more on her guard hereafter against her maid."

"And get me into trouble, too! Surely, my dear Mrs. Benham, you would not do that. You are too much of a Christian to do either of us an injury."

"I find that it takes a great deal of Christianity—more, in fact, than I possess—to tolerate you. I must really beg you now to excuse me. I have several letters to write, and—"

"And I have not yet told you what I came for! One moment, and then I think you will be willing to put off writing your letters for the rest of the day. It was early when I met Lucille. I thought I would like some *wurst* for breakfast, and I was going to Mr. Schmucher's, the butcher's, to get a pound. After parting from her I had gone only a few steps when I saw, lying on the grass alongside of the road, a little leather-covered memorandum-book, such as men use to keep notes in. I picked it up, thinking it belonged to some one about the Works, and not, of course, intending to read any more of it than might be sufficient for me to discover to whom it belonged. On the cover I read the name 'Susan Mullin.' I didn't know any one of that name about here, so I was obliged to open it. I glanced through the leaves, all of which were closely covered with writing, but I saw frequent references to Mr. Honeywood and Miss Honeywood, and so I thought it must concern them more than any one else, and that I would ask you what I ought to do with it."

"Have you it with you?"

"Yes, it is here in my pocket," with which words Miss Pink produced a duodecimo memorandum-book, with the name "Susan Mullin" written in a large round hand on the cover, and handed it to Mrs. Benham.

"I do not think I ought to open it," said that lady. "I think I know who dropped it."

"And I know also who dropped it," exclaimed Miss Pink. "It was the lady who paid a long visit last night to Miss Honeywood, and who was taken to jail by a Philadelphia police-officer. She walked along that road to the station, and must have lost it. Or perhaps she threw it away, supposing that she would be searched, and not wishing to have it found in her possession."

"Lucille, I see, has been very full in her information. Did she also tell you who the woman was?"

"No, for she did not know, except that she had come for the purpose of defrauding Miss Honeywood in some way, but that Mr. Benham and Mr. Wade were too much for her, and that she was exposed and carried off to Philadelphia."

"I think the book should be given to Mr. Wade," said Mrs. Benham. "He will know better than any one else what to do with it. It was very kind of you to bring it to me."

"I am perfectly willing to give it to Mr. Wade. There might be some things in it that it would not be proper for Miss Honeywood to see, and he will know what to show her and what to keep back."

"If it concerns her at all he will certainly show her the whole of it. She is not a child. It may be proper to return it at once to the woman that lost it. At all events, Mr. Wade, by his position and profession, is the man to take charge of it. Shall I send it to him now?"

"I have no objection."

Whereupon Mrs. Benham wrapped up the book in paper, tied it securely, and then, writing on the package, "Found by Miss Pink, and given to me to send to you.—Amelia Benham," sent it by a man who did errands of the kind for her, and who was then in the house.

"Now my mind feels easy," said Miss Pink, rising to go. "I hope you don't think my visit impertinent, since you know what brought me here."

"I never said your visit was impertinent. I thought your statement that you could have married my son impertinent, and I think so still."

"Well, well! we'll not talk about that any more. I think I know how to bear a corroding sorrow without letting the ulcers show on my face." With which pathological comparison Miss Pink took her leave.

She was disappointed, notwithstanding her acquiescence, in the disposition that had been made of the memorandum-book. She had not read it, for she was very sure that Mrs. Benham and she would go over it together; and it was a blow to her, therefore, when that lady proposed sending it to Mr. Wade without reading it. She had, however, looked it through, and had been struck with the evidence it afforded of the relations of an intimate character that existed between the Honeywoods and certain members of the Mullin family. Indeed, to one knowing so little about the matter as did Miss Pink—which was in fact nothing at all—it is doubtful if she could have discovered the full purport of the entries made in the little book, even if she had carefully perused it.

But Mr. Wade had the key, and to him it was all as clear as the noonday sun.   He had not got back from his usual morning's horseback-ride when the package was left on his library-table, but he returned soon afterward, and for more than an hour he was deeply engaged in studying the contents of the little book, stopping now and then to utter some emphatic ejaculation as some point of more than ordinary interest was revealed to him.   When he had finished he locked it up in his desk, and paced the large room for several minutes, thinking of the plan of opera- tions he should initiate, and, he did not doubt, carry on to a successful termination.   Then, having apparently made up his mind what course to pursue, he put on his hat and went to the telegraph-office, where he sent a message to Benham, directed to his hotel at Harrisburg, requesting him to return at once.   In a short time the answer came back that Mr. Benham had gone to Philadelphia.   He sent the message then to the hotel in Philadelphia at which he knew Benham always stopped.   While waiting for the answer to this, he wrote and dispatched several other telegrams—two to Montreal, two to Philadelphia, and one to New York—and then, leaving word that any answers were to be sent to him at his tower, he went to make a call on Alana.

And yet he knew that his visit would in one sense be premature.   The book gave him many important data toward unraveling the mystery connected with her father and the Mullin family ; but he had had such ample evi- dence of the mendacity of all the members of that family who had come under his notice, that he could not regard any information that rested altogether on their assertions as being worthy of credit.   It might be true, and it might be false.

Still, in this case, there was a record that had evi- dently been made for the use of the person making it, and not for purposes of deception. This of itself was a strong point in favor of its truth. In fact, the statements made in the book fitted so accurately with the rather disjointed mass of data in his possession, that he did not believe that there was a reasonable doubt that he had at last obtained all the knowledge necessary for the determination of the questions connected with Alana's father and mother.

But, while this was the case, he did not have that degree of surety that could only be obtained by the confirmation by others of the statements in the book, and hence he had made up his mind to say nothing on the subject to Alana till he had received answers to the telegrams he had dispatched, beyond, perhaps, giving her certain vague assurances that ere long her doubts would be relieved, even if in certain points her fears were confirmed. He knew the terrible, wearing influence on the mind of the anxiety that comes from uncertainty, and he was also aware of the fact that Alana was experiencing it in its most intense form. Besides, there were several business matters in regard to which he wanted her action.

She had just returned from her visit to Mrs. Benham, when he entered the library in which she was sitting, trying to interest herself in a recent novel. But the book was stupid, a fault that no amount of fine writing will atone for, and she was about throwing it down in utter weariness over its platitudes and absurdities, when Mr. Wade came into the room.

"You see," said Alana, as she held out her hand to him, "that I am trying to engage my mind with other things than those that filled it last night. If I had had an interesting book, I might have succeeded, but with this melancholic production I found the task to be more than I could accomplish."

"Tell me about it," said Mr. Wade, wishing to divert

16

her mind as much as possible. "I am interested in hearing your criticism. What's the name of the book?"

"The name? Oh, I can not give you the name; I am afraid there would be a sort of fascination that would make you buy it, if I told you the name."

"That is possible, I admit. When I hear of a book being atrociously bad, I am impelled to get it and see for myself, just as a particularly ugly person draws my eye-sight."

"Doubtless that will be applied to him. The probability is, that you will never hear of this one again as a writer of novels."

"Mr. Benham went away this morning," resumed Alana, suddenly changing the conversation, "to be gone a week. Did he tell you that I have concluded to buy your coal-mine?"

"No, I didn't see him this morning."

"Well, consider the sale made, and please have the necessary papers prepared at once. I'm going to plunge into business now to a greater extent than ever."

"I shall at once attend to it. By securing this mine, you effectually prevent the establishment of any other furnace in this vicinity. I think you are right to devote more time than ever to your business interests. Nothing tends so much to divert the mind from subjects that had better be avoided. I looked at the new stack as I came along, and I think it will be ready for use by the time Mr. Benham gets back. By the by, I suppose he has told you of his discovery."

" No, he has told me very little about himself. He has been too deeply interested in trying to assuage my troubles to think of himself. What is it?"

" A matter connected with the manufacture of iron that he has at last perfected, and that a gentleman told me yesterday in Harrisburg would yield him half a million dollars almost immediately."

"I am glad of that."

"Of course, he has informed you that he refused a partnership in the Juniata Iron-Works of Cummings, Jansen, and Jones?"

"Did he do that? When?"

"Oh, several days ago. He made up his mind then, it seems, that he would ask you to marry him just as he was and as you had always known him, and that, if you refused him, he would go away. Of course, he could not have stayed here as your superintendent after you had rejected him. It was very foolish in him to refuse the partnership in his then state of uncertainty as to what your answer would be. He ought to have asked for time to consider it."

Alana thought for a moment. "Yes," she said at last, "perhaps you are right, from a material point of view; but women like an act of sacrifice and devotion like that."

"Well!" exclaimed Mr. Wade, laughingly, "as matters have turned out, there's no harm done, but most men would have made sure of the partnership."

"Ah! but all men are not like John Benham."

"I came here to talk to you about the mine, but we have settled that without discussion, and then I have another matter which relates to the subjects that were partly settled last night. I have acquired information that I think is of such a character as to take the load from your mind that has crushed you ever since your father's death. I can not, my dear child," he continued, "speak to you just now more definitely, but I think I am warranted in saying that there is hope that your mother's character has been misunderstood, and that she was not the depraved woman we have thought her to be."

While he was speaking, Alana had risen to her feet, and stood looking at him with all the interest that his words were capable of exciting.

"Do you mean to say," she inquired, her pale face, her eager eyes, her half-open mouth expressing the intensity of her feeling—"do you mean to say that my mother was a good woman?"

"How good she was, my dear, I can not tell you. But I do mean to say that I have strong reason for believing that she was not the openly depraved and criminal woman that we have been led to regard her."

"How could she have been so foully wronged? Oh, never mind now, who has done the wrong, so that it is a wrong!"

"In a few hours I shall probably be able to tell you the whole story. In the mean time, prepare yourself for the good news."

At the time Mr. Wade was talking to Alana, John Benham was in Middletown, on his way back by the circuitous route which, as we have seen, brought him to the Works late that night. If they could have communicated with each other, much suffering would have been spared to several of the principal persons with whom this story is concerned. It was only another instance of the fact that the affairs of men often depend for their success or failure upon some apparently trifling and disregarded circumstance.

Mr. Wade, on leaving Alana, went to his house, but found that no telegrams had yet been received from any of the parties to whom his messages had been sent. But he found one from Mr. Layton, the district attorney, requesting his immediate presence in Harrisburg with Miss Honeywood, for that Todd was to be examined that afternoon at three o'clock. There was nothing to do but to obey, and, at half-past two—at about the time that Benham was talking with Miss Veronica Schupp in Linglestown—Alana was on her way to Harrisburg to give her evidence in the preliminary examination in the case of the Commonwealth of Pennsylvania against Alexander Todd.

CHAPTER XXVI

MR. WADE and Alana, on arriving at Harrisburg, went at once to the court-house, where Todd's examination was to take place. She felt anxious and excited, for she did not know how much of her own personal history would come out; and she experienced, as was very natural, a repugnance to making a statement that would in all probability be the means of sending one of her nearest relatives to the penitentiary for a very considerable part of his life. Very much, however, to her relief, there was nothing revealed relative to her relationship to the man, and for this circumstance she knew that she was indebted to his forbearance. He was, of course, present in court, attended by counsel, but it was now evident that he had not made his legal adviser acquainted with any portion of his family history, or of the fact that he was the uncle of the chief witness for the Commonwealth.

Alana gave her evidence very clearly, being careful to state only facts, without indulging in surmises or inferences. She deposed to Todd's attack upon her, to his robbing her of her watch and pocket-pook, and to his threat to cut off one of her fingers. Relative to the homicide of his wife, she testified to the fact that Todd had told the woman to get out of his way, and had slung her across the room with no more force than was necessary to the accomplishment of his object; that she had lost her balance and had struck her head in falling against a piece of furniture. She then went on to state how she had been rescued by the timely appearance of Mr. John Benham, who had knocked Todd down.

There was no cross-examination.

Then John Benham was called, and the district attorney stated that Mr. Benham was absent, and had not been served with a subpœna to attend.

Dr. Arndell was next examined. He testified to the nature of the injury that Mrs. Todd had received, and that it was the cause of her death.

The result was that Todd was duly committed to await the action of the grand jury, and probably to stand his trial for robbery from the person, and murder, at the coming term of the court.

As Mr. Wade was leaving the court-room—Alana had gone at once to Mrs. Priestley's as soon as she had given her evidence—the prisoner made a sign that he wished to speak with him.

"You've treated me very well," he said, in a low tone, taking Mr. Wade aside, while the officers, at that gentleman's request, went off to a little distance, "and Miss Honeywood has told the exact truth, without trying to make things worse for me than they really are. She might have sent me to the gallows if she had chosen, and many a one in her place would have done it, too, just to get rid of a troublesome customer like me. Suppose she had said that when I took hold of my wife I said, 'I'll kill you, damn you!' or something like that, it would have been the end of me. Now, I ain't such a very bad fellow when I ain't drunk as you might think, and I'm going to return her kindness. I'm her uncle, of course, but I'm not going to own kin with her any more. No one will ever know that I'm her mother's brother. I've told no one but her, and you, and the parson. When I told him, I was drunk, and so I let him understand, this morning. He thinks now that I was lying, or didn't know what I was talking about."

"There's nothing ever gained by a lie," said Mr. Wade, gravely. "It was unfortunate that you told him of your relationship, but it would have been better not to have contradicted the story with a falsehood."

"That's all nonsense!" exclaimed Todd. "The man that wouldn't lie to serve a friend ain't worth much, I think. And I've known a lie do a devilish sight more good than the truth! However, that's my lookout, not yours. You won't have to sizzle for it in the next world, nor she either. Now," he continued, as Mr. Wade made no answer to these sophistical remarks, "I'm going to do more for her still. Our little game is pretty much come to an end. I hear my sister has been nabbed, and she's good for anywhere from ten to twenty-five years in the State's prison, which will be as long as she lives, I guess. I'm going to make a clean breast of it, and, if you'll get permission to spend an hour with me in my cell to-night, I'll tell you the whole story. It isn't as bad as you think for —though, perhaps, it's bad enough. I won't ask you to take my word for it neither. I'll refer you to all the proofs, and I've got some of them that I'll give you."

"At last," thought Mr. Wade, "all seems to be converging to one point." "I'll come," he said, aloud. "I may as well tell you," he added, "that I have in my possession a memorandum-book that your sister appears to have dropped while at the Susquehanna Iron-Works, and which was found and placed in my hands."

"Oh, yes, I know that book! That was our guide, so that we shouldn't forget anything. All the dates and plans of operations are there. You see, when people go into an affair like that, they've got to make sure to be consistent and not contradict themselves. She had it all by heart, I guess. Well, you'll be able to see from that whether I tell you the truth or not."

"I shall come at seven o'clock."

"All right, I'll be ready. I suppose there hasn't anything been heard of Rackett, or Johnson, as he called himself here. I'd like to get even with him ! I told Mr. Benham all about him this morning, and I told him I thought
he'd better go back to the Works and make ready for a
visit. You haven't seen anything of him, I suppose—
Mr. Benham, I mean ? "

"No, he went to Philadelphia."

"I guess not. He might have given out that he was
going to Philadelphia, but I'm sure he went back to the
Works. You'd better be on your guard up there, for to-
morrow night Tony will be down on you pretty sure."

This intelligence worried Mr. Wade not a little.
"Where was Benham ? " he asked himself. Certainly not
in Philadelphia, for he had received no answer to his
telegram sent to him at the hotel at which he always put
up. And equally certainly he had not gone back to the
Works. Leaving the court-house, he crossed the street
to the hotel at which Benham stopped when in Harrisburg,
and ascertained that he had that morning left the house
with the expressed intention of going to Philadelphia.
Then Mr. Wade walked down Market Street to the railway-
station, and found that Benham, who was well known to
all the employés, had purchased a ticket for Philadelphia
and had taken his seat in the train. Thus far everything
seemed to show that he had gone to that city. Perceiving
the desirability of his presence at the Works, Mr. Wade
telegraphed to a friend in Philadelphia, requesting him to
call at the principal hotels in search of Benham, and, upon
finding him, to tell him that he was wanted at the Susquehanna Iron-Works immediately. But in the course of the
afternoon he received an answer to the effect that Benham
was not to be found at any of the principal hotels. As a
matter of fact, he was then crossing the mountain-range
between Linglestown and the Susquehanna Iron-Works,

and thinking how he could best act so as to defeat the schemes of Rackett and his men.

The inability to find Benham worried Mr. Wade not a little. He wanted him not only to act, but because he now believed that there would be no necessity for the journey to Montreal. He could only explain the matter by the supposition that Benham had not yet gone to a hotel, having received intelligence that required to be immediately acted upon. What more likely, he thought, than that, on arriving in the city, he had gone at once to the Moyamensing Prison to see Mrs. L'Estrange? What, in fact, could he do better than that, except to come home? This idea satisfied him, and then he went to Mrs. Priestley's to inform Alana that he would not be able to go back with her, but would return in a late train after he had seen Todd.

He found her in better spirits than at any time since her father's death. The assurances he had given her in the morning had evidently produced a beneficial result that was to be perceived in the happy laugh that he heard from her before he entered the room, and which he had not heard before in many a long day. He stopped a moment before going into the room. The door was ajar. There were no secrets being discussed, and he thought he might venture to listen, if only for the purpose of joining more intelligently in the conversation.

"I tell you what it is, girls," Mrs. Priestley was saying, "it's my opinion there'll be a wedding at the Works before the winter is over. Mr. Trevor was here this morning, and he could talk of nobody but Alana."

"Yes," said Colletta, "there'll be a wedding, I've no doubt, but the happy man will be Dr. Arndell, not Mr. Trevor. He spent last evening here, and he also could talk of nothing but Alana. He seemed to think that all he had to do was to say, 'Come to my arms, best beloved of my heart!' and that she would rush forward as though—as though—"

"My dear," interrupted Rubina, "comparisons of the kind you are attempting are scarcely admissible in good society. The only simile you can suggest is, 'as though the devil were after her,' and that would scarcely be proper. Now, I can assure you that Alana hasn't the slightest idea of taking either the parson or the doctor. The one is altogether too bashful and the other too confident, and, besides, she can do very much better. I have given a good deal of attention to this matter, and I can assure you that—"

"Good people," interrupted Alana, laughing, "I'm greatly obliged to you for the interest you take in seeing that I am properly provided for, but you are all wrong."

"Yes," said Mr. Wade, coming forward, "you are all wrong, as Alana says, for not one of you thought of me. Do you think," he continued, as Mrs. Priestley and her daughters gathered around him, for he was a great favorite with them, "that because I have remained a bachelor for —for—well, I won't say how many years, I'm never going to take a wife?"

"Oh, no!" exclaimed Mrs. Priestley, "we don't think anything of the kind, but perhaps it would be indiscreet to inquire of you, after the manner of Lord Chesterfield's son of his father, 'Whose wife are you going to take?'"

"By George!" he said to himself, as he fixed his eyes admiringly on the elder lady, "she looks so pretty to-day that if we were alone I should almost be tempted to answer, 'Joe Priestley's wife!'" Then, aloud: "Madam, I did but banter. God forbid that I should ever so hamper myself! A freeman I have lived till now, a freeman I shall continue to live till such time as it shall please an All-wise Providence to remove me from this sublunary sphere."

"How sweet it is," said Mrs. Priestley, with affected

admiration, "to hear those we esteem discourse feelingly of matters that they don't understand! It gives me renewed assurance that the world is not all bad; that, here and there, there is a man and brother with a heart open to the refining influences that—"

"Now, mamma," broke in Rubina, "you're getting beyond your depth. It's well I interrupted you, for you never would have been able to bring that sentence to a satisfactory end."

"Thank you, my dear," said Mr. Wade, "for pitying the sorrows of a poor old man! But I did not come here to talk of 'marriage or of giving in marriage,' though I admit that I might go further and fare worse. I came to tell Alana that I am obliged to stay here till this evening, and that I shall not be able to go back to the Works till a late train; so that if you," turning to Mrs. Priestley, "will keep her till I call for her, I shall be greatly obliged, unless, indeed, what is not very likely, she should prefer to go by the 5.20 train."

Alana was very willing to stay, and Mrs. Priestley and her daughters were delighted that they should have her a few hours longer with them. Then Mr. Wade took his departure, and she was left alone with her three friends.

She was very fond of the Priestleys. They had been very kind to her in more ways than one, and she began to think that there would be no impropriety in her telling them that she was going to marry John Benham. She felt very sure now that she should marry him. Mr. Wade's assurances had dissipated the one cloud that had prevented her seeing her way clear to becoming his wife. Doubtless she would have married him nevertheless. She had made up her mind to that, but it would have been a marriage into which she would not have entered with a clear conviction that she was not wronging the man she loved. Now it seemed as though she could almost look him in the

face as not unworthy to stand by his side in their course
through life.   It was a great load to take from her mind—
a load that she would have felt all her days, no matter
how kind and loving her husband might be.   Now, it was
off, or almost off.   Mr. Wade, she was sure, would never
have spoken as he had, unless all doubt were removed
from his mind.   Yes, she would tell the Priestleys.

She longed to speak of the event that to her was the
sweetest of all her life.   She had no mother, no sisters to
converse with about the man she loved ; to hear their
praises of him and to sound them herself into their willing
ears.   She was sure of her friends' sympathy.   They all
liked Benham.   She had often heard them descant on his
good qualities.   She wanted to hear them again, and for
them to know that he belonged to her now.

"Sit down," she said to them, for they were still standing in different parts of the room, not having quite recovered from the effects of Mr. Wade's departure.   "Sit
down here, close to me, for I'm going to tell you of something that has made me very happy.   I am going to tell
you, because you are my dearest friends, with Mr. Wade,
and because my heart is so full of the joy I feel that I
must speak of it to some one.   You were all engaged just
now in selecting a husband for me, but not one of you
chose the right man, though you, Rubina, I suspect, would
have mentioned his name, if I had not interrupted you.   I
am going to marry Mr. John Benham."

"I knew it !" cried Rubina, jumping up and throwing
her arms around Alana's neck, while Mrs. Priestley and
Colletta, shoving her aside, were also prodigal with their
caresses—"I was sure of it !   He's the only man I ever
saw who's fit to be your husband."

"He is the only man I ever saw," answered Alana,
"that I would be willing to marry."

"I wish," said Colletta, "that you would tell me what

you see in him to love. Doubtless he is lovable, but I am curious to know how he strikes a woman with your good sense and severity of judgment."

"Oh, my dear!" exclaimed Alana, laughing, "don't expect me to enumerate all the cardinal virtues as being inherent in Mr. John Benham. I love him because—because I love him! I have never stopped to analyze my feelings. He is good and true, and brave and self-reliant. Perhaps I should never have cared for him if I had not seen that he possessed these qualities, but I should love him now whether he had them or not."

"Oh, no!" rejoined the girl, "you surely would not love him if he were not worthy of your love."

"I would," said Alana, with feeling and emphasis in her tone. "I would love him, even though I might not respect him. Is the mother to cease to love her son when she discovers that he has committed a crime? Is the wife to desert her husband when he has dishonored himself?"

"But suppose," persisted Colletta, "he were to beat you?"

"That would be impossible, of course, as would be the commission of any ignoble act, by John Benham; but even if he were to beat me, though I should probably die of sorrow, I should not cease to love him. Do we not in low life hear of instances of wifely devotion for the brutes that kick and stamp upon those they have sworn to love and cherish? That is right; it is as it should be. A woman's love for a man should be absolute, incapable of being alienated by anything he may do. Even the dog loves the master that maltreats it."

"My dear," said Mrs. Priestley, who had been listening with rapt attention to Alana's declaration of sentiments, "it's all very well for *you* to talk in that way, for your opinions are in accordance with your nature. You are one of the clinging types of womanhood—a type that is becoming smaller every day, and that, ere long, will vanish for a time from the face of the earth, to return again, and again to disappear, through successive ages. Such views as those you have expressed are not held now to any considerable extent among what are called the higher classes, though in low life they appear to prevail. Bridget Murphy comes into court with her blackened eyes and bruised breast, and begs that her ruffianly husband may be let off from his justly deserved punishment; but Mrs. Henrietta Stanhope, if her husband snaps his fingers in her face, sues for a divorce. And the public has a contempt for the one, while it sympathizes and applauds the other. The 'strong-minded women' of the day, my dear, will call you a milk-sop, and a poor, mean-spirited creature, if you are known to entertain such doctrines as those you - have just expressed. But when a woman loves a good man after that fashion, her happiness and his are assured."

"Yes, I think so," said Alana, with a happy smile on her face. "John Benham will never perpetrate a mean or dishonorable action, or treat me unkindly; but if he did, I should love him all the same. Because he fails in his duty is no reason why I should disregard mine. Good heavens!" she exclaimed, starting to her feet, "I must go home. I entirely forgot that I have invited Mrs. Benham to tea with me. There is barely time for me to take the 5.20 train."

"You'll have to walk to Market Street," said Mrs. Priestley, "and then you can take the street-car to the station. There isn't time for me to get my carriage ready, and there are no cab-stands in Harrisburg yet. I was hoping we should have you to tea with us. I want you to meet Mr. Broadnax, of New Orleans, who," she added, in a whisper, intended only for Alana's ears, "is very sweet on Colletta. He's a widower, and, it is said, killed his first wife by his ill-treatment of her. That's the reason she interrogated you so sharply. She likes him, for he is a most fascinating man ; but, poor child, she is a little bit afraid."

"I think she has that in her that would make any man kind to her. Men are very much what women make them. Then, of course, she will not be able to go home with me and stay all night. I was going to ask her and Rubina. —You will come with me, my dear, won't you ?" she continued, turning to the elder Miss Priestley. "I can't promise to show you my future husband, but I can at least make you renew your acquaintance with my future mother-in-law."

"Go, Rubina !" said Mrs. Priestley. "The trip will do you good. Hurry and pack your hand-bag."

"Oh, never mind that !" cried Alana. "I can give her all the toilet articles and underclothing she will want. We are about the same size."

Nevertheless, Rubina, who was very willing to accept Alana's invitation, hurried up-stairs, and in a few minutes returned arranged for the journey, and with a little traveling-bag in her hand. In a moment she and her friend had left the house, and at 5.20 were on their way to the Works, arriving just in time to get ready for the six-o'clock tea to which Mrs. Benham had been invited.

Nothing worthy of especial notice occurred during the evening except that, at about eight o'clock, Mr. Trevor entered the drawing-room. He had evidently expected to find Alana alone, and his face and manner gave unmistakable evidence of his disappointment. As a matter of fact, he had nerved himself up to the point of asking her to be his wife, and the reaction from the elation he had experienced was pitiable to see. It would be difficult, he knew, for him to reach another such stage of confidence. All saw his chagrin, and his presence was thus a damper on the little party. After a few minutes of dreary attempts at conversation, he took his departure.

Mr. Wade did not put in an appearance that night. It was twelve o'clock when he got back to the Works, and on the very train that Benham would have taken had he not driven over from Dauphin. He had had a very satisfactory interview with Todd, and this, added to several telegrams that he found awaiting him, put the matters connected with Alana's mother in such a form that doubt was no longer possible. He determined that in the morning he would place before Alana all the facts, capable, as they now were, of being resolved into a connected story, and that he would make renewed efforts to discover the whereabout of Benham. As the reader is aware, that gentleman was at the time in company with Dr. Arndell on his way to the South Fork of Powell's Creek, to obtain information relative to the location and plans of Mr. Tony Rackett and his party.

CHAPTER XXVII.

AFTER Arndell's departure, Mr. Wade had gone back to bed, but there were so many things on his mind that he found it impossible to get to sleep again. He therefore, after an hour's attempt in this direction, rose and, as a first duty, went at once to Squire McElroy's, to obtain warrants for the apprehension of the three forge-men who had been connected with Rackett's gang. They were served, one after the other, by the one constable of the township that lived at the Works, and the men were soon in custody, in irons, and confined in a room adjoining the squire's office, till the arrival of a train to take them to Harrisburg.

Of course, the necessary proceedings created some excitement among the workmen and other inhabitants of the Susquehanna Iron-Works, and Squire McElroy's little office was crowded with men, women, and children, drawn thither by the sight of the constable going down the long street three successive times, with one hand resting on his prisoner's arm and the other grasping the handle of a revolver. Fortunately for the cause of law and order, the men had not gone to their work, otherwise the one legal functionary would not have been able to accomplish his work in so satisfactory a manner. As it was, they were still in bed at their homes, so that he was enabled to arrest them in detail.

But, as only about a tenth part of those assembled in and about the squire's office were able to obtain even a

tolerably correct idea of what it all meant, the most exag-
gerated statements were circulated among the crowd, relative to the crimes of which the prisoners were accused.
Some declared that they had been detected in an attempt to
burn the Works; others, that they had murdered Mr. Benham; and some color was given to this rumor by the facts
that the superintendent was not in his office, and that few
were aware of the circumstance that he had gone away.
Mr. Wade, fearing their stories might reach Alana, and cause
her unnecessary alarm, thought at first of going to her
with a true account of the matter, but upon reflection considered it better to write her a short note, telling her that
there was no cause for apprehension, and then to go home
and get the papers that so nearly concerned her systemati-
cally arranged, so that they could be presented to her in a
form that would at once convey to her mind a correct idea
of their purport.   He was a very methodical man, as are
most old bachelors, especially if they are lawyers.

Besides, he was hungry, not having yet had his breakfast, so that there were plenty of reasons why he should go
home before making his call on Alana. Accordingly, home
he went.

He found Mrs. Schwartz indignant at his failure to
come to his breakfast when it was ready, but he was not in
the mood to resent her innuendoes and lamentations. "Give
me something to eat," he said, "and stop your growling,"
smiling good-naturedly as he spoke.   He felt glad that at
last the matters that had troubled him and Alana were coming to a happy ending, and it would have taken a good deal
from Mrs. Schwartz to have developed even a very mild
emotion of anger.

He finished his breakfast, and then he set about the
work of arranging his data in their proper sequence. It
was not a very easy task. Many of the notes that were
contained in the memorandum-book that Miss Pink had

found were of no consequence, and would only encumber his narration with unimportant details. He was famous for his skill in detecting the salient features of a case, and he brought his experience to bear with effect upon the instance before him.

It was twelve o'clock, and he had not yet got through his labors, when old Schwartz came into the room, his eyes wide open, and his manner showing that he had heard something that he regarded as of great importance.

"There's bad news," he exclaimed, as soon as he had recovered the breath he had lost by the rapidity of movements to which he had not in late years been accustomed. "Mr. Gilchrist has just come over from Lykens, and he says that, just before he left there by a coal-train, Dr. Arndell came in bringing Mr. Benham, who had been shot through the lungs by robbers in the mountains. He could not stop to learn further particulars, for the train was leaving and he had to hurry ; but he saw the wagon in which Mr. Benham was lying, and heard them telling Dr. Green about the wound."

While the man was speaking, Mr. Wade listened without interrupting him. There was every probability that the story was true, and here, just as he was congratulating himself that affairs were coming to a happy ending. this new complication had arisen to throw everything back, and perhaps even to make matters worse than they had yet been. If Benham were wounded seriously, an active element of disturbance would be cast into the current of Alana's life that could not but in the present state of her mind act most injuriously. If possible, she must be prevented hearing anything of the circumstances until they could be told to her with the assurance that they were true. He knew how generally it is the case that exaggeration characterized statements made from knowledge as inexact as that that had evidently served for the basis of the account given by

Mr. Gilchrist. There would be time enough to tell her of what had happened when information in regard to it came, as it certainly would, in due season, from Dr. Arndell.

"Where is Mr. Gilchrist?" he inquired of Schwartz, who still looked the picture of astonishment and fear.

"He's in the kitchen. He's my wife's cousin."

"Has he been to the village yet?"

"No, he stopped here first, thinking that you'd like to hear what had happened."

"Well, and why the devil don't you bring him to me, instead of giving me the news through your thick head? Send him here at once!"

Schwartz hurried out of the room as fast as his old legs would carry him, and in a few minutes returned with Mr. Gilchrist.

"What's this news you bring of Mr. Benham being wounded?" inquired Mr. Wade, as soon as his visitor's head appeared above the hole in the floor to which the spiral staircase led.

"Just what I told Peter," answered Mr. Gilchrist. "I was about leaving Lykens on a coal-train, when I saw a wagon coming along the street, driven by Dr. Arndell. Dr. Green met it, and the two doctors got to talking, and I heard part of what they said. Dr. Arndell said that Mr. Benham was in the wagon, dangerously shot in the lungs, by robbers, on Broad Mountain. Dr. Green insisted on having the wounded man taken to his house, and the wagon drove off in that direction."

"Did you see Mr. Benham?"

"No, the cover was down all around. I forgot to say, however, that one of the robbers was caught in Lykens."

"And what became of the others?"

"Didn't Peter tell you? I suppose he was so much taken aback by Mr. Benham being hurt that he forgot. The doctor didn't mention them in my hearing, but all the people were talking about them. They were all killed, and were lying on Broad Mountain, about two miles distant. A party was going out after them."

"Did Dr. Arndell say that Mr. Benham was badly wounded ?"

"Oh, yes, he said that ; but I heard him say something about nursing and having to stay a long time ; so I guess, from that, that he expected him to get well."

"I am much obliged to you, Mr. Gilchrist. You are a man, I see, who keeps his senses about him. Now, excuse me, please, for I want to go at once to Mrs. Benham with the truth relative to her son. After you've told your story in the village it will grow, and by the time it reaches her, through the medium of Miss Pink, he will have received a dozen wounds in his lungs, and be on his way here as a corpse. I'll be still more obliged to you if you'll stay here about a quarter of an hour longer. I want to tell Miss Honeywood, too, exactly how the matter is with the superintendent.—Peter, get out that bottle of old Monongahela, that I opened last night, and set it before Mr. Gilchrist down-stairs.—You'll find that competent to amuse you for fifteen minutes at least."

Mr. Wade gathered up his papers, although he had not finished his arrangement of them, and, leaving Mr. Gilchrist and Peter, nothing loath, to test the quality of the old Monongahela, proceeded at once to Mrs. Benham's house.

Mr. Wade was not expert at communicating unpleasant intelligence, but he succeeded, after a while, in making Mrs. Benham understand that her son was shot in the lung, that the wound was serious, as all such wounds are, though that there were strong hopes of his recovery, and that it had been received in a contest with robbers, who had contemplated an attack on the Works, and that he was comfortably housed under Dr. Green's roof at Lykens.

"Dr. Arndell," he added, "has probably been detained in getting his friend settled in his new quarters, but will certainly be here in a short time. It is better for him to tell the story in person than to send an outline by telegraph."

Of course, Mrs. Benham was both surprised and grieved at Mr. Wade's account, which was all the more a shock to her, as she had had no idea that her son was in that part of the country. She at once, without losing her presence of mind, declared her intention of going by the next train to Lykens. "There are many things," she said, "that my boy will want done for him, that no one can do so well as his mother. Alana, poor child, will have more trouble! Does she know yet?"

"No; but I am going at once to tell her. Probably she also will desire to go to Lykens. There is a train," he continued, taking a time-table out of his pocket and studying it a moment, "at two o'clock. You will have time to get ready while I go to Alana. I would rather some one else than I had this work to do."

"No one could do it more sympathizingly. I will join you at her house immediately."

She left the room, to make her preparations for the journey, while Mr. Wade started to go across the lawn, when, hardly had he left the porch, than he saw Dr. Arndell coming rapidly toward him.

"I have just met Mr. Gilchrist," said the doctor, hurriedly, "and he told me that he had given you some account of poor Benham's condition. I was on my way to tell his mother. It is a bad wound, but he is doing well."

"I have already told her. She is going to him. Walk with me to Miss Honeywood's, and tell me all about it."

As they went along, Arndell gave Mr. Wade all the necessary particulars of his own and Benham's doings, so far as he knew them. The old lawyer was not a man to show much emotion, but he grasped the doctor's hand warmly when the account was finished, and would have thanked him in words had not his heart been too full for utterance. He said something about Arndell being a hero, and then the two separated, the doctor to go home, and Mr. Wade to perform his mournful duty to Alana.

Rubina Priestley had gone home only a few minutes before, and he found Alana alone in the library, where she had been awaiting him for an hour or more, trying in the mean time to occupy herself with a pile of new books that had come to her that morning from Philadelphia. She was a great reader, embracing in her range almost every subject that did not belong to technical science, and especially fond of every branch of natural history. She had been skimming through the several volumes, merely for the purpose of getting some idea of their scope, and had begun to wonder why Mr. Wade did not come, when she heard the front-door bell ring, and she at once surmised that at last he had arrived. "Now," she thought, as she recognized his step in the hall, "this weight that has rested here"—placing her hands over her heart—"ever since my father's death, will be lifted, and I shall not be ashamed to look into the honest and manly face of my husband, feeling that I am not unworthy of his love." At that moment Mr. Wade entered the room.

He had a good deal of power over his emotional nature when he chose to exercise it. His profession had served to give him experience in controlling his feelings, and he had profited by the opportunity to such an extent that occasionally, when he had been entirely cool and collected, under circumstances that were calculated to cause the strongest natures to give way, he had been called callous. But he was not that, and no one knew it better than Alana.

He came in with the bundle of papers that contained

the facts that he relied upon to comfort Alana, while his
thoughts were busy with the task that he had set himself,
of breaking to her intelligence that he knew would make
her miserable.   To face an unpleasant duty, and to go
through with it as soon as possible, was, however, a cardinal
feature of his character.

"My dear child," he said, after they had greeted each
other, "I told you yesterday that you might hope that the
idea of your mother's depravity, under which you had suffered so long, is erroneous.   I am now able to assure you,
by the most indubitable proofs, that, though she might
have been, and probably was, imprudent, she was not the
wicked woman you have been led to consider her.   But
there is another matter of more immediate importance,
with which it is necessary you should be made acquainted.
Mr. Benham—"

"Mr. Benham!" she exclaimed, interrupting him, while
she looked anxiously into his face—"something has happened to him.   Tell me at once!   I can bear it.   He is not
dead.   *That* I see in your countenance.   I can endure anything else."

"No, he is not dead.   He is wounded, but he is doing
well, and Dr. Arndell expects him to recover."

"Yes, I know that he is grievously injured."   Her
face became pale, her eyes were wide open and filled with
tears, but her voice was steady.   "Tell me all about it,"
she continued, "and then I shall go to him.   My place is
with him."

Then he told her the story as he had heard it from
Arndell.

"It was for us that he got his wound, and it must be
our duty to bring him back to health.   Of course you have
told his mother."

"Yes, his mother knows all.   She will be ready to go
with you to Lykens at once."

"How she must suffer! She loves him so dearly, and is so proud of him."

"Yes, but she is as brave as you are, and as anxious and as able to do her part in nursing him through his illness."

"I shall be ready in a few minutes." She left the room as she spoke, and, summoning her maid, went upstairs to get ready for the journey to Lykens, and, while there, was joined by Mrs. Winebrenner, who, in some mysterious manner, had heard that something out of the way had occurred. "Now," said Alana, after she had told her old friend the chief points of the affair in which Benham and Arndell had been engaged, "you see how unjust you were to the doctor, a few days ago, when you declared that he had no good qualities. He has behaved like a hero, and, if Mr. Benham gets well, he will owe his life to Dr. Arndell."

"You are not going to stay overnight in Lykens?" inquired Mrs. Winebrenner, ignoring Alana's remarks, so far as any reply to them went.

"Yes, I expect to stay there till Mr. Benham is well enough to be moved to his home."

"Will you take Lucille with you?"

"No, I can do without her. She can come to Lykens, however, every day, and bring me such things as I require."

"You know nothing of nursing."

"You forget that I nursed my father."

"Yes, forgive me! I forgot that. But you were stronger then than you are now."

"I am strong enough."

Mrs. Winebrenner left the room in search of Moses, who was to wheel Alana's baggage to the station, and, in a few minutes afterward, the maid was also relieved from further attendance. There were yet ten minutes before it would be necessary to leave the house. Alana locked her

17

bedroom-door, for these minutes she wanted for herself. She wanted to think, to give herself up to the contemplation of this last and greatest of her sorrows, to try to realize her darling's condition, to picture to herself his pale face, his labored breathing, all that there was that showed that his life hung by a thread that at any moment might break. She tried to keep back her tears, but she might as well have endeavored to stay the current of the broad river that flowed past her windows. "Oh, my love!" she cried, bursting into a paroxysm of passionate weeping, as with clasped hands and heaving bosom she threw herself on the bed. "What if he should die! My love, my love! My true-hearted love! My noble, my brave, my generous love! You have risked your life for me. It may be that you have sacrificed it in your attempt to clear my name from shame! May God take me also, if it comes to that!"

Then she rose, and, dashing some cold water into her face, tried to obliterate the traces of weeping. "I will shed no more tears," she said. "They will only unfit me for the work I have to do."

She went down-stairs to the library, where she found Mrs. Benham awaiting her. Accompanied by Mr. Wade, the two ladies went to the station, where they were joined by Dr. Arndell, who was returning to Lykens not only to see after Benham, but to attend the coroner's inquest to be held that afternoon on the bodies of the dead robbers, and at which he would be the chief if not the only witness, for it was scarcely possible that Benham's evidence could be taken. He knew that Alana could never be his wife; not even, probably, if Benham died. In that event, he felt certain that no man would ever call her wife, but he had never felt happier than when, in a few simple words, she thanked him for what he had done, and held out her hand to him. He took it in his, and she allowed him to hold it longer than he had ever held it before. Each knew something of what the other was thinking about, and each knew that they were friends while they should live.

Then, both she and Mrs. Benham plied him with questions about the affair, and more particularly about his friend's wound, till, by the time they arrived at Lykens, they had obtained all the knowledge and all the opinions on the subject that he was capable of giving. He spoke cheerfully of the injury, and while not seeking to disguise its serious character, or the possibility that it might terminate fatally, expressed the strongest hope, based upon what he knew of Benham's excellent constitution, his indomitable courage, and his strength of will, that he would have an easy course to complete recovery.

"Besides," he added, "he has every inducement to live, and that is a great deal in a fight such as he is about to make. Then, with such good nursing as he is likely to get, and a medical supervision that will mainly consist in letting him alone, his chances can not but be increased. One thing, however, I must impress upon you, and that is, don't say or do anything that is calculated to excite him. There was no hemorrhage when I left him, and if he can be kept perfectly quiet it will probably not return."

"I think you may rely on our powers of control," said Mrs. Benham.

"He ought not to speak above a whisper," continued the doctor. "And another thing," he went on, "don't be alarmed if you find him feverish, and even a little delirious. The reaction had fairly begun when I left him, and is doubtless at its height now."

And such they found to be the case. Arriving at Lykens, and proceeding to Dr. Green's, they were told by the doctor that Benham was quite out of his head, but that otherwise matters were progressing favorably. His fever was high, but not inordinately so, and it appeared to be the fever of reaction rather than that of inflammation.

Both the women needed all their powers of self-control, when they looked at the son and lover lying, with flushed face and parched skin, breathing laboriously, and muttering to himself something of which only the words "mother" and "Alana" were distinguishable, but they retained the command of themselves, and went about the work they had to do as methodically as though they had been used to it all their lives. Both quietly, in turn, pressed their lips to his burning forehead, but he made no sign that he had any knowledge of the caress, other than to open his half-closed eyes and look at his mother and at Alana, as though endeavoring to make out who they were and what they had done.

He had a restless night of it. Dr. Arndell did not return to the Works, but remained at the bedside of his friend, watching every phase of the fever, and pouring the quinine into the patient after a manner that his army experience had shown him was expedient, but which almost made Dr. Green's hair stand on end. Nevertheless, the result, as exhibited in the improved condition of the sufferer the next morning, fully justified the practice, and Dr. Green was willing to admit that he had learned a lesson.

There were no violent demonstrations of affection between the two women and Benham. He recognized them at about daylight as they moved to and fro in the room, attending to his needs, and when his mother came to the bedside he stretched out his hand, and, taking hers, raised it to his lips.

"I have been trying for some time," he said, in a low whisper, "to make out who you were; but now I know, and the other is Alana."

"Yes, my dear boy, it is Alana. She is afraid to speak to you, lest you may be excited. The doctor told us that we should not talk to you."

"Tell her to come here."

Mrs. Benham delivered the message, but Alana hesitated. She soon saw, however, that there was more danger of undue excitement from the denial of his request, than from a compliance with it ; so she crossed the floor to his bedside.

"Don't speak," she said, as she drew near to him. "Oh, my darling," as she knelt on the floor, and kissed his lips, and laid her face against his still fevered cheek, "you will get well for me. God will not let you die !"

He threw his arms around her, and held her trembling in his embrace. "Yes," he whispered, "I shall get well. Whatever the doctors may say, I feel that the crisis is past."

"Hush !" she exclaimed, "I must go now." She rose to her feet, and at the instant the two physicians entered the room. Each in turn felt the patient's pulse and counted his respirations. Then they ascertained the temperature, and, finally asking him a few questions, they retired to a corner of the room to consult over the case. After a few minutes they beckoned Mrs. Benham and Alana to them, and Dr. Arndell delivered their joint medical opinion. It was the first deliberate expression of views that they had yet had from the doctors.

"Yesterday," he said, "after Benham was made comfortable, we made a thorough examination of the wound. We found that the ball had passed through the upper part of the right lung, without breaking the ribs, and was lying under the skin opposite to its entrance, whence it can be easily removed. It does no harm where it is, and it is better not to cut it out at present. To-day we find his condition favorable. His fever is within safe bounds, and we shall try to keep it so. He is by no means out of danger, nor will he be, under any circumstances, for several days to come. His strength must be kept up, for when he was shot his vital powers were low, owing to the exposure and hardship and excitement of the past twenty-four hours. He will need careful nursing, and, in order that he may get that, and you ladies not become exhausted, you must take charge of him in turns, relieving each other every six hours. Either Dr. Green or myself will see him several times a day, and one of us will always be within call. Now, I want you both to go into the next room, which Mrs. Green has placed at your disposal, and lie down. You need sleep. I shall stay with him till ten o'clock, and then you, Miss Honeywood, will get your instructions, and will look after the patient, under Dr. Green's supervision, till five o'clock, when Mrs. Benham will take charge, and I shall be again on hand. Now, go and get some sleep. We don't want three patients on our hands." After a few more words of explanation and inquiry, the two ladies left the room. They were fatigued, of course, but interest and excitement had kept them from feeling tired. Dr. Arndell's words had relieved their minds, and they were soon asleep.

As Dr. Arndell was on his way to the station, he met a wagon containing three coarsely made coffins. The driver informed him that they held the bodies of the three robbers that were about to be buried. The day before, the coroner's jury had found a verdict to the effect that these men had been justly killed by Dr. Arndell, and had commended him highly for the great service he had rendered the Commonwealth.

CHAPTER XXVIII

It was not until two or three weeks after the reception of his wound, that Benham had sufficiently recovered to make it safe to move him to his own home. During that period there had been two serious relapses, but, upon the whole, no very untoward symptoms had arisen. His mother and Alana had been in constant attendance on him, though each had made several visits of short duration to the Works. During the latter part of the period of his stay at Lykens, he had been allowed to sit up for a portion of the day, and to converse and to read and to be read to ; and this, he said, was, in spite of his illness, the happiest period of his life. Indeed, he was never tired of expressing his thanks to them for their unwearying kindness, their unflagging devotion. "Of course, mother," he said, "I knew what you would do for your son. I had a right to your devotion ; but how many women in Alana's position would have left everything, as she has done, and have placed herself by the sick-bed of a man, even if she were engaged to be married to him ?"

"What's that you're saying about me ?" inquired Alana, coming forward from a table at which she was heating something with a spirit-lamp. He repeated the observation. making it even stronger than before.

"I think you are mistaken," she said, still going on with her heating operation. "Any well-ordered young woman, such as I pretend to be, would have done exactly as I did, and without being entitled to any special consideration for so doing. People don't deserve credit for doing what is agreeable to them, do they? Of course not!" answering the question herself. "There are many heartless women, as there are many heartless men. If you had been one of the latter class, I am quite sure that I should have been one of the former, and then," coming toward the bed with a little Dresden china vessel in her hand, "I am equally certain that I should not have been here now, making beef-tea for your lordship."

"Nor would I have such an exquisite bowl to eat it out of, either. Every day I see some beautiful thing in silver, or china, or other material, that I have not seen before. To-day it is this tureen, with the Watteau medallions. Yesterday it was the *repoussé* lamp, the day before that this eider-down quilt. What will it be to-morrow, dear?"

"This," she answered, taking from the pocket of her frock a letter, and proceeding to open it. "I received it this morning from Mr. Wade."

"Oh, yes; he hasn't been here for two or three days, has he?"

"No, but he's coming to-morrow, and Dr. Arndell says you are well enough now to hear something very important that Mr. Wade has to say. It is something, I think, that will make you very happy, even if only because it will make me happy. Dear John! it is the unraveling of the whole mystery of my mother, and of the woman-impostor that came to me the night before you went away."

"Yes, if it makes you happy, it will rejoice me also. It makes no difference, otherwise. If you were—"

"Hush!" she said, smiling, and playfully putting her hand over his mouth. "I know what you are going to say, but it does make a difference, for all that. Do you know," she went on, changing the subject of conversation, "that the course of justice is very much impeded by your illness? Neither my uncle, nor Jinks the robber, nor your three forge-men, have yet been tried, owing to the inability to get your evidence."

"I wish the whole thing could be dropped."

"Yes, so do I ; but that is impossible, I suppose."

"Quite impossible, unless we both run away, and take Dr. Arndell with us."

"I think he would be very glad to go with you, any-where."

"He has twice saved my life. Some of these days, perhaps, I will tell you something that will make you form a still more exalted idea of him than any you have now."

"I think I understand," said Alana, quietly, "all that you mean to imply. He has acted very nobly."

"He knows what I think of him. A more unselfish, and, withal, a more determined man, never lived."

The following day, by one of the early trains, Mr. Wade arrived. It was the first time that Benham had been al-lowed to sit up, and he had that morning been told that he might return home the day after to-morrow, if no untoward symptom should in the mean time make its appearance. He was still weak, he was of scarcely more than half his former weight, but it was thought, by both the physicians, that the change would be of service to him.

"You may wonder," said Mr. Wade, almost as soon as he entered the room in which Benham was sitting, with a bright December sun shining in at the window and bathing him in its warmth—"you may wonder where I have been for the last few days."

"Yes," said Alana, "we were talking of it yesterday."

"I have been to Philadelphia. I was sent for by Mrs. L'Estrange, which, as you know, is only one of her many names. She had important information to give me, so she said. It is important, but I could have done very well without it. Nevertheless, it is confirmatory of all that I have otherwise received. I heard her through, received from her what papers she had to give me, and then I left her, arriving home night before last. Before I went away, she begged that I would ask you, my dear, to forgive her the wrong that she attempted to do you."

"It is easy for me to do that," answered Alana. "I forgive her freely. I wish I could help her to be a good woman."

"She was to have been tried to-day for the part she took in the great diamond robbery. But she is now beyond your forgiveness and the jurisdiction of courts, for a few hours after I left her she was found dead in her cell."

"Dead!" exclaimed all three of his listeners.

"Yes, dead. The Philadelphia papers of yesterday morning contain accounts of the matter. Here is one of them."

"'The notorious Sarah Lammy,'" he read, "'with half a dozen aliases, was found dead in her cell in the county jail yesterday afternoon. She had received, at her request, a visit from Mr. Wade, of Harrisburg, and at one o'clock took her dinner as usual. She walked in the corridor till late in the afternoon. At five, when the matron came to make her usual inspection, Sarah Lammy was just breathing her last. Dr. Hanson, the prison physician, was immediately summoned, but before he arrived she was dead. There is little doubt that she died of heart-disease. She had had several attacks of shortness of breath since her incarceration. A post-mortem examination will be made to-day. She was to have been tried this morning, for the great diamond robbery, that she carried out so successfully about a month ago. She has passed the greater part of her life in prison, her first term being for shop-lifting when she was only sixteen years old.'

"I may add," continued Mr. Wade, "that I at once

telegraphed for further information, and was informed, in reply, that the post-mortem examination showed, beyond a doubt, that heart-disease was the cause of her death."

"Poor woman!" said Alana, "I am sorry for her. There was something about her that was very attractive, very winning, in fact. I felt almost irresistibly drawn toward her the night she came to see me."

"Yes," replied Mr. Wade, "it was that feature that made her such a dangerous character. But, my dear, you should scarcely be sorry that she is gone. Her death is a relief to herself, as it certainly should be to all of us. Now, if it would please Providence to take Todd also, another person who encumbers the earth, and inconveniences, to say the least, honest people, it would be a blessing for which I for one should be profoundly thankful."

"I don't think you, or any of us, will be troubled by Todd," said Benham. "He will, in all probability, pass the rest of his days in the Eastern Penitentiary, and will be, to all intents and purposes, dead."

"These doctors are curious fellows," said Mr. Wade, apparently diverted for the moment from the chief object of his visit, by a thought that had suddenly come into his mind. "There isn't anything they won't do in the pursuit of science, from experimenting with the head of a guillotined man, to analyzing the sensations of a man with death staring him in the face. Now, there's Arndell—"

"Don't say anything against Arndell," said Benham, smiling, but still earnestly. "Everything he does is right in my eyes."

"Oh, I was not going to say anything against him. But what do you suppose he's doing?"

"Something for the benefit of humanity, I suppose," answered Alana. "He's the kindest man to the poor I ever knew."

"Yes, I suppose so," rejoined Mr. Wade, hesitatingly,

drawling the words out of his mouth as though each one required a separate thought. "But, it's my deliberate opinion, based on a very careful study of doctors, that they don't care any more for the poor, or for humanity in general, than I do, and that isn't much, I assure you. As to Dr. Arndell, I believe that for humanity, in the abstract, he has the most supreme contempt. He and others like him are willing to help humanity, but they do it for the sake of their science, not from any love for the human species. Of course, the race is benefited, for whatever advances medical science helps mankind, but that is not the primary object of the doctors."

"I, for one, don't care to draw such refined distinctions as that," said Benham. "But what started you in this line?"

"I have just left Dr. Arndell hard at work in his library, preparing a set of questions he designs putting to you this afternoon, relative to your sensations and thoughts as you lay in the wagon the morning that the robbers carried you off, and when they were discussing the question of what disposition to make of you; what you thought of the proposition to give you a hundred lashes; what of the suggestion to tie you, neck and heels, and throw you out on the road; and what of the agreement to kill you on the edge of your grave, etc., etc. Oh, he has worked the matter up very thoroughly, I assure you! Ugh! it makes my blood run cold to think of it all."

"I don't see why it should," said Benham, laughing heartily, in spite of his weakness, though both his mother and Alana looked grave. "I've often analyzed them myself, not only since then, but while the events were going on, from the time I felt myself seized by Rackett, till I heard Arndell's pistol-shots, and felt a stinging feeling in my chest. I shall be fully prepared to answer all his questions. It was quite an era in my captivity when I determined to drop the envelope through a crack in the wagon-bed. If I could go through such a process of introspection and self-examination for my own satisfaction, I don't see why science should not have the benefit of it also."

"That's right, John," said Alana.

"You wouldn't like to read Dr. Arndell's memoir, would you?" inquired Mr. Wade.

"No, I should not like to read it," she replied; "for my feelings are too deeply interested. I should not like to witness a surgical operation either, but I can understand that such things are necessary. I suppose Dr. Arndell knows that a study of the kind is valuable, otherwise he would not wish to have the results. I am willing to be guided by him."

"You seem to have every confidence in the doctor, even to—"

"To any extent," interrupted Alana, warmly. "There is only one man in all the world who stands before him in my heart."

Benham smiled an approval.

"Well, well!" cried Mr. Wade, raising his hands in a deprecatory manner. "I had no intention of upsetting a hornet's nest about my ears. Doubtless, if even the doctor does come next after Benham, the distance between the two is sufficiently great."

"And you come next. Almost on the same plane," said Alana, laying her hand on his arm. "You know I have loved you ever since I knew you."

"I believe you have, my dear," resumed the old man. "I value your affection above most things that belong to me, and I am not complaining. You are right to place Dr. Arndell high in your regard. Now, let us proceed, as they say in the Legislature, to the order of the day."

With these words Mr. Wade moved his chair to a table that stood in the center of the room, and, taking from the breast-pocket of his coat a bundle of papers, laid it down in front of him. Then he wiped his glasses, and, seeing that he had the undivided attention of the three persons constituting his audience, thus began :

"I have so thoroughly mastered these documents, consisting of telegrams, statements, notes, and letters, that I think I can give you a better idea of their purport if, instead of reading from them or referring to them, I should give a connected account of what they prove. The papers will always be on hand at any future time for reference, as I shall, when I have made my statement, give them to Alana for safe-keeping. I shall, it is perhaps scarcely necessary to say, indulge in no hypotheses or inferences. There is ample proof of the truth of every assertion I shall make:

"In the autumn of 1855, Mr. Francis Honeywood, then twenty years of age, was a student in the Scientific School of the University of Pennsylvania. On the night of the 15th of October, 1855, he and two other students, a married man and his wife, and two young women, in all making a party of seven, went to a tavern at the Falls of Schuylkill to take supper. One of the young women was Sarah Mullin, a daughter of the woman with whom Mr. Honeywood boarded. Mrs. Mullin had three other children —a daughter named Susan, a year younger than Sarah, who had not lived at home for several years, on account of the fact that she was serving out a term of imprisonment in the penitentiary for shop-lifting (Mr. Honeywood did not know that such a woman existed) ; a son named Alexander, also a disreputable fellow, and who rarely came to his mother's house ; and another son named William, likewise a bad character, who was killed by a policeman in 1864.

Sarah was not a bad woman, though by no means as perfect as she ought to have been. She was a member, in good standing, of a church, and her clergyman, in a statement that I have here, gives her a good character. The worst that can be said against her is, that she deliberately entered into a scheme to inveigle Mr. Honeywood into a marriage with her, but she professed to be sincerely attached to him, and probably was. The fact that he was not of age, while she was thirty years old, is an unfortunate state of facts. She was an extremely beautiful woman, and possessed of more education than might have been expected.

"Well, the party of which Mr. Honeywood and Miss Sarah Mullin were members, went to the Falls of Schuylkill for an evening's enjoyment. It was seven o'clock when they arrived there. They engaged a private room, and had supper.

"So far as I can learn, all the members of this party were respectable people. I don't mean to say that the married man was a gentleman, as we understand the word, or that the women were ladies, but, for all that, the evidence goes to show that they were certainly not disreputable. They were all, however, in high spirits, and the tavernkeeper seeing this, and also perceiving that the young men had money enough to pay for it, plied them with wine. The consequence was, that they all became more or less intoxicated."

Mr. Wade stopped for a moment. Then he turned to Alana.

"My dear," he said, "what I have to say further will be painful to you, but it can not well be left untold. You must bear these facts in mind. Your father was young, his sin was one into which he was led by others. He bitterly repented, and he was severely punished."

"Yes," she answered, "it was expiated in this world, and is doubtless forgiven by a merciful God. We are all of one family here. There is nothing that concerns me that the man who is shortly to be my husband, and the woman who is his mother, may not hear."

"That is very sensibly said," remarked Mr. Wade, looking over his papers. "Then I will go on :

"Though intoxicated, they were by no means in the last stage of drunkenness, and, in fact, several of them were only in a state of undue hilarity. Mr. Honeywood, who had never been in the habit of drinking, was more affected than any of the others ; and, according to the sworn declarations of two of the surviving witnesses, himself proposed that he should marry Miss Mullin, and that the ceremony should be performed at once.

"Of course the others should not have allowed such an act to take place, but they felt the recklessness that comes from incipient drunkenness, and they entered fully into the spirit of the occasion. An old clergyman, who also ought to have known better, was sent for, came and performed the ceremony. The certificate of that marriage was made out, was witnessed, and is here with the other papers.

"Thus far you will perceive that the account agrees very closely with the story told by Mrs. L'Estrange, the night that she paid a visit to the Works. From this time on she proves a prominent personage in the drama.

"Mr. Honeywood and his wife did not return to Philadelphia for several days. When he became sober, however, he insisted that he had not been married, but he expressed his readiness to have the ceremony performed. Mrs. Honeywood, as she must properly be called, insisted that she was already his wife, and that a marriage would be an acknowledgment of guilt that she had not incurred. There is no doubt that both parties were honest in their opinions, and they held to them with a degree of obstinacy that, under the circumstances, was remarkable.

"When the time came for Mrs. Honeywood to become a mother, her husband, still denying that he was her husband, endeavored by every means in his power to get her to consent to be married, but she showed him the certificate, and brought him other evidence that a legal marriage had already been performed. This he denied, declaring that, even if the ceremony had been performed, he had not been at the time in a condition to understand the nature and consequences of his act, and that he would never recognize the validity of what he stigmatized as a fraudulent performance. All things considered, it was deemed best that Mrs. Honeywood should go into the country until after her child should be born. It was thought, by the friends of both parties, that, after that event, an agreement could be reached. If not, it was determined by Mrs. Honeywood that she would appeal to the law. She went, as these papers show, to the house of a farmer, named Wilson, who lived a mile or so from Media, in Delaware County; and there, my dear child," turning to Alana, "you were born. A few hours afterward your mother was dead."

"Dead!" cried Alana, rising, and approaching Mr. Wade. "Dead then! at—at—my birth? Then she was cruelly wronged!"

"Yes, I think she was. All the evidence in my possession, and there is plenty of it, goes to show that, except in the one act of marrying your father when he was not in a condition to know what he was doing, she had led a blameless life. You will find several letters of hers among these papers, and in them she pleads the sincerity of her love for your father as her excuse."

"But I do not understand," said Alana, excitedly. "My father, on his death-bed, denounced her as a wicked woman, one that had deserted me, and abandoned him for a life of shame. How is that? My father could not have spoken falsely."

"All that your father said, he believed to be true, but at the same time it was not true. Now comes the worst part of the whole matter.

"A few days before your birth, Mrs. Mullin died, and at about the same time Susan Mullin, who had been in prison, was discharged, in consequence of the expiration of the term for which she had been sentenced. Her mother, as I have said, had just died, and she determined to join Mrs. Honeywood at the farmer's house near Media. Your mother received her coolly, but Susan was a specious woman. She stated that she had reformed, and with tears in her eyes entreated that she might be allowed to remain, and finally she gained her point. She had her good traits, she was kind to your mother in her illness, and she promised to care for you till your father could take charge of you.

"But, very soon after your poor mother was laid in her grave, she began to form a deeply laid scheme to deceive Mr. Honeywood. She paid Wilson a sum of money to write a letter to him to the effect that all was going on well, with the exception of the fact that Miss Susan Mullin, while on a visit to her sister, had died almost at the very time that his child was born. Your father made inquiries, and discovered circumstances in regard to Susan Mullin, of whose existence he had previously been unaware, that caused him to rejoice that she was dead.

"In the course of about a month Susan departed, taking you with her, and agreeing to pay Wilson and his wife each a small annuity so long as they lived, on condition that they adhered to the story that your mother was still alive. She continued to pay them regularly till she died. Wilson and his wife are still alive. I have seen them, talked with them, and have their affidavits here."

"Now I understand," resumed Alana; "and that woman was my aunt?"

"Yes, she was your aunt. Mrs. L'Estrange, Sarah Lammy, and by whatever other *alias* she was known, was Susan Mullin."

"Don't distress yourself about it, dear," said Benham.

"Think what has been gained for your mother by these inquiries! You have a right to revere her memory now."

She made no reply, save by a look that was as expressive of what she felt as any words could have been, and, after Mrs. Benham had, without speaking, kissed her, Mr. Wade continued his recital.

"She, Susan Mullin, went away from Wilson's, taking you with her; but, on arriving at Media, she met an old acquaintance, a man with whom she had formerly been unduly intimate, and he persuaded her to abandon you, and to enter with him into a scheme that was being concocted to perpetrate a robbery. You were therefore sent in the night to the Delaware County almshouse, and Susan Mullin wrote a letter to Mrs. Wilson to that effect. When, therefore, your father came to the house, he was told a story that it had been arranged should be told, and was informed of your whereabout. After that time you were properly cared for.

"All the accounts agree in saying that the resemblance between the two sisters—your mother and your aunt—was very great. There was but a year's difference in their ages, so that Susan had no difficulty in passing herself off as Sarah. It was then that your father heard from various sources of her continued degradation, and it was then that, in order to avoid disgrace, he began the payment of an allowance in accordance with his means, on condition that she should not call herself by his name. She had no desire to pass for his wife. He was poor, she had more liberty as Sarah Mullin than she would have had as Mrs. Honeywood, and she mulcted him in the half of his income, given on condition that she kept away from him. He paid it willingly. She went lower and lower, and was several times in prison, for various offenses. Her life was as foul as was possible, and all this time he thought she was your mother."

"Ah, that is the worst of all!" exclaimed Alana. "How keen must have been my poor father's sufferings all this time, up to the very hour of his death!"

"Yes; and yet it is difficult to understand how a man of his great force of character should have allowed himself to be deceived. It can only be accounted for on the presumption that he knew he had not been free from blame, and that he shrank from exposing his private affairs to public gaze—the same source that causes many others to submit to extortion and black-mail.

"Doubtless the fear that the slightest inquiry would reveal her fraudulent conduct prevented Susan Mullin from taking legal proceedings against your father looking to the establishment of her claim to be his wife. She contented herself with threats, and, as they proved sufficient to secure her a comfortable income, free from all the doubts that attended her other sources of pecuniary supply, she was content for a long time—several years, in fact.

"But, finally, she became more intimate than she had heretofore been with her brother Alexander. This man, the Todd of to-day, had received a tolerably good English education, and had been an alderman in the city of New York. But his inclinations were all vicious, and, having considerable natural sharpness, he was enabled to make effective use of them in furthering his schemes. His trade was that of a bricklayer, but he had, for several years, given it up for more uncertain means of livelihood. Todd saw at once that in his sister Susan he had a factor for coercing Mr. Honeywood that had not yet been employed to its utmost extent, and he determined, with her aid, to work it in such a manner as to develop its full power. The business was one that he saw would require the united wits and the most thorough industry of both of them, so he devoted a considerable amount of time to the preparation of an elaborate scheme. This he reduced to writing. Two copies were made, of which he had one, and Susan, *alias* Sarah Mullin, the other. It was this latter that Miss Pink found, and which is now in my possession."

CHAPTER XXIX.

As Mr. Wade uttered the concluding words of the immediately preceding chapter, he turned over the papers on the table and took from the pile two memorandum-books.

"One of these," he said, "belonged to Mrs. L'Estrange, as she called herself on the night that she visited the Works, and the other one was the property of her brother Alexander, now in the Dauphin County Jail. They agree exactly, and, so far as perspicuity and shrewdness are exhibited, would do credit to a general laying out the plan of a campaign.

"In the first place, it was settled that the claim that a marriage existed between Francis Honeywood and Sarah Mullin should not be pressed beyond the point necessary to make him pay a handsome annuity. Although the marriage could undoubtedly be proved, the process of doing so would certainly rouse Mr. Honeywood into a spirit of active resistance. He had kept track of the life of the supposed Sarah Mullin, and would never consent to recognize her as his wife. The investigation that would be instituted by his legal counsel in case a trial should be had, would inevitably lead to the exposure of the plot, to the discovery of Sarah Mullin's death, and to the revelation of the false personation made by Susan. Mr. Honeywood must be frightened, but not angered beyond his powers of endurance.

"At first they contented themselves by announcing to him that they had concluded to accept the proposition made by him to Sarah Mullin several years previously, that a new marriage should take place. This, however, he indignantly refused, and at the same time denied vehemently that there had ever been a marriage. He said, in his letter to Susan, still under the impression, remember, that he was writing to Sarah, that her conduct had been so atrocious, so utterly depraved, that he would rather his daughter should bear the stain of illegitimacy than that such a wretch as she should have the right to stand in the relation legally of mother to his daughter, and perhaps even to endeavor to undermine her goodness. These are almost his exact words. His letter is here, with several others written by him at different times, to a like effect."

Tears started to Alana's eyes, as she thought of the plots that had been directed against her father, and of the suffering he had endured, but she said nothing. She dared not, in fact, trust herself to speak, lest she should give way altogether. Benham held out his hand to her, and she laid hers in it, and sat thus, while Mr. Wade went on with his story :

"But, although he wrote thus indignantly, Mr. Honeywood thought it the better plan to yield to the demands made on him for money, under threat of a suit at law to establish the validity of his marriage with Sarah Mullin. The two confederates had a strong card, and they knew it, but it was one that required to be played with great caution, for, if they endeavored to use it for more than it was worth, the victim might rebel, and then all would be lost. They, therefore, accepted the sum of two thousand dollars, which was to be paid yearly to Susan, *alias* Sarah Mullin, in quarterly installments, and it was so paid regularly during about five years.

"Throughout all this period the woman continued her life of shame and degradation, and was several times subjected to imprisonment. Your father, however, took no notice of her, other than to send her the money that he had agreed to pay her. He was glad enough to be free from her on those terms.

"Then came the resolution to extort a still larger sum from your father. He had never seen the woman that personated his wife, although this was from no action of hers. She was so confident that she could deceive him, through her resemblance to her sister, and her acquaintance with her history, that she had often endeavored to obtain a personal interview. She was sure of her ability to squeeze more money out of him if she could only be brought face to face with him. She had never, however, been able to accomplish her purpose, for he had steadfastly refused to see her. I am inclined to think," added Mr. Wade, dryly, "that in this instance she reckoned without her host, and that had your father consented to see her he would at once have perceived that she was an impostor.

"It was resolved," he continued, after a readjustment of the papers on the table, "that a visit should be paid to your father at the Works. So, accompanied by her brother Alexander, Susan made the journey. He called on Mr. Honeywood, while she remained at the tavern. I believe, my dear, you were present at the interview between your father and this man. It was a stormy one, but it resulted in the increase of the annuity from two to three thousand dollars. Mr. Honeywood persisted in his refusal to see the woman, and she was therefore obliged to leave without accomplishing this part of her scheme.

"They were, however, made to understand that there would be no further augmentation of the annuity, and that if any demand for an increase were made the payment would at once be stopped, and they might proceed to law if they chose. They were satisfied that they had exhausted your father's powers of compliance, and for about ten years they remained quiet, so far as he was concerned.

During this period Susan lived in various parts of the United States, and for the latter part of it in Montreal, Canada. All through this time she drew the allowance regularly, the checks being made out in favor of Sarah Mullin, and she indorsing them with that name, though, as was usual with her, she bore several *aliases*. Then your father died.

"As we all know, nothing was heard of her for over two years. She made no demand for money, nor did she reveal herself to us in any other way. There were two reasons for this. In the first place, she was in prison in Canada, having been sentenced to two years' confinement in the Reformatory Prison at Penetanguishene; in the next, she had heard of your father's death, and she was forming a scheme of still bolder character, to be put into execution as soon as she was released, and that was no less than to come here, and, imposing on you as your mother, claim her right of dower in your father's estate. In due course of time she was released, and immediately she and her brother entered upon the execution of their ingeniously devised plot.

"It was agreed that Todd should come to the Works several weeks before active measures were to be taken, in order that full information in regard to all points of importance should be obtained. He did so, engaging himself as a bricklayer, and very soon thereafter being made foreman of the workmen engaged in building the stack of the new forge. He brought his wife with him, but, so far as I can learn, she was not let into any secrets of the party, though she appears to have had a general idea that something of an unlawful character was contemplated. About this time Susan made the acquaintance of Rackett, the leader of a band of robbers that had been committing depredations in various parts of the interior of the State, and he, wishing to profit by the knowledge that she and her

18

brother possessed, induced them to agree to your abduction
and to the robbery of the Works. It was thought not only
that you would give a large sum of money to be released,
but that your feelings would be so played upon by the pretended intervention of Susan in your behalf, and the pres-
entation of the evidence in her possession relative to Sarah
Mullin's marriage, and identity with herself, as to acknowledge her as your mother. We all know how, through
Todd's drunkenness, an assault on you, and the discovery
of Rackett and Susan on Peter's Mountain, this part of the
scheme fell through.

"Then it was that Susan undertook, very much against
her will, but persuaded to do so by Rackett, to impose herself on you as your mother. The story of her discomfiture
and arrest for a diamond robbery that she had perpetrated
almost immediately after her arrival in Philadelphia from
Montreal, is familiar to all of us, and need not therefore be
retold. She was a bad woman, in every sense of the word,
but she seems, after once having seen you, to have developed within her a feeling of tenderness which might,
had she lived, have led to her reformation, although it
would have been effected within the walls of a prison.
Rackett has gone to his long account, with two of his band,
and the other will probably pass the rest of his life in solitary confinement in the penitentiary.

"Todd shows indications of a desire to lead a better
life, but I place no reliance on him. He is a thoroughly
bad fellow, and is working solely with the object of securing sympathy and a mitigation of his punishment. He is
entitled to some little consideration from the Commonwealth for his disclosure relative to Rackett, by means of
which Benham and Dr. Arndell were enabled to bring that
scoundrel and his gang to grief, and will doubtless receive
his due in this and in other respects.

"That," he continued, gathering his papers together,

"embraces all the essential points of the history that these documents tell more fully. At some future time, my dear, you can look them over. I place them where they belong, in your hands."

With these words Mr. Wade rose and held out the package to Alana.

"I shall never look at a single paper," she said. "Though they clear the memory of my mother, they tell me of other circumstances that humiliate me, and that I would like to blot out of my memory forever. With an aunt living, all through her existence, a criminal life, and dying in a prison ; with an uncle now in jail, and awaiting his trial for murder and robbery, there is little about my family for which I can congratulate myself. Were it not for the kind friends I have found, I should almost feel like hiding my face from all mankind, and—"

"But with them," interrupted Mr. Wade, while Benham, rising, though with difficulty, put his arm gently around her waist and drew her toward him—"with them you will live out in full light of day, blessing all that come within the range of your sweet influence, the type of a noble woman, who, knowing what her duty is, performs it, with full measure and overflowing. Let there be no more sorrow over this matter. The case is closed. It has become what we lawyers call *res adjudicata*. We have all of us other things to think of, and we can not afford to waste any more time on the crimes and punishments of Mrs. L'Estrange and Alexander Todd. To-morrow I am going to Philadelphia, and mainly for the purpose of getting your wedding-present, and—and—"

"And what?" inquired Alana, with a smile, allowing her thoughts to be led away from the subjects that had engaged them.

"I suppose I may as well tell you," answered Mr. Wade, looking a little confused. "You would have to know it soon, anyhow, and I see no reason why you should not know it now. I am going to be married."

"You!" exclaimed all three of his listeners in a breath.

"Yes; it is never too late to mend, and I'm going to begin a new life, with Mrs. Priestley to help me to walk a straight path. It was all arranged yesterday."

"I am not at all surprised," said Alana, giving him her hand, while the others offered their congratulations. "Now that I come to think of the matter, I remember many little incidents that, had I been watchful, would have told me what was going on. You will, of course, continue to live at the Works?"

"No; that is the worst part of it. Mrs. Priestley declares that nothing would induce her to live in a round tower. The fact is," he continued, with a knowing smile on his face, "she couldn't very well get higher in it than the ground-floor, for, while she is not what would be called stout, she is of such fair proportions that I am very sure she could not pass through my spiral staircase. So I shall either have to build an addition to my tower, with more ample means of going from story to story than I have now, or move to Harrisburg."

"Build the addition, then," said Benham, "for I see, by the expression that Alana has put into her face, that she will never agree to your leaving the Works. You have been a second father to her, and it will not do for you to break the relationship."

"Not even if she is going to marry a man who has fought her battles at the risk of his life? Well, well, we shall see."

"I shall try my powers of persuasion on Mrs. Priestley," said Alana, laughing, "rather than on you."

She did, and the result was, that an addition, bearing about the same proportion to the tower that a dog has to its tail, was built. It was essentially different in architecture, especially so far as its staircases were concerned, all of which were wide and straight enough to admit of Mr. and Mrs. Wade passing up and down them abreast, should they desire so to do.

The day but one following that on which Mr. Wade made the revelations concerning Alana and her family, Benham was taken to the Works. It was several weeks before his health and strength were so far restored as to admit of his considering himself as well as he had ever been, and then he and Alana were married. The ceremony was performed in the little church at the Works that her father had built. Mr. Wade gave the bride away, and Mr. Trevor performed the ceremony. Of course, Alana had no right to suppose that he had ever contemplated asking her to marry him, but she nevertheless did know that such had been his intention. It would not have been treating him with courtesy not to have invited him to officiate at her wedding, and yet it was with many misgivings that she sent Mr. Wade to him with the request. He had evidently been expecting the invitation, for he at once accepted, and, when the time came, went through the service without the quivering of a muscle or the slightest tremor in his voice. He afterward told Arndell that it was the most sublime act of self-sacrifice that he had ever performed.

Harrisburg, and, in fact, all Dauphin County, were in a state of great excitement during the trial of Todd, Jinks, and the three forge-men. Todd never, by word or deed, allowed it to be known that he was Alana's uncle. She and Benham gave their testimony, and the latter deposed to the fact that it was through information furnished by the prisoner that Rackett's gang was broken up. The district attorney united with Todd's counsel in asking the consideration of the court, and, as a consequence, a sentence of ten years' imprisonment was imposed instead of the full extent of the law. It is quite certain, however, that he will not live to emerge from the penitentiary, as he is in the last stages of pulmonary consumption.

Jinks was found guilty of several burglaries perpetrated at Linglestown and its vicinity, and was sentenced to twenty years' solitary confinement at hard labor. The forge-men were convicted of conspiracy to commit burglary, and received each three years in the penitentiary.

Alana's secret was well kept. No one outside of her family ever knew the truth except Mr. Wade, and it might as well have been in the grave as in his breast. Miss Pink at one time, in consequence of Todd's statements to Mr. McClure, the prison chaplain, had suspicions, but they were all dissipated by his subsequent assertions that at the time he said he was Alana's uncle he was drunk, as in truth he was.

"Benham's process," as it was and still is called, proved to be of very great value, far exceeding his most sanguine expectations, so that, in the matter of wealth, he was quite the equal of Alana. No happiness can be greater than theirs, for it is based on a love that has its foundations deep in their hearts, and that the memories of the past will never permit to die. A little Benham made his appearance in due season. His father once ventured laughingly to say that he was jealous of his first-born, but Alana was quick to declare by word and deed that all the children in the world could never hold the place in her heart that was held by him.

THE END.

www.ingramcontent.com/pod-product-compliance
Lightning Source LLC
Chambersburg PA
CBHW030819110726
47900CB00006B/1661